THE JACKSON
CONTRACT

BY WAYNE OVERSON

3

Wayne Overson

The Jackson Contract

Book and cover design by Rebecca Hayes
www.beckypublisher.com

Published in the United States

Printed in the United States

ISBN-10: 1-56684-759-1
ISBN-13: 978-1-56684-759-9

A PROLOGUE:
FROM "THE DIXIE CONTRACT"

The main highways through southern Utah, over a period of several years, beginning in the early 1970s, had become something of a "gauntlet" through which illicit drugs passed--seemingly every day. Interstate Fifteen had become the main conduit. Local Utah Highway Patrol troopers, beginning mainly by the young ex-marine Barney Jeppson in Iron County and, increasingly, with veteran Dan Wilde and the youthful Aaron Gentry in Washington County along with others, were becoming more effective at stopping and arresting drug couriers. Marijuana and cocaine shipments were being confiscated, costing Percival Rubinski, a drug kingpin of northern Illinois and his cohorts throughout the Midwest, millions in profits.

Two ex-cons from the Las Vegas area, the somewhat serious, dark-haired and balding, Floyd Barker and the taller, blond-headed Broderik "Brody" Conway, characterized as slower and frequently displaying a wide-eyed, strange, broad grin, were hired by the Chicago drug lord, known only to them as "Rube." Their assigned duties were, after being notified by Rube, to distract the police whenever drug shipments were passing through as well as to learn methods of helping drug couriers escape detection. They were paid by Rube with postal money orders for each successful shipment.

Their first strategy was to simply follow a vehicle hauling drugs through the area driving a plain-looking dark sedan, usually without the courier's knowledge, while anticipating a stop by the officers. On several occasions when an officer showed suspicions and actually stopped the vehicle hauling the forbidden cargo, they thought it would be both clever and practical to drive past at an extremely high speed. Logically, by the time the officer could return to his car and accelerate from zero to well over one hundred miles per hour, the distracters would be miles ahead. Several times, in the early days of their mission to thwart drug enforcement, this maneuver actually worked very well.

As planned, the officer would quickly forget suspicions of drug commerce and pursue the pair of outlaws in the speeding sedan. However, being well acquainted with the highways and byways of Beaver, Iron and Washington counties, Barker and Conway were able to quickly exit the freeway and hide on dirt roads, using the dark green bushy cedar trees as cover, or to quickly blend with traffic on the streets of Cedar City or within the veritable maze of streets in the St. George Basin.

On at least one occasion, the pair of would-be mobsters attended the U.S. District Court, in Salt Lake City for the trial of two hapless Hispanic drug couriers from southern California. However, their demeanor and odd appearance in the courtroom caught the attention of testifying officers and further aroused suspicions. Then, almost beyond the belief of anyone involved, Barker and Conway abandoned traveling in the dark sedan and began using a lime-green Chevy Blazer. It seemed as if they clearly intended to advertise their whereabouts and operations.

Meanwhile, Trooper Aaron Gentry, a young bachelor, having been raised near Parowan, was living in an apartment in St. George and, in his spare time, helping out on the family farm. While patrolling the highway between Washington City and Hurricane, late one night, Aaron had a chance encounter with a very interesting young woman, Naomi Blackstone, who was walking alongside the highway with her large and extremely defensive German Shepherd, Nero. His efforts to find her again were fruitless, that is, until she made it happen, herself. Naomi was a forklift operator in a nearby, big-box warehouse. She, a tall, good-looking and very assertive young woman, through a secret source of information, learned a great deal about Aaron before deciding to follow up. They quickly became romantically involved. In the course of events that followed, Aaron also formed friendships with Naomi's half-sister, Natty Blackstone and Natty's steady boyfriend, the would-be cowboy, Ben Randolph.

Due mainly to Barker's and Conway's inept methods, the officers quickly caught on to their purpose and tactics and increased their efforts to locate them along the main southern Utah highways. By occasionally stopping at a small wayside cafe on old U.S. 91, the elderly proprietor quickly became familiar with their odd vehicle and peculiar travel habits and proved to be very helpful in identifying Barker and Conway. Continuing and increasingly effective drug interdiction threatened to cost them their jobs. The pair of "creative" ex-cons, without Rube's knowledge, tried some tactics aimed at intimidating the troopers. Barney Jeppson's car was actually barraged with rifle bullets, resulting in shattered windows and a deflated tire, while he was engaged in making what he thought was another drug stop. Later, two police vehicles were firebombed during off-duty evening hours. As the ensuing, intensive search for the team of small-time arsonists began to subside with no success, Aaron Gentry, on a routine traffic stop, had his car--and radio--disabled by more gunshots as Barker and Conway happened to pass by while attempting to escape into Nevada. Needless to say, their efforts at intimidation did not have the desired effect.

News of their bold methods was spread nationwide, often posed as peculiar and laughable, by major TV networks. Rube, in his up-scale home in Evanston, Illinois, surmised that Barker and Conway were responsible, and once arrested, would undoubtedly spill their guts to DEA agents and prosecutors in order to get a good plea-bargain. Left with no choice, and employing his favorite technique for resolving such situations, he hired two "old Army buddies"--part-time hit men-- to eliminate them.

The hired killers' somewhat awkward attempt ended in a car chase across Washington County where the two would-be hit men met their demise in a gun battle with Dan Wilde and Sgt. W.E. Walden.

After narrowly escaping death by rifle shot at the hands of the pair of contract killers, Barker and Conway were able to elude their pursuers by turning north on a county road that skirted the western boundary of Zion National Park. The pilot of a small Department of Corrections airplane, upon witnessing the car chase, alerted authorities on the ground. After Floyd Barker, who had had extensive car-racing experience, was able to get sufficiently ahead of their pursuers and make the turn to go north. He decided to drive off the highway into a grove of cedar trees where he got their stolen car stuck in the deep, soft sand. In desperation, they left the car, the trunk loaded with drugs, and hustled to a position on a low ridge where they could see what was happening below.

Meanwhile, Aaron, Naomi, Natty and Ben, on a Saturday's horseback excursion descended the trail along the Left Fork of the Great West Canyon. While taking a break on a high ridge, they had been somewhat alerted by hearing the UDC pilot's voice on Aaron's small mobile radio but had no way of knowing who might be in the large black car that was apparently being pursued on the highways far below. On horseback, the four riders and the women's two large dogs accidentally came into contact with Barker and Conway. Aaron was shocked to recognize the two men he and the others had been looking for. Being unarmed, his immediate intent was to hitch two of the horses to the car and help get it out of the sand and away from them. However, he had forgotten to turn off the small radio he had tied to his saddle.

Being unaware of their situation, while trying to intercept the fleeing black car, Barney Jeppson was driving down the county road from the mountains on the north. His radio call, while trying to make contact with other officers, was overheard by Barker and Conway. They immediately suspected that Aaron and Ben had to be police officers and drew their weapons. In the ensuing scramble and shooting, with the aid of the two dogs and Aaron's friends, the two were finally captured. Barney, surprised at hearing Ben's voice on his radio, was able to help get the badly injured Aaron Gentry and the others out of their plight.

Barker and Conway, arrested and awaiting formal charges to be filed for *"allegedly"* firing guns at two highway patrol vehicles, fire-bombing two others, possession of and aiding and abetting in the distribution of narcotics, and for shooting two dogs in southern Utah, felt very relieved--*and protected*--to be back inside a jail.

* * *

But in Evanston, Illinois, there was no such relief. After numerous unproductive telephone attempts and learning of Barker and Conway's arrests--through some unknown means--and getting no further word from his contract assassins, Rube was in a quandary. He blamed himself, yet could not risk the damage that Barker and Conway would surely do to him and his business.

Wayne Overson

CHAPTER ONE

Left together in a Washington County jail cell to ponder their fate, Barker and Conway quickly came to the conclusion that Percival "Rube" Rubinski, back in Illinois, posed a serious threat to their very lives. Though quite safe for the time being, they were now, in their own reasoning, a major liability--viewed as a threat to a significant portion of the narcotics shipments out of Mexico and destined for the Midwest. Rube, whom they had never met and with whom they had communicated only by phone, would surely be determined that they could not "squeal and deal."

* * *

Several days after their arrest, Floyd and Brody were visited by family members from Las Vegas. Floyd was a little surprised to see his all-but-completely estranged wife, Gennie. It had been over two months since their last contact. Brody's half-brother, Sam, came into the visiting room with her. A second man waited in their car--unseen and unmentioned. Their visit was short. Gennie and Floyd Barker moved to a separate visiting table where their conversation became somewhat tense and hostile. It almost seemed to Barker that she had intended it to go that way by dredging up his past mistakes and his lack of interest in their marriage. She let him know that she was fed up with his long history of criminal ventures and let him know that divorce papers would soon be coming.

As a parting gesture and perhaps as a shallow attempt at an

apology, she withdrew a small bag of M&Ms that she had concealed
in her clothing, undetected by jail personnel. Floyd's mouth opened
slightly in confusion, wondering what she had in mind. But he didn't
speak. She glanced about the room and, forcing a tired smile, quickly
pushed the opened container of candy across the small round table to
him--being careful that their hands made no contact. Floyd was
extremely puzzled but couldn't help but resist his inward tendencies
to breach any sort of jailhouse rules. Willing to accept any minor
distraction from the boredom of lock-up, he quickly tucked the packet
of candy inside his county-issued orange jump suit. But why would
she be sharing the candy? Candy? Could this be some kind of trick?
Could he really trust her? With the package already opened? He
resolved to examine each piece of candy carefully.

Gennie stood, turned her back to him and walked quickly to where
the Conway brothers sat talking. She stood silently waiting for them
to finish. Sam Conway took the hint, grasped Brody's hand and
reluctantly stood to leave.

Outside, the second man, standing by the car and smoking a
cigarette looked intently at Gennie's eyes as she approached. She
gave him a slight nod. He also smiled and nodded in response.

* * *

A little before three o'clock, the same day, a late-model brown
Chevrolet with Utah license plates left the freeway at the first southbound Washington City exit, drove to the town's main street and
parked near a restaurant. A man in an expensive dark suit and a
woman, much more casually dressed, got out of the car and entered
the restaurant. They glanced around and requested a table near a front
window and, while examining the menu, glanced about the street and
the interior of the eating establishment.

While they were eating, a slender young man wearing a black
sleeveless T-shirt and with a shaved head parked a large black sedan
on the opposite side of the main road and sat looking about, as if
expecting someone.

"Well, there it is," said the woman. "That has to be the car."

"Oh, yeah. Looks real good. And right on time."

They quickly finished eating, passing up dessert, and paid cash for the meal and the tip. Outside, they went back to the Chevrolet. The man opened a briefcase, removed a long white envelope, and stuck it in his suit pocket. He bid the woman goodbye and, with briefcase in hand, walked across the street and along the sidewalk toward the young man still sitting in the black car. The youth saw him coming, got out, and walked toward him. They passed each other without a word and the envelope was handed to the youth. After they walked past one another, the younger man, still walking, opened the envelope and examined the contents. Apparently satisfied, he strolled casually to the first corner and disappeared down a side street.

* * *

A little later in the afternoon, the same well-dressed man carrying the briefcase entered the front door of the sheriff's office and approached the receptionist. He smiled behind distractingly large black-framed glasses at the receptionist, Marti Gibson, and introduced himself. He brushed a few flakes from his right shoulder and the lapel of his dark, stylish suit jacket. His full head of strikingly silver hair and neatly trimmed mustache, along with the glasses, gave him a very distinguished and mature "Clark Kent" appearance. Taking out his credentials, bearing the insignia of the Utah Bar Association, he showed them to her and politely requested a visit with Mr. Floyd Barker and Mr. Broderik Conway. He smiled at Marti again as he signed the visitor's register. She cursorily noted his name, "John L. Croft, Jr.," and his address to make certain that they matched those on his Utah bar credentials.

Marti, at the front desk, now somewhat in awe of the man, led him to the jailer's office where he cordially greeted and shook hands with the sergeant on duty. "We don't often get to meet attorneys from out of town, down here, Mr. Croft," the sergeant said, obviously impressed. "If you'll have a seat in the interview room I'll get them for you."

The two surprised inmates were escorted to the interview room. From a loudspeaker, affixed to the ceiling, unpleasant music permeated the small room, making their conversation a little more difficult. But the superfluous noise assured them that no one could possibly be listening to or recording their quiet conversation. Mr. Croft greeted the pair of accused drug runner-arsonists every bit as cordially as he had addressed the sheriff's personnel.

Floyd and Brody, were a little surprised, but nevertheless relieved and glad to be represented by Mr. Croft -- the seemingly suave and apparently competent and experienced attorney--from Salt Lake City. Several of the sheriff's personnel later remembered being quite impressed with the big city lawyer. No one thought to inquire as to who had sent one of the state's legal elite to represent this bumbling team of Nevada's ex-cons.

"Floyd, Brody," he began, "I have been retained to come and represent you. Apparently, there are people with, shall we say, some big money, interested in your case. I'm afraid I can't give you any names, but they definitely want to make sure you will have the best representation available. Let me assure you, I'll be with you every step of the way, which could involve both state and federal courts."

The inmates' spirits were buoyed on his arrival and offer of legal assistance. The men, both feeling somewhat reassured, listened eagerly to his every word. Still, they were both a bit puzzled, having previously, but reluctantly, feared that Rube had, in fact, ordered their deaths. They were quite surprised that he -- or anyone -- would send an attorney to represent them.

John L. Croft continued, "Have you men had any court appearances yet?"

"Yeah, they had us in court once," Barker answered. "The judge just told us what we was charged for. As far as we know, they ain't even set no bail, yet."

Croft looked surprised. "Oh, really. I'll see to it that the process moves along as fast as possible. We can't have you men just sitting here in jail. I'll do my best to have you two out of here as quickly as possible."

Barker and Conway looked at each other. "Mr. Croft," Brody began, with his peculiar wide-eyed grin, "If it's all the same to you... we been talkin' it over and decided we's gonna be better off stayin' in here... for a while, anyways." Croft looked surprised again.

"Yeah," Floyd added, "we might be stupid sometimes, but we ain't crazy! We figgers there's gotta be more people out there that just might wanna kill us! We don't even know who they are!"

"Oh, I doubt there is anything to worry about. The people who've asked me to represent you definitely want to see that you're, uh, well taken care of, I'm sure." He smiled again.

"But we don't even know who they are!" Brody interjected.

"Did Rube send you, Mr. Croft?" Barker asked.

Croft glanced about as if to see if anyone might overhear their conversation and put his finger to his lips. "Can't give you any names," he repeated, in a whisper. "Now, why don't you tell me how it all happened?"

"Yeah," Barker began. "Well, just like Rube told us to... on the phone... we was followin' this big black Lincoln... with two guys in it, that was supposed to be a haulin'... um... some stuff... you know... narcotics, through Utah... outta Mesquite. Everything was goin' okay until we gets past the Arizona line and these two guys, we ain't never seen before, starts tailin' us."

Brody broke in. "Yeah, first we thought they might be cops, ya know. There was this Mexican guy at one a them casinos, he told us there was a coupla cops lookin' to find us. Showed 'im some pictures of us, ya know. Anyways, these other two guys was followin' us kinda close. Then they comes up alongside us and one of 'em points at our back tire like they was tryin' t' tell us t' stop and check it out. Hey! We figgers they was gonna try and do a number on us right there!" Croft nodded as he took notes on a legal pad.

Barker continued. "Brody was drivin'. We couldn't feel nothin' like a low tire or nothin', so we just keeps goin'. Pretty soon there was this Arizona cop sittin' on the side a the road. These guys in the other car, they goes on in front of us and that cop starts followin' us so we just keep goin'. Wasn't nothin' wrong with the tire! No way!"

"So then, we figures there wasn't nothin' wrong with our car, at all. And them guys sure wasn't cops," Brody said. "Then we don't see 'em again until we gits to St. George. The Lincoln pulls into this gas station fer some gas. And that's where we see this other car again."

"So what did you do then?"

Barker picked up the story from there. "Well, we finally figgers out... they was really after the... uh, stuff in the Lincoln! Gonna rip it off, fer sure!"

"Yeah," Brody interjected. "And we sure as... heck couldn't let that happen, ya know!"

"Well, of course not." Croft replied.

Floyd continued. "We're loyal employees, ya know. So, I jumps in the Lincoln... they just left the keys in it! Them other guys were both inside this C-store, and we couldn't have them other guys a stealin' it, so we heads on outta there, up the freeway. Pretty soon we figures we'd lost 'em and so we goes up in one a them side canyons. We was gonna just to hide the Lincoln and go back and get the other drivers for it. We couldn't just leave the merchandise sittin' there so we was gonna put it in our car. Just fer safe-keepin' ya know."

"But we never got the chance to switch it," Brody added.

"So that's the reason the police found all the stuff... still in the Lincoln?" Croft interjected.

"Yeah, that's right," Brody replied, while making brief eye-contact with Barker as if to say that the 'plan' they had made earlier--to steal the cocaine in the Lincoln, sell it, and disappear into Mexico--would never be revealed. "And we figgers that's the last we'd ever see a them guys that tried to stop us back in that big canyon."

Floyd went on. "Well... right about then, I gotta go use the little boy's room, ya know? Out behind a tree?" Floyd and Brody chuckled out loud. "I was just turnin' around to go back to our car when all of a sudden, this bullet hits me in the arm, here. Well, we couldn't see nobody but we gets to shootin' back anyways just to make 'em lay low and maybe give us a minute to git outta there. And the next thing I know, I'm back in the car and Brody's a goosin' it down the canyon! I don't know how he ever kept it on the road!" The two inmates laughed again.

"Then these guys shoots at us again, on the road... busted the side mirror!" Brody added. "We switched drivers cuz Barker, here's damn good at the wheel. He's been in a lotta stock car races, ya know. Anyways, they was a chasin' us until we gets to this little town over on the other side of the valley and headin' up north on this other road... and that's the last we seen a them guys!"

"We heard later," Floyd said, "after we was busted, they got caught and tried to shoot it out with a coupla cops. Guess they just didn't know we'd turned north!" Floyd and Brody laughed loudly at that.

John Croft then asked, "So that's where they finally were stopped and they were both killed? By the three police officers? I understand the police still aren't sure who those guys are!"

"Gee... that's too darn bad!" said Floyd. He and Brody laughed out loud again.

"The police must think those two men were only after the stuff in the trunk of the Lincoln. So... then what happened?" Croft asked.

Brody, still grinning broadly, continued. "We drives north a ways and sees this place where we c'n pull off the road and hide the car... but we gits it stuck in the sand, don't ya know! So, anyways, we gits out and climbs up on this hill and looks back. There wasn't nobody a followin' us. There was this little airplane flyin' around over us, but we hid out in this bunch a big green trees 'til he took off. We musta been stuck there maybe couple hours."

Floyd continued. "We was tryin' to dig the car out with our bare hands when these two guys and a coupla girls come down outta the mountains, by this creek, ridin' on horses."

"And they got these two big dogs with 'em too!" Brody interrupted and held up his bandaged arm. "One of 'em... dang near took my arm off! Man, we ran outta... "

Floyd interrupted him at that point with his eyebrows drawn together and spoke again. "I looks at this one big guy and he looks kinda familiar but I couldn't remember where I'd seen 'im before. They was goin' to just pull us outta the sand with their horses. But then this cop car comes down the road and we could hear what he was sayin' on the one guy's little walkie-talkie. Then we knew they was cops, too! ... sounded like he was sayin' somethin' to another guy. Then he quits talkin'. So, we pulls out our guns... but, dang it, we'd fergot ta reload!"

Brody interjected, "We was... dang near outta bullets, anyways, don't ya know! So anyway we tries to take control of the situation but this one girl screams and lets loose a them dogs! Man, they was after us!"

"Yeah, we musta had only a couple a bullets left between us," Barker continued. "One a them big dogs he gets wounded and the big guy... the cop... he gets shot in the shoulder and we're outta ammo by then and they got us. One a them dogs just about took off my hand. And that one girl... man, she was all over Brody, here! She was nothin' but tough! Damn mad, too! Then they had us all tied up and everything. Then this other cop... he was in a uniform... he comes over and we figgers we was done for!"

"So... what about these arson charges?" Croft asked. "Did you guys set fire to something?"

Floyd and Brody looked at each other in hesitation. "No, we didn't!" said Brody. "We don't know nothin' 'bout no fires! They claims we was burnin' a coupla cop cars! I guess they figgers we musta done it, fer sure! Damn sure wasn't us!"

"We don't know who them other guys were... that was chasin' us," Floyd said. "Maybe they was gonna try to kill us and maybe steal the Lincoln... like we said before. That's why we figgers maybe we'd be better off a stayin' in here."

"Yeah," Brody added with a wide grin. "We figgers just maybe we'd be better off bein' here with the cops lookin' out fer us, ya know?" Again, his remarks were punctuated with his broad, silly characteristic grin and snorting, almost hog-like chuckle.

From there the conversation turned to the events that led the police to suspect their involvement in drug trafficking. The lawyer seemed very interested in that and pressed them for every detail.

"Well, before the deal with this big Lincoln," said Barker, "me and Brody, here, we figgers maybe we oughta lay low for while... a ways from our place in Nevada, ya know, 'cause them cops, was startin' t' look fer us down there, too. So we figgers we maybe oughta just camp out in the mountains a coupla days."

Brody broke in, "Yeah, maybe like a coupla boy scouts! Ya know!" He laughed again.

"According to the news," Croft said, "you guys are supposed to be charged with shooting at two police officers right on the highway, setting fire to a couple of cop cars and shooting a couple of dogs. What about all that?"

"I don't know where them cops came up with this arson story! ... all this other bull crap!" Barker exclaimed, with a straight face. "It sure as... heck wasn't us!"

"When we got busted and they brought us in! Boy, this one big cop," Brody exclaimed. "I could tell, he was really mad! I don't know why. We never done nothin' to him!"

"Maybe it was his dogs that got shot," John Croft said, rising to his feet. "Would you fellows like a drink? How about a Coke, or something?"

They looked at him and each other and smiled. "Sure. Sounds good to me," said Brody, with a wide grin. Floyd nodded his approval. Croft went to the door to summon one of the jailers. He handed the man a ten-dollar bill and politely asked him to bring them the three drinks and not to bother about the change. The jailer was glad to oblige and soon returned with three cold, sealed cans.

They sat quietly for a few minutes and sipped the cold tart liquid. Croft continued. "So, how are your accommodations?"

Brody and Floyd, somewhat puzzled, looked at each other. "Our what?" Brody asked.

"Are your cells comfortable? Are they taking good care of you in here?"

Brody and Floyd chuckled again, then glanced around behind them for a few seconds at their surroundings.

"Well, as jails go, we've seen a few, ya know, it ain't too bad," Barker replied, gesturing around them. "What ya sees is what ya gets. It's kinda new, I guess. And them county cops, they feed us pretty good, too." Both, being puzzled at his question, glanced at one another again.

"Well, men, I can be working on your release, unless you'd rather stay here for a while. It's up to you, I guess."

"Hey, Mr. Croft," Floyd replied, "if it's all the same to you, I think maybe we oughta just stay in here a while."

"Very well, gentlemen," Croft replied. "I understand that time in a jail can get a little, uh, boring, shall we say?" He paused to look around as if checking to make certain that no one else was within earshot. He took a small white envelope from inside the breast pocket of his suit jacket and placed it on the table before them, with a subtle wink. "Let me leave a little something here with you. These little guys will help the time pass a little more quickly... and pleasantly!"

The two inmates were a bit wary for a moment. Floyd ventured to

open the unsealed envelope and his eyes lit up as he opened the
package wider so that Brody could see the capsules inside.

"Go ahead," Croft said, almost in a whisper, while hunching
forward. "Take one, both of you. Wash it down with the Coke. Or,
you can just dissolve it in the can right there. It'll make your day
much more pleasant as long as you're going to be in here all safe and
sound!"

"Golly!" Floyd said, "This is great! Thanks Mr. Croft!"

"Here's my card," Croft continued, "one for each of you. Don't
hesitate to get in touch if you want out... or if you need anything. Oh,
and the courts will notify me of what's coming up for you guys." He
glanced at them and, getting no response, put his notes into his
briefcase and picked up his soda can. "I'll be seeing you men."

At the front desk he signed out, recording the correct time on the
sheet. The young receptionist watched him go and get into the black
luxury sedan with Utah license plates and depart. Becky Scott, a
secretary in the civil operations office, also glanced out just as he was
leaving.

From the jail, he drove directly to I-15 and headed northeast,
passing through Washington City and, exiting at SR-9, drove
eastward to Hurricane. There he entered the parking lot of a
department store and parked the car among many others. No one else
was close by. Glancing around, he got out of the car and walked into
the large store. While doing so, he noted the woman in the brown
Chevrolet enter the parking lot from the street and gave her a casual
nod. The woman smiled back.

Inside the store he was relieved to see that the store was well
occupied with other shoppers. He entered the men's clothing section
and, quickly finding his own sizes, removed a pair of knee-length
shorts, a belt, a sport shirt, a pair of comfortable walking shoes, white
athletic socks, and a pair of sunglasses from the racks. When he saw
that the store sales associates were either busy or absent, he ducked
into the men's room, holding the merchandise behind his back and
locked the door behind him.

Inside the men's room he scanned the upper walls, looking for
cameras that might be recording his face. Seeing none, he entered a
stall and removed his horn-rimmed glasses, the silver-white toupee--

revealing a very short dark brown crew cut--and removed the carefully placed two-piece mustache. These items were wrapped inside his suit jacket. He quickly clipped off all the tags and changed into the new clothing. Outside the stall, he removed the top metal cover of the large trash receptacle, lifted up the white plastic bag inside it and then placed the clothing, including the shoes he had been wearing, underneath the bag. Once fully dressed, he quickly walked back into the shopping area, picked up another leisure-type shirt, walked to a checkout line with a young and busy cashier and paid for the shirt with cash.

After leaving the store, he walked quickly to the Chevrolet and slid in under the steering wheel. He greeted the woman with a quick kiss on her cheek and assured her that everything was going according to their plan. He reached into the back seat for a baseball-type cap with the Utah Stars logo. Noting that the gas tank was nearly full he drove leisurely toward the entrance to Zion National Park. "John L. Croft," with his companion, keeping a wary eye out for police cars, and carefully obeying all traffic laws, made his way to the motel where she had rented a very comfortable room.

CHAPTER TWO

Late that same evening, Barker and Conway both began to experience blurry, double vision. Their speech became slurred and difficult. Aware that something strange was happening to them, they began to feel panicky, yet at the same time tired and groggy and unable to express any alarm. By nine-thirty they began to have difficulty keeping their eyes open and to crave water to drink. Their energy level rapidly decreased and they could do little but lay on their bunks. By eleven o'clock, neither of them could move or speak. Their breathing was meager and shallow.

Was it bad jail food? Yet no one else was having problems. Prisoners in nearby cells noticed their difficulties and began to yell out to the jail staff for help. Before long the main cellblock was in complete bedlam. The jailer and other officers throughout the building could hear the clamor. But most, long accustomed to hearing prisoners yell, curse, and cry, ignored the discord for a full ten minutes.

Aaron Gentry, with his left shoulder heavily bandaged and his arm in a sling, was working late in the highway patrol office to catch up on reports on the slow Tuesday night. He heard the muffled distant chaos. However, not being so jaded in terms of a jail environment, he was able to persuade the night jailer to check on the manifest uproar among the inmates. An ambulance was quickly summoned for the pair of ailing prisoners.

Aaron, as best he could with one hand, helped carry the men out to the waiting ambulance and then ran back into the office and dialed the number for state criminal investigators Andy Jackson and Roger Green. The pair of DCI officers had been sent down from Salt Lake City on a temporary assignment to more thoroughly investigate the activities of Barker and Conway. Arriving back into the area from a week with their families up north, Agents Jackson and Green were in the process of carrying suitcases, freshly laundered clothing, and other personal articles from their car into their St. George motel room.

"Hello?" The response sounded like a question. The phone had rung at least six times before Roger picked it up.

"Roger? This is Aaron Gentry. I'm at the jail. You heard we got Barker and Conway, a week ago Saturday?"

"Yeah, congratulations, man! Way to go! Thanks for doing our job, Aaron! It's been all over the news all week. We heard you got shot! Are you doin' okay?"

"Oh, it should be okay. Still can't use it much. But guess what? Those two guys were just hauled out of here in an ambulance. They're barely alive!"

"What? You're kidding! Are you serious?"

"They're at the hospital right now. They were barely breathing when they hauled them out of here."

"Okay, okay. We'll get over there right away. Anything else we should know?"

"That's all I know, right now. I'll meet you over there."

* * *

Before midnight, in spite of being put on respirators, the emergency room doctor attending Barker and Conway pronounced them both dead. On being questioned by the officers, the doctor's best guess, at that point, after consulting reference materials, was that they had died of an attack of clostridium botulinum, known in the medical community and elsewhere as botulism.

Andy vaguely recalled hearing the name before as some type of food poisoning. Lab tests would likely confirm the exact cause of their deaths. Later, autopsies would be performed as well. Logically, the doctors and officers reasoned, if food poisoning was the cause, then all, or at least some, of the other prisoners who ate the same food for the evening meal should also be sick. Obviously, Barker and Conway had eaten something, or, been given something to eat, that the others had not.

Roger and Andy, along with Aaron, drove back to the jail.

The jailer for the graveyard shift was unaware of anything the two had eaten apart from the others. In a few minutes, he had called the daytime jailer, who, upon being informed that two prisoners had died, became fully awake. He recalled a lawyer, that he thought came down from Salt Lake City, had talked to them for maybe forty minutes or more. His name, address, and phone number should be on the register at the receptionist's desk. He also remembered they'd had family visitors earlier in the day, from Las Vegas. As far as he knew, neither one had eaten anything, other than what the other prisoners had. He remembered that while the lawyer was there, he had bought all three of them a cold soda from the dispenser in the lobby.

"You bought them drinks?" Andy was also on the phone. A tiny thread of suspicion was forming in his mind. "With your own money?"

"Well, no. The lawyer handed me a ten-dollar bill and told me to keep the change."

"Okay," Andy replied. "What happened to the ten-dollar bill? The vending machine won't take a ten. Where is it now?"

"I just stuck in the petty cash drawer and took out a buck-fifty in coins for the drinks. We made eight-fifty on the deal! That's about it. The ten should still be there."

"Can you describe this lawyer? Do you remember his name?"

The jailer gave a very complete description of the mature and distinguished-looking attorney. He had not noticed the man's car. "Maybe Marti, our receptionist, or maybe Becky Scott from the civil and records division had seen it," the jailer replied. "His name should be on the sign-in at the front desk."

"Thanks a lot, Sarge," Andy replied. "We'll be in touch."

Andy quickly explained to the others what the daytime jailer had told him. By then, Sgt. Shane Lowry, an investigator with the sheriff's office had joined them. The sheriff, Ian Cooper, was on the way, also. Andy and Roger examined the register and after a copy was made, collected the page from the previous day and Croft's ten-dollar bill from the petty cash drawer.

"I'm beginning to think that this lawyer, John Croft, wasn't a lawyer at all," Roger said. "We work in the Salt Lake area nearly all the time... and from the way they describe this Croft guy... it's got to be a different person. Let's get that receptionist on the phone and see if she remembers what his car looked like."

"I can call Becky Scott, too," Aaron volunteered. "She might be able to give us something helpful."

The others looked at him quizzically for a moment. "Go for it," Andy said. "Anything may be helpful." The two women, just as the jailer had done, became fully awake on learning of the deaths of the two prisoners. Their descriptions of the lawyer and his vehicle were remarkably similar. Just as Aaron had supposed, once Becky was awake, she seemed to want more conversation with him about the previous weekend, the arrest, and so on. But, he assured her, he'd be free to go over it all with her just as soon as it could be arranged and closed their conversation as quickly as he could.

Reasoning that "John L. Croft," if that was his name, could very well be responsible for the deaths, Jackson and Green directed that a complete description of the man and the vehicle be broadcast throughout the state and into neighboring states.

The wastebasket in the interview area held no soda cans. A search of the cell that the deceased had occupied turned up both containers sitting on a small table along with two business cards belonging to John L. Croft, Jr.. One of the cans still contained a small amount of liquid.

"Opportunity?" Roger asked the others, while they were all looking at the cans.

"Croft could've put something in their drinks when they weren't looking," Shane Lowry responded. "Or maybe he just handed them the pills and told 'em they could maybe get high... or, at least, feel good for a while." A further search of the room turned up an empty white envelope and a half-full package of M&Ms. The plain white envelope by itself in a jail cell seemed oddly out of place. "And... I'm wonderin' where the candy came from. They shouldn't even have any in here. We're not supposed to allow anything like that into the cellblock... and they've been in here close to a week and should have eaten the whole package long before now. But who brought it in for them today? I'm guessin' it had to be the wife... or it could've been Conway's brother. They could've smuggled it in. Maybe there was more than candy in there. We'll have to be testing all this stuff."

"Motive?" Andy queried. "Maybe the wife just wanted to get rid of him... without all the hassle of a divorce, you know. But she'd have to be pretty desperate... you'd think. She could've given them the candy... the M&Ms... and/or what might have been in the envelope. We'll need to get that checked out for sure."

"On the other hand," Aaron responded, "wouldn't it be likely that somebody would be kinda desperate to keep these guys quiet," He added, somewhat self-consciously. Should he even open his mouth-- in the company of several criminal investigators having years of experience? But he went on. "Barker and Conway were heavily involved in drug trafficking. And they would likely have some ties to the drug bosses in one of the larger markets somewhere."

"I'd call that a 'bingo' for sure!" said Roger. "I'd go with that theory first. Somebody at the top of the food chain thought these two bums knew too much to be trusted. We found a phone number in a trash bag where they moved out of that mobile home in Mesquite. The number checks out to the Chicago area code. But then, we turned that over to the feds--the DEA guys."

"That lawyer's business cards look genuine, though," the sheriff observed. "And the phone number matches what he wrote on the registration sheet. But anybody can have cards printed up.

Shane... maybe you could call the Salt Lake number during business hours and see what might turn up. I wonder if it's even the right number for Croft's law office."

The business cards, the envelope, the soda cans, and candy-- along with the entire room--were photographed in the settings in which they were discovered, then secured in sterile containers. "That lawyer must have taken his own soda can with him," Aaron observed.

"My guess is we'll find the poison in these cans," Andy remarked. "And, if we're really lucky, we'll find the lawyer's prints on these business cards and even the sign-in sheet."

Just at that moment, the graveyard shift dispatcher burst into the cellblock. "Hurricane PD thinks they've found the car you're looking for up there in a parking lot!"

"The lawyer's car?" Andy asked.

"Yeah! That lawyer's car! Right there in the parking lot all by itself. The UHP in Salt Lake is looking up the plate for me right now!"

"What the heck would a lawyer's car be doing in a parking lot in Hurricane? Tell 'em not to touch it," Sgt. Lowry said. "We'll be right over there to check it out."

A small convoy of police cars traveled from the jail to the parking lot in front of a large department store in Hurricane. There, not far from the front door, sat the lawyer's car that had been surrounded during the day by many others. Soon the sheriff, Ian Cooper, joined them along with another officer and a sergeant from the city. The officers looked in the windows of the car, hesitant to touch it.

"So then, Sheriff," Andy began, "I guess the murders are now your case... your call."

"Well, yes. Yes, they are, for sure," Sheriff Cooper began, somewhat hesitantly. "Those men were obviously murdered, right inside our jail!"

Just then, the voice of the dispatcher broke the awkward silence. "All cars, the plates on the black car were reported stolen about a week ago in Murray, Utah. They were taken from a similar car up there. If you can get me the serial number on the car we can run that, too."

"Ten-four, thanks," the sheriff answered. "We'll get back to you on that." He directed the deputy to check the number from above the dash. "I'll bet a month's salary the car's stolen, too." The others nodded in agreement.

*   *   *

By the end of the day, Wednesday, preliminary laboratory tests confirmed that Barker and Conway had died of botulism. A number of good fingerprints were developed from the car abandoned in the parking lot. But taken from a stolen car, they could be those of any number of people. The business cards were curiously clean of any prints. Where prints should have been, only slight smudges appeared that had no evidence of friction ridges of any kind. A call to the law office listed on the business cards resulted in determining that their John L. Croft, Jr. bore no resemblance whatever to the man who had visited Barker and Conway in the Washington County jail the day before. The sheriff's detectives along with state investigators Jackson and Green spent literally hours going through the black luxury sedan that had been abandoned in the parking lot. The only sign of personal effects in the car was a partially crumpled aluminum soda can, which, again, where fingerprints should have been, bore the same curious smudges that were evident on the business cards.

None of the store employees remembered seeing him enter or leave the store. One male sales associate remembered noticing a man with white hair and mustache looking at men's shoes and thinking that somehow the really nice dark suit seemed out of place among the typical attire of their early summer shoppers. But even more puzzling was that a custodian had discovered the upscale clothing in the bottom of a trashcan.

* * *

John and Cora Moranski, now calling themselves Collins "Chuck" and Laura Thompson, had spent much of Wednesday, touring the magnificent Zion National Park. They were both satisfied that the job in St. George the day before, with Chuck posing as a high-class attorney, had come off successfully. As a team, they had long since come to know how the other thought and worked. They smiled and joked in their motel room as they watched the TV news reports unfold. The sheriff's investigators reported the deaths of the pair of "notorious drug traffickers" and attributed their demise to "food poisoning."

Chuck and Laura planned to spend one more night near the park. Next, they might drive on to Las Vegas for a few days to play the slots and tables and take in some of the shows before heading back to their more hectic life--managing a lodge in Jackson, Wyoming. There, they would await their next lucrative assignment.

* * *

Aaron Gentry finally crawled into bed around four-thirty on the night of the jailhouse murders and slept until about ten o'clock on Wednesday. Naomi would be working at the warehouse in Washington and he would not be seeing her until later in the day. After a good breakfast and briefly working out, having only one good arm, he decided to get into his truck and make a quick trip through Toquerville where he would take another look at the house that he and Naomi had been considering for several weeks and probably make an offer--if it still felt right. His last-minute check with Naomi, the day before, had confirmed her complete agreement.

After looking at the house again, along with it's large pasture extending to Ash Creek, he felt even stronger that it was the right thing to do. On Thursday morning, he planned to stop at the bank in Parowan where he'd borrowed money for the truck and see about acquiring a mortgage for the Toquerville property.

Sergeant W. E. Walden stopped at the office before the beginning of the four o'clock shift. Aaron had finished reports in the office and wondered what he might do to help the others. It would be weeks before his left shoulder would be sufficiently healed to allow him to resume patrol duties. Sgt. Walden suggested that he could fill in on some vacation time for the officers in the weighing station between St. George and the Arizona border. He was glad to have the chance to help out. His weigh-station experience at Echo in Summit County eliminated any need for training in that assignment near the Arizona border.

The sergeant quizzed him for a while on the murders having occurred right inside the jail and how the "lawyer" had apparently vanished at the department store parking lot. It was obvious that the man had gone to the store to completely change his appearance. Someone had apparently driven him away--or he could have had another car waiting there for him. But they couldn't help wondering why the killer had bothered to drive to nearby Hurricane to abandon the car and perhaps enter the store and get new clothing. It did not seem logical, to say the least, that the killer, whoever he was, would just leave the expensive car in a place that, after the store's closing time, would be conspicuous and then leave his clothing in the refuse container where it was certain to be found. There had to be some loony purpose in doing that. But what would that be?

Later in the afternoon, Aaron stopped at Naomi Blackstone's residence. He was glad to see her black Jeep Wrangler there and quickly walked to the front door. Natty's and Naomi's dogs, Kody and Nero, were happy to see him and left the shade of a small tree in the intense June temperature to greet him with wagging tails. Nero, Naomi's nearly black German Shepherd limped badly due to his injured shoulder. But his tail wagged slowly. Naomi let Aaron in with a hug and a kiss and immediately began to quiz him, while preparing some soup for a quick dinner, about the deaths of Barker and Conway.

"I saw the old guy in Toquerville today and made an offer on the place. He agreed right away... in fact it seemed like he would have even accepted a lower offer."

"Oh, that's great. He seemed so nice."

"Yeah, he really was. He seemed like he really wanted us to have the place."

The word "us" that Aaron had used--it made her think. Was it just an inadvertent use of the word? Or, was he about to formally propose marriage? Did she want him to? Was he really ready? Was she? They had met barely two months ago, she realized, recalling the somewhat awkward circumstances, near midnight, as she was walking along the highway near the bridge over the Virgin River. She felt her pulse quicken and intensify. For a moment they were both silent.

"I'll stop at the bank in Parowan tomorrow and see if they'll combine my truck loan with a house loan. I don't know if they can really do that."

"I think they can. Come and sit up to the table. The soup is hot now."

As they began eating, Aaron continued. "I guess I'll spend the night up there with the folks. If I can get back early Friday night, would you like to go out to dinner with me?"

"Sure, I'd like it very much." Her pulse picked up again. "That would be after we meet with the missionaries. Won't that be about six o'clock?"

"Yes, six o'clock. And Natty will be here. She should be coming home any time, now." She took a deep breath. "But I've decided I want to be baptized, anyway. And I want you to do it for me, Aaron."

For a few seconds, he stopped eating, with a glass of water halfway to his mouth. "Naomi," his voice caught as he spoke her name, "that makes me feel so great! Are you sure... ? I don't want you to do it, if it's just for me."

"No, no! Don't think that. It's the right thing for me to do. I think Natty wants to do it, too. We've talked about it a lot... between us, and with Mom, too."

"What about Ben Randolph? They're getting pretty serious, aren't they? What does she say about him?"

"He was baptized as a child, you know. I believe things will work out for them, somehow."

"I hope so," said Aaron. "I'd hate to see her... "

"See her? What?"

"Oh, well, I was just thinking that after we, uh, were to get married," a flush suddenly appeared on his face, "she would be kind of lonesome here by herself."

Her pulse raced again. "Will that be, um, soon, maybe?"

He dodged her question, but not very smoothly. "Let's talk about it more, later." He stood and took a long drink of water. She stood up, also and stepped into his embrace with her long dark hair gently touching his arm. As they walked to the door, Natty entered the fenced yard and greeted the dogs. Naomi's goodbye kiss was warm and sweet.

* * *

The next evening, Aaron had come from Parowan with the promise from the bank loan officer that he could obtain a clear title to his truck and add the cost to a mortgage on the house. During the following week the house and land would be appraised and the mortgage papers would be prepared for his and his father's signatures. The loan officer made it all sound so simple and convenient.

Naomi was thrilled with the set of rings that he had bought for her, as well. She had accepted his proposal at dinner the night before, but, of course, the date for a wedding was yet to be decided.

But she had a surprise, herself. She had made application to the sheriff's office to become their first female field deputy. Sheriff Cooper was surprised to receive her application and talked about it with her for quite a while. He seemed a bit skeptical and somewhat negative, at first, but slowly warmed to the idea. There would be strict agility requirements, of course, and two months of academy training in Salt Lake that she would have to pass. Her mother, Becky Scott, assured her that her chance of getting the job was excellent. Naomi had picked up applications, also, for a three-hour Thursday evening class in police science at Dixie College. Emotions for both of them were on a high plane.

CHAPTER THREE

The next day, Aaron got into his recently purchased pickup and drove north with the intentions of trying to meet with another trooper, Dan Wilde. As luck would have it he heard on his police scanner that Dan was checking out at Bud Tulley's cafe in Kanarraville. He took the exit to the old highway, U.S. 91, and drove toward Tulley's.

On entering the cafe, he greeted Bud and spotted Dan and a younger, taller man in street clothes, engrossed in conversation, while seated at a table in the rear. The stranger seemed to be a little older and possibly even taller than Aaron with a dark complexion and nearly black wavy hair. Dan smiled as Aaron approached their table.

"Hey, Aaron, this is Johnny Lee Chaffey," Dan said. "He's the trooper in Salt Lake County that I was telling you guys about. Wants to transfer down here." The two men shook hands.

"Pleased to meet you, Johnny," said Aaron as he took a seat.

"Well, likewise, Aaron. I was just saying to Dan, here, that I'd heard it gets pretty hot down here."

"Oh, this is nothing," Aaron replied, taking note of Johnny's southern accent. "Dan, be sure to take him down in the basin. It must be a hundred and ten or more, today."

"Johnny comes from the eastern part of Texas," Dan continued. "Imagine it can get pretty hot down there. He's down here checking us out. His wife, Carrie, is in Cedar City trying to land a job in the hospital."

"Hey, that's super!" Aaron exclaimed. "I hope it all works out for you both. And, speaking of hospitals, Dan, did Jane have her baby yet?"

"Due at any time," Dan replied. "She and the Relief Society's got it all worked out... you know, baby sitters, if necessary... for the boy, and all that. Course the girls are there, most of the time, but they can get pretty busy too. By the way," Dan continued with a grin, "how's it going with you and... what's her name... uh... Naomi, wasn't it?"

"Well," Aaron replied, "as a matter of fact, we haven't set a date yet, but she's agreed to... uh, marry me. And... she's taking discussions with the missionaries. And... she's applied for a deputy slot with the sheriff! Can you believe all that?"

"Oh, really! That's great!" Dan replied. "You got it made, my man!"

Johnny Lee leaned slightly forward across the table. "Hey, congratulations, Aaron! But... not to change the subject, or anything, and don't look now! But have either of y'all noticed that couple sitting over there near the far wall opposite the counter?" He motioned slightly just by moving his head and eyes.

Dan answered, "Well, yeah, they were here when we came in, looks like they're about to leave. Why?"

"Well, back when I first put on the uniform, I noticed right away that just about everybody would turn to stare at me, at least, for minute or two, y'all know what I mean, like sizing me up. Those two haven't looked at us even once. In fact, it looks to me like they're trying hard to avoid it."

"Yeah," Aaron said. "I noticed that, too, then I forgot about it. Who knows? D'ya think they could be up to something?"

"They look like plain old tourists to me," Dan said. "But, then, ol' Bud doesn't get many tourists in here. The freeway has pretty well ended that." Dan motioned to Bud, who had been quite busy, to come over to their table. "Don't look, Bud, but have you seen those people before? That couple over by the far wall?"

"Nope. Never seen 'em afore, Dan. But, I gotta keep movin'. Lotta people in here, today."

The man next to the far wall stood up, drew some cash from his pocket and placed a tip on the table. The woman with him went to use the restroom while he paid for the food and waited for her at the large front window, never once even glancing at the officers. He slid a pair of dark glasses from the top of his dark 'crew-cut' down to cover his eyes. His knee-length shorts and golf shirt marked him as a tourist--just passing through. As soon as the woman, also in typical tourist attire, came from the restroom. They left the cafe, entered a late-model brown Chevy four-door with Utah plates and drove north.

Dan got up quickly and threw some bills on the table. "Let's go, Johnny," he said. "I want to follow those two. I have a really strong feeling they may be up to no good!" Dan headed quickly for the front door then whirled around to seek out Bud Tulley. "Bud! Don't ask questions now but I need to buy the money from you that those people left on the table and in the register... real fast! Do you have an envelope handy?"

Bud, looking surprised, pulled a drawer open and retrieved an envelope, which he handed to Dan. Picking up the money by the edges, Dan took the three one-dollar bills from the table and a twenty from the till and put them in the envelope. Dan put his hand on Bud's shoulder in order to secure his full attention. "Now, this will sound really crazy, Bud. I need you to leave their table just like it is until I get back. Don't touch anything. Don't clean it up. Okay?"

"Well... yeah, sure. Whatever you say, Dan."

Aaron shook his head with a slight smile and left to go south. The brown car was out of sight before Dan and Johnny Lee could get going. But it didn't take long to catch up to where they could assess its speed and other movements from perhaps a quarter mile back.

* * *

The driver of the Chevrolet, Chuck Thompson, upon seeing the white UHP vehicle following them, felt his pulse race. He struggled to calm himself and in his mind reviewed quickly the accessibility of their weapons. His Beretta, a .25 semi-automatic, carrying seven hollow-point, lead rounds was concealed under his right thigh. Laura's weapon, identical in every way, was carried in her purse. He realized that at any moment they may have to use them.

"Sure looks like he's followin' us," he muttered.

"Let's pull off in that town, Cedar City, like we need to get some gas," Laura answered, after looking back. "Let's see what he does. He might be just be going the same way by chance."

"Yeah, you're probably right. He's not gaining on us. Not yet, anyway. I'll just keep going and stop in Cedar City." He entered the freeway and drove at a moderate speed. The troopers followed but stayed well behind. Other traffic soon began to collect behind Dan's car.

"Looks like they're watching us, for sure," Dan said. "They're not going to do more than fifty-five. Let's go on by them and take an exit."

"Good move," Johnny Lee replied. "I'll get the tag number. And we can run a twenty-eight, twenty-nine on it."

"Very good. I know they're up to something."

As they passed the Chevrolet, the couple seemed to ignore them just as they had done at Tulley's. The inquiry on the license plate indicated it was a rental unit out of Salt Lake City. Nothing out of the ordinary? A vacationing couple that had spotted a cop car and didn't want any trouble? Just like scores of others on the scenic southern Utah highways? Still, their actions indicated something odd could be going on.

Dan picked up the mike as he took the exit for Cedar City, now well ahead of the brown Chevrolet. "Cedar, this is One-six-two... is Two-six-eight on the air?"

The Iron County dispatcher quickly contacted Trooper Barney Jeppson, who was north-bound, nearing the Beaver County line, about thirty miles ahead, and advised a car-to-car conversation. Dan re-entered the freeway. The Chevrolet should have been several minutes ahead of them.

Barney's voice sounded weak and distant. "One-six-two, I should be at your location in about three minutes."

Johnny Lee looked quizzically aside at Dan, as he switched the radio over to channel three. "Hey, Mr. Rubble... I've got a passenger you should meet. Can you head back this way? Maybe meet us about halfway? We're just passing Cedar City now."

"Hey, yourself, Danny!" was the reply. "Meet me at Exit eighty-two. Okay?"

"Right. We should be there in about twenty minutes," Dan answered. "You might watch for a brown Chevrolet. The people were acting kind of odd. It's a man and a woman. The car is a rental out of Salt Lake City. We first noticed them at Tulley's. My passenger is Johnny Chaffey, One-eighty-one, out of Salt Lake County. He noticed them acting a little odd in Bud's place."

"What did they do at Tulley's?"

"I'll explain it later. If you see the car going along, you might just take a look at it."

"Very well. I'm getting close to exit eighty-two, now. I'll be going back to channel six."

"Okay, me too," Dan replied.

Dan and Johnny Lee assumed the Chevrolet was ahead of them and increased his speed a little. "That was pretty slick, how y'all switched over to three, that way," Johnny Lee observed. "A little secret code all y'all have down here?"

"Oh, yeah... we learned that some of these little crooks down here use police monitors. So we came up with a way of talking to each other so that they won't be listening in. All ya gotta do is say something with a 'three' in it and then you and your party can switch to channel three... seems to work okay, so far."

* * *

Barney Jeppson took exit eighty-two, figuring he had arrived perhaps ten minutes before Dan Wilde. He made a U-turn on the intersecting roadway and faced west just as a northbound brown car was passing on the freeway.

He picked up the microphone and, without contacting a dispatcher, he spoke to Dan. "Give me three minutes!"

"Hey, Barney? What's happening?" came an immediate response on channel three. "I'm about five minutes away."

Barney was accelerating northward on the entry ramp. "I think your brown Chevrolet just went by. I'm going to follow him a ways and maybe check him out.

"Okay, we'll follow you. Let's stay on three," Dan replied, while increasing his speed.

Barney quickly caught up with the brown car and watched from maybe a block behind. He observed that the car was once again closely sticking with the posted speed limit. Barney's suspicions rose, likewise. He picked up his microphone. "I'll bet he's got something to hide, all right." Two clicks was Dan's reply.

Barney closed the distance between his car and the Chevrolet. The woman in the car ahead turned and looked back. The driver stared into the rear-view mirror for maybe ten seconds. While doing so, the car drifted into the left lane maybe four feet and then quickly swerved back after the driver became aware. Barney, knowing that if a drug case, or if anything else of a serious nature resulted from this stop, if it ever went to court, his "reasonable belief" for the stop would be considered by a judge to be extremely weak. Regardless, he turned his red spotlight to face forward and activated the switch.

* * *

Chuck Thompson gasped and for a few seconds considered the wisdom of accelerating and trying to elude the officer behind him. Why were the cops interested in them? Surely they hadn't connected him to the deaths of the two prisoners, but what? His pulse was racing. Laura Thompson beside him reached into her purse and checked her little semi-automatic. She thumbed the hammer back and for a few seconds fingered the trigger then withdrew her hand from the purse.

"Keep your hands in sight!" Chuck hissed at his wife.

He reached for his own gun and, after cocking it, slid it under his right thigh. He slowly drifted to the right shoulder and stopped the car. As he watched in the side mirror, a tall and broad-shouldered officer was approaching his window. Chuck's hands were shaking and sweating. He pressed them onto his thighs and rubbed them on the fabric of his shirt and shorts. He pictured in his mind what he might have to do. He envisioned grabbing for the gun under his thigh and swinging it up to his open window and discharging a single round into the officer's forehead. It would be very simple. The soft, hollow-point slug would do the job very well. He could just drive away and turn off the freeway at the first opportunity. Then they could toss their little guns into the first body of water they came to--where no one would ever find them.

As Barney neared the window, Chuck began to inch his hand toward the Beretta. At the last instant, he hesitated. It wouldn't hurt to wait a few seconds more. After all, he reasoned, if they suspected that he was the killer of Barker and Conway, wouldn't they have a gang of cops stopping him, not just this one? Laura, keeping her hand close to the top of her open purse, turned to look at Barney Jeppson who was now at the window. She relaxed a bit after he tipped his hat to her.

"Good afternoon, sir, ma'am," Barney began. "The reason I stopped you, sir, is that the law requires a driver to drive within a single lane, except to pass, of course. You seemed to be weaving around a little. May I see your license and registration papers, sir?"

"Yeah... guess I did. Sorry, officer." Chuck Thompson relaxed a little after sensing Barney's friendly manner, realizing that he was not one of the officers that had been in the cafe--and hearing him speak to them so courteously. "Would you get them out of the glove box, Honey?" He kept his hands on or close to his thighs and a wary eye on the officer. To his dread, in the mirror, he noted a second white police car pull up and stop behind the first. A tall, dark younger man, wearing a baseball cap, got out on the passenger side, walked forward, opened the door of the first car, and reached in for something that he kept concealed behind the open passenger door.

Chuck's mind raced. Another cop? Of course! *Those two were at the cafe!* They must know he'd killed the two inmates, after all! But how could they possibly know that? And shouldn't there be more cops? Wouldn't they have a battery of guns out? Shotguns? Bazookas? Pointed and cocked? *Now the third officer is getting out*! I should have done it, he reasoned, when there was just one! Now all we have is our two little peashooters, against their big guns! He could feel the perspiration dripping down across his rib cage.

With hands quivering, he passed his Wyoming driver's license and the car's rental papers to the tall officer at the window. "I guess the sight of a police car so close behind me must have distracted me a little, officer. I'm sorry," he stammered, trying to sound calm. "I'll try to do better." Again, he rubbed his hands on his thighs, trying to manage a smile, and kept glancing back in the mirrors to see what the other officers were doing.

"They've just come up to talk to me for a few minutes, sir. What

I'm going to do is just write up a warning. You won't have to go to court or pay a fine, or anything else. You can wait right there in your car, sir. I'll just be a minute."

Barney retreated back to his car's right side. Johnny Lee had removed the shotgun from the scabbard and placed it on the seat. They introduced themselves and shook hands.

Dan quickly joined them. "What do you think, Barney?"

"My guess is they're hiding something," Barney replied. "This guy's got some kind of eastern accent. I used to hear it in the Marines a lot. He's shaking like a leaf. I'd sure like to get a look inside their trunk. I think I'll ask the driver a few questions and see where it goes."

"Y'all think they may be hauling drugs?" Johnny Lee asked. "Boy, up north, we hear about all y'all doing this all the time."

"He's acting real typical, for a drug smuggler," Barney answered. "I'm going to write up a little warning and then I'll talk to him some more."

Several cars and trucks passed them. "You know," Dan began, standing with Johnny Lee beside Barney's car. "I was just about to start looking around for those two guys we used to see following drug shipments. I had to stop and think. No, wait a minute! We arrested them... and they're dead now. Sure would like to get my hands on that lawyer, Croft, or whoever he is. Course, he's gone and done the world a big favor, that's for sure."

"Yeah. It was y'all and Aaron that caught them, right?"

"Well, actually it was Aaron Gentry and three of his friends. That's when Aaron got shot in the shoulder. They were just out riding their horses over by Zion Canyon and happened to run across them. Those two got away from a couple of hired killers that were chasing them. Then they tried to pull off into some trees and hide. But they got their car stuck in the sand. That's where Aaron and his friends spotted them. I guess they were just out riding their horses. It gets pretty complicated."

"So y'all think this 'Croft' guy slipped right into the jail, posing as their lawyer, and fed 'em some bad stuff?"

"Yeah, maybe put something in their soda cans when they weren't looking... something like that."

"I heard Aaron was right there in the office when they got sick and died! Man, that was some coincidence!"

"Oh, yeah, he helped haul them out of the jail. You'll be meeting his girlfriend, she's really something. She and her sister and her sister's boyfriend... and their two dogs... were with Aaron when they caught Conway and Barker. She is one sharp gal, alright... good sized and strong. You heard Aaron say she's applied for a job with the sheriff's office."

"That's good. Up north, I know there's several women city officers. And, now a couple more in the academy."

At Barney's request, the dispatcher's quick check for "wants and warrants" on Collins Thompson yielded no results. He finished writing the warning and carried it to the driver's window. "Sir, could I have a word with you back here for just a moment... if you wouldn't mind?" He opened the door to invite the driver out.

Chuck was surprised but began to slide out of the seat to go with Barney. As he turned, when his body was blocking Barney's view, he slid the Beretta forward and it fell to the floor. Laura reached over with her foot and pushed it under the seat.

As the two men moved toward the rear of the car, Dan walked toward the passenger door and began to talk to the wife. Johnny Lee followed him and listened. From her, through what seemed to Johnny Lee to be nothing more than casual conversation, he gleaned a synopsis of their itinerary for the past week. The reason that they had flown to Salt Lake City and picked up the rental unit at the airport; where they had been and who they had seen; the name of the movie they had seen on Tuesday night and the names of the actors; and where they were going, including the motel in Ogden, owned by her Aunt Wilma, where they would likely stay for the night were all revealed in her explanation. She answered every question quickly, smiling occasionally, but still seeming very nervous.

Barney requested that the driver resume sitting in the Chevrolet for just a moment. Barney and Dan talked and discovered the Thompson's' stories were astoundingly similar.

"Something's still kinda odd, though," Dan remarked. "Didn't you say that guy had some different accent? The wife sure did. Wouldn't you say so, Johnny? I mean... for Wyoming people. She sure sounded a little... strange. Both you guys've been in the military... you must've heard all kinds of different accents, from around the country."

"Yeah, I noticed that, too," Johnny replied. They looked at Barney waiting for his opinion.

"I could hear it, too," Barney responded. "I asked the guy if he'd lived in Wyoming all his life. He said he had! But it sure sounded like maybe back in the north-east, somewhere... like maybe some big city... definitely not Wyoming." The pair of troopers, still baffled at the couple's actions and nervousness, and without sufficient legal reason to even ask permission to search their car, decided to give it up.

As they talked, the driver, ahead of them, retrieved his pistol from under the seat and put it back under his thigh. This time, however, his hand was around the grip and his finger was lax against the trigger. He began to quake once more as Barney approached the window. Their plan was, if it appeared that he was going to arrest them, to drop him with one shot to the head and then jump out and finish the other two before they could react.

Barney was at the window, once more, still puzzled by their nervousness, and with a smile, tipped his hat and said, "Have a nice day and a safe trip back to Jackson, Mr. Thompson, Mrs. Thompson."

After the brown Chevrolet had departed to go north, the three officers stood outside their cars and talked. Johnny Lee had many questions about the area and especially about the murders of Floyd Barker and Brody Conway.

"Their contribution to the drug trade had been pretty much what I would call a fool's errand... a real farce... from the start," Barney stated. "I've thought and thought about it," he continued. "It seems to me that I remember a time when I was about to stop a guy way back last fall, not very long after Aaron and I busted Santana and Uribe. I had just stopped a car I thought must be hauling dope, when all of a sudden this dark colored sedan passed us going real fast. Course, I jumped back in my car and took off after the speeder. Never saw either car again. They must've turned off or flipped a 'U-ie' on me. And Aaron said the same thing happened to him just a few days before that."

"So you think it was Barker, or Conway?" Dan asked.

"I'm sure it was them, you know, trying to distract me. I guess anything'll work once. I've looked back through my old ticket books, but I couldn't find their names."

"Hey, y'all down here seem to have things a lot more interesting," said Johnny Lee. "Up in Salt Lake County, where I am, speedin' tickets and accidents are about all we ever do."

Dan and Johnny Lee gave Barney a quick summary of how the vigilante group, in some of the northern counties, had been broken up about five years before. And how another trooper's father had been involved. "And, besides that," Dan added, "one of the troopers we worked with, old Claude Maben, was one of the major players in the vigilante outfit!"

"Whoa, I just remembered," said Dan. "I asked Bud not to clean up that couple's table. Their fingerprints may be of some value. Who knows? I'd better get back there and check it out."

"Hey, no kidding," said Barney. "That's good thinking, Dan.

I guess it couldn't hurt to collect the stuff anyway. I'm going to sit down somewhere and write some notes about those people. I think we all should. Something might come of it. You never know."

The others agreed and departed to the south.

* * *

Ken Morgan's retirement party, several weeks later, on a Saturday evening, was turning into more of a "roast" than a party. Many old "friends" brought up some embarrassing occasions and even made up jokes about him. But it was all in good fun.

Aaron Gentry, whose left shoulder was now all but back to normal, and being on duty throughout the party, was able to be with Naomi for a half hour or so as the program was ending. As they sat with Becky Scott and some others from the sheriff's office, they learned that Jane Wilde had given birth to another boy at the Cedar City hospital. Dan was with her.

Sgt. Shane Lowry, the sheriff's lead detective, stopped by their table and sat down. The conversation, of course, turned to the investigation into the murders at the jail. Shane patiently went over some of the pertinent details. His intent was to appear to be baffled and try to see if anyone else may have some ideas that he could pursue.

"What about the wife... from Las Vegas?" Aaron asked. "And that other guy? Wasn't he Conway's relative... a brother? Maybe they really wanted to just get rid of Barker so they could go ahead and get married... or something like that."

"Well, too," Becky added, "I remember seeing this other guy just waiting by their car in the parking lot... out in front. He could've been the wife's boyfriend, or something."

"That's entirely possible," Shane said. "We did call down to Vegas and talk to her and Conway's half-brother. And... you're right, Becky, she told us she only came up here to let him know she was going to divorce him as soon as possible. She had no idea where he had been living before that. And... she even admitted sneaking some candy into the jail and giving it to them. She really didn't know why she did that, just a silly impulse... she told me. At first we thought some of the candy might have been... uh... altered, or spiked with something. But then, after the lawyer's clothing and disguise turned up in the garbage, we knew for sure the wife had nothing to do with it. And... we got hold of the real John Croft, up in Salt Lake... he didn't know anything about all this... at all."

Shane had reasoned, right away, that the purpose for the "lawyer" to go to the store in Hurricane--crazy as it seemed--was to change his identity and to leave the stolen car parked inconspicuously within a crowded parking lot--like leaving a well-crafted "trail" for the police to follow. Certainly even more bizarre was the fact that one of the custodians had found the clothing, toupee, and shoes under the restroom trash bag when he was about to throw the stuff into the dumpster at the rear of the store. It was likely that there had been at least two people involved, since the black car was abandoned in the parking lot.

"What I can't figure out," he continued, "is... why would this man... whoever he was... go to all the trouble of having such an elaborate disguise and all that and then just leave the car right there in the parking lot where he should have known it would be found before very long. If he had just left it in a different place, like maybe leavin' it at a big parking lot at Zion Canyon or Cedar City, we probably would've never found the clothing and other stuff. It's almost like he really intended to leave a trail for us... for some reason." The others at the table remained silent but obviously fascinated. "What has us really stumped, though," Shane added, "is there isn't a single fingerprint on anything! But nobody saw this guy wearing gloves."

"Oh, no," Becky added. "He was definitely not wearing gloves when I saw him. And he handled the ten-dollar bill, the Coke cans, and his business cards, you know."

"It was like he had no fingerprints," Shane said, "... no friction ridges... on his fingers or hands... like he was some kind of alien space-man, or something."

The group was silent for a moment. Naomi spoke first. "Maybe he had put something on his hands to cover up the little lines and stuff on his hands and fingers." The others looked at her in silence. She flushed a little at their sudden attention, but added, "I remember when we were putting in the sprinklers at Mom's house. If you got any of that clear glue stuff on your bare hands it would stick to your hands at least a day. You couldn't get it off!"

The others were fascinated at her theory. "So, you're saying...," Aaron asked, "maybe he put something like that clear PVC glue on his hands and fingers and let it dry, then he'd leave no fingerprints... and nobody would see it on his hands because it's clear?"

"Well, sure," she answered, with an embarrassed smile.

"What do you think, Shane?" Becky asked. "Is that possible?"

"Well, it sounds very plausible," Shane said. "I think I'll try it myself and see if it really works." Those at the table turned to look at Naomi again. Her face glowed anew with some embarrassment from their attention.

Aaron broke the silence. "I've told her all along, she should be in law enforcement." The others nodded in agreement and some of them raised their water glasses in a mock salute. "But, in the meantime, I'd better get back out on the road."

Naomi walked with him to the door and bid him goodbye in the foyer of the building with a quick kiss. "I'll get a ride home with Mom," she said.

* * *

Naomi Blackstone was hired by Sheriff Ian Cooper on the Monday after the party. And after two months spent at the Utah State Police Academy in Salt Lake City, she came back to begin work at the Washington County Sheriff's Office. She and Aaron Gentry set a December date for their marriage. Not long after Naomi had graduated from the police academy, Natty and Ben surprised everyone by returning from a trip to Las Vegas with a certificate of marriage.

CHAPTER FOUR

On an unusually cool and overcast day for late October, it appeared that at least some rain could fall on the dry desert slopes to the west. But then, in the vast southwest, the skies often promised yet failed to deliver.

Naomi Blackstone gave little thought of anything to do with upcoming Halloween. She was enjoying her new job too much.

As she drove the sheriff's white Dodge four-by-four west on old Highway 91 that paralleled the Santa Clara River, she marveled as she had many times before, at how her life and the lives of her mother, Becky Scott, and her half-sister, Natty Blackstone, had played out. Led by Becky, away from the polygamous community of Hildale, near the Arizona border, they had made new lives in the St. George Basin. Occasionally, they would secretly help escort other young girls out into a very different world.

On just such a late-night clandestine operation, early in the spring, Aaron was southbound from the tiny town of Harrisburg and was about to turn toward her on SR-9, walking west from the river. His car, about to make a left turn to go east, toward her, had been illuminated by the bright headlights of another vehicle passing her from the east. In something of a panic, she had quickly hid her much younger companions in the tall mesquite beside the highway. As luck would have it, he had stopped to check on her safety. Her fascination for the tall, blond, young officer had been impossible to dismiss since their chance meeting--late that night in April. For at least the thousandth time she relived that moment.

She had been quite aware, in spite of the awkward situation, of a strong--and mutual--attraction between them. She smiled to herself, remembering how he had strained to bridge the transition from an officer-citizen contact to a more sociable relationship with her and how, on a sudden impulse, she had deliberately given him a false clue to mislead him. But after discussing it with her mother, Becky, had decided to contact him again. She relived their dates and horseback rides with Ben and her half-sister Natty and being involved in the capture of Barker and Conway that had nearly cost Aaron his life. The transition from forklift driver at the warehouse in Washington City to deputy sheriff at times seemed to have been a fantasy. Law enforcement had seemed almost a parallel universe that had been functioning almost beyond her realm of awareness--a change in her life that seemed to her unfathomable. She enjoyed it immensely.

She puzzled again over how the two men, who were suspected of involvement in the transportation of illegal drugs, had died while incarcerated not long after being visited by a man pretending to be their lawyer. The distinguished-looking man, conducting what was obviously a contract killing, had apparently poisoned them by giving them some toxic pills or even slipping a lethal substance into their soft drinks. It seemed to her like a tale out of a James Bond movie. The broad trail of evidence had mysteriously ended at a department store restroom where the man had shed his disguise and changed into other clothing. That made no sense to any of the investigators. The hit man could easily have disposed of those things a thousand other ways--never to be discovered. The stolen car he had been driving was abandoned in the crowded parking lot. From there, he had obviously either driven away in another vehicle or was picked up by a second person.

For several months now, the double murders, practically in the presence of jail personnel, had been the primary concern of the sheriff's chief criminal investigator, Sgt. Shane Lowry. But Naomi was also determined, in spite of being a novice, to help solve the double murder if she possibly could. Everyone assumed the pair of jail inmates, who the officers felt, were not real bright, had been eliminated because of their drug connections. Obviously, they could implicate or be a source of information leading up the chain of command to bigger fish, perhaps in eastern cities, at the distribution level. Still, it was well-known that they had, or once had, connections with the Las Vegas underworld. Shane Lowry had made several trips to southern Nevada to discuss the matter with the Clark County Metro criminal investigators, but had failed to uncover any information that would point to a murder plot originating there.

At the tiny community of Shivwits, Naomi spotted a dust-covered light blue, Ford with a large single red bubble light on top parked at the combination general store and gas station, the only mercantile outlet on the expansive Shivwits Indian Reservation. The second-hand police car was getting on in years and the paint had faded to an even lighter shade. Rust was coming through in places and one couldn't help but notice the darker places on the doors where the Utah Highway Patrol decals, the beehives, had once been. The reservation had a marshal, so to speak, and he would no doubt be inside.

A back room of the little store was basically his "office" where he was afforded a small space. Radio contact, when the apparatus was working, between the young marshal and tribal members was accomplished through a citizen-band radio from inside the store to his car.

Naomi decided to stop in and visit with him. Unlike some others in law enforcement, she was naturally congenial, and instinctively felt that it was good to have friendly relations among all police agencies, no matter how large or small. Besides, in the broad expanse of western Washington County, help from backup officers could often take a long time to arrive.

She remembered Whitney Greyhorse from high school, graduating two years ahead of her. Tall and slender, he had excelled in long-distance running in the spring and was a pretty good halfback for the Dixie High School team. They had taken a few courses together at the local Dixie College in the evenings.

She exited the truck without signing off with the county dispatcher and walked into the store. The lone clerk, a middle-aged woman with black hair pulled back and tied in a bun, on seeing her county uniform, directed Naomi to the back room.

"He's back there," she said. There was something, perhaps a subtle message in her facial expression that conveyed to Naomi a contemptuous reaction as the woman resumed sweeping the badly worn linoleum tiled floor.

"Thank you," Naomi answered, with a smile. The clerk made no response. She'd seen the reaction before in the faces of some citizens, especially women, who expressed--without saying, of course--that she had no business getting involved in *"man's work."* At least, that was the way she interpreted it. Naomi walked back through the door marked "employees only."

Whitney looked up from his paperwork, stood with a smile, and extended his hand to her. "Hey, Deputy Blackstone!" he exclaimed. "Good to see you again."

"Same to you, Whitney. What's going on out here?"

"Oh, just the same old stuff... can't complain, you know. How about you?"

"Just checking out the west side. Some rancher out here says he's missing some livestock, over past the Bull Valley range. The sheriff wants me to go over and look into it. I'll be lucky to find the guy... let alone the cattle. Can I use the phone? I need to call in to the dispatch and let them know where I am."

"Sure, go ahead. Would you like a root beer or something?"

They spent maybe twenty minutes talking about this and that before she rose to go. He congratulated her on her up-coming marriage to Aaron Gentry and asked when the wedding was to take place. The phone rang before she could answer the question. Whitney picked it up.

The call was for her. She recognized the male dispatcher's voice. "Naomi?"

"You can cancel on the stolen cattle deal. The guy found 'em. He must've forgot where he put 'em!"

"Oh, that's neat. Okay maybe I'll go on over to the west anyway... see if anything's going on out there."

CHAPTER FIVE

Nearly back to Shivwits, Naomi asked the dispatcher to contact Aaron for her. She wanted to go to her doublewide, change clothes and meet him at what was to be their home in Toquerville.

"I've got him out on an accident up near the county line. He's with One-six-two. He'll probably be finished before you're ready to go up there."

"Yeah, good idea. He can get me on the CB. I'll be heading up that way in the Jeep."

At her mobile home in Washington City, she greeted Nero, who had to be fed. The animal had been showing signs of being very lonely since Natty's dog, Kody, had been taken away. After Ben and Natty had eloped to Las Vegas and taken up residence in an older house with some horse pasture in tiny Middleton, it had been lonely for her, too.

By the time she had gone most of the way to Toquerville, Aaron's call came on the CB to meet him at Bud Tulley's cafe. One of Bud's hamburgers would be very agreeable. She listened as he put in an order with Bud, using his CB.

To her pleasant surprise, Dan Wilde joined them for a sandwich. "So, was it a serious accident, or what?" she asked.

"Yeah, it was," Aaron answered. "You know how the deer like to come out and graze on the side of the highway this time of the year. California family... swerved to miss Bambi... took out the guardrail and rolled off down a steep embankment. We sent 'em all to the hospital in Cedar."

"Are they going to be okay?"

"Well, I don't know," said Aaron. "One of the passengers flew out of a door and the car rolled on him. People better start using safety belts."

"I think they should all make it, okay," Dan interjected. "He was real lucky he didn't get his head mashed in. So, Naomi, what have you been up to lately?"

"Well... let's see. I just got back from out in the reservation. Talked to Whitney Greyhorse a while. Drove on out to the west some more. Seems like the more I go out there the more awesome it gets. My gosh... there's a lot of wide-open space out there. Sure would be easy to get lost."

Bud Tulley delivered the hamburgers to their table with a big smile and left quickly to attend to other customers.

"So you two are planning to get married next month, I'm hearing," Dan said. "Or, was it December?"

"Actually, it'll be December fifth," Naomi responded with a broad grin.

"That's great," Dan commented. "I highly recommend it, myself. Our firstborn is almost sixteen, now. Seems like it was just a couple of years ago we got married."

"How's your new house coming?" Aaron asked. "I guess you've got the roof on and everything by now?"

"Oh, yeah. Maybe by some time in January, if we're lucky, it'll be to where we can start moving in."

"Sounds great," Naomi said. "You must be getting pretty crowded in the little pioneer house... with the new baby and all."

"Well, we're getting by, I guess you could say. How about your place in Toquerville? I drove by there the other day. I'll bet you're going to really like it there."

"Oh, we're about finished with the painting... and the carpets have been cleaned," Naomi answered. "Aaron's all moved in, already."

"Yeah, we even had some time to go to Brian Head to the lodge a few times," Aaron said. "Hey, if you and Jane like to dance... It's pretty nice up there. Course now that the snow is going to start stacking up, it's bound to get pretty crowded."

"We've decided to take some skiing lessons," Naomi said, smiling.

"Since we're so close to a ski resort, we figured we might as well."

"Oh, really," Dan replied.

"Yeah, who knows? We might even end up going to some really fancy place like Jackson, Wyoming," Aaron said, with a surreptitious wink toward Dan. Saying nothing, Naomi quickly glanced at him. She had been so careful about keeping their honeymoon destination a complete secret.

Dan read their faces and understood his obligation to keep their little secret. But he struggled with something else. "Funny you should mention Jackson, Wyoming. You've darn near reminded me of something, but I can't remember what. Something to do with Jackson. Hmm... Jackson, Wyoming? Now you've got me thinking. Dang it! I know I'll be trying to remember what it was for a week."

A few minutes passed in silence as they ate. They were Bud's only customers now and he, at their invitation and being a gregarious soul, pulled a chair up to their table and seated himself. Bud was proud of his role in helping identify Floyd Barker and Brody Conway, since they had been his frequent customers while driving the bright green Chevy Blazer. "So what's the latest on the Barker and Conway murders?" he began.

"You know," Dan remarked. "I still think the drug people were really stupid to have those guys hanging around in the first place. I mean... what? ... following drug shipments just to watch what we were doing? I guess they must have thought we were the stupid ones."

"Anybody have any idea who it was that bumped 'em off?" Bud persisted. "I mean, you gotta admit it was pretty slick, not to mention pretty, uh... darn bold. I mean to just slip into the jail and poison 'em like they did."

The three men looked at Naomi. "Well, Shane Lowry's been working on it just about full-time, I guess. He's recovered the clothing and the hairpiece that were used. They went over the black car completely. It had been stolen from up around Salt Lake somewhere. They took some prints off the steering wheel and the back side of the rear-view mirror. That's about it... so far. I guess you could say... right now, we're stumped... in capital letters."

"I've wondered how come he just left the car there at the store," said Aaron.

"Yeah," she answered. "If he was so smart... I mean, leaving the car there practically *invited* somebody to find his clothes and stuff in the garbage can. He, or they, would have had plenty of time to get rid of it in lots of other ways."

"I guess they all seem to do something really stupid, somewhere along the way," Aaron said.

"Yeah," said Dan. "Like Conway and Barker did... thinking they could scare us off. And shooting my dogs wasn't all that bright, either. I could've strangled both of them!"

After they had finished eating, Dan said he would go north and check out the freeway. Aaron walked Naomi to her black Jeep Wrangler and they exchanged a kiss. "I guess I'll be seeing you on Wednesday morning? Maybe we can get the rest of the painting done. I got that old lawn mower tuned up that he left for us. It works fine now."

"That's nice. I brought the list of stuff to get from the hardware store. Have you thought of anything else we'll need?"

CHAPTER SIX

By the middle of November, Aaron and Naomi were counting the days until their wedding in early December. On a couple of their dates they visited the ski lodge at Brian Head. The lodge was not crowded and the small dance-floor afforded them a chance to be away from the cares of their jobs. A quiet dinner and a few coins fed into the old jukebox gave them an opportunity to dance to Perry Como's "And, I Love You So," Jim Reeves' "Welcome to My World," and other romantic ballads. Being close to six feet tall, herself, Naomi always enjoyed being next to Aaron, who at six-feet-four, made her feel very cozy and protected. Each time she placed her hand on his powerful shoulders and felt the strength in his arms, she sensed the quickening of her pulse and a peaceful realization of sweet, unconditional belonging.

Aaron had moved from the apartment in St. George to the house in Toquerville. In off-duty hours, they worked to clean, scrape, sand, and paint to make up for the years of neglect of the nearly thirty-year-old house and yard. Old and over-grown shrubs were pruned or removed and old fences restored. Their horses, "Mancha," Naomi's bay-and-white pinto mare and "Pepper," Aaron's red roan gelding, now occupied the pasture that had been renewed with additional seeding and irrigation. The combination tack shed and hay barn, along with the house, would soon have to be re-shingled.

On top of all that, planning their wedding and receptions, in both St. George and Parowan, and taking a police science course together at the college one evening each week kept them very busy.

* * *

The day after meeting with Aaron and Dan at Tulley's was Tuesday, the last day of Naomi's workweek. She worked on reports for the week in the late morning when Sgt. Shane Lowry stopped by her desk.

"So, how's it going?" Shane began.

"Oh, everything seems to be okay. It's been a lot of fun. I was just mentioning to Dan Wilde, yesterday, traveling out to the far end of the county... You just don't realize how much open space there is out there!"

"Well, I've been hearing only good comments, so far."

They were surprised as Whitney Greyhorse joined them. "I'll drink to that," he said, with a grin and a soda can in his hand.

"Hey, Whitney, what brings you to the big city?" Shane asked.

"I'm due in court in a half-hour or so, unless they cancel it. I was backing up one of the deputies about two months ago on a DUI."

"I was just going to mention to Naomi," said Shane, "that I tried out her theory on how that lawyer 'John Croft' got into the jail and killed those guys without leaving any fingerprints on anything."

"Oh, really, what theory was that?" Whitney asked.

"Did you try out the PVC thing?" Naomi inquired.

"Yes, I did, and it worked perfectly. The cement dried on my fingers. It's quite flexible and you can't see it unless you look really close. No fingerprints or palm prints. It starts to peel off after a day or so."

"So you've got nothing to go on?" Whitney asked.

"Well, we've got the man's signature, his handwriting on the registration sheet and there were two of his real hairs from inside the toupee he had on. His hair was fairly short and brown. The clothes, the shoes and the phony horn-rim glasses could have come from anywhere."

They were interrupted by Naomi's obviously upset mother, Becky Scott, and Marti Gibson, the receptionist. "Naomi, there's a really strange man out in the lobby," Marti said. "Says his name is Preston Blackstone. He talks funny and says he's looking for anyone in the area that might be a relative of his."

Becky said quietly, "I'm thinking he could be looking for me. Go take a look at him, Naomi. I'm scared. Ever since Andrew died I've been afraid of this."

"Just calm down, Mom," Naomi cautioned her. "We don't know any Blackstones named... what was it? Preston, do we?" She put her arm around her mother's shoulders. "Just settle down. I'll go see who it is."

"You be careful!" Becky exclaimed.

"Oh, Mom," Naomi said in sympathy. "We are in the sheriff's office, after all!" She looked at Becky for a few seconds, remembering her father's large frame and dark features, then calmly walked toward the lobby. It had been several years since anyone from the border town of Hildale had stalked or bothered them in any way. Actually coming right up to the sheriff's office struck her as being rather bold and it made her extremely curious. She looked through the doorway at the man sitting in one of the upholstered chairs in the lobby.

His short, neatly combed hair was stylishly graying at the temples. It was immediately obvious that he was not a local person. An older man, a complete stranger, he had a pleasant face which reassured both Naomi and Becky. He was dressed impressively in a nice suit with a light blue shirt and a conservative tie that appeared to be nearly choking him. His face sported a neatly trimmed gray mustache. He sat with his legs crossed at the knee, studying names in a local telephone directory. Naomi, followed closely by Becky, walked across the lobby toward the visitor who politely stood up at their approach.

Naomi extended her hand to him. "Good morning, sir," she said. "I'm Naomi Blackstone." His lower jaw dropped slightly at her name. "And this is my mother, Becky Scott."

"Good morning to you, ladies," he responded, with his friendly smile directed at Naomi. "Please allow me to explain. My name is Preston Blackstone. I believe we would most certainly be distant relatives." His accent was unmistakably British and his manner was greatly animated. "This so extraordinary. I have come all the way from Lancashire to Salt Lake City, where they sent me down here to St. George. Such a curious name for a city in the desert. And, unbelievably, the first event after my arrival, I find two lovely ladies who have got to be my distant relatives."

"Oh, who sent you down here?" Naomi asked with a pleasant smile. Becky stood a little behind her, just far enough to the side to see the man.

"Oh, I am so sorry," he replied. "Please allow me to explain."

"Sure. Please do," Naomi said.

"I retired from the position of Assistant Chief Constable in Lancashire, approximately three years ago. My wife died soon after and I am alone now, with a lot of time on my hands. It seems I've taken up a hobby of sorts, you might say. I have thoroughly documented the names and pertinent dates surrounding all the relatives and ancestors as far as possible in England, at least back to where some of them had followed Sir William out of Normandy." With wide eyes, Becky, now fascinated, moved out a little more from behind her daughter. Preston smiled at her warmly.

"Please continue, Mr. Blackstone," Becky said. "So, now you've come to the U.S. to find some more, uh, relatives?"

"Exactly! Over a hundred years ago, one of my great uncles, several times removed, was converted by the preachers from a small, new church in Illinois, or maybe Missouri, it's a little confusing, you know. I believe they were called 'Mormons.' He was my great-grandfather's older brother. Their grandfather was Sir William Blackstone. Perhaps in your studies of the law, in preparation for your employment, you may have heard of him. One of the great legal minds of the eighteenth century, both in England and the United States. Well, in the colonies, shall we say."

"Well, no, can't say that we've ever heard that name before," said Becky. The visitor's eyebrows raised slightly for a brief moment.

"Well, at any rate," Preston continued. "I discovered that the Mormons had moved west to the Utah Territ'ry and have now spread out, practically all over the world. So I have come to this place to find out what happened to him. His name was Hanford Rushton Blackstone." Preston paused to look quizzically at their faces for any sign of recognition.

"Oh, yes," Becky replied, with a smile. "We're very familiar with that name."

"Ah, perhaps we are, indeed, cousins," Preston continued. "Somewhat distant, however. In Salt Lake City, at the grand genealogical reposit'ry, they searched for the name and found that he had matured and had a small family. In fact, they mentioned that he had acquired three more wives and was sent by the Mormon leader to this place to help grow grapes and cotton. Presumably, this young lady must be a descendant of his?"

"He was my great-grandfather," said Naomi. "Let me put it this way, sir," Naomi said. "I probably am your relative, but like they say, it would be a long story. A very long story."

"Oh, I am so sorry," he said. "I am keeping you from your official duties. I am so sorry."

"Oh, that's okay," said Becky. "This is really fascinating."

"What prompted you to start your search at the sheriff's office?" Naomi asked.

"Oh, I suppose that was only natural, of course. You know there seems to be something of a common bond among constabulary, no matter where we might go."

"Oh, yes, of course," said Naomi. "You were a constable, in England... where... did you say?"

"Lancashire. That's on the west, the Atlantic coast... well, actually next to the Irish Sea."

Quickly Naomi tried to recall some of the details of the lectures she'd sat through in her night class about the origins of U.S. law enforcement. Indeed, it made a lot of sense for him to seek out the "Shire Reeve" in another country.

"Would you like to get together this evening?" Naomi asked. "We could tell you the whole story."

Preston's face glowed. "Why, certainly. I would love to do that."

"I know!" exclaimed Becky. "Why don't we all get together at my place for dinner, about seven. I'll see if Natty and Ben can come, too. She's Naomi's half-sister."

"Oh, my," he responded. "I wouldn't dream of causing the slightest inconvenience for you."

"Hey, it would not be any problem at all, Mr. Blackstone."

"But your husband, madam?" he said.

"Andrew's been gone. He passed away... over two years, now."

Her tone sounded almost enthusiastic. Naomi gave her mother a quizzical glance.

"Oh, I am so sorry," he replied. "But, please, allow me to take you all to dinner, completely at my expense, of course." Naomi's glance shifted from one to the other, back and forth, smiling to herself and sensing that something just might be going on beneath the surface of their verbal exchanges.

"No, no, I insist. It's no trouble at all," said Becky, with a very wide smile. "I insist. We'll all meet at my place!"

"It's no use, Mr. Blackstone," Naomi said. "Once she wants us to come to dinner there's no changing her mind. And she's a great cook, too. Why don't we exchange phone numbers, now, and I'll pick you up for dinner. You'd never be able to find the place, yourself. Maybe I can get my fiancé to drop by, too. He's working the evening shift. Where are you staying?"

"Very well," he answered. "I'll be waiting for you in the hotel lobby... the Howard Johnson... at half-past six. And, by all means, please call me Preston."

"Very good, Preston," Naomi said, smiling broadly. "Look for me around six-thirty."

* * *

Near the end of her shift, Naomi initiated a call to Aaron. "Washington, this is Seven-ten, I need Two-eighty-nine, on three." She didn't wait for a response from Aaron but switched over to the "car-to-car" channel. There was another conversation going on, so they waited for a time.

"Seven-ten?" was his quick inquiry after the others had finished.

"Aaron, something's come up... for this evening, where are you right now? Can you meet me in the city somewhere?"

"I'm on the east side, not too far from your place. I can meet you there. Is that okay?"

"Okay, give me about fifteen minutes."

He tapped the talk button twice to acknowledge, then switched channels and started to head in that direction, wondering what it could be. He met her at the doublewide as Nero in his eagerness to greet them jumped against the chain link fence. Aaron reached over the fence and massaged his ears and jowls to his pure delight.

"So, what's up, Naomi," he asked.

"We'll have to postpone the rest of the painting until tomorrow morning. Mom has invited us and Natty and Ben to dinner tonight. And she wants you to drop by, too, if you can." He seemed somewhat disappointed at the delay at first.

She explained the details of meeting Preston Blackstone and the plans for dinner. "I think Mom is quite impressed with this guy," she said, grinning. "... know what I mean?"

"Oh. No kidding! Hey, that sounds fun. I'll check out for dinner out there around seven-fifteen, if I can. Guess, I better make a run to Zion's and check up around the county line first. Oh, and by the way... you can feel free to use our little code thing. When you need to go to channel three, just say something with the word 'three' in it." Naomi looked a bit puzzled. "You could say, 'I'll meet you in about three minutes' or 'three PM' or anything. Dan and Barney started doing that when they figured Barker and Conway might be listening in on them."

"Well, that sounds simple enough. Pretty cool. Okay, I'll be seeing you, then." Naomi glanced around them and, seeing no one, tipped her face up to his and planted a smiling kiss on his lips.

* * *

Promptly at six-thirty that evening Naomi parked near the front door of the white two-story Howard Johnson's Motor Inn. Preston Blackstone, slightly less formally attired in a sport jacket and another too-tight tie, met her just outside the door.

"Ah, good evening, Miss Blackstone," he said, with a broad smile. "It is so very hospitable of you to transport me about."

"Howdy, Mr. Blackstone," she responded, feeling somewhat uncomfortable. "The transportation's no problem. But, please, can't we be a little less formal? We can all use first names, can't we? Preston?"

"Oh, I'm so sorry. We can, for certain. Absolutely," he said. "I must remember to remember. This is not exactly the 'wild west' anymore, I suppose, but formalities are quickly dispensed with, nevertheless. I'll try to remember that, Naomi."

"You got that right. Come and meet my friend, Nero."

He looked at her quizzically as they walked to her Jeep, which seemed to be unoccupied. But as the passenger door was opened, Nero stood in the back seat and eyed the stranger silently but with evident apprehension. His tail stood straight out and still while the hair behind his skull rose slightly.

Naomi reached in to massage his ears. "Hey, boy this is my cousin, Preston. He's a good guy, for sure. He's going with us to Mom's house."

* * *

As soon as they stopped at Becky's home in Bloomington, Nero was on his feet barking and whining to get out of the Jeep. Naomi, seeing Ben's truck at the curb, knew what he was excited about. As soon as she let him out he sprinted around the house to the gate to the fenced back yard. His old pal, Kody, Natty's dog, no doubt recognizing the sounds of her Jeep and Nero's bark, was already at the gate. Naomi opened it and let him in where the grinning dogs began to chase and bite and wrestle in highly energized mock ferocity on being together again.

"My goodness," Preston exclaimed. "Such a remarkable display of canine congeniality!"

"Yeah," said Naomi, smiling to herself. "They've been together practically since they were just pups. At least until Ben and Natty got married and took Kody away with them."

"A most singular display!"

"Come on in the house and meet the others." At the door was a surprise for Naomi. The door burst open and a tall, broad masculine figure stood before her.

"Naomi!" exclaimed Paul Blackstone. "Get in here! ... got a hug for your favorite brother?"

"Paul!" she exclaimed, as they came together and she kissed his cheek. "When did you get here? You didn't even let us know you were coming!"

"Well, I've decided to go to college, courtesy of the U.S. Navy, and I expect to get a commission out of it. I'll tell you all the details, later. So this must be our cousin from England! I've been to London several times. A 'right jolly good' place to visit, I must say!" He put out a hand to Preston. "I'm mighty pleased to meet you, sir. I'm Paul Blackstone, Petty Officer, second-class, U.S. Navy."

"The pleasure is mine, to be sure!" said Preston. "It is such an honor to make your acquaintance."

"Come and meet the others, Preston," said Becky, smiling broadly and introduced Natty and Ben.

A white police car arrived as they were getting past the introductions. Aaron Gentry notified the dispatcher and walked quickly to the front door where Naomi let him inside and introduced him to Paul and Preston.

Halfway through dinner, the phone rang and Aaron looked at it with apprehension. Sure enough, he had to leave to check out a report of a possible drunk driver coming south that would soon be approaching the basin on the freeway from the north.

"Not much chance of finding the car, but I gotta try, anyway," he said to the others as he gulped a glass of water and ran for the door with a handful of raw vegetables. "Maybe see you later."

He was out the door in mere seconds. "Ah, yes," remarked Preston. "Operating while inebriated. I remember it very well."

"Oh, yes, you were a, um, constable, in Lancashire." Becky remarked. "I'll bet it was very different from what we do here."

"I'm sure you're correct, Becky. I'm beginning to surmise it was *very* different. I see that Aaron and Naomi are in different police organizations. That's very curious. Are there others?"

"Oh, yes, every county has it's own elected sheriff, you know. Then the state has a number of organizations with police powers. Practically every city or even some of the little towns, if the people want it, can have their own police and even their own court." Preston's eyes widened at that. "Then there's a ton of federal agencies. They're all over the place. What's it like in England?"

Preston began to chuckle. "I knew the Americans were assuredly in favor of keeping control of the police at the local level. And you can credit the English, from centuries past, for that. But, I simply had no idea! It would seem so cumbersome and perhaps even competitive. In the UK, a Chief Constable is more or less a political appointment, of course, but all of the constabulary are joined at the national level."

"No kidding. That all sounds really, um, efficient, I guess," Becky replied. "Down here, though, it's like we're all practically one big happy family, well, most of the time."

The others finished the meal and, thanking the hostess, left Becky and Preston to themselves. Natty and Naomi found their favorite board game and invited Paul and Ben to join them.

"So tell me about Hanford Rushton Blackstone," said Preston. "Apparently, after he left England, there were a couple of letters that he sent home to his parents. He talked about meeting his, um... prophet and how much the Mormons were suffering from extreme persecution. What a curious set of circumstances."

"Yes, I guess there were a lot of hardships they had to go through. Do you like to read? I have a couple of books on the history of the Mormon Church. And there's a library in St. George where there's a biographical sketch of 'H. R.' Blackstone. That's what he went by. I guess, here in the west, the name 'Hanford Rushton' seemed a bit long and awkward."

"I'm afraid I'm a bit confused," Preston said. "You are Naomi's mother? However, your name is Scott. I don't mean to be excessively, um... nosey but... "

"Oh, sure, I can understand. Naomi's father, along with his several wives, lives in a small town, down near the Arizona border. You can see from the looks of Paul and Naomi, he is a very large man. We were never actually married, that is, not in the eyes of the law... not legally, anyway. And I've only had the two children." Preston's eyes widened noticeably, but he remained quiet and fascinated. "Back when Naomi's grandfather was a child--one of H.R's twenty-seven children--they and a lot of others had to flee to Mexico or Canada to get away from federal officers. Back then the government was eager to prosecute the polygamists, you know. But then, the president of the Mormon Church issued a declaration that banned any additional polygamous marriages in 1890. But several groups split off from the main church and some of them even left the country, for a while, anyway. Over the years, since then, most of them have come back into this country and set up their own communities, mainly in Utah and Idaho... and Arizona. Now, it seems the government authorities have decided to pretty well ignore them."

"Am I to understand, then, that you were once in one of these small communities?"

"Oh, yes. I was the third wife to Naomi's father. I guess you could say that I became somewhat rebellious. When Naomi was about fourteen, I discovered that she had been 'spoken for.' Like I had been, back when I was only sixteen. That was the last straw for me. I guess I'd been in what is now called 'denial' about a lot of things. I just up and left one day, and took Naomi and Natalie with me. Hey, let me tell you, they were hopping mad and tried to get us back. My son Paul, on the other hand, was basically told to leave. He wasn't buying into their doctrine either, same as me and Naomi. Natty was always so close to Naomi that it was easy to persuade her to come along with us... with the approval of her mother, of course."

Preston's lower jaw had been sagging, somewhat. "How utterly remarkable. Astounding!"

"After I went to work for the sheriff, they pretty well quit bothering me. Before we got the big dogs, they were even stalking the girls. Natty went back to be with her mother for a while when she was about seventeen for just a few months but soon became disillusioned with it. The girls really missed one another, that's for sure."

"I'm terribly sorry, but this is all so fascinating. Am I correct, then, in assuming that you don't really belong to any church, right now?"

"I guess not. My husband, Andrew Scott, died a couple of years ago last May. He was baptized as a child in the main Mormon church. Aaron, that was just here, baptized Naomi and Natty this last summer. He was actually a missionary in Puerto Rico a few years back. I just haven't really felt the need. Maybe someday. Who knows. What about you?"

"Well, Anglican, all my life."

Becky took a photograph album from a shelf in the living room and opened it for his inspection. Preston was fascinated. Becky had managed to keep some early pictures of H.R. Blackstone and several of his wives and children, some letters to him signed by Brigham Young and other memorabilia.

"I'm sure a lot of people out in Hildale would like to get their hands on these things!" Becky commented.

The conversation among the young people seemed to be ending and Ben and Natty bid the others goodbye for the evening. They departed into the darkness. The sounds of the dogs as they were being separated penetrated the walls of the house.

Paul and Naomi joined Preston and Becky. "So, tell me," asked Preston, "what sorts of big cases are you working on at the moment? You've only been on the job a short time, I take it. Are you experiencing any difficult times, as yet?"

Naomi smiled and related the episode of being sent to locate the skeleton of "Ira Hoakes" in the desert, over beyond the reservation. Preston found it "most perplexing" and "appalling" that her fellow officers had played such a "nawsty" trick on her, but eventually came around to understand the humor. From there, she related the history behind the murders of Floyd Barker and Brody Conway inside the Washington County jail.

"It's not really *my case* but I am completely fascinated by it. I wish it were my case, but so far, I've been on routine patrol... vandalism, domestic disputes, barking dogs and so on."

"My job is strictly in the office," said Becky. "I keep the records in order and look after civil matters, like Sheriff's property tax auctions and evictions."

"So, Preston, how long do you plan to be around?" Paul asked. "It's going to be expensive to stay at Howard Johnson's for very long. You could soon run up some really big hotel bills. What all are you planning to do while you're here?"

"Yes, well I thought I might find a room, nearby, and perhaps rent a small automobile for, say month or so, before going back to England. I wanted to kind of map out all of H.R.'s progeny. Just a hobby, mind you. Eventually, you see, I'm planning to write a complete history. Well, sort-of complete history of the Blackstone family as far back as I can. Aside from that... I find that this is such a glorious place. There is so much to see... so different from my homeland. I'll be taking a large quantity of photographs, of course. I only wish my two daughters and their families were here to see it with me."

"Spare rooms may be a little hard to find this time of year," said Naomi. "This is a real popular place in the wintertime. A lot of 'snowbirds' will be flocking in, as usual. Mom, do you know of any place like that around here?"

"Not, um, off-hand. But, Preston, you don't need to rent a car." The others looked at her questioningly. "You can use Andrew's truck, I haven't been able to sell it yet. Haven't really tried, I guess." She raised her voice as if to overcome the objections that Preston's face was conveying. "No, no. It's just been sitting out there on the curb with a 'for sale' sign in the window for several months. Somebody needs to drive it. It's really nice, with a shell on the back. You could even camp in it if you go somewhere overnight. I'll need to follow up on the insurance, though. ... and the registration papers."

"Ah, Becky, that is so very generous of you. But I couldn't possibly impose on..." Paul and Naomi smiled at the exchange.

"Hey, Preston, you'd better take the offer," said Paul, cutting him off. "Trust me on this. You don't want to get my mother mad at you. You can take my word for that."

"Just make sure you remember to drive on the right side," said Naomi. "You could get yourself killed." Paul and Becky laughed.

Preston opened his mouth to object again, but Becky cut him off before he could speak. "Then it's settled! Paul, why don't you see if the truck needs attention right now? Let's see... what did I do with the keys?"

"This is so very generous of you, Becky, I shall be forever in your debt."

"What nonsense! You will not!" she exclaimed. "When you drive it around with the sign in the window, it'll give me a lot of free advertising."

The two men left the house and attended to the truck, which required a jump-start to get it going and recharge the battery. While they were gone, Naomi and Becky began to clean up the dishes and the kitchen.

"For a minute, there," Naomi remarked, with a smile. "I thought you were going to offer him free room and board, too."

"Well, it did occur to me." Naomi's mouth opened in shock. "But I guess it wouldn't look right... would it?"

"Mom, you're really asking me!?"

"No, I was just thinking out loud, I guess. He's seems like such a nice man, though."

"Yes, he does. But, Mom, I'm getting married in about three weeks. We've got so many things to think about."

"Yes, I know."

"I'm taking some of my stuff up to the house in Toquerville, in Aaron's truck in the morning. Hey! I just thought of something! You've got a couple of extra bedrooms here. Paul will be here for a couple of weeks. Won't he? What if I moved in here until the wedding? Then Preston could live in my house for a while. That Idaho couple won't be taking possession until after New Year's. He could stay there 'til they get here."

"That's brilliant! That would work out just great!" They explained the deal to Preston when the truck was ready. He objected at first, of course, but changed his mind when Naomi agreed to accept payment for a rental arrangement.

CHAPTER SEVEN

The next two days were hectic. Aaron and Naomi moved a lot of personal items into the house in Toquerville and some essentials into Becky's house in Bloomington. Preston moved into the doublewide in Washington City, then gave a hand with furniture, using Becky's truck. Driving on the left all of his life required a considerable amount of undoing. But a couple of near misses quickly left a lasting impression. Paul Blackstone helped shuffle things around, as well. The interior of the Toquerville house was essentially ready and they were able to start cleaning and repainting the exterior doorjambs, window trim, and the soffit and eaves. December was unusually mild, even for the 3,200 ft. Ash Creek bottomland, in Utah's Dixie.

Many of the neighbors stopped by to chat and bid Aaron and Naomi welcome. Some women from the church even brought food and talked at considerable length about the town and the ward and how glad they were to have a couple of law enforcement officers move into the neighborhood.

Dan Wilde, while spending nearly all of his off-duty time working hard to finish his new house, stopped by for a few minutes to talk and survey their progress. He mentioned to them, again, that he had been trying to remember why Aaron's allusion to their honeymoon in Jackson, Wyoming, had reminded him that there was something very significant about it.

"I've even spent some time looking back over my notes, ticket books and log book for the past couple of months. Guess I'll have to keep digging... if I can ever find the time. It's really got me going...

between that, trying to finish the house, and trying to teach my daughter how to drive! Whoa!"

"Well, it must have been something important," Naomi remarked. "Did your friend from Salt Lake ever get his transfer to Iron County? I assume his wife got the job at the hospital."

"Yeah, he did. You'll probably meet both of them before too long. I saw her in the ER about a week ago."

"I understand she's really small," said Aaron. "Like about five feet tall, or so?"

"Oh, yeah, and Carrie's real pretty. She's quite dark. You might even think she was Hispanic. Well, come to think of it, her mother is. And Johnny's about your height, not as heavy, though. Well, you met him once, back in the summer, up at Tulley's place." As he said that, Dan suddenly remembered the interior of Tulley's cafe and the couple acting a little odd at a table next to the far wall--the couple that Barney Jeppson had stopped and talked to north of Parowan.

Aaron's response distracted his thoughts. "Yeah, that's right," Aaron said. "He's dark, too."

"Why don't we all get together with them sometime?" said Naomi. "After Aaron and I get all settled in here, we could have everybody get together for a Christmas party or something."

"Hey, that would be great!" said Aaron. "Course the whole district will be doing a Christmas thing about the middle of December, I understand."

"Yeah, I think it's going to be at a restaurant in Cedar City this year." Dan looked at his watch. "Speaking of Cedar City, I'm due up there for court in about an hour. I'd better be heading that way, 'mucho pronto.' Anything new on the jailhouse murders, Naomi? Has Shane Lowry come up with anything?"

"No, not really. We, uh, I hear he's run out of leads and he's about ready to rip out what's left of his hair!"

"Well," said Dan. "I'd best be going. By the way, your house is looking real good."

"Oh, well, thanks a lot." Aaron said, as Dan turned to leave. "See you later."

As Dan drove north to Cedar City, his thoughts returned to the man and the woman that he and Barney had briefly talked to after leaving Bud's place. Could they be the Jackson connection? And what if they were? Why would that be of any importance? Maybe he should go back and find his notes from that day and talk about it with Barney.

* * *

Detective Lowry had come to feel quite comfortable talking to Naomi about the murders of Barker and Conway. He liked her creative ideas--sometimes quite unorthodox but often very interesting. Early Friday afternoon they happened to meet in the hallway near his office.

"This is about to drive me nuts," Shane remarked. "All we've got so far to go on is two lousy brown hairs from the wig."

"Don't forget, too, we know the size of his shirt, jacket, and trousers. Probably his shoe size, too."

"Yeah, him and maybe a few million other guys."

"Don't you think that if he was smart, he would've found some place locally to maybe 'lay low' for a few days. Until some of the heat had dissipated."

"What do you mean, Naomi?"

"Well, he might very well reason that the police would be watching the Interstate, really close. Where do you think he could've come from? Las Vegas? Maybe he... or they... would just get a room in a motel not too far away. On the other hand, maybe take one of the back roads like maybe Eighty-nine through Panguitch or maybe even take off across Nevada. Maybe he went south. He, or they, would have had quite a long time to get a long ways away... maybe six or seven hours... by the time somebody realized it really was a double murder."

"Or, maybe he, or they, just became part of the tourist crowd at Zion's, or maybe the North Rim at Grand Canyon. Like you just said, the poison worked so slowly, there was plenty of time to do either one."

"If he did that, there's a real good chance he had a partner. They could even be husband and wife, or at least pretending to be."

"And, they would likely have been staying in some motel or hotel in the area, at that time. I have to say, Naomi, I like the way you think. That sounds like a very plausible theory. I think I'll start checking hotel and motel registers around that date."

"But then, he could have been alone," said Naomi, with a sigh. "And just got into another car and drove away on the interstate. He could've even made it maybe as far as Barstow or Salt Lake City before Barker and Conway even got sick."

"Quite possible. But there wasn't any reports of any cars stolen anywhere close to where he left the black one."

* * *

Shane and Naomi were both about to leave the office after having talked for a few minutes before she was to go back on patrol. They were surprised when the sheriff, Ian Cooper, a tall broad man, younger than Shane, with wavy black hair stopped by the detectives' office.

"Hey, Sheriff," Shane said, with smile. "How's it going?"

"Not bad. How's it with you two?"

"You know... the murders of Barker and Conway has been driving me nuts. Naomi has made some suggestions that may turn up something. And, I've decided that we should go over the physical evidence again... the clothing and even the shoes, for more clues. Maybe there really is something that I've missed. I don't know."

"You've found the hair," Naomi observed, "that was inside the wig he'd been wearing. We know he has brown hair."

"And like you said, we know his clothing sizes and shoe size and all that."

"How closely did you look at the trousers?" Ian asked.

"What do you mean?" Shane replied. "His suit jacket and trousers seemed to be very clean. I suppose we could take all that stuff all the way up to Weber College in Ogden. They've got that new crime laboratory. I'm hearing that Millard County takes stuff up there a lot, now."

"Maybe you should," the sheriff replied, "at least, you could give the crime lab a call and see what they might think about it."

"Okay. I'll do that," Shane answered, "right away."

"Sometime before you leave today, Shane," said the sheriff, "could you stop by my office for just a minute?"

"Yes, sir. I'll do that."

The sheriff left them and they continued talking for a few more minutes. Naomi stood up to go and resume her patrol duties, which would take her to the west end of the county. Becky Scott quickly emerged from the civil and records office and met her in the hallway with a big smile.

"Guess what?" she blurted. For an instant, Becky seemed transformed from being Naomi's mother into a sister or girlfriend about to share some very personal confidence with her. Naomi had a pretty good idea of what it was going to be. And she was glad for her mother. It had been a lonely time for her since Andrew Scott had passed away.

"Gee, I don't know. What? I could never guess."

"Preston wants to take me to dinner tonight!"

"Gosh, Mom," said Naomi, faking astonishment, "what a surprise! That's really neat!"

"He wants to learn all he can about the H.R. Blackstone family. I told him he'd have a hard time getting anything out of your father."

"I'm sure of that. I guess that means you'll have to be his only source of information. Course there are others around that have left the order and 'gone astray.' But that's beside the point."

"Oh, Honey, I know you've been angry about it all. But it's way past time to be over it. Preston has been such a breath of fresh air, you know."

Oh, I know," Naomi said. "He seems like such a nice man. I think you should help him all you can. Who knows, maybe..." Naomi smiled at her unspoken thoughts.

Becky understood. "Well, I'd better get back to work," she said with a smile of her own. "I can't be worrying about the work here over the weekend. I'll let you know how it goes."

* * *

Sergeant Lowry stopped by the sheriff's door on his way out to leave to go home. "You wanted to see me, Sheriff?"

"Yes, I did. Have a seat. I was just dictating something for the secretary. How's Naomi doing?"

"Hey, she is really smart. I'll tell you what, if we were a big department with a whole bunch of detectives, I'd almost kill to have her for a partner."

"You want to explain that to me, Shane?" Ian said, with a somber and puzzled expression. He rose from his chair and closed the door.

"No, no! It's not that she's so attractive, and all that." He paused for a few seconds and smiled. "Oh, I see what you're getting at. You used to be a bishop!" Ian looked at him intently in silence. "Don't worry about that, Sheriff. She's almost young enough to be my daughter. And besides that, she's about three inches taller than me and tough as nails."

"Well, I'll take your word for all that, Shane. What I was really thinking about is that some of the other deputies have mentioned that they would like a shot at being a criminal investigator. But I'm hearing that they think Naomi seems to have some kind of inside track with you. They see that she has been spending some of her time helping you, or at least talking with you on this double murder."

"Yes, that's true. But I've never been around an officer that seems to have the abilities she has. I was dead in the water. She put me onto the idea that maybe 'Croft,' or whatever his name is, may have been using PVC cement on his fingers, so he'd have no fingerprints. And just today, she came up with the idea that his accomplice, if he had one, may have been a woman, maybe even his wife. And they may have just assumed the role of being tourists at Zion's or the Grand Canyon."

"So what would that lead you to?"

"Well, I was planning to check out the guest registration books for couples that might be 'possibles' for that date. You know, see where they came from and if they used a credit card, and so on. Most tourists would either be older couples or bringing the kids with them."

"Well... that just might take you somewhere," the sheriff said, thoughtfully. "Anything else?"

"Right after you came by, she said maybe there'd be some old soil particles sticking to the bottoms of the shoes... just in front of the heel. Maybe a mineral analysis could tell us where it might have come from. I'll tell you what, Sheriff, she's really something."

"That sounds great, Shane. Go for it. Still, that doesn't solve my problem, does it?"

"What's that, Sheriff?"

"I'd like to have our best people moving into criminal investigations and we badly need another one now. But Naomi's not even dry behind her ears. I can't transfer her... ahead of some of the others."

"Oh, I agree. I'd say for the time being, you could go ahead and pick another deputy for the job. But, from time to time, I could, uh, let's say, bring her up to date on what I'm doing and maybe get her input. But yeah, I agree, she does need more experience first."

* * *

On Tuesday afternoon, the fifth day of December, Naomi and Aaron were married by the bishop of the student ward in the Relief Society room where they had been attending. Mostly family members were present. Of course, Becky was accompanied by Preston Blackstone. Everyone who knew her had become accustomed to seeing them together frequently. The Gentrys were there from the farm in Iron County, along with Aaron's grandparents and other close relatives. Natty and Ben stood up with the bride and groom. Naomi found herself wishing that perhaps her half-sister could have waited and they could have enjoyed a double-wedding ceremony.

Naomi's dark wavy hair, that she kept tied back out of the way while on the job, flowed down around her shoulders. Her blue-gray eyes and brilliant wide smile easily set her apart from all the other women. Natty, a little smaller, with a lighter shade of hair had the same high cheekbones and gorgeous smile. Aaron and Ben, however, in matching dark blue tuxedos, were a sharp contrast. Aaron was large and blond, while Ben Randolph, obviously ill at ease in the rented "monkey suit," stood more than half a foot shorter and was deeply sun-tanned with dark wavy hair and a substantial mustache and sideburns.

The bishop, while conducting the ceremony, talked at some length about the importance of focusing on a date for an eternal marriage the following year. His comments received Preston's full attention at once.

He turned to Becky and whispered, "What is that about?"

But she just smiled and "shushed" him, whispering, "I'll explain all that later."

* * *

Their reception was held that same evening in the recreation hall of the same church. It was a pleasant evening. The winter temperature in the St. George Basin was unseasonably agreeable. Many guests were arriving in suits and light jackets, and just a slight breeze played among the palm trees.

The newlyweds, each having a full week off from their jobs, planned to get a night's rest at their home in Toquerville and then drive to the Ruby Springs Lodge in Jackson, Wyoming.

* * *

Aaron and Naomi had both quickly mastered intermediate skiing on Brian Head's groomed trails and were looking forward to improving their skills on the slopes surrounding Jackson Hole. They both understood the trip would be a great adventure.

On the morning after their wedding, they began the long trip to Jackson. By the time they had progressed to Bear Lake, before passing into Idaho, they began to wish they had chosen a closer destination, or perhaps had bought airplane tickets. Aaron's Chevrolet pickup, with a borrowed shell on the back, required chains and four-wheel-drive to get over the higher mountain passes. The warm and sunny St. George Basin seemed a distant and all but forgotten universe.

Still, it was an adventure, and with an eight-millimeter movie camera that had belonged to Aaron's grandparents, they recorded the trip for future memories. By Thursday afternoon they were finally at the Ruby Springs Lodge in Jackson. They had chosen that particular establishment since they liked the idea of relaxing in the naturally hot water of Ruby Springs that filled a spacious swimming pool behind the lodge and looked so inviting in the brochure that the lodge management had mailed to them.

Once there and settled in, they agreed that the lodge was a good idea. Having their own transportation made it easy for them to tour the area, including parts of Yellowstone Park. It was an exciting diversion to see the elk herds that were fed on bales of grass in the meadows of Jackson Hole where the snow wasn't so deep. It was a most enjoyable trip. They hoped the old movie camera was working properly.

On Saturday morning, the sun, at its lowest winter angle, shone brightly into the wide valley. They decided to make a sweep of some of the tourist attractions in the town of Jackson. On the icy streets, while waiting for traffic to clear at a stop sign approaching the main street, they felt a substantial bump, as a car behind them had been unable to stop quickly enough. The other driver was very apologetic and insisted on having the police investigate the slight damage to his grill and a broken headlight. He walked to a nearby store to use the phone to summon an officer while Aaron and Naomi waited and enjoyed the warmth of the sunlight streaming in through their windshield. Several other cars drove around them as they waited with emergency flashers operating.

The officer who came to investigate, Sergeant Bender, seemed old enough to be a veteran of substantial years. He was an out-going and seemingly tourist-oriented officer with a folksy manner.

"St. George, Utah!" he exclaimed, with a wide grin. "And you want to be up here in the middle of the winter?" He laughed at his own question.

"Only for a week," said Naomi. "We just learned to ski and thought it would be fun to come up here and try it for while."

"Well, welcome to Jackson Hole. I hope you enjoy it here. I don't see any damage to your truck. You've got a pretty tough bumper, there. Scratched the paint some, I guess."

"I don't see any damage, either," commented Aaron. "It really wasn't that much of a crash."

"What do you folks do, down there in sunny southern Utah, Mr. Gentry?"

"I guess you could say we're both in your line of work," Aaron replied, with smile. "Naomi's a deputy sheriff and I work for the highway patrol." They looked casually at the officer's face, in anticipation a friendly reaction. An unmistakable fleeting look of concern appeared on his face. Naomi quickly glanced at her husband attempting to sense his reaction.

"Hey, really!?" the officer exclaimed after the slight pause. "No kidding! Two police officers married to each other? You don't see that every day. Well, consider the red carpet rolled out!"

"Well, thanks a lot," said Aaron. "We're just looking around the town today. Where's a good place to eat?"

Their conversation ended, as the other driver seemed to be eager to finish and leave the area. The officer quickly finished his work on the non-reportable collision.

* * *

Not long after the investigation was completed, the phone rang at the manager's office of the Ruby Springs Lodge. It was a separate line into the lodge that guests had no access to. Chuck Thompson, a blond man approaching middle age, reached for the transceiver.

"Yes?" was his abrupt response.

"Thompson?" It was a familiar voice, but the manager was somewhat uneasy being contacted by the man in this manner.

"Yes, chief. Go ahead."

"Just thought I'd give you a little 'heads up' on a couple of your guests. One of my men, not more'n a half hour ago spoke to a young couple staying at your place. They're from down in southern Utah. They're both cops, workin' in the St. George area." The manager struggled to stay calm and sat down behind his desk in a firm leather chair. For a few moments he was totally mute. He rested his elbow on the chair to keep his arm from shaking.

"What are their names?" the manager asked after the initial pause. "What do they look like?" He struggled to keep the panic from his voice. "Are you sure they're stayin' here?"

"That's what they told us. It sounds like they must be on their honeymoon. They were involved in a minor accident with their truck.

My guy, Sgt. Bender, took down their names as Aaron Gentry and Naomi Blackstone, but he said they talked like they just got married. She probably hasn't had time to change the name on her driver's license yet. They're both quite tall, early twenties, he's blond and she's got long dark hair. They mentioned to Bender they were stayin' at Ruby Springs."

"Okay, yeah, I've seen 'em around. I'm sure they're not here on any kinda business, though." A thoughtful silence followed. "For one thing, they seem to be just having a good time. They even had me take their pictures a couple of times. They've got this old movie camera... gotta be twenty-five or thirty years old. They wanted me to show them coming down the stairs... you know, stupid stuff... like that."

"Well, just the same, I'd be real careful. If they were to get wind of our little, uh, arrangement..."

"Yeah, you're right." the manager said. "They'll be gone in a few days... none the wiser. Thanks for callin', chief."

The manager racked his memory to try to reconstruct scenes that the movie camera might have included. He resolved to do all he could to avoid further contact with the young couple from Utah. But could they actually be here to find out about his little gaming operation? He decided to make some slight changes as long as the Gentrys were around.

* * *

After spending more time in the outdoor heated pool that Saturday night, the Gentrys took in a movie and then returned to their room. The large window in their suite on the second floor faced the front of the lodge. Aaron looked out at the wide expanse of the valley and admired the mountains far to the east. On the previous two evenings, he had noticed one or two large hotel vans pull up to the front and pick up a number of guests of the Ruby Springs Lodge, and drive away. He thought about asking the manager where they were going. He never saw them return. This Saturday evening he saw no vans arrive and wondered about it.

After a time, with the television on, Naomi began to have an uneasy feeling. "Aaron," she said. "I'd swear that someone's been in our room. Things seem to be, maybe, rearranged."

Aaron looked at her quizzically. "What do you mean?"

"Well, look at the closet! Our clothes have all been pushed to one side. We didn't leave it that way... did we? The camera, on the top shelf. I'm almost sure it was facing the other way."

"Really? Are you sure?"

"Yes, I am. Well... I think so. And, look at this. My suitcase has something sticking out from the edge of the lid. The dirty clothes bag. I don't think I left it that way."

"Are you sure?"

"You said that before, Aaron." She sounded somewhat annoyed.

"Well, maybe we should mention it to the night manager, or somebody, in the morning. Maybe one of the maids went through our stuff. We'd better look around and see if anything's missing."

A quick inventory of their belongings indicated that nothing had been taken. Their sense of having been violated seemed to be soothed somewhat.

"I don't know," said Naomi. "Maybe I'm just imagining things. What are you looking for?"

Aaron was studying the local phone book. "I just realized tomorrow is Sunday. I don't want to skip church. I'm trying to see if there's a number for somebody we could call and get the time and the directions."

"That's a good idea."

CHAPTER EIGHT

At that moment, Preston and Becky sat talking in her living room. Paul Blackstone was away at Logan, staying with friends for the weekend and on Monday would be starting the process of registering for several winter-quarter courses. Preston had brought his notebook along, as usual. They had eaten another superb dinner at her house and were relaxing in front of the television after cleaning up. Becky liked the way he pitched in to help with just about any task.

"I think I've told you about all I can remember about the Blackstone ancestors," she said. "We could try to look up some of the other relatives. I think Naomi's father has some cousins that live around here." Preston reflected for a moment on the fact that he had never heard her actually speak the man's name. Living in and leaving Hildale must have been very traumatic for her.

"Maybe later. However, presently, I'd like to see more of the country. I'm getting a bit weary, at the moment, of this family history endeavor. Perhaps we might do something a bit more, um, recreational?

"It's a nice night. Why don't you take me for a drive? I'll show you some of the local sights."

"Yes, that's a splendid idea. Where would you like to go? I'm going to need to stop for petrol soon, however."

"We can stop along the way. It's not far."

It wasn't long before they sat looking over the city of St. George from the roadway that skirted the tops of the cliffs high above the town. In the chilly evening, a full moon was rising in the east and casting an eerie glow across the valley. Preston's light jacket that he had brought from England had been replaced with an extra-large, heavier Levi jacket with a quilted and insulated lining. As they stood on the bluff above the valley he unbuttoned the jacket and wrapped her partially inside it with him. She stood facing him and clasped her arms around him inside the warmth of his jacket and smiled contentedly to herself while tucking her face under his jaw.

"Tell me," he said, pointing toward the central part of the city, "about that large white building that is so substantially illuminated? It somewhat resembles some architecture that I've seen on the continent of Europe."

"That building is a Mormon temple. It's a very special building that belongs to the Church of Jesus Christ of Latter-day Saints. That's the official name of the Mormon Church. The name is so long that people don't use it very often."

"It seems to be such a lovely edifice. Have you ever had an occasion to go inside it?"

"No, I've never been in it. I understand they don't allow anyone to go inside unless their bishop gives them some kind of permission. You remember what the bishop said at Naomi's wedding? About being married... forever?"

"So, you're saying... they will be married again... in there? Why next year? Why not now?"

"Well, I'm no authority on the subject, but apparently there is some sort of waiting period or probationary period, so to speak. Naomi and Natty were baptized just this last summer. She told me they would have to wait a year after that."

"So... are you telling me that you would not be allowed to go with Aaron and Naomi into the temple on that occasion?"

"Well, that's our understanding," Becky said, with some sadness in her voice. "They baptized us out in Hildale, of course, but I really don't have any membership in the main Mormon church."

"Perhaps we could go down there tomorrow," said Preston, "and find out more about it. Would you like to do that? This is making me very curious."

"Oh, I suppose we could," said Becky. "Last summer Aaron lost no time in getting Naomi and Natty involved. He was a missionary...

you know... in Puerto Rico... for a couple of years, I understand. Most Mormon young men do that, I think."

"Aaron was a mission'ry you say? That is so very remarkable... being a mission'ry, then a police officer. Natty's husband, Ben? What about him?"

"Ben's not much interested, I guess. Like so many others. When he was a child he was baptized. But then his parents apparently didn't have any real interest and I understand he's just never been involved. I don't know what those two will end up doing about it, if anything."

"Have you received any sort of communications from our honeymooners, yet?"

"No, they haven't called or anything. I expect they'll be in touch if they need anything. Naomi said something about having some kind of Christmas party at their house in a week or two, after they get back." She paused for moment. "Have you decided how long you might want to stay here in the U.S.?" Her emotions rose to the surface, awaiting his reply. The choking feeling in her throat somewhat surprised her.

"Well, that's a question that I haven't really been prepared to face, as yet. There seems to be so much more to this peculiar expedition than I had ever anticipated." He paused for a few moments. "It's getting cold out here, maybe we should get back into the truck and turn on the heater." He led her back away from the high bluff. The heater felt good and she sat closer to him this time.

"I'll tell you the truth, Preston," she said. "We just met maybe three weeks ago. I've enjoyed the times we've been together so much. I hope you feel the same. I'd like it very much if you decided to stay... for while longer. Of course you'd need a place to live after New Years Day."

"Yes, Becky. I do feel the same way. Our time together has been just simply splendid. Truthfully, I... I had been thinking that perhaps I was destined to live the remainder of my life, uh, by myself. But now that we've met, I've begun to wonder." He turned to face Becky, and considered kissing her.

Anticipating his thoughts, Becky turned away and looked out at the city lights again. "Let's drive by the temple. Maybe we can go into the little building out in front. Tomorrow, if it's open then. Want to?"

"Hmm, yes. I'd be delighted," Preston answered. "The entire business has stirred my curiosity immensely. It would be very interesting to find out just what attracted my great-uncle... H.R. Blackstone... to leave the lush, green homeland... and settle here in this semi-barren, desert land."

* * *

The Gentrys attended Sunday school in Jackson and introduced themselves in the morning, and were surprised and delighted to accept an invitation for Sunday dinner with another young couple that lived in the valley. Sacrament meeting, in the evening, was a good experience, as well. Upon arriving back at the lodge, the heated pool looked really inviting to them, but they decided against it anyway. They were both beginning to feel less and less enchanted with the idea of staying for the full week.

"I still wonder," said Aaron, relaxing in one of the upholstered chairs, "what Dan was trying to remember about Jackson?"

"Maybe it had something to do about police work or somebody he met on the highway. Maybe he's remembered by now. What if we gave him a call... and see what it was... see if he's remembered? Maybe it's something we could look into."

"Good idea. He should be home tonight." Aaron took out a notebook with names in it, found Dan's home phone number and made the call. He was disappointed that Dan was not at home.

"Are you thinking what I'm thinking?" Naomi asked.

"And... what's that?"

"Well, we've been here three... what's it been? ... three, four days, now? I'm starting to get anxious to get back to our house. A whole week of skiing is looking less and less, um, wonderful. Know what I mean?"

"Yeah, I know. What if we give it one more day and then head out on Tuesday morning. How does that sound?"

"Sounds good to me. We're not due back to work until Friday."

* * *

That Sunday night, in their first-floor apartment not far from the front desk of the Ruby Springs Lodge, Collins "Chuck" Thompson recounted with Laura, once more, how they had gone looking for an out-of-the-way place to stop for a sandwich prior to leaving southern Utah.

Collins and Laura Thompson, of course, were not their real names. Coming from near the east coast, Collins, who had taken to calling himself "Chuck" was born John Moranski, in Newark, New Jersey. Attracted into "the mob" by the lure of friends and the easy money, he had escaped a lengthy prison sentence on federal charges of extortion and racketeering by skipping bail. From Newark, they had fled to southern Alabama, where he assumed the identity of a recently deceased white man about his same age.

It had been easy. They found the man's obituary in a local newspaper, containing the names of parents, a spouse and children, along with a birth date. Moranski had then gone to the capitol at Montgomery and told the authorities he had lost his wallet containing his driver's license while fishing off the coast and needed to renew. Of course, his social security card was also in his lost wallet and he couldn't remember the number. He had been issued a new card--for employment purposes. Having obtained those documents, he then applied and got a duplicate birth certificate. He was then a new man, Collins Thompson--a native of Chickasaw, Mobile County, Alabama.

Nevertheless, he had been well connected in the criminal underworld in the east and cleverly maintained those ties, albeit, at a long distance. The real Laura Thompson mysteriously drowned, while swimming alone late one evening in the family pool not many months after her husband, Collins, had died. John Moranski's common-law wife, Cora, a name she detested, assumed Laura's identity in much the same way.

They immediately left Alabama and ended up in the resort town of Jackson, Wyoming, taking jobs in the Ruby Springs Lodge where they were able work their way up the staff to the top management level. Meanwhile, the Thompsons had another--far more private-- enterprise going for them. They had developed some ingenious techniques that they used to eliminate, on a freelance contractual basis, competitors or anyone else who could be a "liability" to mobsters, basically anywhere in the country. Along the way; running from federal marshals, stealing another man's identity and accomplishing their occasional "contracts," Chuck had acquired an ingrained and slowly increasing case of paranoia--not a mere case of persecution complex. His state of mind and sporadic behavior irritated his wife to no end.

Laura didn't necessarily *enjoy* their occasional outside jobs and was not, personally, involved in the "dirty work." But since their targets were, after all, such unsavory characters, she went along with it--and the extra money was fabulous. As hotel manager and secretary/book-keeper--a husband and wife team--no one questioned their occasional, short "vacations."

Eventually, Chuck was able to persuade the owners of the Ruby Springs Lodge to establish a clandestine gambling casino at a separate location within the city, complete with poker tables, slot machines, and roulette wheels. It was a perfect setup to take advantage of the numerous wealthy tourists, who became bored in the long dark hours of the winter evenings, to drink and unload large amounts of cash. Trusted employees of other hotels, along with selected cab drivers, were paid to discretely steer gambling clientele in that direction. And, of course, some cash was diverted to easily persuading the local police to look the other way. What was the harm, anyway? After all, money from hundreds of wealthy tourists, spent in Jackson, helped ensure a substantial budget for all city operations.

Aaron and Naomi, quickly assessed by Chuck and Laura, to be law-abiding youngsters, very likely on a tight budget--and now discovered to be police officers--were, of course, never invited to join in the gambling excursions. But the fact that Chuck had found that they were cops from southern Utah made him very nervous and he discontinued having the vans stop at the lodge until the newlyweds had departed.

* * *

Monday was, indeed, a long day of skiing. Later in the day, the naturally heated pool felt good. They marveled as large snowflakes fell on their heads and on the surface of the ninety-eight-degree water. They were alone in the pool surrounded by a thick mist that had formed above their heads.

"I didn't see the manager anywhere, today," said Aaron, as they clung to the edge of the pool with their chins on the water's surface.

"Yeah, maybe he's taken the day off. He was so accommodating and helpful before. We'll probably see him when we check out in the morning."

"You know, this is really a great place. We'll have to come back again. Maybe we could come back and celebrate our fifth anniversary, or something, up here."

"Hey! It's a deal, Mr. Gentry!" she replied. He put an arm around her waist and pulled her close for a wet kiss.

"I've thought about the night we met, out by the river bridge, so many times. I think your dog wanted to have me for dinner. Did I ever tell you how beautiful you looked in the beam of my flashlight, that night?"

"I couldn't see your face very well. Did I ever tell you I was trying to see if you had any rings on your left hand?"

"Well, I was checking out your hands, too, you know."

"Yes, I figured you were," she said, laughing. "I'm so glad you tried to find me afterward. When I asked Mom about you she almost went berserk trying to think of some way to introduce us... I mean, she really wanted to get us together!"

"Oh, she would have succeeded. Eventually."

"I'm sure she would have." They kissed again. "I try not to think about when we caught Barker and Conway... when you got shot. I was sure you were going to die right there!"

"You guys saved my life! You and the others... and your dogs, of course. It was miracle they ran out of bullets so fast!"

"It was a miracle any of us survived. I remember... I was sooo mad when that... that... ignoramus shot my sweetheart... and my dog! I was nothing but ready to kill him!"

Aaron put hand on the back of her head and drew her face toward his and kissed her again. "Speaking of the pair of ignoramuses... or would it be 'ignorami'? Is Shane Lowry making any progress on the jailhouse murders?"

"Well, I told you we talked about it again the other day. Shane was going to follow up in the next few days and take the clothing up to that new crime lab in Ogden. He may even know more when we see him again. He's nothing but diligent, you know."

"Yeah, he's a good man, all right."

* * *

When Aaron and Naomi checked out early Tuesday morning, the manager watched from a shadowy location on the balcony of the second floor as they paid their bill and left. He smiled and breathed a sigh of relief as he watched them get into their truck and drive away.

"Well, they're gone... and good riddance," Laura said, when he told her he had watched them leave. "Right? Mr. Thompson?"

"Yeah," he replied, turning to go down the stairs to the lobby. "They had their minds on each other all the time, for sure. Just a couple of love-struck honeymooners, I'd say."

"Well, good. Maybe we can get back to business as usual."

* * *

The drive back to southern Utah took all day and a good share of the night. Taking turns driving for the nearly eight hundred miles, they arrived shortly after two o'clock Wednesday morning and slept soundly until almost noon.

"Well, we can't stay in bed any longer," Naomi said as they relaxed.

"Yeah, well... Mrs. Gentry... I need a shower, and I'm hungry."

"Okay, why don't you start shaving, while I'm in the shower and then I'll find something for us to eat." Aaron groaned in protest as she rolled him out of the bed.

CHAPTER NINE

Preston Blackstone worked feverishly at the electric typewriter that he had borrowed from Becky. Thus far, he had produced about twenty pages of the history of Hanford Rushton Blackstone's family after leaving England.

As he typed he smiled, recalling how Becky had dropped by with something to eat the previous evening. The more they were together, the more he pondered--where would this lead? Should he pursue the relationship? Why not? After all, his wife of thirty-seven years had been gone nearly three years. And Becky seemed definitely interested. Perhaps she hadn't thought it entirely through. Of course, she didn't seem like the type of person to ruminate at much length on any given subject. She was definitely more spontaneous and unpredictable.

Their time at the St. George Temple's visitor's center on the previous Sunday afternoon had proved fascinating. The guides seemed to be overtly competing for his attention, especially after finding out that he was researching the history of one of his pioneer great-uncles--a contemporary of so many other immigrants from England, Wales, Ireland and Scotland.

No matter what was to happen between him and Becky, he definitely decided to find out more about the church that had been severely persecuted and driven practically halfway across the continent into territory that, at the time, had been part of Mexico, and had now spread around the world. What, he wondered, would become of the card he had filled out, giving his name and a local address? As they had walked around the temple, the older lady guiding them mentioned a few things that were accomplished inside. Marriages and baptisms for dead people? To Preston, it seemed *preposterous* until the lady reminded him that this practice was mentioned in one of Paul's sermons to the Saints at Corinth. Becky, on the other hand, had not shown so much interest since the historical aspects were mostly quite familiar to her. Was the old bitterness she had held onto over the years still so strong?

What if marriage came of their dating? Would they remain here in the U.S. or go back to England? Ah, that would be the ultimate question. But then, why not keep a residence in both countries, spending summers in the U.K. and winters in the mostly sunny St. George Basin, or even farther south? She had talked of visiting the southern reaches of Nevada and California while he was here. What was the name of that town? Someone had rebuilt the old London Bridge somewhere down there! He looked forward to seeing the bridge that had spanned the Thames River for 136 years until it was replaced just a few years ago. He decided to invite her to go down there--maybe a Saturday or Sunday. Walking across the bridge again would be absolutely splendid.

On top of that, he had to reckon with a deadline of sorts. Naomi and Natty's mobile home would soon be turned over to the new owners and he had to decide whether and where to find new lodging or leave the country. He suspected that Becky was probably dealing with the same dilemma. She seemed to drop perhaps not-too-subtle hints now and then--alluding to the fact that, "Now that Naomi is married and Paul will be leaving again, I guess I'm going to be all alone in this three-bedroom, split-level house" or "It's sure quiet over here, now." It all gave him a sense of urgency that he had never contemplated. In phone calls to his two married daughters back home he confided that he had met a woman he "liked." But he didn't get any impressions from their comments that they had any particular feelings one way or another about their father's "somewhat extraordin'ry dilemma."

Besides that, this business about two murders right in the county jail--by a man posing as a barrister--intrigued him no end. And to think that Becky and her daughter, Naomi, afforded him an access to information about the investigation. It must be frustrating, he thought, to have no crime scene specialists, evidence technicians, or scientific laboratories available nearby. Sending bundles of evidence to the F.B.I. laborat'ry in Washington, D.C.? What a colossal bother that must be! And the maize of multi-level law enforcement agencies with over-lapping responsibilities and jurisdictions? It seemed a miracle to him that anything of importance could ever be accomplished.

These crazy Americans! Leading the world in industrial wealth, military strength and space technology, yet seeming at times so primitive and backward, it seemed to him, in law enforcement organization and methodology. Furthermore, he was certain, the rights of the accused and other legal barriers posed by decisions of the American courts, no doubt, contributed to higher crime rates. Not wanting to seem intrusive or arrogant, he had thus far kept his thoughts and questions about it to himself. Still, whenever the subject of the jailhouse murders came up, he listened with intense interest. Maybe he would get a chance to hear more when he went with Becky to the other wedding reception in Aaron's locality of origin.

* * *

The old rock church out in the farm country west of Parowan had, in recent years, become a treasured antique. After being abandoned and overgrown with weeds and wild Olive and Asian Elm trees for more than fifty years and after newer chapels were built, it had been recently purchased and renovated as a quaint and now beautifully landscaped reception center. People from three counties--and oftentimes beyond--patronized it for wedding receptions, family and high school reunions and other gatherings. The thick walls were made from dark reddish-brown lava boulders that pioneers in the broad, nearly-flat valley had chiseled into building blocks. Massive wooden beams served as the bases for the sturdy, fully exposed trusses that supported the roof. Some of Aaron's ancestors, three and four generations back, had helped erect the sturdy old building.

The reception was a happy occasion but seemed somewhat anti-climactic for many attendees. Aaron and Naomi, his parents, along with Becky Scott stood in the reception line while most everyone else sat at tables and were served the traditional cake and light refreshments.

Preston Blackstone waited patiently through it all, staying at a table close to Natty and Ben and Aaron's younger sister as much as possible. Many of the Gentry's relatives and friends were introduced to Naomi's "distant cousin from England" who exhibited heroic patience in answering their seemingly endless questions. Becky often glanced at him in sympathy. He had been hoping that he might be able to meet the sheriff's sergeant from St. George again, whereupon he might casually ask a few questions about the investigation of the jailhouse murders. Sgt. Lowry never came.

* * *

The next morning was Friday and both Naomi and Aaron resumed working. Naomi was eager to get back to St. George and find out what Shane might have been able to come up with. After a couple of hours of patrolling she heard him check in with the dispatcher at the detective's office. In her absence, the sheriff had decided to transfer another deputy, a seven-year veteran, to work on a trial basis as an assistant to Sgt. Lowry. This would give Shane more time to devote to the double murder.

Naomi walked into his office grinning broadly, happy to be back on the job and happy to see Shane, as well. He looked up as she entered and smiled.

"Hey, Naomi," he exclaimed, half-rising from his chair. "Good to have you back! How've you been?"

"Good, good! We had a great time. We skied a lot and they have this fantastic heated pool that we swam in. It was just amazing. You can be in this swimming pool right in the middle of a snowstorm! And we saw all these big elk herds and several moose. We even went up to Yellowstone Park. Some of the park is kept open in the winter. We rented a couple of snowmobiles, too. You should see all the buffalo and the elk herds!"

"Whoa, that sounds like a blast!"

"Oh, yeah, and we took some pictures with Aaron's grandpa's old movie camera. Maybe we can all get together and show some of them sometime."

"Well, hey, that sounds mighty interesting."

"I'm dying to find out what you've got on the murders. Did you send the clothing and stuff to the crime lab up in Ogden?"

"Oh, yes, we did. In fact, I took it up there myself. I guess the main lab guy was teaching a class or something but I spoke to this woman that was working there. ... had a really loud voice. Sounded like she had some kind of Brooklyn accent."

"A Brooklyn accent?"

"Yeah. She seemed to know what she was talking about. They should be giving me a call any day now. Oh, and I've been checking with hotels and motels around here and I've got four possible names, so far. You know, couples without family. In fact one of these couples registered under the name of Laura Thompson from... guess where?"

"I give up. Where?"

"Jackson, Wyoming!"

"Really? You've got to be kidding! You're not? Did it show the husband's name?"

"No, but they had her driver's license number. And I called up to Cheyenne and got her full address and birth date. Looks like she's just barely past forty-one."

"You should have called me. Maybe we could have located her for you. But surely you don't think they'd be stupid enough to register under their real names, do you?"

"Hey, I've had criminals do dumber things! They can get really over-confident or really nervous, like a bank robber who hands a note to a teller that he wrote on the back of a credit card receipt or something like that! But there were three other possibilities like her, from all over the country."

"Was she alone? Or what?"

"I don't know. They only had the one name, but there must have been a husband, or a friend. Nobody I talked to could actually remember her. Course she could have had a couple of her kids... even grand-kids, her mother, or maybe anybody... or, I guess, nobody."

"Yeah, that's true."

"She's quite interesting, though. She checked in during the

afternoon before the murders and checked out two days later. But you never know. She might just have been down here to attend the wedding of a relative or just to see the parks or for any one of dozens of reasons. I've even called all three of the Thompsons around here in the phone book, but they've never heard of her."

"But if her husband had been with her, he would likely have been about the right age to be this 'John L. Croft,' the lawyer."

"That's probably right. She is the most interesting of all the names I've come up with so far."

"And if she had a husband with her..." Naomi reasoned, "and if her husband really was this 'John Croft,' we have a general, over-all description, don't we? Approximate age, height, weight, even his shirt size. And we know he has brown hair. And probably brown eyes."

"Hey! Naomi," the sergeant exclaimed, with a wide grin. "You're getting way ahead of me. You're a genius!"

"Well, it's just speculation. This Laura what's-her-name could be an old maid, traveling by herself."

"Hey!" said Shane, sternly, in a mocking tone. "I'll have you know, forty-one is not 'old'!"

"Oh, sorry," Naomi said, putting her hand over her mouth to cover her smile.

"I oughta know! I was there once!" Shane exclaimed. "And not very long ago!"

"Hey, I just thought of something," Naomi interjected. "We met this police officer up in Jackson. Some guy slid on the ice and bumped into the back of our truck and damaged his grill. He insisted on having it investigated by the city police. I guess he must have wanted a ticket or something. Anyway, I've got the name of the officer somewhere. You could give him a call and see if he knows this Laura Thompson. Maybe he would tell you if her husband might fit that description."

"And if he doesn't know of her... Maybe he would try to find her for us. And if her husband, if she has one, was to, more or less, fit our description, maybe the sheriff would authorize a trip up there to check them out!"

"Aaron should still be at home. He could find the officer's name for me. I'll give him a call."

While she was on the phone, Shane asked quietly, "I'm going for a Dr. Pepper. Want a drink?"

"Aaron?" she said, shaking her head at the detective. "I'm here in the office with Shane Lowry. He's got a line on a possible murder suspect. He found the name of a woman who might be the wife of... what's-his-name... 'Croft'... that was supposed to be a lawyer! She lives in Jackson! Can you believe that?"

"No kidding!"

"I need the name of that officer that we met up there. Shane wants to call him and see if he knows any Thompsons up there."

"Well, I guess that's possible. It's not a really big town. He probably would know a lot of the permanent residents."

"I think I stuck a copy of the driver's exchange information in my purse. See if it's still there for me, okay?"

"Okay. Hold on a minute."

"He's looking for the officer's name," she said to Shane. "You could probably get him on the phone, right now." After a pause of maybe thirty seconds, Aaron came back with the name. After she wrote it down along with the departmental phone number, she said, "Thanks, Aaron. I'm off at five. Let's get together for a chicken sandwich, okay?"

"Sounds great."

"I'll give you a buzz. Love ya, bye."

Shane was studying the name she had copied down. "Looks like 'Kenneth Bender' to me," he said.

"Yeah, Aaron spelled it out for me. Ken Bender, as in, 'fender-bender'." They both chuckled. "And here's the number for the police department," Naomi continued. Shane, smiling at the possibilities, dialed the Wyoming phone number. After several rings the line opened.

A female voice answered. "Jackson City Police. How may we help you?"

"This is Detective Lowry. I'm with the Washington County Sheriff's Office, in St. George, Utah."

"Oh, good morning detective. How may we help you? Oh, St. George! I wish I were there! Tell me, how's the weather down there?" Shane pictured an older lady, perhaps anxious to retire and flee to a warmer climate. It was a question frequently asked in winter by people in the northern zones.

"The weather's great," he responded, and continued in a more jocular mode. "It's real sunny and about eighty-five right now. We can't pick the bananas fast enough. And the coconuts are lookin' real good this year!"

"Stop! You're making me crazy! I would die to be there right now! But anyway, how may we help you?" she asked, for the third time. This time she waited for an answer.

"I need to speak to Officer Bender. Do you have a Sergeant Kenneth Bender? Would he happen to be there right now?"

"Give me a minute. Ken was here a short while ago."

"Sure, I'll hold." The line was silent for a full minute. Shane sipped from his Dr. Pepper a couple of times. "She's trying to find him now," he said to Naomi.

Suddenly a jovial-sounding male voice replied. "This is Ken Bender. How may I help you, detective?"

"Good morning, Ken. I was hoping you might be able to give us a hand with an investigation. One of our officers was up there on a vacation... her honeymoon, actually. She tells me she met you when some guy collided with the back bumper of their truck."

"Oh, sure. I remember them," Bender replied. "The husband told me he was state trooper, too. Yeah, seemed like nice folks."

"Yep, that's them. Anyway, the reason I called is we're looking to find a woman from Jackson... or maybe a couple, likely both in their early forties, from Jackson. She, or... they were down here and stayed in a motel for about three days last summer. I forget the exact dates, right now. All we know, so far, is that the name she used to register at the motel is Laura Thompson. She used a P.O. box for an address." He paused for a few seconds, expecting a response, then continued. "This may sound a little strange, Ken, but we assume there was also a Mr. Thompson. We have a general description for him, but not her."

"Um, well, there are three Thompsons in our phone book. I'm checking it right now. There's no Laura listed here. But it seems I recall a woman who teaches in our elementary school, by that name. She might not even be married. No, I don't think so. Divorced, most likely. Could be that she and another teacher... Maybe two women, or whatever, got together and decided to take a little vacation before the school year started in September."

"Hmm, interesting. That sounds very plausible. The people we're looking for probably weren't school teachers." Shane felt uneasy about Officer Bender's response. "You say this Thompson woman is most likely an unmarried school teacher? Sounds like just one more dead end."

"So, what sort of case are you working on, detective?"

"Oh, didn't I mention that? It seems they may be important witnesses to a fatal traffic accident down here. The county attorney really needs to talk to the Thompson woman, he says." Naomi looked at him in astonishment. "I guess the officers were in such a sweat they forgot to get the complete address."

"Oh, I see. Sorry we couldn't help you on that. But I'll do some checking around and give you a call if we find anything. Call back anytime, if we can be of any assistance."

"Will do, Ken. Thanks anyway. Catch ya later."

Neither party to the conversation felt satisfied with the other's response. Ken Bender, of course, would pass the word along to the chief. He was pretty well satisfied that he had successfully deflected the inquiry on Laura Thompson, but he didn't buy Shane Lowry's story about the traffic accident for a second. If the manager of the Ruby Springs Lodge and his wife were involved in anything, it could very well be something far more serious, he reasoned. He would talk to the chief about it.

Shane Lowry, on the other hand, having interviewed hundreds of victims, witnesses, and criminal suspects over the years, keyed in on the hesitation, change in the tone, and even the pitch of Officer Bender's voice at the mention of Laura Thompson's name. This, of course, made the Thompsons all the more interesting. But why would a police officer in Jackson, Wyoming, *possibly* be protecting them? From what? Certainly not from a murder investigation!

"Well, what did he have to say," Naomi asked. The sergeant explained it to her and they speculated about Bender's seemingly elusive response. "Wow, I sure wish we'd have known about this 'Laura Thompson' name when we were up in Jackson Hole. Maybe we could've looked into it. Maybe even found her. But don't you think she would've used some fake name... checking in at a motel?"

"Oh, yeah. I'm sure of that. Name... and address, too. But, still, why would Sgt. Bender be sounding so evasive when I asked him about the name? But then why would 'Croft' leave evidence in the trash basket at that store in Hurricane?"

Naomi was beginning to feel that she should get back on patrol when the telephone on Shane's desk startled them both. Marti, the receptionist, asked Shane to pick up line four. The voice was somewhat familiar.

"Detective Lowry?" It was a woman's eastern, nasal twang.

"Yes, ma'am. This is Sergeant Lowry."

"Hey, this is Margaret Radowicz, at the Weber State Crime Lab. We found something quite interesting on this clothing you brought in. Are you ready for this?"

"Very good! What've you found?"

"The hair inside the wig you guys found appears to be from a man with brown hair. But we got looking inside the trousers and found three different hairs, you know, from the man's leg. Whoever was wearing these pants is very much a blond-haired person... presumably a man."

"Hmm... that's very interesting," he responded, glancing at Naomi who was now standing at the office door with car keys in hand. "So, maybe this guy planted some brown hair in the toupee just to throw us off?"

"Very likely. I'm betting it was the hair in the wig that was planted. He probably wouldn't even think about hair inside the trousers, at all."

"I agree. He could have disposed of his clothes in a lot of other ways. But he probably decided to leave it where we could find it and think we were looking for a guy with brown hair."

"Yeah, pretty dumb scheme, I'd say."

"Maybe he's outsmarted himself! Anything else?"

"There's some residue in some of the pockets that looks interesting. Can't really tell anything about it yet. And we're getting the soil particles on the bottom of his shoes analyzed right now. It may give us something more to go on."

"Great, let me know as soon as possible."

CHAPTER TEN

Nearly a year passed with little change or progress in the investigation of the double murder inside Washington County Jail. Shane Lowry had had no response from the Jackson police. And after discussing it with the elected county attorney and county commissioners, Sheriff Ian Cooper was not convinced that sending investigators to the resort city in Wyoming would be worth the expense. For all they knew, the "lawyer," Croft, may have been any light-haired man who had dyed his hair brown.

From time to time the local and sometimes statewide newspapers featured stories about the unsolved crime. Reporters from the Salt Lake City TV stations occasionally called and requested interviews with Sheriff Cooper or Sgt. Lowry. Most of the time those requests were declined. All of the sheriff's personnel felt embarrassment to one degree or another.

Both Aaron and Naomi Gentry acquired more experience and self-confidence in their law enforcement skills, making fewer errors and misjudgments. But it would be a long time before they had sufficient seniority to schedule their days off on weekends. Their love grew stronger and matured and they appreciated the townspeople of Toquerville and enjoyed their new LDS ward immensely. Many of the people they met complimented them on the improvements they had made to their property.

To Becky Scott's great relief, Preston Blackstone returned to St. George after spending four months of the summer in England and other parts of Europe. In spite of their steady exchange of letters, it had been a lonely time for her and she took every opportunity to draw Paul, Naomi, and Natty to her home. But in Preston's absence-- without his initiative to nudge her along--the chance to be with her daughter and son-in-law when they made their temple vows escaped her.

* * *

On the last weekend of November, Aaron, whose Sunday shifts varied considerably, was happy to attend church with Naomi. She had been able to arrange a later patrol shift almost every Sunday.

After a light lunch, they both prepared for work and agreed to meet at Becky's house for the Sunday dinner at six o'clock as usual. Becky had, long since, issued a standing invitation to Naomi and Natty and their husbands for dinner at her house every Sunday evening. They only had to let her know if they were not able to be there. The weekly gatherings at Becky's house were always a welcome opportunity to get together. And they were all glad that Preston Blackstone had returned from England and hoped he would not only be there for dinner but would find a way to stay around longer--much longer.

* * *

Becky and Preston seemed ecstatic as they talked about the trip they had taken through Las Vegas, on their way to Lake Havasu City, Arizona. Having put it off for over a year, Preston had been "absolutely delighted" to stroll across the old London Bridge and he raved about how he had done it before, both as a child and later as a young man when the same structure was in England. They marveled at the crowds of older people that were there, as well as in all the dry and sunny towns along the way.

"How's the H.R. Blackstone history going?" Aaron asked as the meal was getting underway. "Have you had any luck getting anything out of the people at Hildale?"

"Well, um, I went out there again, the other day. Our Becky refused to accompany me. Can't say that I blame her. I tried to inquire of some children where any Blackstones lived, but they ran away from me. I knocked on a couple of doors, but nobody answered. A decidedly inhospitable lot, I'd say."

"Anyone around here could have told you that," Natty offered. The others smiled and nodded in affirmation.

"So, I suppose it would be useless to go back," Preston replied. "I've found some others in the county of Washington that would presumably be willing to speak to me, however."

"I doubt you could get any more than I've already told you... and what's in those books," Becky said.

"Have you visited the temple grounds, yet?" Aaron asked. "The visitor's center?"

"Why, indeed we have," Preston answered. "Certainly a most impressive edifice. Actually, Becky and I visited there over a year ago. I suppose we didn't mention it before. A fellow called me just yesterday and wanted to know if I would welcome a visit with your mission'ries."

"So, what did you tell them?" Becky asked.

"They're arriving on Tuesday night," Preston said. "Would you want to be there, too?"

"Um, okay," she replied, with little enthusiasm. "Sure, I can be there. What if I come over to your place and make us a little dinner first. Okay with you?"

"Certainly," Preston answered with a broad smile. Naomi was pleased that Preston seemed to be taking an interest in the church. But she kept quiet and was slightly embarrassed to be privy to her mother's personal matters.

But Preston was bursting with curiosity about what progress, if any, had been made concerning the murders that had taken place inside the local jail, apparently committed by a man posing as a lawyer. He was very pleased that Becky opened the subject.

"Naomi, I saw you talking to Shane," she remarked, "first thing on Friday morning. Has he been able to make any more progress on the Barker and Conway murders? I know the sheriff is downright frustrated... wants to get something going. I guess he's still feeling pretty discouraged about it."

"Oh, yeah," Naomi answered. "We have, um, that is, Shane has a general, well, no, I'd say quite a specific description of the man. We know his hair color. He's actually blond, probably with blue eyes."

"That description would seem to fit a lot of guys, me included," said Aaron. "Is there anything else to go on? You mentioned the woman from Jackson, Wyoming, before."

"Yeah, here's a coincidence for you," she continued. "Seems there was this woman who checked into a motel over by Zion's Park and gave her address as a P.O. box in Jackson, Wyoming, of all places. I guess this is 'old news' to most of us, but maybe Preston hasn't heard it. She stayed two days at the motel. She probably had a husband with her, but hers was the only name the motel had. Anyway, Shane called up to the police department and spoke to that officer Bender, that Aaron and I met... trying to find out if he knew anything about anyone by that name. Shane had a feeling that the officer gave him a bum steer for some reason. He claimed he didn't know a woman by that name. Said she might have been a local school teacher. Sheriff Cooper apparently told him that there really wasn't enough to go on, to justify spending the money for a trip up there. Not yet, anyway."

"Do you have this woman's name and address?" Preston wanted to know.

"Her name's Laura Thompson," Naomi said, and immediately wondered if she ought to say more. "The motel where she stayed didn't have an exact address for her, only a Post Office box." Why would Preston want to know the address, she wondered? But then, he had been a British constable for many years. Probably just out of habit. It was an awkward situation. Could he be helpful? He and the others looked at her expectantly. But she decided to say no more about it.

Becky's telephone was ringing. Aaron and Naomi looked at each other. Becky answered and handed the phone to Aaron. He took the phone and listened for a moment. "Got to go," he said and headed for the front door. "Thanks a lot, Becky." He gave her a one-armed hug at the door and waved to the others.

"I'd best get going, too," said Naomi. "Thanks again, Mom."

* * *

Since the Christmas party they had contemplated the previous year had not come to fruition, Naomi and Aaron set a date for a party at their house for the following Thursday evening. Many from Aaron's family, including grandparents, parents, and three younger siblings came. Becky and Preston and Natty and Ben were there. Dan and Jane Wilde, along with Johnny Lee Chaffey, and his wife, Carrie, whom none of them except Dan and Jane had ever met, came also.

It was somewhat startling to the others when the Chaffeys arrived. At six-foot-four, Johnny Lee towered above everyone except for Aaron, while his wife, now a nursing supervisor at the hospital in Cedar City, stood just a little above five feet. She seemed all but "lost in the shuffle" until her gabby humor got started, relating some hospital stories.

The business of the traditional and delicious turkey dinner was expeditiously handled by seven-thirty. Afterward, the living room was quickly converted to a mini-theater.

"We hope you're not too bored with the movies from our trip to Jackson last year," Aaron said, as he focused on the small white screen. "We finally got around to getting the films developed. But they're really short, so bear with us."

Everyone sat back to relax and enjoy some of the scenes from Aaron and Naomi's trip to Jackson. The old "silent" movie projector that apparently had been used very little over its many years seemed to function perfectly. Scenes from the snowy slopes that included a few spills they had taken were quite humorous and entertaining, since none of the others, except for Carrie Chaffey, had any skiing experience. The guests had a lot of laughs.

Aaron re-wound the film and changed reels while the others talked and laughed about the skiing scenes. During the second short reel, with scenes of the heated pool and inside the lodge, Aaron and Naomi alternately narrated. Some of the guests couldn't help but notice that Dan and Johnny Lee seemed to be engaged in highly animated conversation and pointing at the screen in earnest. Quickly, the scene on the screen changed to outdoors again and soon ended where Aaron was smiling and talking to the Jackson police officer at the rear of their truck and then grinning for the camera while pointing at the damage to the grill of a car behind.

"Well," Aaron said, smiling broadly, and preparing to rewind the reel, "that's about it. You don't have to sit through any more of our, um, vacation adventures!"

"Hey, Aaron," Dan said, "Johnny and I would like to see those scenes inside the lodge again." All heads in the room turned back toward them. "Can you roll it back there for just a minute?"

In silence, except for the soft clickety-click of the old projector, the group watched again with heightened curiosity. "There's something about that man, right there!" Dan walked quickly forward and placed a pointing finger on the face of a man in the background, behind the check-in counter. The man, of average size and build with short blond hair, looked wide-eyed, directly at the camera for an instant, moved quickly to the side, turned his back and then disappeared into an office. It was as if the man, out of embarrassment--or perhaps for a more urgent reason--had "ducked out" and appeared to be making a hardly concealed attempt to avoid being filmed.

"That was the manager of the lodge. During the day, anyway," said Naomi. "He was really friendly and helpful, for a couple of days, anyway. We didn't see him after Saturday, though." All eyes were on Dan Wilde.

"He looks kind of familiar," Dan said. "Why d'you suppose he'd try to avoid a camera. When he looked directly at the camera, he was like a deer caught in your headlights. Johnny, doesn't he look sorta familiar to you?"

"Yeah, he sure does," was the response. "Did y'all mention to him that y'all were cops, from Utah?"

"No, we never did," Naomi said. "Did we, Aaron? The only person we mentioned that to was that city officer at the little fender-bender." Naomi paused a few seconds. "Oh, you know what? That reminds me! That officer's name was 'Bender', Kenneth Bender, as in 'fender bender'!" Everyone in the room laughed.

"Really," said Aaron. "That really was his name!"

Naomi went on. "Back about a year ago, I gave his name to Shane Lowry and he called up to Jackson and talked to him."

"What about?" Dan asked.

"Well," Naomi answered. "Shane found where a woman from

Jackson, had registered at a local motel at the same time that Barker and Conway were poisoned in the jail. Shane wanted to know if Bender might know the woman." Everyone in the room was quietly anticipating her further response. Preston Blackstone had been quietly listening and watching the goings-on like the proverbial cat watching the birdie in a badminton match.

"Well, he ended up feeling like our Officer Bender was being somewhat evasive," Naomi continued. "Said he might have heard about someone by that name, who was maybe a divorcee, that could've been a local school teacher. He said possibly she and another teacher may have made a trip down here at that time."

"What was the name?" Johnny Lee asked. "Y'all remember the name he was asking about?"

"Seems like it was Thompson... Laura Thompson... I think." Dan and Johnny Lee looked at each other in silence.

"Laura Thompson, from Jackson, Wyoming." Dan scratched his head. "Does that mean anything to you, Johnny?"

"I know I've seen that guy, somewhere before," Johnny Lee replied. "And the look on his face... like he didn't want to be recognized." For several seconds there was silence in the room again and they all looked around at each other.

At last Becky broke the brief silence. "Well, c'mon, Natty, let's let these super-cops sort it all out. We need to get started on the di..."

"Wait a minute!" Johnny Lee exclaimed. "The first day I was ever down here! I was riding with y'all, Dan. And we met Aaron up at Tulley's! In Kanarraville!" Everyone's attention was on Johnny Lee. "Man! What's it been? A year ago last summer!"

"Oh, yeah!" Dan answered. "You're talking about that couple in there that was acting really suspicious... like we made them really super nervous? Do you remember them, Aaron?" Dan asked.

"Well, vaguely, I guess." Aaron said. "I guess I turned back south, from there. Didn't you guys follow them north a ways?"

Dan spoke up again. "After you told us you went to Jackson, Wyoming, on your honeymoon... I remember it rang a bell for me somehow." All attention in the room focused on him. "It bothered me so much that I finally went through my files at home and at the office and found some notes on those people from Jackson that we first noticed back at Bud's place. You remember, Aaron? Johnny was with us? Well, he noticed this couple acting kind of funny. I bought the money they spent and had Bud save their dishes and stuff from the table, possibly for some fingerprints."

"So, did you ever get any prints, or anything off the stuff?" Naomi asked.

"No. I was just waiting to see if your people came up with any suspects, or anything," Dan replied. "Never heard anything from the sheriff's people. I think I must've spent the money, myself. I'll bet Bud's forgotten all about it, too. So we had Barney stop them up north of Parowan. He wrote up a warning. Maybe he's still got copy of it. That should have an address."

"So you think that hotel manager could be the same guy!?" Carrie exclaimed.

"Yeah," Dan replied. "We talked to them quite while, but couldn't come up with anything. Man, they were nervous! You keyed on that right away, didn't you, Johnny?"

"Yeah, they sure were. I noticed that right away. And Bud told us he'd never seen them before. We'd maybe best get together with Barney and compare notes."

"Are you saying," asked Preston, unable to contain his curiosity, "that the manager of the hotel--the man in our little cinema--might be your Mr. Thompson? That he might even be Sheriff Cooper's jailhouse assassin? What did he call himself? 'John Croft'?" All eyes in the room turned to their British guest. "Didn't someone say that the hairs inside the wig indicated that the man had brown hair? Perhaps our Mr. Croft thought it would be consummately clever to leave the automobile and his clothing where it could easily be found, and then plant the brown hair inside his toupee as a fraudulent manifestation!"

"Now that would be a 'hair-brained scheme' if I ever heard one!" Becky commented. Her wit seemed to dispel some of the tension of the conversation. Some in the room even laughed.

Naomi smiled, too. "Well, it's all very plausible, to me," she said. "But Shane got a call from the crime lab, and... Guess what? They told Shane that the *brown* hair in the wig had just a tiny sliver of *blond* just above the roots! *And*, there was a couple of *blond* hairs from his legs inside the trousers! What do you think, Preston. You've had a lot of experience, I'm sure."

"That scenario certainly has possibilities," Preston replied. "I've known some dastardly scoundrels in my time. Some who seem to have concocted a rather brilliant scheme only to sabotage themselves with a consummate blunder or two. However, with blond hair inside the trousers, it seems almost certain that the man planted the brown hair in his toupee in order to deceive everyone. But he, undoubtedly, did not fully comprehend that the hair on his head would continue to grow!"

Johnny Lee, who had been sitting with the diminutive Carrie on his lap--looking as though it was her favorite place to be--spoke again. "Naomi, maybe y'all oughta have one of the frames in the film blown-up. And have this manager's face put on a large photograph."

"You're right!" she responded. "An excellent idea! We could even have a photo-shop put a silver wig and big dark-rimmed glasses on him."

"But then," said Dan, "you could do that with just about anybody's picture and you'd get people that would swear it was Croft, for sure."

"Yeah, you're right," said Naomi. "Maybe I'll do both and see how they turn out. All we have, so far, is that the hotel manager appeared to be somewhat shy. And he *might* be the same man you guys talked to on the highway last summer, a couple of days after the jailhouse hit job. But from what I recall, he was about the same size as the clothing that Sgt. Lowry found in the dumpster. I'll run all this by Shane tomorrow, and see what he says. And, I know a place that can turn this film into a regular photograph for us. But we've got to come up with something really solid before the sheriff would finance a trip to Jackson."

"The plates on the car they were driving... wouldn't do us any good. Seems like it was a rental unit... as I recall. But if we had some fingerprints from the hotel manager..." said Dan. "We've still got the dishes and things they were eating with, at Bud's place. Bud should still have them in a box somewhere. Anyway, I *hope* he still has them stored somewhere!"

"But still," Aaron said. "There's really nothing to connect the manager, Thompson, if that's his name, to the crime scene, at the jail."

Jane Wilde broke the silence. "Why don't you just call the lodge and ask for Mr. Thompson? The manager."

"Sure," said Carrie. "If you did that, it would close one more link in the chain, so to speak." The officers looked at them and at each other.

"Yeah, sure," said Aaron. "Naomi, why don't you call right now, and just, oh, say how much we enjoyed our visit there? We've got some brochures with the phone number. They're put away in a box somewhere. I'll bet I can find them."

"But it's been a whole year, Aaron," Naomi said. "He won't even remember who we are. Besides that, we should talk to Shane about this first, shouldn't we?"

"But that's all the better," Aaron replied. "You could just give them another name, anyway. And it would save Shane going to the trouble."

Becky, Natty, and Aaron's mother had begun to clear the dining room table and clean the dishes. Ben Randolph, as usual, was paying close attention but had kept quiet thus far.

Naomi returned from a bedroom with the Ruby Springs Lodge brochure. She picked up the telephone to dial the long-distance number. Everyone else listened intently to what she was saying. "Hello," she began. "Is this Mr. Thompson?"

A man's voice responded. "I'm sorry ma'am, he'll be here in the office first thing tomorrow. I understand he's gone out for the evening. His wife, Laura, is in their apartment, I believe. But she don't like to be disturbed unless it's really urgent. May I help you?"

"Oh, no, I just wanted to thank him for the enjoyable time we had at the Ruby Springs Lodge a couple of weeks ago."

"I'll be happy to give him the message," the male voice answered. "May I tell him your name?"

"Oh, just tell him we're the Wilsons, from Utah. And we had such a wonderful time. And thanks, again."

"I'll be very pleased to relay the message, thanks for calling. Goodbye."

Naomi hung up the phone and exclaimed to the others, "It's gotta be them, all right! The wife's name is Laura. He never did say what the husband's name was, though."

"Okay," said Dan. "So... it's a pretty sure bet they're the same people we saw at Bud's place, over a year ago. And, the same ones we talked to up by Parowan. But that still doesn't make them the killers!"

"True, but they *could* be!" said Johnny Lee. "But why would he be so nervous in the hotel? He wouldn't have known who Aaron and Naomi were. And y'all say he was never around after Saturday? Didn't y'all reckon he was really hiding? After Saturday? Didn't y'all say that was the day y'all met the city officer? But then, maybe he just had some vacation coming?"

"Oh, yeah!" said Aaron. "That may very well be the day that Thompson found out that we were cops."

"From southern Utah!" Naomi added. "But how would he have known that?"

Preston spoke up. "You're certain you only mentioned your law enforcement profession to the local constable?"

"That's right," said Aaron. "You think he told Thompson?"

"I'm afraid it is entirely possible," Preston answered. "It seems as though your Mr. Thompson may be a bit of a shady fellow after all. Even if he's not your killer! I'm saying, if the police officer felt it was necessary to take the trouble to apprise him of your constable status, it would seem likely that they just might have some... shall we say... some shady sort of mutual interest?"

"What are you saying, Preston?" Naomi asked. "What could this 'shady mutual interest' possibly be?"

"Well, I believe you Americans would call it being 'on the take' or simply a 'protection' operation."

"Yeah. I've heard of stuff like that," Aaron said. "But not around here, not in the west." The other's seemed to agree.

"Are you telling me that corruption and complicity of the constabulary is strictly an east-coast phenomenon?" Preston asked. "That seems to me to be somewhat unlikely."

"Well, yeah," said Dan. "The east coast, or, maybe big city stuff. Course we've had Las Vegas, but I hear it's a lot cleaner now than it used to be. But... Jackson? Wyoming?"

Preston smiled and nodded. "I see," he said, and didn't press the issue further.

Well," said Naomi. "I'll get a picture made and run all this by Sgt. Lowry as soon as possible. I'm sure he'll want to get together with you, Dan, and you too, Johnny. And probably Barney Jeppson, too."

"What dy'all think, then?" asked Johnny Lee. "Would the sheriff be willing to send someone up to Jackson and check this guy out some more?"

Naomi responded. "Shane gave me the impression that Ian Cooper is really careful about his budget. He likes to keep reserve funds on hand for emergencies and things like that. Maybe if he gets desperate enough, or if anything more turns up. But all we know now is that the Thompsons were nervous around cops. He matches our general description... besides being blond, and all... and doesn't like to be photographed. And this Officer Bender may have--or may not have--told him who we were, and he stayed out of sight until we were gone. Or, who knows, maybe he had a little vacation coming. Winter would be a good time to get away from there, but then it's probably the busiest time of the year, too. That's not much to go on. I mean, to lay out a big chunk of change out of the sheriff's budget for a trip to Jackson? I doubt it."

"I seriously doubt he'd go for it," said Dan.

"But don't forget the hair from the guy's leg was blond, according to the crime lab people," Naomi said. "And... too, the manager of the lodge definitely had blond hair. I guess the next move is up to Sergeant Lowry. I know he's been looking at a few other, less promising leads, as well."

"Your sheriff," Preston began, "Ian Cooper, you say? What sort of fellow is he? What's his, um, experience?"

"Oh, he's a good man," Naomi replied. "He hasn't had a lot of experience, though. He's been sheriff since he got elected back in '72. He was a deputy for maybe a year before that and ran against the old sheriff and got elected."

Preston's eyes widened a bit. "So... are you telling me that any deputy can be *elected* sheriff, the chief constable, uh, chief officer of the county?" The others in the room began to pay close attention to their conversation.

"Well, actually, the sheriff isn't required to have any experience at all," she answered. "None whatever."

Preston was incredulous. "No experience? *Any* man can become sheriff?"

"Or woman," Naomi replied with a patient smile.

Preston sank back in his chair. "Surely you jest!" His gaze swept the room, studying their serious expressions as if seeking any indication of betrayal of the deception they had to be playing on him. "You have to be jesting! Are you telling me that just any bloke... who...? For example an attendant at a petrol station, or perhaps a cabinet maker can be elected sheriff if he gets a majority of the votes?" The others stared back at him. Some smiled nervously.

"Well, sure." Naomi answered. "I guess so. I remember Ian Cooper, he took some time off from the job to run for office. He wanted it really bad. Mom said it really caused a ruckus in the office to have one of the deputies running against the old sheriff. Most everybody was real cautious and quiet about it around the office. But some were having some really bitter arguments. I remember Ian going around knocking on doors, with his little baby son in a carrier on his back, shaking hands and handing out his campaign brochures. Everybody likes the guy."

"This simply cannot be!" Preston exclaimed. "And here I've often thought we Brits have clung to some rather foolish customs! Sir Robert Peel would be simply aghast!"

"It's been that way forever," said Naomi. "Well, I guess since we were just a bunch of England's colonies, anyway. I remember from a class I took at Dixie College that the tradition of an elected sheriff goes back in English history for hundreds of years. He was called the 'Shire Reeve,' I think."

"I'm afraid England abandoned that practice long ago," Preston allowed.

"So, Preston," Becky asked, having rejoined the group. "How do they do it back in England?" The others listened with intense interest.

"Well, of course we no longer have a sheriff, per se. We're a small country, you know. And here you seem to have, what, three? No, actually, four levels of constabulary operating somewhat independently. England's police are more or less joined at the national level. There are no elections. The Chief Constable for each county or shire is appointed by a board made up of government officials and prominent citizens. Their decision is based on the candidate's experience, qualifications, and demonstrated leadership ability."

The brief thoughtful silence that followed was suddenly interrupted by quiet notes on the old piano that had been left in the house. Everyone in the group turned in disbelief to see the quiet Ben Randolph--whom they all had figured for a dedicated "cowboy"-- softly stroking the piano keys. With some encouragement and broad smiles from Natty and Becky at the kitchen door, Ben began to play a Christmas carol from memory. Many joined in singing along for a good forty-five minutes before the party began to break up.

CHAPTER ELEVEN

Naomi was a little surprised to look up at the tops of the Pine Valley Mountains to see the first dusting of snow on Signal Peak. It had rained in the depths of the Ash Creek drainage in the early hours after Thursday night's party. Returning from the west gate of Zion's Park where there had been an attempted burglary at the ranger's office, she was elated again to remember what had transpired at the party while watching the short film from their trip to Jackson.

She had arranged with Shane Lowry to meet her at the Red Rock Cafe at four o'clock, which was near the end of his shift and the last day of his workweek. Earlier in the day, she had stopped at a photography shop and after some explaining, arranged to have several frames of the eight millimeter film, focusing on the hotel manager's face, blown-up and developed into prints.

Shane was waiting in the parking lot. They entered the small cafe on the south side of the city and went inside together. The place was nearly deserted.

"Well, Shane," she began, as they sat down at a table in the rear, "I've got something you're going to find very interesting. Something I learned at our party last night."

"Oh, really. Well, let's hear it." They ordered sandwiches from the server and relaxed. From the jukebox, the Marty Robbins rendition of "El Paso" softly played.

"Well, Aaron and I brought back some movie films from our trip to Jackson about a year ago. He didn't really want to show them last night, but I talked him into it."

"I'll bet everyone at the party was thrilled to see them, all right." Shane was grinning broadly. "I mean, it isn't every day you get to see movies of somebody's honeymoon!"

Naomi faked a smile. "One of the scenes was inside the lobby of the lodge where we stayed. The manager was in the shot, along with me and Aaron. He was in the background. Dan said it reminded him of having a deer in his headlights! Well, when this guy, the manager, realized he was in the background he ducked into the office mighty fast!"

"Sounds interesting. Why would he do that?"

"That's what we all wondered last night. Dan Wilde was there and this new trooper, Johnny Chaffey and his wife Carrie, from Iron County that Aaron invited. Anyway, Dan and Johnny both said the manager looked kind of like this guy they stopped and talked to a year ago last summer. When Dan found out we went to Jackson, he got real curious and found the notes he'd made back in the summer of '74 on these people. Bet you can't guess what his name is!"

Shane was 'thinking hard' and snapping his fingers, as if it would help. "Don't tell me! You've found our Mr. Thompson?"

"Yep! And his wife's name is Laura!"

"How did you find that out?"

"I just called the lodge last night," she said, proudly, "and asked for Mr. Thompson. You know, to tell him what a great time we had. And how good the service was."

Shane was suddenly deeply concerned. "Did you actually talk to him? The actual Mr. Thompson?"

"No, he wasn't there. So, I just left a message with one of his assistants. The guy said he was out for the evening. But I didn't leave my name, or anything. I just said we were 'the Wilsons'."

"Um, that's good. Did you ever mention to him, while you were there, that you and Aaron were cops from southern Utah?"

"No, we didn't. But that's another thing, like I was telling you before, some tourist slid his car into the back of our truck. A city officer investigated it. Remember Officer Bender? And we did tell him. We think maybe, now, that the officer may have told Thompson."

"And that would be that Ken Bender that I talked to on the phone?

Whoa, that *is* interesting." Shane said, in consternation. "Why would it be important for Bender to tell Thompson who you guys were? Could've been just some casual conversation over coffee. But on the other hand... maybe there's something going on in Jackson... "

"Well, Mom's boyfriend, Preston was there. He's that retired constable from England, you know."

"Okay, yeah. What did he have to say about all this?"

"Well, he thinks that Thompson could very well have some kind of 'criminal enterprise' on the side... going on... right there in the city and the police are in on it. You know... looking the other way... maybe for some of the 'action' so to speak."

"Yeah, taking some kind of payoff... under the table," Shane responded. "I guess that would be entirely possible. If he's dirty... And... if he's our jailhouse killer... maybe even a professional hit man? No tellin' what they might do. They could take off and we'd never find them. Or, he just might get real paranoid about you two." A thoughtful silence ensued. "You'd better watch your back, for a while, anyway."

"Oh, yeah. I see what you mean. I guess I shouldn't have called up there. Oh, my gosh! What was I thinking, anyway?"

"From now on, Naomi, please don't make any more moves without talking to me first. Promise me?"

"Oh, shoot!" she responded. "I shouldn't have done that. I'm sorry, really!"

"Okay," Shane said. "Now, we need to get photos of this Thompson guy. Why don't you... ?"

Naomi cut him off. "I've already taken the film to get some large prints made of Thompson's face. They should be ready by tomorrow morning."

"Hey, great! That's good thinking! I'll see if I can get together with Dan and this new guy on Monday afternoon. Is there anyone else we need?"

"Oh, I almost forgot... another thing! In the movie... in the blowup, you'll see that Thompson has blond hair! Just like the crime lab woman told us."

"Hey... that's fantastic! Another piece of the puzzle!"

"The guys mentioned another trooper from up north of Cedar City,

Barney Jeppson. He's the one who actually stopped the Thompsons after they left Bud's place. They'll all have notes and Dan said you could probably even get some fingerprints they would have left from their meal at Tulley's place."

Shane's eyebrows fairly leaped upward. "You've got to be kidding! Fingerprints?"

"Sure, on their glasses... and the silverware. Aaron was there too, at first. He told me the Thompsons were acting really nervous in Bud's place. So Dan and Johnny, he's the new guy--sounds like he's from Texas or somewhere down there--decided to check them out. Barney Jeppson was real sure they were hauling drugs. That's his thing, you know. Dan said Bud was keeping all the dishes and other stuff in a box for him. I hope he still is."

"Okay, can you and Aaron be at Bud's on Thursday, around noon? I'll contact the others and let you know if we have to change the time? See if you can bring the 'blow-up' of Thompson's face."

"Okay, we'll be there, unless something else comes up."

* * *

That same Friday afternoon, Roger Trebecque, the assistant manager arrived at the Ruby Springs Lodge to assume his duties for the evening. Chuck Thompson, doing his best to suppress any hint of concern on his face, confronted him, attempting a grin. "So, Roger," he began. "Tell me about this note. It says some lady from Utah called to make some positive comments?"

"Well, yeah. She just wanted to tell you how much they enjoyed their time here, and the service was great. And she wanted to wish you a merry Christmas."

"Oh, I guess that's not so unusual. Did she happen to mention what part of Utah they were from?"

Roger looked at him, quizzically, wondering why Chuck seemed to have any concern. "No, she just said Utah, as far as I can remember. We have a lot of guests from Utah, don't we? Did I write down her name? I can't recall what it was. Something really common like Watson, or Wilson, maybe. Could've been Smith or Jones for all I know. Sorry, Chuck. Can't remember."

"Yeah, guess we do get a lot of Utah people." Chuck folded the note and put it in his shirt pocket. Roger shrugged and went about his duties, wondering why the note would raise any concern for the manager.

"Everything seems to be in order for another busy weekend," Chuck said. "I've got to run a few errands. If Laura comes looking for me, tell her I'll be back before five o'clock."

Roger turned to reply, but Chuck had suddenly vanished from the doorway. The sound of his rapidly retreating footsteps on the tile floor of the hallway preceded the slamming of the door leading to the parking lot.

Thompson's anxieties increased as he drove quickly to the local office of the telephone company, hoping to get there before the secretarial staff had left for the weekend. A familiar face greeted him with a smile. "Mr. Thompson, you're back again?" said the friendly and attractive, middle-aged woman.

"Linda!" he began, with relief in his voice. "Glad I caught you before you left! I need the number of a party that called the hotel last night. It was about eight-thirty. It was a call from Utah. Can you get it for me?" He stuffed a twenty-dollar bill into her purse, which she had placed on the counter in preparation for leaving.

"Sure thing," she answered with a tired smile. "But I'm not Linda. My name is Judy. Linda left us, weeks ago. Just give me a minute."

"Oh, sorry about the name, Judy."

She puzzled again about his apparent urgent concerns with people calling the hotel from out of state--especially calls from the eastern half of the country. What could possibly be of such great interest in a call from Utah? In addition to his accent that seemed a little odd to her, Chuck Thompson was something of a man of mystery, but she figured by his nervous mannerisms and strange requests of her that he just might be a little off-center. She quietly complied with his puzzling requests, though somewhat amused. Besides that, she appreciated his generous tips.

It took her a few minutes to get the Utah phone number and write it down for him. "Don't know where the call originated, Mr. Thompson. The whole state has only one area code, you know. But I could pin-point the prefix, if you'd like."

"No, no need," he answered, with an effort at looking relieved. "I'd just like to call these people back. My assistant didn't write down the name. Thanks again, Judy."

"Anytime, Mr. Thompson."

He and Laura had discussed getting stopped by the Utah troopers many times, but could never come up with a reason that they had been stopped and questioned for at least twenty minutes. The cops couldn't possibly have known that he had fatally poisoned Floyd Barker and Brody Conway. It was true that he had allowed the rental car to wander out of his lane just before he got stopped. No, there had to be more to it than just a minor driving goof-up. But, on the other hand, what could they have actually known, or even suspected?

He had been ready to raise his little .25 semi-automatic and kill the officer at his car window with a bullet to the brain--being actually on the verge of doing it. Chuck and Laura acknowledged to each other that it had only been the presence of that third cop who had stayed back behind the door of the cruiser--presumably holding another firearm, likely a shotgun--that had stayed their hands. Just two quick shots would have done the job. Chuck had even insisted that they rehearse such a maneuver in the event that it might become necessary in the future.

After a year and a half had passed, they had both assumed that they were in the clear. But now it seemed to Chuck that some disconcerting loose ends could be the start of the unraveling of their very lives! With his nerves on fire, his right foot began to quiver on the gas pedal as he tried to hold his speed down on his way back to the lodge. He would check recent registrations from Utah tourists for the phone number that Judy had given him. His body seemed to tingle and a strange heavy feeling of numbness crept into his hands. Was he over-reacting? Going crazy? It was nearing five o'clock and Laura would probably have something prepared for their dinner. But he couldn't put off checking recent registrations just to eat something!

He entered the lodge, went immediately to the office and quickly scanned through several months of registration records, carefully scrutinizing any from Utah. Finding no recent record of Utah guests with a phone number that matched the one Judy had given to him, his hands gradually stopped shaking. Chuck jerked around as Roger entered the office with no warning of his approach. The registration records slammed shut, seemingly without any thought or effort on Thompson's part.

Chuck tried to sound relaxed, but his movements were jerky and awkward. "Roger," he stammered. "How's everything going?" He was suddenly aware of the warm flush of his face and wondered if Roger had noticed.

"Oh, well... good. Everything's under control far's I know. How's it with you, Chuck? I thought you and Laura would be chowin' down by now. Is everything okay? Are you sure you're not coming down with something? Your face looks a little... "

That sounded to Chuck like a good excuse for his flushed face, not to mention the sickening feeling in his mid-section. "I don't know. Could be. I'd better get out of here. I hope you don't catch it, too, whatever it is."

"Yeah, I think you'd better take something for it. Get some rest... or whatever. Let Laura take care of you, ya know what I mean, boss?"

"Yeah, yeah. I will... I'll be fine. ... could be something I had for lunch."

Chuck hurried to the apartment that he and Laura shared. He quickly found the box of older files. He searched for the better part of an hour for other records of Utah guests. There, at last, was the registration of Aaron and Naomi Gentry, showing their Toquerville address and a phone number that matched the one that Judy had given him. Why would the woman call after more than a whole year had passed? These people had to be the cops that the Jackson chief had told him about. And the phony name! Calling herself "Mrs. Wilson," or "Watson," according to Roger, clinched it. His pulse raced and his hands shook uncontrollably. But why would that woman be calling now?

Laura had prepared a salmon dish for their dinner, which was on the table. Normally the smell of it or just the mention of it would have made his mouth water and hasten his movements. She looked up as he strode into their apartment and blurted, "They're onto us! We gotta get out a here! We gotta disappear! Now!"

"What are you talking about, Chuck? Who's 'they'?" Over their years together she had witnessed similar fits of what she considered to be his baseless paranoia. "What's the problem, now?" was her exasperated response.

"I told you before, a year ago, that young couple from Utah were both cops, from down by St. George, in southern Utah." His voice began to rise to a higher intensity. "Does that all ring a bell... at all?"

"Yeah? So? I hardly noticed them before you mentioned gettin' a call from the chief. Wasn't he the tall blond guy and she was quite tall... long dark hair? Just kids on their grand honeymoon, weren't they? They seemed to be all wrapped up in each other, from what I could tell. How'd you know they were cops, anyway?"

"Well, they got involved in a little fender-fight downtown, in their truck. They told Ken Bender they were cops. This kid, Gentry's a highway patrol guy and she said she's a deputy sheriff. Like I told you before... the chief called and gave me a 'head's up' on them. We wouldn't have known, otherwise."

"So, what's the big deal? They were just here on their little honeymoon vacation. And what would Utah cops care, or do, about a little gambling, anyway? Seems to like they just skied a lot and swam in the pool about every night, didn't they? What are you so excited about?"

"Don't you get it? Laura! They were here about our little job in the St. George jail! That had to be it! They were checkin' us out! Don't you get it!?"

"Oh, for cryin' out loud!" Laura exclaimed, "If they'd a had anything they would've busted us back then! That was a year ago! What's got you so upset about it, Chuck? It was a clean job, wasn't it? You're all upset over nothin'. Those guys were just a couple of scumbags, anyway. I'll bet nobody down there even cares."

"Oh, d'ya think? What about this? That woman, the Gentry woman, who happens to be a deputy sheriff... called here last night! Asked for Mr. Thompson! She gave Roger a phony name!"

"How did you know it was her? I say again, Chuck, what are you so excited about?"

"I didn't tell them my name!"

"Well somebody must have--probably the clerk. Besides that, your name is on your nameplate on the front desk! Honestly!" She poured some liquid from a large, dark green bottle into a glass tumbler. "Here, have a drink... and settle down!"

He gulped several swallows and thought about it some more. "No!" he exclaimed, suddenly. "She called and asked for 'Mr. Thompson' just to verify that was my name. They got our name from somewhere. They're onto us, Laura! I know it! We gotta get outta here, I'm tellin' ya!"

"All right!" she exclaimed. "I repeat: How do you know it was her, that called? And... why the heck would she wait a whole year?" She marveled again at how upset he was, remembering how calm and professional he always seemed to be whenever they were on an assignment away from the lodge.

"I can't explain why she would wait a year. I went to the phone company office and they looked up the number of the caller." Chuck poured himself another glass of wine and drank some more. "Then I came back and looked up the phone number they used on their registration!"

"And it was the same number?"

"*The same number*! Laura! Just as I thought! We'd better get packin', right now! There onto us, I'm tellin' ya!"

"So, it's the same number! Same woman! She just called to say thanks. Somebody used your name or told them your name while they were here. Probably one of the maids or a bellhop, who knows? And it's on your nameplate, for cryin' out loud! Right there on the desk! Look. It's Christmas time! I'll bet she'd had somethin' to drink and was feelin' a bit merry... rememberin' their honeymoon... and decided to give you a call. Get hold of yourself, Chuck! Now sit down and eat! It's salmon... your favorite... it's gettin' cold!"

Now a bit more relaxed, most likely from the wine rather than from Laura's suppositions, Chuck started toward the dining table. He stopped, took another drink, and his shoulders sank lower. "I just thought of something else!" he exclaimed.

"What now?" she demanded, rolling her eyes at the ceiling.

"That day that they first got here, they had one of our flunkies take their picture right in the lobby with that old movie camera!"

"Yeah, so?"

"They caught me in the background! I was in the picture! He was aiming the camera right at my face! I remember that like it happened yesterday!"

"Are you sure? What did you do?"

"Well, first I moved aside so they were between me and the camera, but they started to move and I just walked back into the office. They've gotta have my face! Right there on the film!"

"So then you think that somebody could connect your face and your name with what? Chuck? You ain't thinkin' this Gentry guy is one of those cops we saw at that little cafe down by St. George?"

"Well, he could've been. But I don't think he was one of the ones that followed us. They were both older... maybe in their thirties... you remember? Maybe even early forties. And that other guy had really dark hair, you know. That big Gentry kid was blond, for sure."

"Well," Laura responded, forcibly leading him to the table, "if you ask me, it's just a string of coincidences. Give me some time to think about it. C'mon, let's eat and think it over for a few days. Let's not do anything rash."

"Well, maybe you're right," he said, as he sat down. "I've got to remember to give Bender a little something for his Christmas stocking. I'll have a giant fruit basket delivered to the PD and the sheriff's office. Got to remember to take care of the troopers, too, though."

CHAPTER TWELVE

Chuck Thompson couldn't get what he figured to be a very mysterious phone call from southern Utah out of his mind. Shortly before eight o'clock that evening, he parked his car at a downtown location, glanced around, zipped his down-filled parka with the hood over his head and walked a block and a half. With a glance over his shoulder, he slipped into the alley behind one of the city's major restaurants. Halfway through the block, he looked both ways, walked down several steps, and, taking a key from his pocket, opened a metal security door and stepped inside. Now within the back stairwell, he looked through a small window of a second door at the interior of the basement casino and spotted the floor manager. Using another key, he opened the second door and stepped inside.

Everything seemed to be in order among the thirty or forty customers. As he meandered among the patrons, he pondered again the business of the phone call from southern Utah. Maybe Laura was right, he thought. Why was he getting so spooked over a few coincidences? Was he making too much of the strange phone call? Maybe that Gentry couple had just moved to another residence and some other people had been given their phone number? What was that name Roger mentioned? Wilson? Watson? Or something like that. Yeah, that had to be it.

The casino had just about everything that any Nevada gaming establishment had, but on a much smaller scale, of course. Paying out an average of thirty percent, the profits were immense, especially on weekend evenings. It was not unusual to have high-rolling guests from just about anywhere in the world.

The drinks he'd consumed helped calm his anxiety, but the phone call from the previous evening hung in his consciousness. Was it a call from a county cop in Utah to verify his name? Or was it really just a call from a satisfied customer to compliment him on the service? Maybe Laura was right. Maybe there really was no need to get upset. On the other hand, it might pay to have a plan, just in case.

But should they flee and make a new life? Or would it be better to go down there and simply eliminate the classy young lady deputy? After all, that was what he did best--for pretty good money, of course. But how, he pondered? Poison? A bullet? What about an "accident?" That made sense--an accident. On a car chase? That could do the job. But then what about her husband, the road cop? And there would surely be others she'd told about her suspicions. Or maybe he and Laura could just start a new life somewhere else? In another country? Mexico? Canada? Getting a new identity would be easy. There were so many ways. But then, could he convince Laura? Why did women like to stay stuck in one place so much? In his line of work, maybe not such a good idea.

He went to the bar and was handed a drink, which calmed him even more. He strolled around for a half hour talking to the employees but grew restless and decided to leave. Maybe he would drop by the police station and try to find officer Bender. ... try a little more shmooze and maybe grease a few palms for the Christmas season? He considered walking, since he figured he'd probably register pretty good on the breathalyzer. He decided to wait until he felt a little more steady and sober to visit the police station. He drove back to the lodge instead.

* * *

Becky Scott had planned to do some serious Christmas shopping on Saturday, but Preston's invitation to make a trip to Mesquite, Nevada, was just too tempting. She would put off shopping until Monday--and maybe Tuesday--after work. That would be cutting it pretty close, she decided, but, as in years past, she could pull it off. Christmas Eve was Tuesday night.

Saturday, after a light lunch, they departed for Mesquite and spent some time in the afternoon at the slots and tables. She was getting the impression that Preston was pretty well-fixed for money--frugal, perhaps, but certainly not stingy. She liked it that way. Toward evening they found a buffet. Feeling well-fed, they strolled to a small stage deep within the casino and enjoyed a young aspiring comic and a bluegrass group on tour.

She half-expected him to offer to take her to church on Sunday as they drove back north in the darkness. But he didn't mention attending church at all. On the contrary, he seemed to be unusually preoccupied with something far away.

"Okay, Preston," she asked, turning to him and sitting close. "You're being really quiet. What's on your mind? Are you back home in England?"

He turned to her for an instant. "Oh, I'm so very sorry," he replied. "Um... Yes, as a matter of fact, I was. I was just wondering, at the moment, about my daughters, Polly and Alicia. They each have a small son, you know. But I've told you that before. They are such delightful children. I haven't seen them in a very long time."

"Oh, I'll bet you just adore them. You've never shown me their pictures." She was surprised at how the thought of his longing for home and family affected her. How would she handle it if he were to go back to England permanently and leave her alone--again? Suddenly, she turned to him and asked, "What about us, Preston? What's going to happen to us?" The sudden question just came out and it surprised her. She reprimanded herself, hoping she hadn't sounded like she was pleading with him. He glanced at her but remained silent. "Sorry to be so blunt. But I was remembering from the other night, that we were saying that we had grown fond of each other. The truth is, I'd like to keep you around for a long, long time." She took his right hand in hers, clutched it tightly on her lap, and took a deep breath, trying to quell her emotions and smile at the same time. She wondered, could he be thinking of bringing up the "M" word? Should she?

"Becky... you know I'm feeling the same way. Now, I'm facing a monumental dilemma. It's driving me absolutely daft." It sounded almost like a groan to her. "What am I to do?" was spoken almost as a sigh of desperation.

"No, Preston. It's 'we,' what on earth are *we* going to do? Can we afford all that traveling back and forth and maybe having two homes?"

"Here in the U.S., I believe they would call my home a 'town house' in Blackpool on the west coast of Lancashire. Alicia lives nearby and she's been looking after it for me. But I could sell the place and get something less expensive outside the principal metropolis, I suppose."

They rode in silence for a time, each one deep in their own thoughts while crossing the "Arizona strip." The rising full moon ahead of them filled the Virgin River Gorge with a lustrous glow.

* * *

"Hi, Mom," Naomi said, as she stopped at the door to the civil and records office. "How was your weekend?"

"Well, it was really nice," Becky replied, with wide smile. "Preston took me to Mesquite on Saturday. We dumped a bunch of quarters down the old slots then we had dinner at a buffet and saw a show. It was great. He's such a nice man... and kind of fun to be around."

"Well, I'm glad for you both. How's he doing with the 'mission'ry' lessons? Have you been involved in that, too?"

"Oh, he seems excited about it, but he decided to put it off until January for some reason. I thought he was going to drag me to church with him yesterday. But I haven't heard anything from him since Saturday night."

"I hope it works out for him. And you should give it a chance, Mom! If anything ever comes off between you two, then you know you'd better be on the same page, church-wise."

"Well, my dear, I appreciate the advice! But you're right, of course."

"You've been seeing a lot of each other, haven't you," Naomi said, smiling back. "Have you two been having any, um, serious talks?" Becky's face began to glow. "I don't mean to pry, Mom, but you know, we're all starting to wonder... just a little."

"As a matter of fact, we have."

"Ah, ha! I knew it would happen. Tell me all about it!"

"Well, we're just talking a little. Now and then. It really is a problem for him. For us, I guess. He's got two daughters and two little grandsons back in Lancashire. And he owns a townhouse there in the city of Blackpool on the coast. I don't know if he'll want to stay here or what. It's a big dilemma for him, I know. Would I want to live there? And... I won't be able to get any retirement for quite a few years, you know. If... if something happened to him, I'd have no income."

"Oh, yeah. That could definitely be a problem."

"He said it was driving him 'abs'lutely dawft!'" They both laughed out loud.

Suddenly Sergeant Lowry stood beside Naomi. "What's all this frivolity, I'm a hearin'? What's goin' on with you two, now?"

"Oh, we were just discussing Mom's love life," Naomi replied. "You've met Preston Blackstone... at our reception, remember him?"

"For sure. Yeah, I remember. The very distinguished and 'propah' gentleman from England. Somebody said he had been an English 'bobby.' Or was he a 'coppah?' Has he decided to stay around a while? Wasn't he researching his Mormon relatives? That could take a while."

"Yes, he is," Becky replied. "And he'll be meeting with the Mormon missionaries, too. He told us he had been an assistant to the chief constable of Lancashire."

"Really? That's great. Oh, seeing you two here together reminds me, Becky. Did you ever sell that pickup truck your husband used to drive? You were trying to sell it, at one time, I think."

"No, I still have it. It's for sale. Do you know anyone who might be interested in it? I've been letting Preston use it. But I don't know for sure how long he'll be here. Why do you ask?"

"I just remembered seeing it early this morning," Becky looked a bit puzzled.

"Oh, really," said Naomi. "Where was that? You know he's been staying in my mobile home until it sells. We thought we had it sold about a year ago to a couple from Idaho, but the sale fell through when the man got really sick. Preston usually just stays at home and does his typing early in the morning."

"Well, I saw the truck parked up by the airport, this morning. The 'for sale' signs were still in the windows. That's what drew my attention to it, you know." Shane's words had a sharp and apparent impact on Becky. Her face became pale and drawn. Her breathing became slightly irregular.

"The airport?" Naomi asked. "Up on the bench?"

"Yeah. Right there where passengers usually park their cars. Is there something wrong? Do you think he might have taken a flight somewhere?"

"Well, if he did," Naomi said, noting the alarm on her mother's face, "he never said anything about it to Mom... or anybody else!" Becky leaned her elbows on her desk and covered her face with her hands. She seemed to be saying something that they could not understand. Shane realized that he was stumbling into matters that did not concern him. After stating an offer to help, if needed, he excused himself and started to leave.

He stopped and turned to ask, "You're planning to be up at Bud's place... Thursday, at noon?" Naomi nodded and Shane left them quickly. She placed a hand reassuringly on her mother's shoulder.

Becky took a deep breath and raised her head. Her fingers rubbed a tear that was about to fall from her cheek. She took hold of Naomi's other hand and held tightly to it. "He's gone, Naomi," Becky sighed. "I knew he'd go. My gosh! I just knew it! I knew I shouldn't have... Oh, my word." Her voice trailed off in a choking whisper.

Naomi, afraid that her mother's fears were on target, tried to console her. "Oh, I don't think he'd just go without telling you... without saying something... to somebody. He wouldn't do that. I know he wouldn't. He must have at least left a note somewhere."

"Well, I guess we'll see," Becky said. "We'll just have to wait and see, won't we."

"Mom, I'll go up there and talk to the Sky West people and see what they can tell me. He'll be back, Mom! I'm sure he will." Naomi gently massaged her mother's shoulders in consolation. "Why don't you try calling his house?"

"Oh, I don't know if I should do that. I don't want him to think that I'm checking up on him." She sighed again. "But this has me concerned. Maybe he'll call me. I was really looking forward to spending Christmas together!"

"He'll be back, Mom. I know he will."

* * *

Naomi managed to stop at the Sky West ticket counter where she talked to a high school classmate later in the morning. But all he could tell her was that Preston had purchased a one-way ticket to Salt Lake City on Saturday morning and had boarded a twelve-passenger prop-jet--taking only one small carry-on suitcase--early Sunday. From the Salt Lake International Airport, the ticket agent told her, he could have gone virtually anywhere in the free world. Glancing in and around Becky's locked truck in the parking lot, she found no note or other indications of his intentions.

So he'd bought a plane ticket even before taking Becky to visit Mesquite, she reasoned. Could it really have been a "last date" in his way of thinking? And he'd said nothing about it to her! That would take some nerve! But then, he couldn't possibly have carried all his belongings in just one suitcase. And Sunday would be such an odd day to leave--or travel.

Her first thought was to go to the mobile home in Washington City and check on what he may have left behind. Maybe that would give her some clues as to where he was going, and for how long. Perhaps he'd left a note or a letter of explanation. She could go inside and look around. But then, his rental wasn't complete until the end of December and going inside could almost be considered meddling--an invasion of his privacy--and probably for no good reason, she decided. After all, it had only been one day. He must have had some urgent business that he wanted to keep private. Perhaps by Christmas day, if he hadn't contacted them, she would look into it further.

* * *

For a Monday morning, the radio had been fairly quiet. Naomi drove by the photography shop to pick up the pictures that she hoped had been made from the movie film.

CHAPTER THIRTEEN

Having retired after more than thirty-five years in the British constabulary, and working his way up to Assistant to the Chief Constable of Lancashire, Preston Blackstone was not a wealthy man by any measure. But his monthly retirement stipend check was mailed to him regularly and he had "adequate means," as he might have commented. He was living comfortably. His formerly sharp investigative skills were somewhat rusty, to say the least, and he realized that his activities taking him away from dear friends in Washington County could--and undoubtedly would--be criticized when he returned. But he felt certain that he could be very careful to cover his tracks.

He sorely regretted leaving without telling anyone where he was going or when he would return. But there was a good reason for that. Frequently, he thought of Becky Scott and her family and the new friends he had found. He had developed a deep fondness for them, especially Becky. Furthermore, he was continually enthralled with the variegated beauty of this part of the United States. He hoped to return quickly, hopefully, on or even before Christmas Eve. Gradually, the thought of leaving Becky and going back to England on a permanent basis seemed more and more inconceivable.

On arriving at the Salt Lake City International Airport, the first thing he did was to drop the letter he had prepared for Becky on Saturday morning into a mail slot. He hoped to have it reach her on Monday or Tuesday afternoon at her home in Bloomington. He was sure that she would understand when he was ready to begin explaining his reasons.

He then went back and purchased a one-way ticket to Sun Valley, Idaho on another small airline. From Sun Valley, with a separate new ticket he made it to Jackson, Wyoming, by late Sunday evening. At his request, a taxi took him from the airport to the Ruby Springs Lodge.

The taxi driver, who introduced himself as Sal, was a talkative and an inquisitive young man who practically related his life history. Preston's strategy was to affect an "Aussie" brogue. He'd even considered registering at the lodge under an assumed last name. But then, he reasoned, Aaron and Naomi would have written "Gentry" as their last name, anyway. There would be no way that anyone could connect "Blackstone" to the young honeymooners from the previous winter. The charismatic young driver, who said he was saving money for college, eagerly furnished Preston his name and a home phone number. He also pleaded with Preston to call anytime--day or night--for quick and efficient transportation--anytime--anywhere. Either he, Sal Maracek, or his roommate would be at his complete disposal.

Sal managed to glean from Preston that he had been to ski resorts from the Sierra Mountains, to Park City, to Sun Valley, and now to Jackson, in hopes of meeting a friend for a short vacation. There had apparently been some mix-up in directions and they'd been unable to make contact for the past three weeks. He explained to the driver that, having lost his wife several years ago, he had been doing a great deal of traveling.

"Do you like to gamble?" Sal asked, just prior to turning into the parking lot at the Ruby Springs Lodge.

"Gamble?" Preston asked. He did his best to sound nonchalant at the idea, but his pulse quickened at Sal's question. *Of course! Just as I suspected!*

"Yeah," Sal replied. "You know, card games, slot machines, roulette, and stuff like that."

Preston remembered Mesquite and the good time he'd had there with Becky. "Oh, certainly! I've managed to indulge a bit, in my time. Why do you ask, mate?"

"Interested in doing some this evening? It's a great way to pass the time, you know. And if your friend shows up. Hey, all the better."

"I would have suspected that most gambling would be illegal in this state. This isn't Nevah-da!"

"Oh, well, yeah, I guess it is illegal, technically. But here in Jackson, nobody seems to care much. It's a tourist town, you know. The police pretty much look the other way. Besides that... the police, well, everybody here, has a stake in keeping the tourists happy. Know what I mean?" Sal parked the car and quickly got out and ran around to the passenger side. His movements were quick and he smiled continually. "Don't pay me yet. First let's make sure you can register. The lodge may be full-up by now. There's a lot of people in town for the Christmas week, and all."

"Oh, certainly. How very thoughtful of you, mate." Sal held the door open for Preston. "Thank you, Sal. You almost make a man feel like royalty."

Once inside, Preston couldn't help but glance casually around the lobby for the man whose face he'd tried to memorize from the film he'd watched just three nights before. But the man at the desk, whom he presumed to be the night manager, was definitely not the Mr. Thompson he was looking for. But it was just as well, because the lodge was completely full and probably would be for at least the next week.

"Hey, Roger!" said Sal. "My man, Preston, came all the way from Australia to be here. He was supposed to meet a friend. Can you tell us if he's here already?"

"Sure thing. What's his name? I'll check our records. What's his name? Where's he from? What city?"

"Well, mate, *she's* from Melb'n, we both are." The night manager's eyebrows raised somewhat and his smile widened.

"The name's, uh, Abbey Hughes." His late wife's maiden name was convenient. Roger looked briefly in his records.

"Um... no, she doesn't seem to be here at Ruby Springs," he said. "Let me call around and see if some other hotel might have a room for you. And I could call and see if anyone has Abbey Hughes, from Melbourne, registered, if you'd like."

"Blimey! You mates are so exceptionally accommodating!" Preston exclaimed. "I've never encountered such a splendid degree of hospitality!"

"We aim to please," said Roger. He was dialing the phone to reach another hotel. "We all call amongst ourselves if we're full-up." While Roger was on the phone and Sal was engaged in a conversation with another patron of the lodge, Preston glanced at the desk behind the counter, seeing that there was a second nameplate sitting on the desk that appeared to have been hastily placed there. He moved subtly to the right in order to read what it said. Reassuringly, the nameplate belonged to "Chuck Thompson-Manager." He glanced around the lobby again, but did not see the man. Within minutes Roger had found a room in another hotel for Preston, but could find no record of Abbey Hughes.

"Thank you so very much!" Preston exclaimed, smiling broadly. "I'll try to find Abbey on my own and if she stops by you'll know where I'll be staying, at least for a night, or two."

"Certainly, sir. Sorry for the inconvenience. Sal, here, will take good care of you."

"Oh, I'm certain that he will. And thanks, again, Roger." He offered the night manager a five-dollar tip, but it was refused.

Back in the taxi, Preston relaxed in the back seat for the short trip to another hotel. But his brain was at work. If Chuck Thompson was not at the lodge and was involved in the illegal gambling then it seemed logical that he could very well be at the casino--or whatever they called it--at this very moment.

"What was this you were telling me about gambling, Sal?"

"Sure! After you get settled in a room, you can give me a call and I'll take you over there. It's a nice place. A little out of the way... out of sight too, you might say. I can get you in... *no problemo*! Just give me a call. And yeah, they have food and drinks too, if you want."

CHAPTER FOURTEEN

As promised, Sal picked up Preston at his hotel and drove quickly to the "casino" in the basement of The Grand Teton Chuck Wagon. Sal accompanied him to a partially concealed door that was down a flight of concrete steps and proceeded to knock in what Preston perceived to be a peculiar cadence. He had to repeat the knock before the door finally opened. Preston smiled to himself at what he considered to be a rather cartoonish, secret procedure.

He tipped Sal generously again and was left on his own. The combination bar and casino was quite crowded and the patrons decidedly jovial. Having studied the blown-up photo that Naomi had shown to him, it didn't take him long to spot Chuck Thompson, with his strikingly blond hair. The man was friendly, relaxed, and engaged in conversation with some of the patrons. Preston remembered someone saying that Mormons made a big thing about abstention from alcoholic beverages. And, though it had stuck in his mind, it was somewhat puzzling, since, as he recalled, Jesus himself, and his followers used wine in religious practices and at weddings. He accepted a glass of wine from the bar and proceeded to sip at it as he maneuvered closer to the hotel manager.

Keeping an eye on Chuck Thompson, Preston moved about the large room from the roulette table to the slot machines while carrying his wine glass. After a time, he made a gradual move toward Thompson and began to engage him in conversation.

"G'day, mate," he began. That sounded pretty lame and corny, he thought, especially since it was now evening. Nevertheless, he extended his hand in greeting. "You seem to be the mate in charge, here." He tried to effect a bit of a slur in his diction.

"Good evening sir," the blond man replied. "You've come halfway around the world, just to be here with us? What an honor it is, my friend!"

"S'right. Name's Blackstone, from down under, as you 'Yanks' would say. Didn't get your name."

"Oh, I'm Chuck Thompson," was the smiling reply. "I'm here a lot, but not really managing the place. My wife and I run the Ruby Springs Lodge during the day. That's over by the mountains, you know. We get lots of skiers. Not often anybody shows up from Australia, though."

"Oh, really," Preston replied. For a few seconds, he was amazed that he could now be speaking with the man responsible for the double killing in the Washington County Jail--a contract murderer. He forced the thought from his mind in order to engage the man before him in pleasant conversation. "Never skied, m'self. Bloody good fun though, I hear. S'posed to meet me ol' sheila up here, all a way from Melb'n. Blimey! mate, we just can't seem to make c'nections!" He thought of his deceased wife again with a degree of sadness and hoped she wouldn't mind him using her name.

"That's too bad, Mr. Blackstone," Thompson said with a wide grin. "But no sense wasting the evening. Can I get you some more wine? Drinks are on the house you know."

"Certainly, mate! 'preciate it! This is a such great place, mate!" Preston wondered if he was maybe over-playing the "mate" charade and doubted that he had the accent and lingo quite right. Well, they wouldn't know anyway, he reasoned. "Right now, though, I'm afraid nature's calling!" He made his swaying departure to the restroom.

"Later, Mr. Blackstone," Thompson called after him, laughing.

Once in the restroom, which was deserted, Preston poured the remaining wine from his glass down the sink drain. He exited the restroom with his empty glass and walked, once more swaying a little, with his feet wide apart, to the bar. After obtaining another glass of red wine, he spotted Thompson, across the room.

"Blasted wine you have here. Goes straight to a man's head, for sure! Powerful stuff, mate!" He moved closer to Thompson and placed the glass to his lips with some apparent difficulty. He took a long swallow from the glass, which left it nearly half empty. Coming still closer to Chuck Thompson, he determined that the time was right. He stumbled, lurched forward, and swung his hand holding the glass toward the man, as if to steady himself.

The liquid from his glass spilled onto the upper portions of Thompson's light grey wool trousers and deposited a large red stain. That should do it, he surmised.

"Blimey, mate!" he exclaimed. "I am so sorry!" He took a handkerchief from his pocket and tried to wipe at the blotch. Thompson's face was livid. He jerked away from Preston. "*Keep away from me! Idiot!*" he exclaimed, and went straight to the restroom. A woman from across the room rushed toward the restroom after him, but stopped to wait outside as he pushed through the door. Preston surmised that she must be Laura Thompson. He reeled toward her and apologized profusely.

"Crikey! What in the... what's in this wine? I've never... ! I'm so sorry, madam! Please 'llow me to pay for the cleaning! I'll get 'im a new pair of trousers! I am so sorry! It was all my fault! Please lemme pay for it!"

"Oh, it'll be okay," said the woman. "I'm Chuck's wife. He'll be fine, really. He's easily upset. But he'll get over it quickly, I'm sure.

So this was Laura, the wife of Chuck Thompson. Again, he wondered, could they really be the contract killers? Thompson stuck his head out of the restroom door and motioned to his wife. His face was highly animated as they exchanged a few words. She nodded to him and turned toward Preston with an amused smile, "He wants me to go home and get him another pair of pants! I guess you really did a number on the grey ones. The port is going to leave a dark stain, I'm afraid."

"Oh, please 'llow me to pay for the purchase of a new pair," said Preston, pulling some cash from his wallet. He extended three twenty-dollar bills toward her, still swaying, feet wide apart. "Will this be suff'cient?"

"Hey, it's okay. Don't worry about a thing, mister! Please don't," she pleaded. "These things do happen. He'll be over it in no time." She left the casino quickly and Preston glanced around the room taking note of several amused smiles. He noticed Thompson's face peering around the door again. This time the face seemed more relaxed--friendlier, even possibly amused. Chuck motioned him nearer. Preston reeled toward him and apologized again, extending the money toward him.

"Hey, sorry for yelling at you. These things happen. I know you didn't mean to spill the 'vino' on me. These things happen, my friend." He was smiling now and waved Preston away. "Now you go on and have some fun, and be sure to let me know when you're ready to go back to the hotel. I'll see that you get a ride. Know what I mean?"

Preston couldn't believe his luck, hoping, of course, that Thompson would simply swap trousers in the restroom and discard the soiled pair in the waste receptacle. "Utterly unbelievable!" he muttered to himself. Thompson's face disappeared back into the restroom to wait for a fresh pair of trousers to arrive. Preston slowly sauntered back toward where Chuck had been sitting and glanced around the room at the other customers who seemed fully intent on gambling. Covering Chuck's wine glass with a clean napkin, he picked it up and slipped it into the pocket of his jacket. He chose a spot at one of the slot machines and sat watching for Laura's return while dumping quarters into the machine.

Laura Thompson was not long in returning and carried a shopping bag toward the restroom door and knocked. Soon the door opened and Chuck took the bag and disappeared inside. Preston saw from the corner of his eye as Thompson exited the restroom smiling. He was carrying nothing in his hands as he approached Preston.

"Hey, sorry Mr. Blackstone," he said, extending his hand. "Sorry to yell at you that way. But don't worry about it."

"But, the red stain! Won'cha please 'llow me to compensate you for that, mate!"

"No, no, no!" Thompson protested, again. "You go on now, and have some fun. And be sure to find me when you need a ride back to your hotel."

"Yer shore?" Preston replied, with a grin. "You Yanks are certainly a hos... hos... 'spitable lot! I don't care wot ever'body says!" He swayed toward the restroom again, laughing to himself at his words, as if he'd said something supremely witty. "Gotta make the

W-C! The boy's room! Bloody quick!" he called over his shoulder.

He went into the restroom and took his time, waiting for the room to empty. He then walked quickly to the wastebasket and snatched the shopping bag from inside, and took it immediately to a stall to inspect the contents. Sure enough, the bag contained Thompson's grey wool trousers with a dark, moist stain below the left front pocket. He could feel a small comb in the right-front pocket. He closed the bag and secured it under his left arm beneath his red and tan, plaid, polyester sport jacket and went back out into the casino. He paused at the bar and handed Sal Maracek's phone number to the server.

"Would you be s'kind as to call this number and jus' tell 'im ol' Preston is drastically in need of conveyance back to his lodging?" He waited for the young woman to make the call, gave her a two-dollar tip and then sauntered back toward the slot machines. His left arm clutched the package under his jacket tightly and he carried his wine glass in his left hand as he dumped more quarters and pulled the handle--waiting for Sal.

It was still just Sunday night, he could even be back in St. George by Monday night, if things worked out, he reasoned. Maybe he'd be back before Becky got his letter--maybe before she even realized he was gone. She probably wouldn't even know he'd left St. George. How careful do I need to be? Will this guy, Thompson, be checking to see why I left so soon? Will he be suspicious? If he discovers that I've taken a direct flight out of Jackson, would it leave too wide a trail?

He was just beginning to get a little nervous when he saw Sal Maracek look inside the room. He walked quickly, trying to remember to sway a little as he walked. Just before reaching Sal, he felt a hand upon his shoulder. It felt as though his nervous system froze as he stopped and turned to face Chuck and Laura Thompson, together.

"Leaving so soon, Mr. Blackstone?" Laura said, with a wide smile. He studied their faces intently, trying to read their thoughts. He began to relax, noting their congenial smiles.

"Hope we see you again soon," Chuck added. "And please don't worry about the trousers."

"Think maybe I've reached my limit fer t'night, mate!" he

answered, trying to display a crooked grin. "Lemme say one more time. Sorry 'bout that. Jus' 'membered, there was a number we was s'posta call if we couldn't find each other, ya know, me and m'lil sheila. She's got a cousin in Colorado. I better go back to my room and make a call."

"Sure," Chuck answered, smiling. "Hope you find her. Sal, here, will take good care of you. Right, Sal?"

"You bet, no problem at all!"

Sal began talking once again in the car. Tired of the charade, Preston feigned a yawn, slumped in the seat, and leaned toward the door and closed his eyes. Sal smiled and kept quiet during the remainder of the short ride. As they stopped at the front door, Preston didn't stir. Sal shook his shoulder.

"Oh, short ride, mate," Preston muttered, as Sal opened the door for him. The cold air refreshed his awareness. He opened his wallet and handed it to the driver. Sal removed his fare and gave it back.

"Sure you can make it back to the room, sir?" Sal asked. "Need any help?"

"Crikey!" Preston exclaimed. "You blokes're certainly a friendly lot. I c'n make it, Sal." Once more, he swayed as he walked toward the elevator.

Sal got back into his car and started the engine. His CB was calling from the apartment he shared with a friend. It was a call to go back to find Chuck Thompson. Another drunk, he supposed.

As soon as he walked into the main room of the casino, Thompsons approached him quickly. "Get him back into the hotel room?" Chuck asked, with a grin.

"Just left him at the front door," Sal replied, wondering where the question would be leading.

"He seemed to be quite, um, intoxicated, wouldn't you say?" Chuck asked. "Did you notice anything unusual about him? Besides being from Australia... and all that 'bloke' and 'sheila' nonsense?" Thompson seemed to be straining to appear relaxed. Yet the question seemed a bit odd.

"Well, I guess he seemed pretty well plastered, all right. But in the car he didn't seem to smell much. What was he drinking, anyway?" And why was Thompson so interested? He thought he detected more than a slight degree of concern on Chuck's face and in his manner.

"I guess the guy put away his share of wine--and then some," Chuck said. "Anyway, that couple over there by the roulette tables was asking about a ride back to Ruby Springs. I'll tell 'em you're here."

"Hey, thanks a lot, Chuck!"

* * *

Chuck Thompson didn't sleep much through the night. He kept thinking about the drunken "Aussie" who had spilled wine on his trousers and ruined them for him. The man had seemed odd enough, over and above the obvious. Sal was right. For a man who seemed that intoxicated, there was little apparent odor on his breath. Of course, with others drinking in the room, including him, maybe he had simply become quite accustomed to the aroma. He tossed and turned through the night, getting two or three hours of sleep.

In the morning, after taking over the manager's duties, he decided to look further into Preston Blackstone's activities. About ten o'clock in the morning, he informed Laura that he would be gone maybe an hour. The extra help they had hired for the holiday season had not been adequately trained and she was more than a little irritated with him.

"Here we go again," she said, rolling her eyes in his direction. "What was it about the man that has you so worried?"

"I don't know. Maybe it's nothing. Can't put my finger on anything in particular, just a feeling. We can't be too careful! *Can we? Cora?*" His emphasis on her old name was intended to remind her of their critical need to be supremely cautious.

"Well, of course not! *And don't call me that, anymore! Dammit!* And keep your voice down!" Her irritation was near the boiling point. "You know I always hated that name! Somebody might hear you! Besides that, your idea of leaving that stolen car... and all your clothes... and that wig in that department store, in that little town down there. *What a colossal brainstorm! Good grief!*"

Chuck was silent for a moment, digesting what she had just said. "Yeah, sorry. But we were John and Cora for a long time, you know.

I should be back in an hour or less."

"If you must! Why don't you just call the hotel where he was staying, Chuck? He's probably still there, sleeping it off. Maybe he's found his 'Lil Sheila' and they've gone somewhere, already."

"Not a bad idea." Chuck was dialing the phone. The manager of the other hotel informed him that Preston Blackstone had departed early in the morning, apparently for the airport.

"Well, he's gone," Chuck remarked to his wife, "probably to the airport. He's gotta have one heck of a hangover, I'd say. He's probably headed out for Aspen, maybe. He mentioned he had to call someone in Colorado."

"Well, so he's gone," Laura replied. "Now what?"

"I'll be back in a little while." Chuck didn't wait for her reply or objections but went quickly out the back door to the parking lot. He drove quickly to the small Teton County Airport.

The Sky West ticket agent informed him that a Mr. Blackstone had come from Sun Valley, Idaho, on Sunday morning, stayed overnight, and departed early in the morning for Aspen, Colorado. Said he was meeting some woman there. Chuck breathed easier. The man's story checked out.

"I talked to him last night," Chuck said. "He didn't seem to be doing well at all. A little too much of the "old vino." Was he a little, uh, under the weather, this morning?"

"No, he seemed okay to me. Perfectly normal, well, for an Englishman. 'Rawthah chippah,' I'd say," said the ticket agent, attempting to mock the accent.

More alarm bells sounded in Chuck's brain. He struggled to maintain a calm manner. "Oh, really! I guess the man can handle his booze better than I thought."

CHAPTER FIFTEEN

It was close to midnight, Monday, December 23, when Becky Scott finally finished wrapping the presents she had purchased that afternoon and evening. Even though shopping had consumed her time, her mind was mostly occupied with wondering about Preston Blackstone. She had thought of the worst, of course. Had he just up and left her? How long had he been planning to leave? She would have understood if he'd just mentioned that he wanted to see his family and be back in England for Christmas with his daughters and two little grandsons.

Still, it seemed so uncharacteristically thoughtless of him to leave without saying anything to her. Maybe she didn't mean that much to him after all, she thought, sadly. Still, hoping for the best, she wrapped his present and tucked it under her tree, hiding it under the others. At last she slipped into a flannel night gown and knelt by her bed to pray. She asked the Lord out loud to keep Preston safe wherever he was. She considered pleading with the Lord to bring Preston back, but decided not to say it. No, he would have to make that decision himself.

* * *

It was nearly half-past one o'clock in the morning of Tuesday, December 24th, when the pilot switched on the landing lights of the twelve-seater over Cedar Breaks. The nearly full moon in the western sky illuminated the snow-laden mountains below. Preston sighed in relief as the brilliant gold and white lights of the St. George Basin lit up the ground ahead and to his left. The headlights of a few weary travelers enabled him to make out the major route--Interstate 15-- entering the valley from the north and exiting into the Virgin River Gorge across the Arizona Strip. He noted the lights illuminating the white LDS Temple in the center of the city. The temple was old, by the relatively brief American reckoning, he mused. But he smiled, thinking of touring ancient artifacts such as the Stonehenge near the river on the wide Plain of Salisbury and the stone fences built during the Roman occupation, long centuries past.

The small propjet settled onto the runway with only a slight bump and he thought of Becky again, doubting that she'd even been aware that he had been away. She may have tried to call him, or perhaps she'd gotten his letter. No, that would not be possible for the postal system--especially at Christmas time--he thought. He relished the thought of seeing her again.

Her truck was parked just as he'd left it. Back at the rented doublewide, he decided to shave and shower before settling down for a much-needed long sleep.

* * *

Naomi had explained her mother's predicament to Aaron over breakfast on Tuesday morning.

"He'll be back," Aaron said, confidently. "He's probably just gone to Salt Lake to do some more research in the genealogy files up there."

"Oh, well, that's certainly possible. But he couldn't expect to do that on a Sunday... and why wouldn't he say something to her. Or somebody? He's always seemed to be so thoughtful of others' feelings, you know?"

"Yes, I guess he has been. But I think he's in love with your mom. At least it seems that way to me. I'm pretty sure he'll be back. He must have had a good reason to go without telling her. I'll bet anything he's left a note for her and she hasn't found it, yet."

"Well, *I'll* bet he's missing his family back home. Christmas is tomorrow. He would've had maybe just enough time to make it home for Christmas."

"Yeah, but I'd bet he didn't go back to England. He'll show up. Anyway, Christmas is tomorrow. Are we ready?"

"Oh, yes. What a nice coincidence that it comes on our days off. Mom wants us to come down to her place for dinner and to open our presents down there."

* * *

Most of the sheriff's office staff would work just half a day on the 24th of December. Becky arrived at her office very early and rushed around for the first three hours in order to get her work done.

Halfway through the morning she looked up to see Naomi at her office door, watching her in the midst of her hectic efforts. Naomi smiled at her mother's typical last-minute rush. It would be useless to lecture her on making more timely efforts.

"Hi, Mom," she said in greeting. She decided to let her mother bring up Preston's name, if she wanted to. "I guess we'll be down for dinner, tomorrow. We'll open our presents at your house."

"Oh, that will be very nice. Natty and Ben should be there, too." Becky froze and brought her hand to her open mouth as she gaped with wide eyes over Naomi's shoulder. Her eyes suddenly began to glisten. Naomi whirled around and, taking a step backward, stared into Preston's smiling face.

"Surprised to see me, ladies?" he said, smiling broadly.

Becky stood up and walked quickly on unsteady feet toward him. She flung her arms around him and buried her face in his chest. He returned the embrace, looking somewhat embarrassed. "There, there," he managed, looking quizzically at Naomi, who was wishing she was not a witness to her mother's emotional release. She smiled at him over Becky's shoulder and turned to retreat.

Preston motioned her to remain and rubbed Becky's shoulders. "There, there," he said, trying to comfort her. "What's all this?"

"We were afraid you had gone away," Naomi said, while quickly wiping the moisture from her own eyes. "Someone said they saw Mom's truck up by the airport. I guess... uh, some of us assumed you had gone back to England, without even saying goodbye, or anything."

"Ah, of course. I am so sorry. Naturally one might reasonably be led to believe that." Becky drew back, dried her eyes with a tissue, and waited for further explanation. "There was an errand I felt compelled to undertake. And I couldn't let any of you know what I was trying to do. I simply didn't count on anyone seeing the truck at the airport while I was gone. I mailed a letter from Salt Lake City on Sunday. I was hoping you'd get it yesterday. I assume you didn't."

"No, no. There was no letter," Becky replied, her voice thick with emotion.

"Well, I'm so very sorry. I hadn't the slightest notion of the time it would require. Or whether I would have any degree of success. But it all seems to have turned out rather well, I believe. I tried to ring you late Monday night, but there was no answer. I knew Naomi and Aaron would be working, but I finally did get through to Natty's husband, Ben Randolph. He apparently neglected to tell you, it seems."

"What on earth were you doing?" Becky demanded. "You couldn't tell anybody? Where did you go?" There was an unmistakable tone of pleading--and demanding--in her voice. Naomi unconsciously reinforced Becky's demands by folding her arms and waiting patiently while leaning against the wall.

"Ah, yes, we'll get to that forthwith," Preston replied, with a slight smile. "I'd like to have your Sgt. Lowry present, as well, if he happens to be in the vicinity."

The women stared at him again. "Well, I'll see if he's still here," Naomi said, and disappeared down the hallway to the detectives' office. Preston picked up a package from where he had placed it on the floor, entered the civil office and sat down beside Becky. Presently, Naomi returned with Shane Lowry in tow. Preston rose and extended a hand in greeting.

"You wanted to see me, Mr. Blackstone?"

"Please, call me Preston, Sergeant," he said. "Please have a seat, this will take a few minutes, I'm afraid. And, Naomi, this concerns you, too." Shane and Naomi pulled chairs into the civil office and sat waiting.

"First of all," Preston began. "Allow me to say that it's most gratifying that my absence was noted by anyone." He squeezed Becky's hand without pausing. "And I apologize for the slightest degree of concern that any of you might have felt." He paused to take a deep breath. "I spent from Sunday afternoon until Tuesday morning in Jackson, Wyoming." The others in the room stared at him, incredulously.

"What the h...!" Shane began, but stopped himself mid-sentence. "You went to Jackson? What for? What did you do there?" he demanded.

"I was well aware that you'd have deep concerns." Preston answered calmly. "I hope this doesn't make me look too much like the proverbial jackass! I saw and had a conversation with a man by the name of Collins Thompson. And I've returned with some evidence that may be of assistance."

"*You what?*" Shane blurted.

"*You did what?*" Naomi gasped.

Preston raised his hand as gesture for further patience. "Let me assure you, Sergeant, I've taken every precaution that would prevent said Thompson--they call him 'Chuck'--from discovering that I arrived from this part of your country. For all he, or anyone else up there, knows, I was a tourist from Australia, trying to meet a friend for a few days of vacation at a skiing destination." He went on to explain his circuitous travel on separate one-way tickets in order to defeat at least a cursory attempt to trace his movements, should anyone bother to try. Sgt. Lowry shook his head and rolled his eyes but seemed to be somewhat relieved. Naomi's mouth remained open in amazement.

"I've spent some time researching American jurisprudence," Preston continued. "As near as I can determine, a person is free to gather evidence, unencumbered by the restrictions imposed on the government, or the constabulary. However, if I had told any of you where I was going, or asked for your approval, in any way, and for what purpose, I would have, in the eyes of American case law, become your agent. Therefore, I would have been under the same restrictions on privacy as would apply to any of you.

Shane's eyes narrowed, apparently skeptical. "So you've got some evidence? You could wind up a hero, you know. Or maybe a real dunce. *And me, too! You just may have blown our whole case!*" Shane stared at Preston, letting the weight of his words penetrate. "If Thompson's our man... If he gets suspicious and finds out, or even suspects that you came from here, he could take off to who knows where! *We might never find the guy!*" He paused again to let his lecture sink in. "Now, what is this '*evidence*' you're talking about?" There was more than a hint of sarcasm in his question.

Preston reached down and picked up the paper bag that was sealed with clear tape. He opened the bag and, using a tissue from the box on Becky's desk, retrieved the wine glass used by Chuck Thompson. "This is his wine glass. You should be able to get fresh fingerprints from it."

"Just set it on the desk," Shane said, with more than a small amount of irritation in his voice. "What else?" he demanded.

Preston picked up the shopping bag and opened the top for Shane to see. "This is a pair of Thompson's trousers. They just may contain, um, certain, um, evidence that would compare to that which was in the trousers that were left in the refuse container at the retail establishment in Hurricane."

Shane Lowry stared at Preston. "I'm afraid to ask, but I guess I gotta know. How in the...? Okay, so how did you manage to get his pants?" The women listened in rapt and silent, open-mouthed, anticipation.

Preston explained in some detail. Somehow, as he explained it, the plan he'd concocted began to seem all the more idiotic to himself. He ended up feeling somewhat apologetic, but tried to bolster his actions with a final comment. "I know this sounds like a rather dubious scheme, but it worked."

"I have to say," Naomi remarked, attempting to sound somewhat supportive. "You certainly are creative, Preston. Is this how the British police would do things?"

"Well, not exactly. But creative, perhaps. But our rules are somewhat similar." He glanced at Sgt. Lowry, looking for any hint of approval.

"Preston," Shane began, with a mere suggestion of a smile. "That is the most fascinating tale I've heard in a long time. We'll have to see if the county attorney will buy it. We may already have sufficient fingerprints from the things that Dan Wilde said he collected up at Bud's place. This will certainly confirm that it was the same man they saw in Bud's cafe. But that may not do us much good, you know. There's still nothing solid to positively tie this Thompson guy to the murders. About all we have, so far, is that the car, *the stolen car*, we processed over in Hurricane matched the description we got from our secretary, Marti. But, I'll send the pants you've got, there, to the crime lab up north. Or maybe take 'em myself. There just might be some hair that would match what we already have."

"Well... that would be conclusive evidence, wouldn't it?" Becky asked.

"No. Not entirely," Shane replied.

"Can't they prove whose hair it was?" Naomi asked. Shane shook his head and glanced at Preston.

"Afraid not," said Preston. "At the present time, there is no test or procedure that I'm aware of that can prove that a specific hair came from a specific person. Only that it is the same *type* of hair."

"But if it proves to be the same color and the same type," Shane said, "then we would have a pretty good case. The wig and mustache, and the clothing that we got out of the dumpster all connect to 'John Croft' for sure. Along with the body hair and the clothing sizes. All that *almost* links Thompson to the murders. Would it amount to 'probable cause'? Maybe, maybe not. That would be the County Attorney's call. He just *might* approve of an arrest warrant, though. Then we'd have to see what the judge thinks. We should be able to get fingerprints from his wine glass and send them to the FBI. If he's been arrested before, they'll have his prints and probably an old 'unlawful flight' arrest warrant for him. That's our safest bet."

"So we don't know for sure if we're further ahead, or not, at this point?" Naomi asked.

"Not until the lab people look at the hair... *if there is any*... in these trousers," said Shane. "And don't forget, we'll know, too, if the trousers match up for size with the others. I still haven't got any results back on any residue on the bottoms of the shoes."

"Course if it turns out that this Thompson is the wrong guy," said Naomi, "we'll have wasted a lot of time and Preston's travel money."

"We'll have to wait and see," Shane replied. "None of the other people I've looked at have panned out, at all. Preston, now that I've heard the full story, it sounds a lot better than I was afraid it was going to be."

"At the very least," Naomi added, "if the prints on the glass that Preston brought back match the ones that Dan collected, we can connect Chuck and Laura Thompson to the episode in Bud Tulley's place. Then, with the pair of trousers--the same size and everything-- to his dumping the clothes at the department store in Hurricane."

"You're absolutely right," Shane replied. "I'm assuming he thinks his trousers went out with the rest of the trash. Let me get some evidence paperwork going. And as soon as you can, I'd like you to sit down and write a thorough narrative of your activities from Sunday morning until now. And please. Don't make any more trips up there without clearing it with me or the sheriff first, okay? No more trips... no phone calling! *Understand?*" Shane's stern glance shifted back and forth from Naomi to Preston.

"Certainly," Preston answered, smiling. "I shall commence writing the narrative at once." He turned to the women. "Even if my efforts prove fruitless, it was not a waste of my money. I was afforded a grand opportunity to view a significant amount of America's most exquisite real estate." The others laughed. Preston looked puzzled.

A glance and a head movement from Shane conveyed to Naomi that they should leave the others alone for a time. She gave a slight nod and they prepared to retreat to another office.

"There's something else you should know," Shane began, as he closed the door behind them. "I got a call yesterday from a woman in Jackson. I sounded like she was probably calling from a pay phone on her lunch break."

"Oh, really? Who was she?" Naomi asked.

"She didn't give me her name but left me a number where I could get back to her. She's the same woman that answered the phone at the PD when I called to talk to your Officer Bender."

"No kidding? What did she have to say?"

"It seems she's overheard some talk around the department to the effect that there's a protection deal going on between the PD and somebody in town that runs an illegal gambling operation."

"Oh, yeah, that's what Preston was just talking about. He told us he suspected that at our Christmas party."

"Yeah, I remember you telling me that. I guess the old guy's got a lot of sense, after all. Anyway, she said she's just a secretary and hasn't been on the job very long. But she gave me the name of a sheriff's deputy in Teton County that she says we can trust. Name's LaMont Hawley."

"Have you talked to him, yet?"

"No, I haven't. I tried yesterday. She gave me his home phone number. Say's he's her nephew. There wasn't any answer at his house. She overheard Thompson's name mentioned and since I'd called to ask Bender about the name, she figured we'd like to know about it. She seemed to be implying that we hadn't oughta trust the PD, where Thompson's concerned, unless it involves something more serious than gambling."

"You didn't mention our suspicions about the murders?"

"Oh, no. Absolutely not!"

"So what's next? What do we do now?"

"Well, I'll mail this wine glass and Thompson's trousers up to the crime lab and try to get a hold of this deputy Hawley."

"Guess that'll have to wait 'til Thursday?"

"I'll call up there right now and make an appointment. It could be Monday or who knows when, before the lab people are back from their Christmas break."

"Sounds like a good plan, Shane."

"Well, it's all we've got to go on right now. But Naomi, be a little careful. If Thompson really is our man... he could be mighty suspicious of your call up there... sayin' you was Mrs. Wilson? It wouldn't be hard to have the call traced back to your home phone. He could very well be our professional killer. If he's our guy, there's no telling what he might try. If he gets real paranoid about it, he might at least consider doing who knows what. Or, like I said before, he could just up and leave the country. Course, I think we can assume he's not stupid. He'll know that you're not the only one down here that knows about him. More than likely, if he gets real scared he'd probably just up and disappear to who knows where."

When considering the possible threats to her own life, Naomi felt a wave of intense warmth surge through her body. At the same time, her hands felt cold and damp. "But then, all this could come to nothing," Shane continued. "I just hope the lab people can give us something... one way or the other! I'll get them on the phone right now."

"Good idea, Shane. This thing is starting to creep me out!"

Shane checked his Rolodex for the number. "Let's see... Margaret What's-her-face? Margaret... Margaret? Oh, yeah... here it is... Radowicz."

While he held the receiver a few inches away from his ear, Margaret Radowicz, in a very loud voice, informed him that, unlike the professors and students, she and a few others would be in the laboratory through the holidays. He smiled in relief. "Hey thanks a lot, Margaret. I'll get it up there, myself, soon as I can!"

CHAPTER SIXTEEN

Christmas eve was fairly quiet in the basin. Many families crowded into the open spaces surrounding the stately St. George LDS Temple to hear the concert by a community choir and to view the scene of Jesus' birth portrayed by live people and animals. Aaron Gentry, of course, was completing his normal late shift on and around the freeway while Naomi, Becky and Preston, joined by Ben and Natty, sat in the temporary bleachers and enjoyed the spiritually uplifting music.

Naomi felt sad that Aaron could not be there, but was slowly getting accustomed to the life-styles that required their frequent and irregular separations, often at special occasions--times when most others were afforded time together with loved ones. Naomi had been quiet through the evening. As they stood gazing at the nativity scene for a few moments after the concert, Preston put his arm around her shoulders in consolation. "I know how it is, believe me, Naomi," he said, quietly. "I went through it with my family for a lot of years. When our daughters were small, they couldn't understand why their father couldn't be there with them."

Naomi slipped her arm around his waist and pulled him against her for a brief moment. "Thanks, Preston," she replied, softly. "I guess it'll be this way for quite a long time."

Becky walked beside Naomi to her truck. "We'll be seeing you guys tomorrow, right?" she asked.

"Sure, we should be down by ten, or so."

"Us, too," Natty said, on her other side. At her truck, the women paused and engaged in a three-way hug. They quietly expressed words of love for one another before Naomi hugged both Ben and Preston, got into the truck and departed.

* * *

At her home in Bloomington, Becky prepared hot chocolate for herself and Preston. They relaxed on the couch together. "I can't believe I still have some gifts to wrap!" she said, with a big sigh. "It's the same thing every Christmas. I'm never really ready for it." The television was featuring a Glen Campbell and Dean Martin Christmas Special, with a guest appearance by The Osmonds.

Preston took her hand in his while he finished his cup and set it aside. He rose to his feet, walked to the television and reduced the volume during a commercial message. He turned back toward her and said, "I must confess, there's one present I have neglected to wrap, also." He sat beside her again and placed a small box into her hands. Her mouth opened in surprise. "You may wish to open it now," he said, smiling at her. "I've been hoping that you would accept this."

Inside the box, resting on a tiny satin pillow, was a set of rings. "I'm proposing marriage, Becky," he said, quietly. "In case you haven't realized it by now."

"Oh, my heavens!" she gasped. "You are? I don't know what to say! Oh, my word! Yesterday, I was sure you'd gone back home to England! I was so sure you'd gone!" Her eyes began to moisten. "It's been such a roller-coaster ride. I don't know what to say!" She put the rings on her finger and admired them. "I just don't know what to say! There's so much to talk about, so much to discuss!" She sat for a moment just looking into his smiling face. "Oh, Preston, I was hoping this moment would come. Now... I don't know what to say!"

"Well," he responded, holding her hand again. "You don't have to give me an answer just yet. When you're ready, we can certainly talk about it. But I've been considering the myriad of implications, too, you know. I would like to keep my feet in two places at once. If you wish to continue working until you're eligible for a retirement stipend, I can certainly understand that. And, of course, it would make a lot of sense, in financial terms. I could sell my townhouse in

Blackpool and sort of travel back and forth. Then at some point in the future, as I see it, we could have a summer home in England and spend the winters here."

"Oh, my goodness! I just don't know what to say!"

"Yes, Becky. That would be approximately the fifth time you've told me that. Maybe it would be practical," Preston offered, "to let this remain our little secret, for now. We could discuss it... um, periodically, and in time arrive at an entirely satisfactory agreement."

"Oh, Preston," Becky replied. "I want to say yes, now, but you're right, of course. The rings are so beautiful! Oh, my heavens! Andrew died almost three years ago... But still, this seems all so sudden. I knew I was going to like you a lot from that first day you came in the office trying to find some of your distant relatives. Oh, my heavens!" Her eyes moistened again. "I need some time to think about it. Not that I haven't, already! Oh, my goodness! There's so much to talk about."

"Certainly," Preston said, "If you like, you can just keep the rings in the box for now, or maybe you'd like to shop for a more satisfactory assemblage of stones."

"Of course not! They're beautiful! I'm going to wear them tonight, but they'll be put away in the morning. Okay?"

"Certainly!"

"Maybe you'd best be going before I get too mushy." He gave her a quizzical look, but she didn't explain further. "Like I said, I need to wrap some more things for tomorrow. You'll be here by ten o'clock, or so? Unless you have some more surprise trips planned?"

"Well, not really, not just yet!" Preston said, pretending to consider it. "But there's a whole twelve hours... I could make arrangements, perhaps."

"You'd better not!"

* * *

It had been almost two in the morning before Aaron Gentry had crawled into bed. At eight-thirty, Naomi, having been up for over an hour, bent down and held her long dark hair aside to kiss him awake and wish him a Merry Christmas.

Before breakfast, Aaron and Naomi opened and shared gifts for each other that were too personal to share in a family setting. "Did I mention," Aaron said, afterward, "that I love you without measure?"

"Oh, not for a few hours!" Naomi replied, her blue-grey eyes moistening. "Words cannot express my love for you, Aaron. I'm so glad you found me." It felt good to both of them to not have to work on Christmas Day. Two days off--together--was fantastic.

* * *

"Shane's making a trip to Ogden on Friday to take some stuff to that crime lab," Naomi said, as they drove south. "I told you when we were having a sandwich last night, what Preston brought back with him."

"Yeah, the Crazy Brit!"

"Yeah. Maybe we should be calling him 'Double-O-Seven'!"

"What has Shane said about it?"

"I guess Shane doesn't have real high hopes. He says the most we can find out from the fingerprints, is that the Thompsons really are the ones you guys saw in Bud's place last summer. And that the hair, if there is any, is the same type of blond hair as there was in the clothes he found in the garbage can."

"It's looking more and more like he's your jailhouse hit man, though!"

"Yeah, for sure. I'll bet Shane is spending every waking minute thinking about it."

"Maybe you should make the trip to Ogden with him. On Friday." Her head turned quickly and she stared at him for a moment. "I was just thinking it would be a good experience for you to learn more about the crime lab and to meet the lab people up there."

"Well, I guess so, but... "

"It was just an idea. Besides that... Dad wants me to come up there some time and help him make a new manger for the horses, or the steers. I can get up there early on Friday afternoon. It would feel good to do some real physical work for a change. You'd be welcome to come and help us... or... maybe we could do something else."

"Well, I guess if I went with Shane, you could help your dad, on

Friday. The trip would take us about all day, though, you know."

"Maybe you could give Shane a call when we get to Becky's house and see what he thinks. I don't know what his wife would say about it, though."

"Guess this means you trust me, huh? Spending the day with Shane Lowry?"

He turned his face toward her and winked. "That old duffer? Sure. He must be... what? Goin' on forty-five years old? Sure."

"Well, maybe that's a good idea. Let's see what he says about it."

* * *

At Thursday's meeting in Bud Tulley's cafe, Shane Lowry, leading the discussion, was surprised and pleased at the copious amount of notes supplied by Dan Wilde, Barney Jeppson, and Johnny Lee Chaffey, regarding their impressions and the details about the Thompsons. He decided to take all the notes to Cedar City and make copies of them at the office, so that the originals could be retained by the troopers.

Bud was highly irritated when other customers entered his cafe for a noon meal and distracted him from listening in on the meeting. He was proud of his contribution, having helped to identify the pair of Nevada's ex-cons, Floyd Barker and Brody Conway, who had stopped in his place of business numerous times.

He was listening eagerly to everything the officers had to say until Dan Wilde mentioned the unwashed eating utensils and drinking glasses, used by the Thompsons, that Bud was to keep stored as he had requested. At the mention of the stored plates and cups, Bud's jaw dropped and his face reddened. "Aw, shucks! Dan, I kept that box fer dang near a year! I got t' thinkin' maybe you didn't need it anymore! You never told me what it was for... far's I c'n remember."

"Well, I guess I can't really blame you for that," Dan replied. "That's really my fault. I should've followed up on that. Don't go blaming yourself for that."

"I don't recall hearing anything about any dishes stored in a box," Shane said, smiling. Aaron and Naomi grinned also. "We may have some more recent prints, anyway." Dan and Barney looked puzzled but began to relax as Shane related the exploits of Preston Blackstone on his recent trip to Jackson. "We're sending copies of Thompson's prints on his wine glass to the FBI records office in Washington, D.C. for a check on any possible history they might have on the Thompsons. There just might be some kind of 'fugitive' warrant on him... and his wife, too. If there actually is, they could both be arrested and held, at least for a time."

Shane, however, reasoned that there was little chance that *anything* the notes or any fingerprints could reveal that would positively tie the Thompsons to the murders of Barker and Conway. All they knew about the Thompsons at this point was that, except for his hair color, Collins Thompson fit the general description, that they were there in the area at the right time, and that they had acted suspiciously, both in the cafe and on the highway. If Mr. Thompson was, indeed, a contract killer, he would likely have an arrest record for other crimes in the FBI files, that could be discovered using the prints. Still, having made no positive identification as yet, it was a flimsy connection at best.

Shane knew, without asking, that Ian Cooper would not authorize a trip to Jackson, Wyoming, on that basis. And the county attorney would not authorize an arrest warrant.

Also, he doubted that the Jackson PD could even be trusted to gather any further evidence for him after talking to Officer Bender on the phone. Perhaps Preston's theory was correct. Maybe the gambling casino actually was operating with the full knowledge--and cooperation--of the Jackson Police Department.

* * *

Shane Lowry arrived at the rendezvous point in Parowan just before six o'clock Friday morning. At a small truck stop cafe, Naomi sipped a cup of hot chocolate with him. The more Naomi thought about a trip to the college-sponsored crime lab, the more excited and interested she became. So far, her job as a deputy sheriff fascinated her and the more she could learn about any facet of her chosen career she saw as a challenge and an opportunity.

They were fortunate that the weather was cooperating on their dark-to-dark road trip. Naomi spoke first. "So Shane, what did the sheriff have to say about making this trip? I'll bet he wasn't real excited about it."

"No, he tries to keep the expenses down, you know, which is good. But I told him that there was some possibility that this Thompson guy just might suspect that we're looking at him real seriously. And there's no telling what he might do. Anyway, I was able to convince him that we had to get all the evidence we could as fast as possible. But it would sure help speed things up if the FBI could come up with a positive ID and a fugitive warrant!"

"That's for sure," Naomi said. "If there actually is one."

"Besides that, Millard SO has some stuff they want us to pick up and take to the lab with us. We'll be there before long and you can meet some of their people, too."

* * *

The three-hundred-plus miles passed slowly. Naomi had never been to Ogden before. She'd heard it was a city with something of a "colorful" reputation, having a history as a tough railroad town. But, in taking the U.S. 89 short-cut from Farmington to the college on Ogden's east bench, Shane and Naomi saw very little of the city, itself.

The college was practically deserted. Shane parked in the delivery port of a large building off Harrison Boulevard next to an open, snow-covered practice field. He went to an outside telephone and called up to the laboratory to be allowed into the locked building. Margaret Radowicz, seeming to be habitually jovial and friendly, opened the door and escorted them to the laboratory.

"Okay, whatcha got for us?" she queried, in what sounded to them to be an overly loud and nasal Brooklyn accent. "You've been traveling half a day just to see me, Shane. It's gotta be real important!" Naomi scanned the large room and realized that it was as much a classroom as it was a laboratory.

"This goes along with the murders of two jail inmates that we had a year ago last summer in Washington County. A guy posing as a lawyer apparently poisoned them by leaving them with some botulism pills."

"Oh, yeah!" she responded. "And then he switched clothes and left them and his shoes and a wig where you could find them. This guy sounds like a real brainiac!"

"Well, we were able to get a pair of pants and possibly some fingerprints from a guy that we're pretty sure did the foul deed. Don't ask how we got 'em from him. It's a long story. And he doesn't even know it yet."

"What?" Margaret exclaimed. "He doesn't know!"

"Like I said, it's a long story," Shane said. He and Naomi laughed out loud. Margaret looked questioningly from one to the other with a furrowed brow.

"Some day you'll get the whole long story, I promise!" said Naomi. "What we were hoping for today, Margaret, is that you'd have time to examine this pair of trousers for hair or other evidence. Then maybe you could at least tell us if it compares to the hair you found in the other pair of trousers. We have a kind of an emergency going... we think."

"So you haven't busted this guy yet, I take it?"

"That's right," said Shane.

Margaret started to say something, then rolled her eyes, ever so slightly. "Okay, let's have a look." She put on a fresh pair of thin white cotton gloves and removed the wine glass from the brown bag and set it on her desk. She then rolled out a length of clean white paper, carefully removed the light grey trousers, and spread them on the paper. Naomi and Shane stood quietly watching. "What's the red stain? Any idea what that is?" Margaret asked.

"That's the red wine that Preston told us about," Shane said to Naomi. "Like I was saying, it's a really long story."

"Hmm... " Margaret replied, as she examined the outside of the trousers and then proceeded to turn the pockets inside out. There was a soiled white tissue in one of the back pockets. A small white comb was retrieved from the right front pocket. "Oh, hey, this is nice," Margaret said. Shane and Naomi looked at each other quizzically. "You've got a couple of hairs here from his head, too. They sure look blond to me." Margaret finished turning the pants inside out and examined the insides, front and back, with a large square magnifying glass. Using a pair of tweezers, she plucked a single hair from the inside near the pockets. "That's all I can see," she said, finally. "You've got one hair from his leg... and two from his head in the comb. Plus a lot of lint. And we can surely get some prints from the wine glass. We can just about guarantee that!"

"That's great!" Shane exclaimed. "More than we bargained for. How about that, Naomi?"

"Okay, let's see if they match up with the others," Naomi answered. "Don't get your hopes up too high."

Margaret secured the evidence in separate envelopes and retrieved the hairs previously obtained by Shane. She used a comparison microscope to look at them. "Oh, yes, they're the same type of hair, all right," she said. "I'd say these are identical. Any fingerprints on the comb should be positive, too. I'd bet on it. Plus, folks, both pair of trousers are the same size!"

Shane's face still reflected his skepticism. "Okay," he said. "This is great but we still don't have the guy put away."

"Yeah," said Naomi. "We're one tiny step closer, but... " Margaret was still looking into the microscope eyepiece. "Well, maybe... " She moved the hair around to look at the root ends. "We could... maybe..."

"Maybe what?" Shane asked. Margaret moved aside to give him a look into the microscope.

"I don't want to get your hopes up too much," Margaret said. The others looked at her in expectation. "The boss, Dr. Hunter, mentioned the other day that he'd read in a criminalistics journal recently that science is looking into the possibility of maybe identifying a person on the basis of individual DNA. Somebody finally figured out that, since each person's DNA is unique, a positive identification could be made from crime scene evidence... fluids like blood or even flesh... maybe other things. I guess nobody, until recently, had thought to apply it to criminalistics."

"What is this D-N-A you're talking about?" Naomi asked, while vaguely recalling something from her high school biology class about genetic material.

"Yeah, what's that?" Shane asked, still skeptical.

"DNA is the term used for dioxyribo-nucleic acid," Margaret answered. "There has to be... well, there could very well be some complete cells attached to the roots of some of these hairs. That's what I was just looking at... the roots."

"So what do we have to do to find out?" Shane asked with renewed interest. "Who can tell us any more about it?"

"Well, we're not sure. We may have to send the hair samples to a big lab somewhere to get it analyzed."

"You don't know where?" Naomi asked.

"Well, no. Let me call the boss and see what he says. He's not supposed to be back to work until Monday."

Margaret was dialing the phone as they spoke. A woman on the phone informed Margaret that her vacationing supervisor had left long before sunrise to shoot some geese and likely wouldn't be back home until late in the evening.

"We'd really like to find out what can be done as soon as possible and get the tests expedited," Shane said, exhibiting agitation. "We're also waiting to hear from the FBI to see if they came up with a criminal record... and, maybe even get a fugitive arrest warrant... from the prints we sent them for an ID... if the prints are any good."

Shane stopped talking and with intense frustration walked back and forth, looking around the room and out the window, while trying to think of a quicker solution. Facing the window, he paused to run a comb through his thinning hair, shrugged his shoulders, and hyperventilated in deepening exasperation.

"Hey, Shane," Margaret said, sympathetically. "I'm positive you've got the right guy. I mean, like I said, the hairs are all identical. The brown hair in the wig had been dyed, you know."

Shane stopped pacing. "Could you send the sheriff a letter stating that? Get your boss to sign it, or something? I'm just afraid this guy could up and disappear on us."

"Yeah, we could do that," Margaret answered. "Let me get him on the phone tonight. I'll write up the letter right now and get him to sign it and get it in the mail tonight. I'll see what he knows about the DNA stuff... and what we might be able to do for you. We'll try to find out if there's someplace that can do the DNA analysis for us. We don't even know if anybody can really do it. For all I know, maybe somebody could do it right here on the campus. Maybe somebody in the biology department. I really hate to hold you up, like this." The room was quiet for a moment.

"Okay," said Shane. "I guess that's all we can do for now."

The paperwork was quickly finished. Naomi and Shane walked to the car. "Maybe you'd better drive for a while," Shane said, handing the keys to her. "I'm still too frustrated to concentrate on driving."

"Sure," Naomi replied. "Be glad to." This facet of his personality was new to her. He had always seemed so calm and analytical.

"It's good you're always the one to hold yourself together," Shane said. "Maybe I just need to get something to eat. It's close to one o'clock and we need some gas. Why don't you stop at that Texaco station and then we can go next door to that fish place. Okay with you?"

* * *

Shane conferred with Ian Cooper at his home the following day. The sheriff seemed interested and excited about the results of the trip to the crime laboratory. He assured Shane that he was stopping at the office every day through his week of vacation to check his mail. He'd never heard of DNA analysis either, but agreed that it sounded like a plausible pursuit.

"So, Shane, what do think should be done, now? We've got a trail for sure on the type of hair, body size and a description of what we think was Thompson's car. But nothing solid to tie him with the murders."

"I don't think we should wait any longer. If we can't get a warrant based on the hair samples, somebody needs to keep a close eye on this man... and his wife, too, until the FBI comes through. If Thompson really is our killer and he starts to suspect that we're seriously looking at him, he could disappear real fast. On the other hand, if he's crazy, he might even come right down here and... "

"What do you mean? Do what?"

"Well, I mentioned to you that Naomi actually called up there from her house last Thursday night and asked for 'Mr. Thompson.' She was pretending to compliment him on the service at the lodge where she and Aaron stayed on their honeymoon. She didn't actually get to speak to him, but left a message with the night manager, using a phony name. We now believe he knew that Naomi and Aaron Gentry were from this area and that they were both police officers. Now, if he happens to get a little nervous and was halfway smart, he would have some way of finding out where the phone call came from... connecting the dots, you know. I hate to say this, but Naomi... and Aaron, too, could be in danger. After all, this guy had the gall to come right into the jail and knock off Conway and Barker."

"Yeah, I see. I see what you're saying. But she and Aaron were up there over a year ago, weren't they? I really doubt he'd figure out any kind of connection."

"Probably not. Anyway, there may be a Teton County deputy up there we can trust to work with us. I haven't been able to get him on the phone, yet. But I got his name from a reliable source, I believe. I could maybe ask him to keep an eye on Thompson until we hear from the FBI on those fingerprints we sent them. Oh... by the way, we sent the FBI a photograph of Thompson, too."

The sheriff was incredulous. "You're kidding me! How the heck did you get the picture?"

Shane explained the movie film exposed in the lodge on the Gentry's honeymoon skiing trip. Ian Cooper shook his head with a broad grin. Shane continued, "Just maybe this deputy's boss would put him on it full-time. If Thompson's our killer... If he's a contract killer, a hit man, he would very likely have an arrest record, probably under some alias. It might help if you'd call and see if the FBI would expedite the search."

"Let's go to the office and I'll call them right now. I'll see if Special Agent Gates, up in Provo, can help speed it up. We can't afford to wait any longer than what's absolutely necessary. I agree, somebody needs to watch the Thompsons around the clock. Let me think about this."

"Sheriff, I don't see any other logical way to handle this except to send me up there. Between me and this Deputy Hawley. If he checks out okay we could take turns keeping an eye on Thompson until the FBI comes through."

"What if Naomi went with you?" Shane's mouth opened slightly and he turned to stare at Ian. "She'd recognize the man. You and she could get rooms at the lodge where he works and take turns watching the guy and maybe the deputy, too."

"But he'd recognize her right away. Wouldn't you think? I mean, she's tall and she's very... "

"Attractive? Yes, I know. She does indeed stand out in a crowd... any crowd. She could do something to change her appearance, you know. She's had over a year's experience, now... and she's smart and very capable of handling herself. Our new investigator can handle things while you're gone."

"Yeah, maybe. Let me think about that." Shane was shocked at the sudden turn-around. *Cooper is actually trying to convince me to make the trip to Jackson? But with Naomi? Maybe with changing her hair color and style and a pair of large dark glasses? Maybe in a large, more or less ordinary parka?* "Well, let's have her come to the office and talk about it," he said. "We'd need to see if Aaron will go along with it."

"Let's go to the office and get on it right now," Ian said.

* * *

A search of fingerprint files, even in the office of the Federal Bureau of Investigation at the nation's capital, routinely took days and sometimes even weeks, depending on the priority and workload, but more especially on the quality of the latent prints submitted for a comparison and records check. In theory, at least, having very likely been arrested several times during his teen years and beyond, John Moranski, having assumed the identity of Collins "Chuck" Thompson, would surely have an FBI arrest record. The problem was one of locating the "needle" in the proverbial haystack.

Ian Cooper had been able to convince FBI Special Agent Jon Gates to call Washington, D.C., and get a top priority on the search using the photograph and fingerprints taken from Thompson's wine glass.

CHAPTER SEVENTEEN

Chuck Thompson couldn't help but focus his attention, whenever she was in view, on the tall young woman with short blonde boy-cut hair. He watched her walk across the lobby of the Ruby Springs Lodge and sit down in one of the plush chairs next to a coffee table. She picked up a copy of the local paper and opened it. Had she stayed at the lodge before? Why would she be staying in a room all by herself? She seemed to be waiting for someone. Would they be driving up in front? Or, would someone come down to the lobby from a room in the lodge? But then, what if she really was going to be all alone? Maybe she was really lonely! He decided he might try to speak to her--when Laura wasn't around, of course.

The lodge was crowded. New Year's Eve, coming the next day, brought many people especially from the surrounding states and left little time to speculate about any particular guest. He was very busy and the temporary help had to be supervised more closely. But as he registered guests, hustled their luggage, and saw to their needs, he wondered why the young woman seemed even remotely familiar. Was she alone? Why? Maybe after Roger arrived in the afternoon, he might have time to talk to her.

Unobserved by the lodge manager, Shane Lowry kept her in sight, also, from the mezzanine above the lobby. He patiently waited for her to look in his direction. After fifteen minutes of waiting she directed her gaze in his direction and he motioned to her. She turned back to the newspaper for a few minutes and then, putting it down, she rose and retreated to the staircase that led to the mezzanine.

She walked toward him and spoke. "He's the man at the desk," she said. "There's a lot more people here now. It looks like he's going to be pretty busy this week."

"I wasn't sure that was you, down there!" Shane exclaimed. "Okay, let's meet in two-thirty-nine. Give me ten minutes."

When no one else was in the second-floor hallway, Naomi knocked softly at the door. Shane let her in. "That deputy, LaMont Hawley, is supposed to come up and meet us here in a few minutes. If it feels right we'll tell him the whole story."

"You think it will be safe to do that? What if he's getting paid off, too?"

"The local police might look the other way considering a little gambling going on but not if Thompson's really our killer. Anyway, Hawley's probably heard about the case already. It doesn't appear that anything has panicked our Chuck Thompson. Not yet, anyway."

"No, you're right. We don't have to watch him that closely. He could get suspicious if we hang around too much. Have you spotted their car yet? The white Mercury?"

"I can see it in the back parking lot," Shane replied, motioning toward his window. "We both got lucky, you know. You have a room with a rear view, too. The license plate checks out... registered to the Thompsons. But they'd probably have a second car around."

"Have you seen Laura Thompson, yet? I'm not sure if I would recognize her. She probably takes care of the books in the office. But they must have an apartment in the lodge somewhere. Probably down close to the front desk. I'll see if I can find out where it is. That would be good to know."

A soft knock at the door silenced them. Naomi walked quickly and silently across the carpet and stepped out of sight into the bathroom. As Shane greeted LaMont Hawley and closed the door she returned and introduced herself.

Hawley was a rather large, middle-aged man dressed in western style casual clothes that didn't quite fit in with those of most of the vacationing hotel guests. Naomi and Shane felt very comfortable with him at once and that he could be trusted. After warning the deputy that the details must be kept absolutely secret, Shane spent the next ten or fifteen minutes explaining the events that he strongly felt

Chuck Thompson was involved in. LaMont Hawley was surprised and shocked at what he was told. He confided to them that he had several days of vacation coming and that he'd be glad to donate some time to their cause. But, since the sheriff's routine responsibilities ended at the Jackson city boundaries, he was not at all acquainted with the manager of the lodge or its employees. He acknowledged, however, that he was aware of rumors concerning illegal gambling operations within the city. Also, ultimately, that his boss, being elected by the people of the county, was especially sensitive to their wishes as to which laws were to be enforced and which were to be largely ignored. As long as the operators were discrete and kept a lid on things, the sheriff didn't seem to have any real concerns.

But a double murder, accomplished right inside another sheriff's jail, was certainly not to be dismissed. LaMont was excited to be working with the two Utah deputies.

* * *

The next two days passed slowly. Each day, Naomi, using a pay phone, called home in the morning to stay in touch with Aaron. Shane, likewise, called his home and Ian Cooper. There was still no word from the FBI.

On Wednesday, the first day of the new year, the night manager was summoned to his duties early and worked alongside Chuck Thompson for some time. When asked if he remembered registering a tall young blonde woman the previous Sunday, Roger acknowledged that he had. He quickly looked up the name she had used along with a Boise, Idaho, address and phone number.

"Is there a problem with her?"

"Oh, no problem. Was she alone? I see her around the lobby once in a while, she's always alone and acting like she's just waiting for someone. She reminds me of someone, but I can't remember who."

"Yeah, I've seen her hanging around, too. Good-lookin' lady, I'd say. Almost makes me wish I was single again, you know?"

"Yeah, you're right about that."

When Roger was busy elsewhere, Chuck copied down the name, phone number, and the Boise, Idaho, address written on the registration sheet. The name, "Mrs. Betty Livingston," bore no familiarity. More curious, and becoming more paranoid still, he used a pay phone and dialed the Boise number. The man who answered became annoyed when asked a second time if he was sure he had not dialed the Livingston home. Chuck repeated the number to the man who acknowledged that it was his number, but he had no knowledge of anyone by that name. Chuck's pulse suddenly began to rise and he fought to keep his emotions under control. According to the man on the phone, the address Chuck read to him was in a different section of the city of Boise.

He began to reason to himself. Why would she register using a phony name? Then again, maybe Roger had written the number incorrectly. Or, perhaps she couldn't remember the right sequence of numbers. But the more he thought about it, the more worried he became. Could she be a cop from the Wyoming Attorney General's office? They would certainly be interested in illegal gambling! She was sent here to investigate me--to watch me--he concluded in anger! But, she surely wouldn't be here by herself! There had to be other state vice cops around! I know it! I'd best stay away from the casino until the heat blows over, he reasoned.

But then, maybe Laura was right. Maybe he really was worrying too much. Thinking of the casino reminded him of the drunken Aussie who had spilled wine on his good grey trousers less than a week ago. Another stranger, alone in a city made for having fun with spouses? And families? Or Lovers? Odd things seemed to be taking place. Chuck was becoming more troubled.

Chuck went back to helping Roger and the others. But all the while, he kept thinking, trying to connect the two unusual people. Was that guy really Australian? He certainly talked like he was. Did he give a phony address too? And why would the sort-of odd and friendly foreigner, now that Chuck thought about it, seem to have been bent on talking to *him*? Spilling the wine? Was that really an accident? What was that all about?

Chuck's nerves got the better of him and *he had to find the answers*! He frequently studied the rear-view mirror in the Mercury as he drove toward the hotel where Preston Blackstone had spent the night of December 23rd. He parked in the rear and strode quickly through the long hallway and into the front office.

"Hey, if ain't ol' Chuck Thompson," exclaimed the young and energized night manager. "So, how're things... at Ruby Springs?" He laughed, having just made a clever little poem.

"Hey! Got no time for chit-chat," Chuck shot back. What'll this dolt come up with next? "Do you remember that fellow... an older guy... here by himself about a week ago? Said he was from Australia?"

"Sure I do, came back from *el casino*? Drunk as a skunk. Only stayed one night. Paid his bill... with cash... no problem. Why do you ask?"

"On his bill... did he make any calls from his room?"

"Well, let me check it out, Chuck!" The other manager laughed again as though he'd just said something funny. Chuck didn't laugh. "Let's see, yeah. He did, for sure. Made a call to an 801 area code. That's gotta be in Utah, I think. Ain't it?" Chuck, his pulse racing, remained silent. "Here, I'll copy the number down for you. What's the problem, Chuck?"

Again, Thompson did not answer. He then remembered that Preston had told him he was going to call Colorado, not Utah. "Was that the only call he made that night?"

"Just one call... that's all!"

Chuck took the paper with the Utah number out of the other man's hand and exited the building. He got back into his car and headed into the street. After a few blocks, he suddenly noticed a flashing red light in his rear-view mirror. Oddly enough, the flashing light calmed his nerves a bit. It almost felt as though an old friend was reassuring him. After pulling to right shoulder and stopping, he recognized Officer Bender walking up on his left side. Suddenly, it occurred to him, as it frequently had before, that these officers would literally go into "spazz" mode if they ever found out who he really was and the things he'd done.

"Guess I was going a little fast?" he offered, before Bender said anything.

"Yeah, nearly double the limit, you know."

"I guess that's two I owe ya for, Ken." He proffered his driver's license in a plastic folder with a fifty-dollar-bill tucked inside it.

"Appreciate the heads-up on those two cops from Utah. What's it been? About a year now? Just a couple a kids on a honeymoon trip, you know. Harmless enough."

"Well, can't be too careful. Oh, by the way, did I ever tell you... ? It must've slipped my mind. I got a call from this county detective in Utah... gosh, it's been more'n a year ago... asking if I knew any Thompsons up here." Chuck jerked his head around and confronted the officer's face not more than a foot away from his. His eyes were wide and his mouth was open. "I guess I never told you. Sorry 'bout that. And the chief didn't mention it?"

"What did this Utah detective want?" Chuck demanded, straining to control his anxiety.

Bender handed the license back without the currency enclosed in the folder. "Well, seems like he said that a couple by the name of Thompson from up here were witnesses to a fatal traffic accident down in the southern part of the state, last summer, and the troopers were trying to find out a full name and address."

Chuck was now out of his car and grabbed the officer by his shoulders. "What did you tell him?" he demanded.

Bender broke free by raising his hands together between Chuck's arms and rotating them outward and stepped back. He was very upset that Thompson had grabbed him. "*Didn't tell him anything*! I just said there were a couple of Thompsons in the phone book and I would contact them to see if any of them were down that way in the summer." He continued, somewhat more calmly. "Seems like there's this school teacher, or single woman... might have been her. Maybe on vacation with friends. I assumed it was her. He never called back. What are you getting so upset about? You weren't there... were you?"

"No, no, it wasn't us! We've never even been there!" Chuck's pulse had slowed a little and he stared at the officer for a few seconds before he got back into the car and drove away.

Sgt. Bender called after him in futility, "Keep the speed down, Chuck!"

Now Laura had better be scared, he thought, as he sped toward the lodge. His tires slid sideways on the snow-pack as he swerved into the parking lot. He didn't bother parking straight with the back fence, but shoved the gear selector into PARK, ripped the keys from the ignition and sprang from the car. Roger looked up in surprise as he walked briskly from the back hallway.

"Hey, Chuck! What's goin' on, man?"

Thompson made no reply but strode past him and entered his apartment and closed the door behind him. He had to think! This was not supposed to be happening! That was it, think! Think!

That blonde woman? Was there a connection to the drunken Australian? A phony Idaho address! Was she from Utah, too? I could go to her room right now and take care of her, right now! No, he'd have to make it look like an accident. But who was she? Then it suddenly clicked. Oh, yes! Phony blonde hair, too! She was that woman, that woman cop, from Utah. But where was her husband now? Could he be around, too? They damn sure wouldn't send her by herself! Surely he would have noticed the large young man who'd been with her on their honeymoon!

Chuck Thompson strode from the apartment and into the office to look up the registration records. He quickly found the right date and studied the names for the day. There they were! "Aaron Gentry" and "Naomi Gentry." He saw that he, Chuck, had started to write a last name for her that appeared on her driver's license. Her last name started with "Bla" which had been crossed out. He cursed again. "Blackstone! Miss Naomi Blackstone!" he repeated. That phony 'Aussie!' Had to be... what? Her father? An uncle? Certainly some relative. That phony accent! But why would the relative of a cop... ? Was she the one Blackstone had called from his room in the other hotel? He rifled through the papers in his top drawer and found the number that he had obtained from Judy at the phone company office--the call that Roger had taken--the same number the Gentrys had listed when they registered over a year ago. Badly shaken, he walked to a pay phone in the lobby and dialed the Utah number he'd just obtained from the manager of the other hotel. As the phone rang he tried to calm himself by taking deep breaths.

It was a young-sounding female voice that answered. "Hello."

After a momentary pause, Chuck said, trying to affect a pleasant inquiry. "I'm calling for a Mr. Preston Blackstone?" It was more a question than a request. Who could this woman be? Another daughter?

"There's no one here by that name," Natty responded.

"Do you know anyone by that name? A gentleman of maybe fifty-five or sixty years of age?"

"Well, yes. Yes, I know the man. Who's calling, please?"

"Oh, sorry. This is Jim Bates calling from Sky West. We think he might have lost some personal items on one of our planes. The name we have is Preston Blackstone. Are you acquainted with him?"

"Well, yes. But he doesn't live here. He lives over in Washington City, right now. I can have him call you back, or maybe get his number for you."

"If you would just give me a number, please," Chuck said, trying his best to remain calm as his pulse pounded. "I'm sure we can expedite the matter."

Natty Randolph supplied the number and hung up. Then she began to wonder about the call. This is crazy! Surely, when buying a ticket for a flight, Preston would have given his own phone number? Or, the airline personnel could easily have looked it up in the local directory. No, wait, the phone at the doublewide was still in her and Naomi's names--and unlisted. Wouldn't Sky West call there? And why would they be calling a number listed to Ben Randolph?

* * *

It was, of course, one of those very busy times and Chuck did not know where Laura was. He could take care of the problem without her help. He would have to make a plan during the night when he could think. Besides, he knew he wouldn't be getting much sleep. He would first, however, take certain precautions, just to make sure he was not getting upset over nothing. The attractive blonde Blackstone, or Gentry, woman could even be completely "innocent." Chuck imagined that she could even be at the lodge in disguise, by herself, having planned a cozy rendezvous with another man. But where was he? And... so soon after getting married? He smiled to himself. But then, maybe the "husband" would show up, too. *Yeah, right!*

Strangely, and he realized it, himself, whenever he was contemplating a homicide a degree of calmness settled over him and he could think more clearly. If she was still hanging around tomorrow, he decided, he would take care of her then. It would be an "accident," of course.

* * *

Naomi awoke Thursday morning dreading another day away from Aaron and Nero, the chores of taking care of the horses and the daily challenges of her new career. She missed her mother and others in the office back home. Only the brief meetings with Shane and LaMont, usually in the evenings kept her spirits up somewhat. Surveillance on the manager of the Ruby Springs Lodge, which had sounded exciting at first, had become extremely tedious and dull. Even the few times that she had actually been able to speak to Shane Lowry or LaMont Hawley, for a limited amount of time, had become monotonous. What was the FBI doing about Thompson's prints? Hadn't they given this case a high priority?

Shane had obtained a room on the rear of the lodge which afforded them a view of the back parking lot where the Thompsons' Mercury was routinely parked. Sheriff Cooper had stated very emphatically that he would continue to maintain contact with the FBI and call Shane the minute any word came through. They could finally know for sure if an arrest warrant was in the works, or, if Thompson, in fact, had no criminal record.

Naomi wondered again what had suddenly changed the sheriff's mind about sending them to Jackson. The crime lab had confirmed the obvious fact that Thompson had blond hair and the body hairs were identical. The clothing sizes were the same. Didn't they all know that? After seeming so adamant about what the trip--that the sheriff felt was based on questionable evidence--would do to his budget, he had suddenly all but demanded that they go. What had turned him around? It was apparent to her that Shane was also baffled by Cooper's change of thinking.

Loathe to even get out of bed, Naomi began to think about Aaron and tried to imagine what he would be doing at that moment. Most likely, Thursday, being one of his days off, he would be having an early breakfast, taking care of Nero and the horses, and getting prepared to continue working on expanding the barn. The tedium was taking its toll. She wondered whether having a career in law enforcement was really what she wanted. It would be wonderful to have children and stay at home to love and care for them.

Aaron was a good man whose love she treasured and would someday be an excellent father. She wanted to pick up the phone in the room and call him right then, before he would be going outside to work. But Shane had cautioned her against using the phone in her room that would give Thompson a way to quickly become suspicious should he discover that she had called southern Utah. But then, was Chuck Thompson really the hit man--the contract killer they were waiting to arrest? Or, was he just a blond-haired hotel manager who happened to be the same size as "John L. Croft, Jr." and who got nervous around police officers? Would all their time and expenses turn out to be for nothing?

She got out of bed hungry and determined to do something that day to get her spirits out of the doldrums. Maybe she could spend some time skiing in the afternoon. That would help a lot. Pausing to glance out the rear window of her room, she could see that the Thompsons' white Mercury was still in the same parking stall, facing the back fence.

By ten o'clock, she strolled through the lobby to the front door, carrying her parka. Out of the corner of her eye, she noted the presence of Chuck Thompson at his usual post--the front desk. He casually noticed her, too, as she walked out the front door and beyond, as if she would be going for a walk in the bright sunlight that barely cleared the low mountain to the south of the city. She was only gone for maybe fifteen minutes in the near-freezing temperature of Jackson Hole before returning to the lobby and sitting down to look at the morning papers that the lodge provided.

Chuck noted her return. And after few minutes, he took the elevator to the mezzanine, and walked to where he could see her from the shadows. She seemed absorbed in reading the paper while occasionally glancing about. Chuck took his short-range walkie-talkie out of it's case on his belt and called an assistant at the front desk. "This is Chuck," he said. "I'm on the fourth floor... talking to a guest who is trying to find a lady he thinks is in the lodge somewhere. Would you page Naomi Gentry for us?"

"Sure," the girl at the desk replied. "I'll have her come to the desk for you." The page for "Naomi Gentry" sounded loudly through the lobby and on each floor. Chuck watched the blonde backside of Naomi's head above the back of a large couch. There was no apparent movement. "Try it again in a few minutes," Chuck said to the assistant.

At the sound of her name, Naomi's face suddenly flushed and her eyes opened wider. Careful to make no physical response, she sat wondering who it could be. Surely Aaron wouldn't be calling and having her paged, using her real name! Shane certainly wouldn't be using her real name. LaMont Hawley? Ian Cooper? Her mother? It had to be her mother.

She waited a few minutes then rose, as Chuck watched from the mezzanine. She walked calmly to the pay phone and dialed her home number. As she listened to the ring, she slowly turned around and her eyes swept the large open lobby. Where was Shane?

Where was the manager? The ringing continued. She would have to find Shane and see what he thought.

It's her! Chuck concluded. It's got to be her! She had just tried to call someone who might be trying to have her paged! Naomi gave up on the call and walked to the elevator, she went to the fourth floor then walked down the stairs to the second. At room two-thirty-nine, she knocked softly. The door opened and she walked inside and closed the door behind her. She told Shane she'd just been paged, by someone using her real name.

"It would have to be someone from the sheriff's office. You gave Aaron your alias, so, it couldn't have been him. Couldn't have been the sheriff."

"I'll bet it was my mother. I'm sure it was."

"I'll go down to the lobby and call the office. ... see if it was somebody there. Could've been your mother. Maybe they've heard something from the FBI. But they surely wouldn't have used your real name. You'd better stay out of sight for the rest of the day."

"What if I went skiing for a while? I've got to get out of this place!"

Shane thought it was a good idea and agreed that he or LaMont would be around. "Why don't you just take the whole evening off?

LaMont should be coming in pretty soon. Let me take your walkie-talkie. He can use it if we get separated. You can just relax and do whatever you want."

* * *

She left the lodge after a light lunch, purchased a half-day lift pass and rented skiing equipment. It was something of an extravagance and she mentally apologized to Aaron for playing while he worked. But an afternoon of skiing in the bright sunshine proved exhilarating. Admiring looks from several male skiers made her feel a little self-conscious. She smiled to herself at their obvious interest and attempts at conversation with her. A solitary soak in the heated outdoor pool afterward would be just the thing. She could compensate Shane for the break tomorrow. Maybe he would want to relax a bit, too.

CHAPTER EIGHTEEN

The late afternoon sun had swung around to the southwest and put long shadows on the low mountain south of Jackson before sinking out of sight. The day had been sunny and bright. By seven o'clock, long after dark, Naomi had settled into the pool of extremely warm spring water behind the lodge. Two couples were there in the pool for some time, also.

Chuck Thompson briefly watched from a third floor window. He took note of electrical lines leading from a pole, crossing the pool and attaching to the lodge. If the wires were detached from the wall of the lodge, he figured, they would fall into the pool. But then, that would not be an "accident." No, he thought, his previous plan would do very well. He disappeared from the window.

* * *

Skiing always seemed to put a painful strain on muscles in different places on her body, and the extra-warm water felt soothing and wonderful. The others left the pool after a while and Naomi was alone. The hot water relaxed her body and seemed to sap her energy. She used different strokes to propel herself lazily from one end of the pool to the other. She decided to take one more lap and then get out. Maybe she'd take a hot shower and then watch television.

While she stroked toward the deep end of the pool, a man emerged from the silvery mist above the water and stepped quickly to the edge of the pool behind her. He slipped quietly into the four feet of water and immediately submerged. Attached to his bathing suit was a small cylinder filled with compressed air and a hose leading to a mouthpiece that enabled the man to inhale through his mouth and then exhale through his nostrils. A large pair of goggles covered most of the upper part of his face and a black rubber bathing cap covered nearly all of his hair. The man propelled himself along the bottom of the pool beneath Naomi.

She stopped at the far end--the deeper end--to catch her breath for a few seconds. The man watched and waited near the bottom for her no more than six or eight feet away from her as she clung to the edge. She noted for the first time the tiny air bubbles rising to the surface a few feet in front of her but paid them no mind. She turned toward the pool's edge and slowly began to backstroke to the shallow end with her mouth and nose just slightly above the surface. It reminded her of the hot, lazy summer days with Paul and Natty and friends from high school at the municipal pool in St. George and later at the motel where she had worked part-time and had used their pool free of charge. She enjoyed lounging in a pool.

Swimming on her back, maybe ten feet out from the edge, she felt a sudden violent pull on the back of her bathing suit that yanked her straight down. She barely had time to gasp, mostly from surprise, a single breath before the ninety-degree water closed over her face. Strangely, her first thought was of Paul, and how he, also an excellent swimmer, would play such pranks on her and Natty. But this was no prank!

She knew it was Chuck Thompson! He'd had her paged that morning to see what her reaction would be. Had he been watching her all along--just as surely as she, along with Shane and LaMont, had been keeping him in their sights?

The jailhouse killer was now beneath her, pulling her down with one hand while stroking the water with the other to maintain a steady downward pull. She floundered helplessly for a few seconds until she realized what was happening and began to react. While rotating somewhat to her right side, she swept her right arm in a wide circle away from her body and down behind her back. Her right arm locked elbows with the arm that was pulling on her bathing suit and pulled the arm toward her right side. His grip on her bathing suit caused her to rotate inside it somewhat. With her left hand she could now get a grip on the man's wrist. Five feet below the surface, her lungs began to ache for fresh air. Chuck's left hand formed into a fist and began striking her head and shoulders while he struggled to continue pulling her down.

Chuck was surprised at the strength and agility she possessed. Her grip on his right wrist felt almost bone crushing and a wave of panic enveloped him. This was not at all what he had expected. The pain in his wrist quickly overcame his will to fight with her. It had been so easy the first time, when, using the same homemade equipment and the same methods, he had pulled the real Laura Thompson under the water in her pool to her death. Intent only on breathing, his first drowning victim had panicked and struggled helplessly to regain the water's surface. It had been such a quick and simple "accidental" drowning. But this was different. He simply had not counted on her size and strength.

Naomi's lungs began to scream for air and her grip began to weaken. Her only thought, now, was to reach the surface. She tried to take the man with her, but he, encouraged by her now relenting grip, rotated his hand out and away, which caused her to lose the grip. Naomi, almost totally disoriented, at last found the bottom with her feet and shot upward to the surface for air.

On rising to the surface, she gasped twice then stroked slowly in the direction of the shallow end of the pool with her face in the water to look for her attacker. The sulphur from the hot spring stung her eyes and blurred her vision. She would have to wait for him to come up. He had to come up somewhere! Had he drowned? Surely he couldn't stay under water that long, could he? How was he able to do that?

A sudden splashing at the shallow end of the pool caught her attention. She whirled around to see in the mist the dark silhouette of a man with the dim light in front of him lunging out of the pool and rushing for the door leading to the dressing room. In the thin mist over the water, the shock of blond hair that Naomi expected to see was not evident. Before she could make it to the side of the pool to get out and pursue the man, he had disappeared through the door.

In the dressing room Chuck Thompson paused only to snatch a

damp towel that had been discarded on one of the benches. Running down the tiled hallway, he quickly wrapped his crude miniature SCUBA gear in the towel. In case he encountered someone in the hallway, he thought it best to keep the goggles and the swim cap that kept most of his hair dry in place. But he saw no one. It was not far from there to the apartment that he shared with Laura. He was relieved to find that she was not inside. He changed quickly into his usual working attire, having left his other clothes in a dressing room locker. He could later conceal the wet bathing suit, the breathing device, the cap, and goggles in the same locker. He paused only to run a comb through his almost completely dry hair and reach into the refrigerator to retrieve the half-eaten sandwich that he hadn't had time to finish at lunchtime.

* * *

Not ten minutes later, Chuck Thompson burst through the apartment door into the hallway, still holding the sandwich. Naomi and her large-bore, short-barreled revolver were all he saw. His mouth dropped open in shock.

"*Stop right there, Mr. Thompson!*" she screamed into his face with her heart pounding.

"*What is this!?*" he exclaimed. He dropped the remains of his sandwich. "*Who are you!? What are you doing!?*"

"You're under arrest, Mr. Thompson," she responded more calmly. "Turn around and put your hands up on the wall."

"You must be joking!" His response was laced with curses. "Who are you? What's going on here?"

"Turn around!" she repeated, raising the tone of her voice. "I'm a police officer. Now grab the wall!" Glancing at her revolver, he slowly turned to comply. "Now put your right hand behind your back." He complied again with a sinking feeling in his stomach. In panic, he wondered where Laura was. Could she help? But what could she do? Their small guns were hidden inside the apartment.

There had been no time for Naomi to go to her room to get her handcuffs. She'd been able to stop in the dressing room just long enough to slip on a pair of jeans and a shirt and to grab her gun from her locker. Still having bare feet, she'd been able to trace his wet footprints on the tile floor of the hallway almost to the apartment. Unable to think of any way to contact Shane or LaMont Hawley, she'd decided to wait outside the locked door for Chuck to emerge from the apartment on his own. With his right hand now behind him, she grasped his thumb and two fingers with her left hand and, satisfied that she had him in control, un-cocked her gun, placed it into her back pocket, and began a partial frisk of areas that might be accessible to his left hand. Finding no weapons, she steered him in the direction of the elevator and took him to Shane's room. There was no response to her knock at the door. Where would he and LaMont be right now?

Much meeker now, Chuck asked her, "Officer, what is this all about? What am I being arrested for? I'm the hotel manager. I'm sure there's been a big mistake."

"Mr. Thompson, I have plenty of reason to believe that you just tried to kill me!"

"What?" Chuck exclaimed. With a slight nervous chuckle, he continued. "That can't be! Are you crazy? I just stepped into my apartment for a sandwich! Is this some kind of gag... or what?"

"No joke, Mr. Thompson," she responded, noting that the bottom of his hair and his sideburns were still damp, she steered the manager toward the elevator. Two couples, obviously having a good time, got out of the elevator on the second floor and as they passed they turned to stare at the way Chuck and Naomi's hands seemed to be connected behind his back.

At her room, she was able to handcuff him to the metal bed-frame while she got on the phone and dialed the Jackson PD number. She informed the dispatcher that she was a police officer from out of town that had just arrested someone at the lodge. A local police officer would soon be on his way to assist.

"Please, officer," Chuck begged, now more humble. "I haven't tried to kill anyone! What are you talking about? Are you nuts? I don't even know who you are? Why would I try to kill you?"

Naomi made no reply. Where was Shane? She desperately needed to have him with her. And what about LaMont Hawley? He'd seemed so willing to help. She considered having them paged. Probably in the coffee shop, talking, as usual. Surely the boredom must have taken its toll on them, too. Wouldn't they have noticed that the manager had been out of their sight for such a long time? She decided the best option was to leave Thompson and try to find the others in a rapid sweep of the lobby and cafeteria. First, however, she tried to get Shane on the phone. There was no reply from the phone in his room. Suddenly a wave of dread swept over her. Had the Thompsons done something to Shane? She took a few seconds to run a comb through her damp hair and walked quickly out into the hallway.

By the time she had looked in the restaurant and the lobby, not finding either Shane or LaMont Hawley, she decided to look outside for a police car that should soon be coming. The city car was there, with vapor from the exhaust pipe rising in the back. A young officer was at the front desk, talking to the assistant manager.

"I'm the officer who just called you," Naomi said, showing them her police identification. Roger's eyes were wide in amazement. The officer took it from her and examined it more closely, comparing her face to her photograph.

"From Utah?" he queried. It wasn't really a question. "A deputy from Washington County. You've arrested somebody?"

Naomi glanced at Roger, whose attention was riveted on her. "Yes, I have," she said. "You'd better come with me."

"Let me see if I can get the manager," Roger called after them. Neither of them turned around.

"Have you made the manager aware of this?" the officer asked. "Where are we going?"

"He's definitely aware of it." They walked quickly to the elevator and rode it to the fourth floor. "He's in my room, now."

On seeing the lodge manager handcuffed to the bed frame, the officer's jaw dropped. "This is the man who just tried to drown me. I'm charging him with attempted murder."

"That's ridiculous!" Chuck exclaimed. "I never did anything to her, I've been working all day... and evening too. I haven't even had a break all afternoon! I have no idea what she's talking about, officer."

Naomi read the officer's name plate above his right shirt pocket. "Devin," she began, suddenly beginning to realize that she might not have an airtight case of attempted murder. And where the heck was

Shane? "It's a long story. For now, let's just say that I was in the pool and this man grabbed my bathing suit from behind and pulled me under the water... trying to drown me. I got away from him in the water, but he ran to his apartment and changed into these dry clothes."

"Whoa! You're sure it was him?"

"Absolutely!"

"No! No!" Chuck groaned, now sounding desperate. He was still sitting on the bed, handcuffed to the frame and gesturing wildly with his free hand. "Whatever happened, officer... it had nothing to do with me. You can see the wet spots coming through her shirt and jeans. I guess... apparently she was in the pool behind the lodge. But as you can plainly see, I am perfectly dry!" Chuck and Naomi both looked expectantly at Devin as though they expected him to either find the manager "guilty" on the spot or let him go. Naomi made a more careful inspection of Chuck's hair and sideburns. They were now dry, of course.

"Maybe we'd better go down to the station," Devin said in frustration. "We'll have to see if the sergeant can maybe sort this all out for us."

Naomi had a sinking feeling in her stomach. Chuck was right! She had no real physical evidence to back up her assertions. Had she just blown the whole case? If Thompson were to get free of her "attempted murder" accusations, he and his wife would surely disappear and would likely never be found again.

With both his hands cuffed behind his back, Chuck was escorted into the hallway and the elevator. Naomi maintained a secure hold on the handcuff links between his wrists as the Jackson officer, Devin, followed.

As they passed through the lobby of the lodge toward the waiting police vehicle, Shane Lowry watched in surprise through a screen of indoor plants that separated the restaurant from the hotel lobby. LaMont Hawley also watched from behind him, as did several other hotel guests throughout the lobby. The two made no move to intercept them--deciding on the spot to maintain their anonymity for the time being.

"You reckon she maybe got word from your sheriff? Or from the

FBI? While we were out?" LaMont asked, as they watched the police car pull away from the curb.

"That could be," Shane responded. "How can we find out what's going on without blowing our cover? Any ideas?"

"C'mon. My truck's out back. Let's go crank up the monitor. Maybe we can figure out what's going on from that." From the monitor they were able to hear that a Sergeant Kofford was being summoned to the station to meet Officer Devin Burleson, who had just helped escort Thompson through the hotel lobby.

The sergeant turned out to be a man Naomi judged to be at least sixty years old. There were seven small gold stars over his gold nameplate. His thirty-five-plus years in law enforcement did not portend a favorable attitude toward women officers from the start, she figured. But was she unfairly prejudging him? Probably not.

Sergeant Kofford looked at her for a moment, making no effort to introduce himself. He then looked at Thompson. Naomi surmised that the two would know each other, perhaps very well. But she could detect no hint of recognition between them.

"I'm Naomi Gentry," she offered to the sergeant. "I'm a deputy sheriff from Washington County in the southwest corner of Utah." She extended her hand to him. He accepted her handshake insipidly with only a glance and no facial reaction or verbal response.

"What's seems to be the problem here, Burleson?" he asked of the city patrolman, quite obviously dismissing any authority or validity Naomi might possess. She was now even more dispirited.

"Well, Mr. Thompson, here... he's the manager of the Ruby Springs Lodge, you know. The deputy, here, tells me that... " Burleson hesitated and glanced at her.

"He tried to drown me!" Naomi exclaimed. The sergeant looked at her with a blank expression.

"What did you say, um, deputy?" The sergeant's expression seemed to border on indignation. "You're accusing this man of trying to kill you?" Naomi opened her mouth to explain. "These your cuffs, lady? Let's get 'em off." His eyes narrowed and his eyebrows seemed to come together. The wrinkles in his forehead deepened. Naomi removed the handcuffs and Chuck rubbed his wrists vigorously with some relief--almost grinning.

"Can we talk privately, sergeant?" Naomi requested. Leaving Thompson alone in an interrogation room, the three officers went into the hallway where she began a lengthy explanation of the events at the pool.

"Say, Burleson," the sergeant said, interrupting her, "make sure this man gets his one phone call and keep an eye on him for a few minutes while I talk to this lady." Kofford motioned for her to follow him into an office. "So why would this man, this Mr. Thompson, try to kill you?" Kofford asked. Not waiting for an answer, he continued. "And if he was under water and then running away from you, you didn't get a look at the man's face, did you?"

"Well, no. I didn't actually see his face."

"What about his hair, he's got a lot of blond hair. The man who tried to drown you, did he have blond hair? You could see it easily from the back as he ran away from you, I suppose?"

"No, I can't remember any blond hair. The light wasn't very bright back there and there's kind of a mist over the pool. But I followed his wet footprints on the tile floor leading toward the manager's apartment!"

"Are you telling me the wet tracks didn't actually lead right up to the apartment door? Or did they?"

"His tracks... his feet... got dry before they got all the way to his apartment." Her discouragement increased, realizing that she had just made a rookie's major blunder. She had to get word to Shane!

"So why do you think this man would try to drown you?" Kofford asked it with a straight face, but Naomi perceived the sarcasm in his tone, or, at least, thought she did. Knowing that he would probably not take it seriously, she launched again, into a lengthy explanation beginning with the murders of Floyd Barker and Brody Conway inside the Washington County jail.

"And you really believe your 'hit man' is actually Chuck Thompson, the manager of the Ruby Springs Lodge?"

"Yes, we do. We're just waiting on word... or an arrest warrant... back from the FBI, based on the fingerprints we sent to Washington. We figured we should come on up here and make sure he doesn't skip out before we get word from the FBI. Somehow he must have found out who I am."

Sgt. Kofford leaned back in his office chair in silence as he studied her face. His fingers and thumbs tapped together across his chest for a few seconds. "So you're not here by yourself. Where's all your help? Who's here with you? Who's this 'we' you're talkin' about?"

"My sergeant has been with me all along and a deputy Hawley from Teton County. I don't know where they are at the moment. I guess we all got too bored after several days. I don't know where they are. Apparently, Thompson must have figured out who I was," Naomi repeated, "and decided to take me out and make it look like a drowning accident."

"Lady, your story sounds, um, plausible, but very iffy. As far as this, um, *attempted murder* goes, I suppose it could have been anybody. Maybe some dimwit 'pre-vert'... maybe gets his kicks out of drowning women... stayin' at the hotel? Who knows? Oh, we'll investigate it, for sure, based on what evidence, though?"

"I just thought of something. He would have to have a wet swimming suit in his apartment. And he would have had some goggles and some kind of basic SCUBA gear. He was under the water a long time!"

"Well, maybe I can get a warrant to look in the apartment," the sergeant said. "You and I could stop by the city attorney's house and see if he'll go along with it. Then, if we can get the judge to sign it, we'll have a look. I'll have Burleson put him in a detention cell while we do that."

* * *

Shane Lowry and LaMont Hawley had followed Devin Burleson's police car to the center of the city and then parked a short distance from the police station.

"There goes the wife," LaMont murmured, as the Thompson's Mercury sped past them. "She's gotta be one upset little lady!"

"Yeah. They're pretty clever people. Makes me wonder how they're going to plan their escape." Shane was torn between walking into the police station, introducing himself to Sergeant Kofford and the others in order to find out what was happening or remaining out of sight for the time being. LaMont offered to go in on some pretense.

After several minutes of considering their options, Shane decided to make one more phone call to Ian Cooper.

He made the call from a nearby mid-town service station. To his consternation, the sheriff asserted that he had still not heard a thing from the FBI. He had not spoken to Naomi and knew nothing about Thompson's arrest. Before much could be said, LaMont, still sitting in his truck, honked the horn to get Shane's attention and motioned for him to come over. Shane let the phone dangle by the cord and sprinted to the truck.

What baffled him more than anything else was the arrest, itself. Had Naomi's patience simply worn thin? Did she just get tired of the constant waiting? He approached LaMont's open window. No, she wouldn't *do that*, he decided!

LaMont explained quickly. "I just heard Sgt. Kofford tell his dispatcher that he and the Utah deputy were out of the car at the city prosecutor's house."

"Well, that's gotta be for a search warrant," Shane said. "But for what?

"Yeah, it'll take some time. I heard their city attorney is real particular. Then they'll have to take it to the judge."

"I'd better let my sheriff know. He says he hasn't got anything back from the FBI yet." A voice on the monitor silenced them momentarily. It was Devin Burleson signing out at a small cafe that was frequented by the city police. "Do you know the place?" Shane asked.

"Sure. We could drop over there in about a minute, if you... "

"No, take me back to the lodge first. Then you can stop in at the cafe and see if the city officer will tell you about it."

"Good plan!" LaMont said, as he started the engine.

"Let me get back on the phone and I'll let the sheriff know what's going on. Back in a second." Ian Cooper was still waiting on the line. After a brief explanation, Shane promised to call back soon.

* * *

Chuck Thompson paced nervously in the detention cell. Sounds of women's voices could be heard through the locked door. That would have to be Laura arguing with someone who wouldn't allow her to see him. He felt a degree of solace that she had come.

Laura had, of course, stubbornly demanded an explanation on the phone. But his stern rebuke, along with a promise to explain later, had persuaded her to comply with his directions.

* * *

A meticulous search of the apartment, authorized by the city judge, proved fruitless. In disgust, Sgt. Kofford quickly drove back to the police station. After making an NCIC records search, which turned up nothing in the name of Collins "Chuck" Thompson, he all but apologized to Chuck for the "absurd inconvenience" and released him quickly. "I'll have to do a little paperwork and then you'll be free to leave with your wife, if you like. Guess she's been waiting for a couple of hours now."

"Thanks a lot, Sergeant. I just hope we can catch whoever it was that tried to drown one of our guests. I'll bet she still believes it was me that did it, though."

Sgt. Kofford had decided not to relate anything Naomi had said to him about why she was in Wyoming. "Well, maybe she does. Guess she just assumed it was you, based on the wet tracks that went in your direction. I'd wager she'll be leaving the lodge in the morning. Kind of a strange girl... young... inexperienced. Never did say why she was staying at the lodge all by herself. She'll get over it. You know how women are, right?"

* * *

After the futile search of the Thompson's apartment, Naomi felt devastated. She even considered handing over her gun, badge, and police ID to Shane Lowry and going home in disgrace. And where was he? She hungered to have Aaron's strong and comforting arms about her and loathed trying to be so stoic and sure of herself in a 'man's world.' Was it all just an act on her part? Was it time to hang it all up, stay home, and start a family? How would she be able to explain how she had botched the deal with a premature arrest. She even began to question whether it really was Chuck Thompson, the manager, who had tried to drown her. Could it--in fact--have been some "nut job" on a depraved mission to kill tall blonde women? Why hadn't she waited to consult with Sgt. Lowry? *And where was he?*

It was close to eleven-thirty when she came out of a long, hot, comforting shower. She wiped a space in the steamed-over mirror and looked at herself, hating her wet and clingy short blonde hair. What a dope! What was she thinking--making a premature arrest? She had managed to turn a really cool and exciting assignment into a major fiasco. In the first place, what made her think that Thompson wouldn't recognize her? She'd seen how he'd ducked out of range of the old movie camera. Her eager phone call back to the lodge from the party at her home had, of course, alerted him. The man wasn't stupid. He'd connected the dots, all right, and probably recognized her--even expected her--the minute she'd set foot into the hotel lobby. At least, she figured, Shane was still out of sight. That was a good thing after all. But Thompson would surely know that she wasn't here to watch him by herself! Where in heaven's name, she wondered again, was Shane Lowry anyway?

She dressed in pajamas and emerged from the bathroom, knowing she would not be able to sleep. At the soft knock on her door she quickly put on a robe, tied the waistband, and picked up her revolver. She checked the load in the cylinder and stepped to the side of the door in almost complete darkness. "Who is it?" she called out.

"It's me, Shane." Not willing to take any chances, Naomi stepped to the peephole and, seeing Shane's face, she removed the chair that she'd placed with it's back under the doorknob, unlatched the safety chain, shifted the dead bolt, and opened the door. Shane glanced up and down the hall before entering. LaMont Hawley followed him. After the door was closed and the dead bolt secured she turned on a light.

Unable to conceal her anger and frustration with him, she demanded, "*Where have you been!?*"

"Look, Naomi, I'm sorry you had to go through this by yourself. We've been watching ever since you took Thompson through the lobby to the police car. We didn't want to blow our cover... just in case it was still necessary. LaMont, here, was able to find out what happened from that officer, Burleson, that came here to help you. Nobody can blame you for arresting him."

"It would have helped if I'd known you were even around!" she exclaimed, near tears. "I had no idea! For all I knew, the Thompsons might have killed you before he got to me!"

"I'm so sorry. Really, I am! I guess, after all the days of waiting, we all forgot what a clever man he is. We, no, I should have been more careful. I guess I got bored with it, too."

"I'm sorry, too," said LaMont, pushing his hat back and scratching his forehead. "We decided to drive out to a restaurant and grab a hamburger. These hotel prices are really something," he added weakly. "Can we go over exactly what happened?"

Naomi spent the next ten minutes explaining in every detail all she could recall from when she had told Shane that she would like to spend some time skiing. "But his swimming suit and the other stuff he used *has got to be in their apartment! Somewhere!*"

After a few moments of silence, LaMont asked her, "Do you know if they let Thompson make a phone call?"

"Well, yeah. As I was leaving with Sgt. Kofford to get the warrant," Naomi answered, "I heard him tell Devin Burleson to make sure Thompson got a chance to make a call. I don't know if he... " Naomi stopped talking. The three of them were silent for a moment. *"He called her!"*

"That's what I'm a thinkin'," LaMont said. "Called his wife and told her to get that stuff out of the apartment and hide it!"

"Holy cow! Of course he did!" Shane exclaimed. "Where'd she hide it though?"

"Garbage can? Maybe?" Naomi ventured. "We know he likes dumpsters! Or she could've put the stuff in their car."

"Why don't you get dressed, Naomi," Shane said. "We'll check it out, right now."

Naomi quickly changed into a pair of jeans and a shirt. Her hair was still damp and straight. She took a few minutes to use her blow dryer and a brush. She put on a thick sweatshirt and took her down-filled, hooded parka.

"I was thinking," she said, as she emerged from the bathroom. "I doubt he'd want to throw those things in the garbage can or a dumpster. He'd probably figure we'd know to look there. My guess is he'd have her put them back in a locker in the women's dressing room by the pool or something like that."

"You're probably right," Shane said, as they prepared to leave her room. "Let's eliminate the garbage cans first though."

Using LaMont's flashlight to search the garbage, nothing was apparent. Of course Laura likely would have had time to put the stuff inside a garbage bag before discarding it. In the freezing midnight temperatures, opening garbage bags didn't seem to be that urgent. Both dressing rooms had been locked.

"Let's call it a day," Shane offered as he and Naomi re-entered her room. LaMont had already departed for his home. "I'll call the sheriff in the morning and see if he has any ideas. You'd better get some rest and I'll watch the parking lot... the Mercury. There's no telling what these people have in mind now."

Before slipping into bed to try to get some sleep, Naomi knelt down to pray that their actions would be guided and successful and that Aaron and the others at home could be kept safe and assured that she was okay.

CHAPTER NINETEEN

At seven o'clock Friday morning, Chuck Thompson was on duty at the front desk, acting as though nothing had happened to disrupt his routine. From the shadows of the mezzanine, Shane watched him carry two suitcases out of the office and set them down by the front desk. The manager then retreated to the rear of the desk and made a call to the number provided by Sal Maracek. In ten minutes, Sal's roommate showed up at the front of the lodge, left the engine running, and walked quickly to the manager's desk.

"Got something for me, Mr. Thompson?" he asked, with a wide grin. "Sal's still asleep. He was running around pretty late last night. What'cha got for me?"

"I had a couple of guests check out early this morning. It seems they got a ride to the airport with a friend. But I guess they left in a big hurry and forgot these two pieces of luggage. Can you take these to the airport for me. Here's a ten for you, okay? They should be inside the terminal. They said you could just leave their things on the curb and they'll run out and pick them up."

"Hey, leave it to me."

"Better hustle. They said their plane leaves pretty soon. They'll be waiting for you."

"I'm on it, Mr. Thompson." The taxi driver grabbed the suitcases and headed for the front door. "Thanks a lot!" he called back, over his shoulder.

With a great deal of anxiety, still waiting for word from the sheriff--or the FBI, or anyone, requesting Thompson's arrest on a "fugitive warrant"--Shane Lowry left the elevator on the ground floor and walked past the front desk to the restaurant entrance. He sat down at a table where he could see what the manager was doing most of the time. It was nearing eight-thirty and he'd had no sleep when he ordered breakfast and looked over the half-wall with potted plants on it. The hotel manager was nowhere to be seen. Shane was not especially concerned for several minutes. Thompson's daytime assistant, a slim woman of maybe thirty, was in plain sight and seemed to be very busy. Shane watched her look around the lobby and into the office, as if searching for someone.

A sudden feeling of dread and unease swept over him and he got up from the table and walked, trying not to seem to be hurrying to the hallway that led to the rear of the lodge. On the way down the hall, out of curiosity, he paused to quietly check the door to the manager's apartment. It was locked. He picked up his pace toward the rear parking lot.

The Mercury was gone. Had Naomi seen it go? A light snow had fallen in the dark, early hours of the morning and he could see tire tracks showing that the car had been backed out of the stall and driven around toward the front of the building. There the tracks blended with others. Shane ran back to where the car had been parked. From footprints in the skiff of fresh snow he could see that one person, no doubt a woman, had apparently cleaned the windshield, gotten into the car and driven it away. There were no footprints on the passenger side. That was somewhat reassuring.

LaMont Hawley would be showing up anytime to help look for the man. Shane walked back into the lodge, half-expecting to meet the Wyoming deputy in the restaurant. Chuck Thompson was still nowhere in sight. Laura could have picked him up at one of the side entrances. Shane was reluctant to call the city police, remembering what had happened the night before, and the chagrin that Naomi had painfully experienced. LaMont Hawley met him at the restaurant, smiling.

"You ain't lookin' real good this morning," Hawley remarked. "Anything wrong, deputy?"

"I haven't seen Thompson for fifteen minutes and his car's gone. Did you see his white Mercury leaving on your way up here?"

"No, I didn't," LaMont said, glancing to his left as Naomi approached. "Did you see the Mercury leaving?"

"Yes, I was looking out my back window and saw the wife get in it and drive around to the north side just a few minutes ago."

"Are you thinking what I'm thinking?" Shane asked, turning toward the side entrance. They walked quickly to the north door. In the half-inch of snow, a single set of medium-sized footprints led from the door and was lost in the confusion of tire-tracks. The three officers walked quickly back into the lobby.

Shane spoke first. "We still don't know anything for sure. If we call the city cops to help us, they'll think we're crazy. Then Thompson will walk out of his apartment and resume his job at the front desk."

"I think he's gone, for sure," Naomi said. "We've all got our radios. Why don't I stay here. I'll stay out of sight... and you guys can get in the truck and look around Jackson for the Mercury. What do you think?"

"Good idea," Shane answered. "C'mon LaMont, let's get out and have a look around. But where would she, or they, go? They don't even have any luggage... unless they loaded it up in the dark when I wasn't looking! But then, if they did that, there would be more tracks around where the Mercury was parked."

As they were about to split up, two men walked in the front door and glanced around as if searching for someone. They seemed out of place at the vacation lodge in dark suits and white shirts--and with grim expressions on both their faces. Shane and LaMont couldn't help but notice the men as they passed.

Outside the front door, LaMont turned to Shane with a grin. "Hey Shane, how does an FBI man go undercover?" Shane stopped walking and looked at him with a blank expression. "He loosens up his necktie!" His grin quickly faded.

Shane ignored the joke that he'd heard many times before and turned to look through the glass doors. "C'mon. Let's get back inside," he said, grimly. "Those guys are FBI, I know it!"

* * *

At the Teton County Airport, a ticket agent looked up from her paperwork and watched as a late-model white car, driven by a woman, stopped at the curb. A man got out from the passenger side and opened the trunk. He then picked up two suitcases that had been left by the front door, placed them in the trunk, and closed the lid. The luggage had been left there by that flirty taxi driver, who had assured her that he'd been paid to deliver them to the airport door, and that some passengers would be picking them up.

The ticket agent walked around the desk to explain to the man in the white car that the early flight had already departed and no passengers had spoken of having left their luggage at some hotel.

"It was all a mistake," Chuck exclaimed. "I guess the taxi driver must've been confused. These were supposed to go to another hotel... we'll take care of it."

The ticket agent shrugged her shoulders as the car drove quickly away from the curb and disappeared. "Oh-kay. Must have been some mistake," she repeated, to herself in half-amusement.

* * *

From the airport, the Thompsons, with Chuck now driving, went west on Highway 22, toward the Idaho border. They passed a highway patrol car near the small community of Wilson. Chuck and Laura watched him nervously, but the trooper made no effort to stop them. That was an apparent indication that there was nothing broadcast about them as yet and, also, that the 8,430-foot Teton Pass was open which would take them through the Targhee National Forest toward Rigby and on to Idaho Falls.

* * *

Six special agents of the FBI, in pairs, had converged from several entrances on the Ruby Springs Lodge to arrest John and Cora Moranski, also known, of late, as Collins and Laura Thompson. The latent fingerprints, taken from the wine glass and submitted by the Washington County Sheriff's office had enabled the bureau to identify the pair of federal fugitives--wanted on the east coast for jumping bail on charges of extortion and racketeering. Led by the

Special Agent in Charge for Wyoming, the agents were just minutes too late. Among them was Special Agent Jon Gates, from Provo, Utah. As Agent Gates later explained to Shane, the federal agents had known of the Thompson's whereabouts for two days--plenty of time to make a more complete investigation and to obtain the necessary federal warrants. And, at least according to Gates, FBI agents, had been aware of his whereabouts for most of the preceding forty-eight hours.

Gates had been pressing his superiors to expedite the fingerprint search. Furthermore, as soon as the Thompsons' true identities were known, he had wanted to get word to Sheriff Cooper. But his superiors had prevailed in keeping word from reaching local officers. This matter, he had been assured, was, first and foremost, a federal case--not to be "botched" by the "antics of half-trained, local" police officers. Jon Gates, however, was well aware that the real reason for not telling Ian Cooper was that FBI administrators wished to take the credit for the arrest of a long-term fugitive from justice.

Shane recognized Gates and approached him in the lobby. The agents had been successful in getting the assistant manager on duty to open the apartment, which the agents searched, again. Shane couldn't help but utter a soft curse under his breath when Gates confided to him that the FBI had made a positive ID two days before. "This 'Collins Thompson' is really John Moranski. Comes from New Jersey. He's got quite a long history and could very well be your jailhouse killer, Shane."

"*We had him right in our hands, yesterday!*"

"What? Are you telling me you arrested him? Yesterday?" Gates demanded quietly, not wanting the others to hear.

Shane glanced around the lobby and motioned Naomi and LaMont closer. "He's gone now," he said. "LaMont, would you get an APB going on the Mercury?" He scribbled the Wyoming plate number on a page from his notebook, tore it out and gave it to LaMont. "My guess is they're a good half-hour out of Jackson by now, in any direction." He took Naomi and Jon Gates into the restaurant and sank into a booth out of sight of the other agents. Nearing complete exhaustion and very angry, he turned to Gates and began to pummel the table top with his index finger. "*We've been here for goin' on five days now!*

Waiting for word from your people! What in the... What's going on?"

"Sorry, Shane, really," Jon said, not actually apologizing. "It's just the way the bureau does things. You know how it is! These people were wanted on federal warrants, too, you know. Besides that, a couple of our agents were in the area. Supposed to be keeping an eye on this guy!"

"Well where in the... heck were they last night when Naomi and a city cop strolled through this lobby with Thompson... or Moranski... or whatever his name is... in handcuffs? We could've had 'em for you guys!"

"What's this you said about arresting him yesterday?" Jon asked, quietly. "Our people didn't mention that! How could they have missed that?"

Shane turned to Naomi. "You tell him. I'm tired."

Naomi patiently rehearsed the events of the previous evening, beginning with the boredom and the time she'd spent skiing. At Shane's prodding, she admitted that Sgt. Kofford had seemed more than a little inclined to discredit her story from the beginning. Gates was shocked to learn of the casino operation in the basement of a local restaurant, along with the apparent collusion of the city police. Naomi was somewhat reassured to know that Shane believed in and supported her. She hadn't actually seen her attacker's face after he tried to drown her in the pool. And she couldn't say she'd noticed his mop of blond hair under the pool lights. The man's wet footprints only led in the *direction* of the Thompsons' apartment--not all the way to the door.

A search of the apartment had turned up nothing related to the *attempted* murder by drowning that she had alleged. She had felt that Sgt. Kofford had simply dismissed her as a hysterical female. Still, they had been assured that the attempted drowning would be 'investigated' by the Jackson police.

"So the goggles, the swimming suit, and the other stuff are still missing?" Gates asked. "And... you think that he must have called his wife and had her dispose of them?"

"Yeah, that's right," she said. "Maybe they gathered them up before they left. And took the stuff with them this morning." Shane nodded in agreement. "We think she either must have put the stuff in the garbage or in one of the lockers in the women's dressing room."

"Well, let's have a look," Gates said. "The dressing room would be easiest to eliminate first. And now that he's apparently fled the scene, he hasn't any more privacy rights around here."

"I'll get the assistant manager," said Naomi. "We may need a master key."

* * *

The conference at the Jackson Police Department wasn't long. Jon Gates and the SAC from Wyoming, along with Shane, Naomi, and LaMont, met with the chief of police, Sgt. Kofford, and the young city attorney. The equipment that Moranski, aka, Thompson, had used in the pool had been recovered from a locker in the women's dressing room. All of the details were ironed out. Almost seeming to be nothing more than a formality, a few obviously insincere apologies were extended. Naomi readily agreed to swear and sign a complaint for attempted murder which would give the federal agents the additional charge against John Moranski for the unlawful flight to avoid prosecution, based on the assumption that the Moranskis would be leaving the state.

Shane Lowry was tired and ready to crash. LaMont drove them back to the lodge and offered to take them to the airport, if needed. He waited while Shane and Naomi checked out, and arrangements were made for the flight back to Salt Lake City and on to St. George. At the small airport, LaMont shook Shane's extended hand and turned awkwardly to Naomi. She thanked him and gave him a hug. As they sat waiting to board the plane, Shane quickly fell asleep.

* * *

John and Cora Moranski had easily traversed the Teton Pass on a smooth, but somewhat icy surface, that had been plowed several days before. The early morning light snow had posed no problems. They followed Idaho's Highway 33 to Driggs and stopped in a parking lot among several other cars behind a fast-food restaurant. Keeping watch for local police officers, they went inside to have some lunch and to think through their next moves. They had cleaned out all the cash from the Ruby Springs Lodge safe. Never trusting their personal finances to banks, they also had their own considerable pile of cash that had been kept hidden in their apartment.

"Well," said Cora, "we had a good deal going there at the lodge in Wyoming. Where do we go from here, Chuck? I guess I should go back to calling you 'John,' though."

"I got to liking 'Chuck.' Course we'll have to get us some new names, you know, and we've got to change our looks, too."

"Well, yes, of course. You can change your hair color to brown and grow a beard and I guess I'll have to be a blonde for a while." They both laughed. Somehow just being away from the Ruby Springs Lodge was a relief, in itself. Being over the pass and into Idaho seemed like entering a new world. "Don't look now!" she gasped, glancing to the exterior of the establishment soon after the server brought their meal. "There's a cop car driving around this joint!" There were two officers, who appeared to be local, in the green police car, not paying much attention to anything except their own conversation.

"Ya know, maybe we *should* look at them, just like everybody else does," Chuck said, quietly. "I've thought a lot about that time we got stopped in Utah. I think they only stopped us because they figured we was acting suspicious. I mean, everybody notices when cops come around. It's just natural. Look at all these other people. Everybody's takin' notice... ain't they?"

Cora looked around the room. "Yeah, you're right," she said, watching the police car. "We should just act naturally. I guess I hadn't thought about that before." The police car drove back into the street and went south.

"I'd better get the plates changed real fast," Chuck said. "I've been keeping another set in the trunk, just in case. We'd better find a place to switch them right after we eat."

"You've got some other Wyoming plates? Where did you get more plates?"

"That's easy. Hey! I grew up in Newark, remember? Any junkyard has a bunch of cars with license plates left on them. You can just walk through carryin' a screwdriver."

"What about Idaho plates, then? Or maybe you could find some others when we get to Oregon?"

"Sure. We can do it anywhere. But I think we need to get them replaced as soon as possible." He paused for a moment. "What would you think about slipping down into Utah?"

"Chuck! You can't be serious! We can't be goin' there! That would be crazy!"

"Well, think about it. It's the last place they would expect us to go. Course we could maybe go on down to Vegas. Some of the guys back in Jersey have friends down there. We could get new names and stuff down there, just like we did before... get another car. We've got plenty of money... and when some more assignments come along, we'll be all set."

"Well, sure. But, why Utah?" He struggled to craft an appropriate reply. "Oh, no, you're not thinking of... Chuck! Everybody and their cats would know who did it! You can't be serious! How come you have such an obsession with that... that woman deputy?"

"It's unfinished business! I take a lot of pride in my work! I'll find a way. You'll see."

"Yeah, you'll find a way to get the electric chair! Besides, there's that other guy... that old guy from Australia! What was he? Some kind of relative? She's not the only one that can trip you up, you know. You're crazy to even think about it!"

"Okay, okay! Give me some more time to think. Maybe I can get her out of my system. And... yes. As a matter of fact there are other relatives. I went over to where he stayed that night and found out he'd made a call to southern Utah... from his room. Did I tell you, that deputy, she was a Blackstone, too. He coulda been her father, for all I know. ... had to be maybe an uncle... or some kinda relative."

"So... he really wasn't from Australia, after all? Sure had everybody fooled."

"But either one of 'em could get us busted. I ain't spendin' the rest of my life in no lock-up! I'm tellin' you, we gotta do somethin' about them two!"

"But, Chuck... Chuck, listen to me, please! She ain't like all those others we did. Those Mafia dudes! They're nothin' but a bunch of big old crooks, you know that! But, this woman cop is different, she's just doing her job. They're just newlyweds! She could even be carryin' a baby... who knows! She doesn't deserve it, Chuck!" He made no reply but took a deep breath and wiped his mouth with a napkin while glaring at Cora.

They paid for their food and departed from the restaurant. "We might as well find a place to stay around here for a few days," he said, as they drove away. "We'll need to find a quiet little motel, where we can park off the street. I can switch the tags after dark."

* * *

Shane Lowry was sprawled in his seat, still asleep, when the Beechcraft propjet landed at Salt Lake City. Naomi, in a window seat beside him, seeing no reason to wake him up, stepped over his feet into the aisle. After a short delay, the plane would continue on to St. George. It was in the early darkness of winter. Snow had been pushed into piles higher than the windows of their aircraft.

At the first pay phone she could find, she made a call to her home phone. It was Friday night and Aaron should be at home. He'd mentioned that with the new year, his 'weekend' would be changed. If not there, he could very well be at his parent's farm, she thought. There was no answer at their Toquerville home. She next tried the Gentry farmhouse. Would they be having the evening meal? Aaron's mother quickly answered the phone.

"Oh, Naomi. How are you? Aaron's here now. It's his day off, you know. Where are you? Are you coming back soon? I know he's really missed you."

"Oh, I'm fine," she answered, actually pondering the question. Well, maybe not, she thought. Their surveillance mission had been a bust. Sabotaged by her own over-zealous actions? "And how are you?" she inquired, trying to sound upbeat. She thought of her hair and how she had been so enthralled with changing her appearance and remembered the strange looks that Aaron had given her--with her hair cut and dyed, wearing dark glasses. Her skin was naturally a darker tone than most. The "blonde" ruse had been dumb from the start. She had reluctantly agreed to let him take her picture. That would certainly be something for the family album!

"Well, we're doing just fine," was the reply. "We were about to sit down and eat. But, here, you can talk to Aaron, first."

She waited just a few seconds before he answered. For the first time, since arresting the man who tried to kill her, she felt her emotions start to go. She wanted so much to be with Aaron, just the two of them, alone, where she could get completely unglued, just to cry and love him. It was a few moments after he said "Hello" that she could respond.

"Hello!" he repeated, louder this time. "Naomi! Are you there, Naomi?"

"Hello, Aaron," she answered, softly--her voice thick with emotion. "I'm on the way back. We're at the Salt Lake airport, now. Shane's still asleep on the plane. It's so good to hear your voice again."

"So you should be home in a few hours? I was going to stay here one more night, but I'll meet you at our house, tonight. How did it go? What about the Thompson guy? What happened?"

"Well, they've escaped. They cleared out early this morning, just before the FBI agents showed up. It's a long story, Aaron. I'll tell you all about it tomorrow. But tonight, I'm just dying to be with you. I need you so much."

"I've missed you, too," he said, quietly. "But you'd better get back on the plane before it leaves without you. I'll be waiting at our house!"

"Okay. See you in a while, Aaron. I love you."

"I love you, too. Now get going!"

CHAPTER TWENTY

Saturday morning in Toquerville held the promise of a warm day, at least for mid-winter. Compared to the Jackson Hole, the sun's angle to the earth's surface was more than six degrees greater and the elevation was more than four thousand feet lower. That combination, plus the southward tilt of the land along Ash Creek, produced a considerably higher temperature. And though Naomi enjoyed the sun's welcome rays, always in the back of her mind she could not help dwelling on the Moranskis' escape--and blaming herself. She even dreaded turning on the television, half-expecting that news reports would be covering the story--perhaps high-lighting Thompson's attempted murder and her botched arrest--and their escape.

That morning, as well as the night before, Nero greeted her with unbounded affection and affected a tongue-lolling wide "smile" as only a loyal and loving canine can. It felt good for Naomi to feed and water the horses. After breakfast she inspected the new barn that Aaron had nearly finished while she was gone. Together, they saddled Pepper and Mancha for a ride in the hills for a few hours. On a low ridge, they sat on a large black volcanic rock, ate a sandwich, and kissed again while Nero scampered about and the horses scavenged in the dry grass.

After Aaron had gone to work in the early afternoon, Naomi took the truck and, with Nero, headed for St. George to get her hair back close to it's natural color before anyone she knew might see her as a "blonde." Becky was home when she got there and was overjoyed to see her. Nero seemed glad to be back in Becky's fenced backyard and ran from place to place hoping to catch the scent of his old friend, Kody. Meanwhile, Becky, never having seen Naomi's hair so short in many years, kept looking at her to reassure herself that it really was Naomi.

"I guess you had to try to look different. It was actually blonde?"

"Uh huh. Well, Aaron took some pictures so you'll be able to see how disgusting it was. Even with that, our Mr. Moranski, aka, Chuck Thompson, finally figured out who I was. I don't know how he did it! But he sure did!"

"Oh, my gosh, I was so worried about you! And Aaron was, too, I know that's for sure! He would call me... then I would call him. 'Have you heard anything yet? No, have you?' How did it all go anyway? We heard late yesterday... I guess Shane called the sheriff and let him know that the Thompsons got away. I had the impression he was blaming the FBI for not telling us anything."

"Well, that was part of the problem." Becky was shocked when Naomi told her the whole story. No one had mentioned to her that the man had tried to drown her only daughter on Thursday.

"Oh, my gosh!" Becky exclaimed, giving her daughter a hug. "I know you can take care of yourself, physically, that way, and all, but my gosh, what will he try next?"

"Oh, well, we're not worried about that anymore. I doubt he'll ever want to get within a thousand miles of this place again. The FBI agents told us he and his wife came from the east... like, New Jersey... or maybe New York. It was back there, somewhere."

"Oh, I sure hope he stays away! But just to think that he's on the loose now!"

"Actually, Mom, there are tens of thousands of fugitives out there, all around us, hiding out all over the place."

"Yes, I guess that's true," Becky replied, with a deep sigh. "But I'm still concerned for you. One of them tried to kill you!"

"Thanks, Mom. I'll be just fine. What's new with you? And Preston?" she asked, with a grin. "Any news? Anything I should know about?"

"Well, as a matter of fact, he's asked me to take trip to England with him."

"Whoa! And you said...?"

"And, I said I would. But he wants to wait until spring, when it's not going to be so cold. They have so much rain in the winters, you know."

"Oh, Mom, that is so neat. How's it going with the missionary discussions? Have they started yet?"

"Well, actually we're starting this week. He's still very interested. I think more all the time. I guess he's decided he's about ready to be baptized, and all... even before they've even taught him much of anything."

"What about you, Mom? You don't sound really that excited."

"I'm really not, I suppose. I'm not sure why, either. But he's coming over in the morning and we're going to church here in Bloomington. That should raise a few eyebrows! I'll bet a lot of people will be commenting on that."

"Oh, Mom, I'm sure the story about Preston has been spread all around by now! I'll bet your neighbors have taken care of that! You know you only have to tell one curious neighbor and word gets around. Besides that, all your neighbors have seen him coming and going."

"Well, probably. The Relief Society president stopped by one day. We talked for quite a while. She's very nice."

"Just stop worrying about it! I know what the problem is, Mom. I think, deep down, you're still bitter about my father and all that. I don't think I've ever even heard you speak his name to anyone."

"You're absolutely right! And you never will, Naomi. And you know something else? I've never told Preston this, but I even hate the thought of being married to him and having that same last name, again!"

"Maybe you could just keep the last name you have now. No, that wouldn't work. Course you could even go back to your maiden name. Sure... you could be Becky Madsen again."

"Well, I suppose so. Maybe we'll talk about it. But, in the meantime, he's found a new place to live not very far from your mobile. And, by the way, those people from Idaho decided to move down. They're all moved in now and they've called me three times. They're really eager to close the deal... the title and everything... on your doublewide. Why don't you call them now and make arrangements? I guess you'll need to coordinate with Natty, too."

"Oh, great, I will. I'll call her now. Then we can meet in town and go see the new people then we can find a restaurant for dinner. Just the three of us."

* * *

Preston Blackstone's first time at church, some months before, in the St. George Basin had proved to be a major culture shock for him. He could not recall a time when so many people had offered a friendly hand in greeting. Word had, of course, spread rapidly that he had come all the way from England to find out what happened to his distant relatives--the progeny of Hanford Rushton Blackstone. He quickly became aware that he had created a minor sensation.

Almost as if by design, the theme of the talks centered on the restoration of the gospel--commemorating 155 years since the First Vision of Joseph Smith, Jr. One speaker illustrated the ways in which the world had been prepared for the restoration and another concentrated on the experiences of young Joseph and his visitations with Moroni, the translation of the gold plates, and other events that led to the establishment of the Church.

The presence of families, surrounded by small children, many of whom were being somewhat fidgety, was disturbing at first. But after the initial shock, the Sacrament Meeting soon became a "rawthuh pleasant affayuh," as Becky jokingly explained to her family afterward.

But this Sunday was a bit different. He had persuaded Becky Scott to attend meetings in the ward in which she lived and take him with her. They quickly became aware of the intense interest they were generating. Preston was again taken aback by the enthusiastic handshaking and the welcoming greetings. It felt very good to him and Becky enjoyed it, too. Recalling what Naomi had said just the day before, she thought maybe she really had allowed her old feelings of bitterness to keep her depressed.

What had become the traditional Sunday dinner at Becky's house brought the family together again. Aaron was able to get there earlier than usual. Naomi was already there, since the sheriff had allowed her to take the weekend off before resuming her routine on Monday--with Thursdays and Fridays off. Natty and Ben were there and there was ample time for Naomi to rehearse the events of her trip to Jackson with Shane Lowry.

"That reminds me," said Natty. "A few nights ago, we got this strange call from Sky West... at least, that's what he said. Some guy was trying to find Preston Blackstone. Said he thought Preston might have left something on the plane." All the others looked at her questioningly. "But why would he call our house, anyway? Why wouldn't he just call Preston's number? Wouldn't he have had that number instead of ours?" The room was quiet.

"Ah! I'm positive," said Preston, "that it was not Sky West, at all. That would most assuredly have to have been our Mr. Thompson... or, rather, Moranski, from the state of Wyoming. The man is most clever. He undoubtedly discovered where I was lodging in Jackson. That would easily be accomplished by inquiring of a most accommodating cabby. What was his name? Sal, something. This Mr. Moranski then went to my hotel and obtained the number that I had rung down here to inform all of you that I would shortly be returning. I should have anticipated his most clever inquiries!" With a glance at Ben Randolph, he continued. "No one answered at Becky's residence... So I called the Randolph residence. It appears that Ben, here, neglected to inform the rest of you."

"I guess I figured you would've called Becky, too," Ben responded in his defense. "Couldn't imagine why you'd be a callin' our place." Now the others looked at him quizzically. "Well, I guess I musta been really tired. It was kinda late, anyway, ya know."

"Of course, Ben," Preston replied. "That makes a lot of sense. I didn't mean to impugn your reliability. Actually, it was my fault. I had no idea he'd even attempt to have my telephone conversations traced. Now, that wasn't exceptionally bright of me, was it?"

* * *

Aaron had kept quiet about it, but he continued to blame himself for not objecting to Naomi's trip to Jackson. He had figured she would be in little or no danger from the Moranskis since Sgt. Lowry was along, and, as he learned later, a deputy sheriff of Teton County had joined them in watching the man. But the major focus of his anger was with John Moranski, himself. The man had somehow figured out who she was and tried to drown her--his precious Naomi. It was a dilemma. Was she the intelligent and capable police officer that could be the equal of most men he knew? Or was she his tall and lovely wife, to be protected and cherished? Would the time come when she would become the mother of their children, stay at home, and be the traditional and most capable housewife? His emotions stormed inside him, just to think that Moranski had even touched her! He envisioned meeting the man and battering him with fists or choking him with his bare hands--but he said nothing. After all, he remembered, he had encouraged her to go.

* * *

Together, Aaron and Naomi had already studied maps of the various routes out of Jackson and into the several surrounding states. While it might be tempting to think that the fugitives would want to head back east, to a more familiar territory and culture, the Gentrys decided that the Moranskis would have departed Jackson--and Wyoming--as quickly and quietly as possible. And under that assumption, the most obvious route would have been to leave the state by taking a "back road" into Idaho. But then, a white Mercury with Wyoming plates should not be hard to spot in small-town Idaho.

To most police officers--including the FBI and U.S. Marshals--the Moranskis would constitute just another pair of federal fugitives from the east. But the Gentrys had personal reasons. They decided to spend their next Thursday and Friday "weekend" together in Idaho--on the extremely slim chance that there was something they might learn of the Moranskis' departure. After all, the fugitives had to eat somewhere. They would have to find lodging and certainly a different car.

* * *

Sheriff Ian Cooper arrived at his office early Monday morning, eager to meet with Sgt. Lowry and Naomi Gentry in order to discuss more fully the details of last week's surveillance assignment. He had barely removed his jacket when the phone on his desk began ringing. He expected it would be a news reporter. The dispatcher had taken the call and routed it to him.

"This is Sheriff Cooper," he said, into the phone while sinking into his high-back, black leather chair.

"Sheriff Cooper!" the familiar male caller echoed, with no introduction of himself. "How are you, sir?"

"Just fine, my good man! And you?"

"Never better, sir! I've been quite thoroughly informed of the Jackson episode. I've been extremely curious as to your thoughts about our little, uh, arrangement, shall we say?"

The sheriff, of course, knew very well who it was. "Well, as of now, it looks as though our agreement is leaning in your direction. At this point, though, we can't be absolutely sure that the man who tried to drown our deputy is the same man who murdered our jail inmates. We do know he's wanted by the feds. But, on the other hand, he could be just another paranoid lunatic. Or some kind of pervert that has an aversion to tall attractive blondes. Maybe Naomi reminded him of his mother who was a prostitute. Who knows? All bets are... at this point, anyway, uh, pending, shall we say?"

"You may be right, Sheriff. However, I just wanted to let you know that my offer still stands. If it's ever proved that your Mr. Thompson or Moranski or whatever he's calling himself these days, is not your jailhouse-killer, I'm taking care of the budget for the surveillance trip to Jackson."

"Well, I'm almost positive he's the man. But the problem still is... what now? Every cop in the western states has been alerted. They might've even crossed over into Canada. He's a clever man, my friend. We may never hear of him again. But as far as our little, um, shall we call it a 'wager,' goes... It looks like you're off the hook, at least, for the moment. We'll just have to see how the story plays out."

"Let me assure you, Sheriff, I am a man of my word. But what about this DNA business? I've heard mention of that."

"I understand the lab people up north were looking into it. We haven't heard any more, so far. I'll have my investigator contact them again and see where it might lead us. But... anything to do with DNA still wouldn't positively tie him to the murders. Not as far as I can see, anyway. That lawyer, Croft... Moranski, whatever he called himself, left absolutely nothing to go on that we found... that would have anything to do with DNA."

"Yes, that seems to be true, Sheriff. I'm planning to research the topic, myself. It does sound extremely promising. Good luck with it, sir. I shall positively make contact with you later."

CHAPTER TWENTY-ONE

In the pre-dawn hours of Thursday morning, Aaron and Naomi swept through the Salt Lake Valley on the new freeway. Naomi had slept nearly all the way and they agreed that she would take over driving at dawn. It was a cold clear morning. The rising sun brightened the tops of the Oquirrh Range on the west side of the broad and populous valley. Meager flakes of snow had powdered the valley floor in the early morning darkness and now billowed around the traffic flowing north with them. They stopped for gas and a light breakfast in Layton before continuing northward. By noon, they were in Idaho Falls, where they left I-15 and took Idaho 20 to Rexburg.

What had appeared to be a relatively simple matter from looking at the highway map of Idaho, to follow the probable route out of Wyoming and across Idaho now appeared to be an onerous puzzle. Now becoming somewhat perplexed, they discovered that the Snake River Valley, in contrast to their highway map, was a veritable maze of roads of every description. From Rexburg, they took Idaho 33 east into the Teton Basin, a smaller agricultural area with another tangled web of highways and lesser roads going in all directions.

"My gosh, Aaron," Naomi lamented. "So many ways they could have gone. I guess the best thing is to concentrate on the major routes. But I don't think they'd stay in Idaho."

"Well, you're right, of course. I didn't realize this was such a long shot. The first thing we need to look for is some place where they might have stopped for some fast food. I'm getting kind of hungry, too."

"Yeah, me, too. They'd want to go to a place where they could park the car out of sight from the street. Why don't we go all the way to Victor, that would be the first town they would come to in Idaho, then we can work our way back west."

"Good idea. I'll bet they would be looking for a way to ditch the Mercury and get another car. Maybe just steal one along the way. What do you think?"

"Well, I'll bet they'd have plenty of cash. They cleaned out the safe at the lodge and they probably had a stash of money of their own. I mean, who knows when their last hit job was and how much they got paid for it."

"Yeah, you're right. Wonder what their fee was for taking out Conway and Barker... and who paid for it?"

Naomi drove from one end of Victor to another and saw no fast-food merchants in the small town. Nor were there any through most of the valley. Discouragement began to settle over the pair of would-be detectives.

"Okay, let's go on back to Sugar City and keep an eye out for the Mercury," Naomi said. "They wouldn't try to trade the car in on a new one, would they?"

"Come to think of it, no, I doubt it. They'd most likely try to hide it some way, somewhere. They'd have to deal with their names, taxes, registration, and all that stuff if they went through a dealer."

"And stealing a car would stir up a big stink and arouse the police," Naomi reasoned. She drove much slower, thinking about the snow-covered side roads and places where the Moranski's may have ditched the car. "So what else would they do, Aaron?"

"Well, I was just thinking. Most of the time, Chuck what's-his-name, is really smart, but really stupid at other times. If it was me, I'd look in the want-ads and try to buy a car from a private owner. That way, they could just pay cash, take the title and go. If the seller didn't take off the license plates, they'd be down the road and gone. All of a sudden, they'd at least appear to be legit' and everything. But then, they could always steal plates from another car. I've found that the police don't pay a lot of attention to stolen plates, anyway. It's kind of like the old needle-in-the-haystack situation."

"Yeah, they'd be long gone by now. It's been a week already. But if we could find a newspaper from last week or so, we could check out any cars that had been sold."

In several small towns along the way west, they stopped at fast-food joints, had lunch at the first one and--on a long chance--showed the slightly fuzzy blown-up picture of "Chuck Thompson" to all the employees at each place. None of them recognized the picture. At Sugar City they were directed to the office of a weekly county-wide newspaper where they obtained a copy of the classified ads of the previous three editions. They patiently called each of the numbers for cars for sale. None of the vehicles listed had been sold in the last week.

"There should be a daily paper in Rexburg," Naomi said, with a sigh of frustration in her voice. "But we need to find a place to stay tonight."

"Yeah, you're right. We need some gas right now, though."

Back on the road to Rexburg, Naomi began, "Maybe they just saw a car with a sign in the window and bought it right on the spot."

"Could be. Maybe this wasn't such a good idea after all. Let's find a room for the night and a Rexburg paper. We can make some local calls from the room."

At a motel on the north side of Rexburg, Aaron and Naomi obtained a room and with the help of a desk clerk salvaged some old papers from the recycling bin. The classifieds were over a week old and dozens of vehicles were privately advertised. After an hour's worth of calling, four possibilities emerged. All four sellers gave local addresses. Taking the picture of the man they sought, they set out to find the addresses. Again, none of the four vehicles that had been sold in the past week panned out. No one recognized the picture of Chuck Thompson. Their spirits sank even lower as darkness settled into the Snake River Valley.

Back in their room, Naomi took the Idaho map out. "Maybe they took a different route out of the Teton Basin. The map shows this Highway 31 going down, out of Victor, then over a mountain. It goes south down to this big long reservoir and then west on Idaho 26, over to Idaho Falls."

"Very possible," Aaron responded, as they settled on the bed with the pillows behind them. She handed him the map. "We could check out the papers down there tomorrow. And we need to plan our time getting back home for Saturday... to get back to work. I hope Dan had time to take care of the animals for us."

"Well, I'm sure he'd see to it one way or another." She picked up the front section of the local paper, looked at it for a few minutes, put it down, and asked. "Aaron, what do you think about Preston Blackstone?"

"Ah, yes, Preston Blackstone," he replied, smiling, "an absolutely splendid individual, I may say. A rawthah pleasant chap, for certain!" Naomi laughed at his attempt to sound British.

"I think he's about to marry my mother. What do we think about that?"

"I say more power to 'em. They would make an utterly delightful, magnificent couple." Naomi laughed again.

"I've thought a lot about this, Aaron. What a difference the last year and half has made. Ever since we met that night... out by the river, a year ago last spring. Natty and I were baptized. I married the perfect man! Natty and Ben got married, I think they're expecting a baby. She hasn't said anything to me about it, yet, though."

"Are you jealous of her?"

"Oh, gosh. I really haven't had time to think about it. But Mom was so lonely until Preston showed up. I'll bet none of this would have happened if you hadn't come along and found me walking along the highway by the river that night. I feel that the Lord has really blessed us. Wouldn't you say so?" She gazed at him in silent admiration and they kissed softly.

"Indeed, I would." A fairly recent movie called "The Sting" had already begun to play on the television.

* * *

In Bend, Oregon, John "Chuck" and Cora Moranski were likewise settled into their motel room for the night. The several drinks they'd consumed at the bar next door helped them relax and more serenely reflect on their situation. Their tan Chevrolet four-door sedan with Idaho plates was parked in front of their door. The previous owner had absent-mindedly, or ignorantly, allowed them to drive away with his plates on the car, the registration papers in the glove box, and the "signed-off" Idaho title for $3,000.00 in cash. With any luck at all, as Cora had wanted, they could make it to the Oregon Coast in just a few days, assume new identities, and find a new life in some little town, or maybe drift south toward southern California. If they were ever stopped by the police, John Moranski would just say that they were the registered owners, but he had run off and left his wallet at home. They would simply say that, "The trip was just a 'spur of the moment' thing."

John Moranski, having decided that he preferred being called "Chuck," at least for the time being, had taken an opportunity along the way to call some of his eastern contacts and apprise them of his changed status and let them know that he was still available should any needs arise--anywhere, anytime. Strangely, when he tried to call the man he knew only as "Rube" in the Chicago area, a woman answered the phone and, sounding somewhat irritated, said she didn't know anybody named Rube. That was strange, since the double hit-job in Utah had been paid for by the Chicago group. Moranski tried the number again, thinking that he must have mis-dialed. The same woman answered and yelled obscenities at him and slammed the receiver down. "What the...! What was that all about?" he muttered to himself.

In spite of Cora's urging, he could not fully dismiss the deputy sheriff from southern Utah from his mind. He struggled almost constantly between the grip of paranoia and his obsession with completing what he had failed to finish in the pool behind the Ruby Springs Lodge. How, he wondered, had the Utah cops come to suspect him in the double murders in the Washington County jail? He had no idea. But then, did they? Really? Even when the female deputy had arrested him, nothing had been said to him about any other crimes. And no federal officers showed up with arrest warrants. But still, his fingerprints were everywhere in the lodge and the Jackson police would--or somebody would--surely have his prints checked against those in the FBI's old booking documents back in New Jersey.

He knew he was too scared about it and, furthermore, almost continually dwelling on it in his mind didn't help at all. Maybe when they were settled into the new life that Cora talked about so much, he could take care of that woman cop from Utah. He'd plan it--and carry it out--quietly, and get it done before Cora could object. Then, again, why should he even tell her about it?

As they contentedly settled in to watch "The Sting" on the television, Cora commented, "I hope we can spend some time at that Crater Lake tomorrow. I've heard it's so beautiful there."

"Yeah... guess it is," Chuck replied absently.

"It's pretty high up there, though. I hope the roads are open. Speaking of lakes, I can't help but keep thinking of our good old Mercury. I can close my eyes and still see it going through the ice and sinking into that lake. I shudder to think about it. I really hated to lose that car."

Chuck couldn't help but express his relief at seeing it disappear by cursing under his breath. "I was beginning to worry the ice on the lake might hold it up!" he exclaimed with a grin. "Maybe somebody'll see the tracks in the snow and think there's got to be somebody in the car that made the tracks."

"I'm sure somebody'll eventually fish it out. How deep d'you think the water is? And couldn't somebody identify the car and trace it to us?"

"Well, maybe in time," Chuck responded. "But I took off the plates and the serial number from the dashboard. I doubt they could do it in time to be of any problem for us. As cold as it is, the ice has probably covered the hole by now and more snow has likely covered the tracks. They'll probably wait 'til spring comes to fish it out, anyway."

"I like your hair that way," she commented while playfully running her fingers through it as they reclined against the pillows. "It was getting too long, anyway. Besides, I always liked dark brown hair on a man."

He smiled to himself. "I like yours, too. You look real good with the honey-colored hair... makes you look... um, maybe twenty years younger."

"Oh, yeah... the gray was starting to show too much, wasn't it. You're right. It was time to give it a little help, anyway."

CHAPTER TWENTY-TWO

A good night's sleep helped a lot. Aaron woke up quietly and lay still listening to Naomi's deep, steady breathing in the semi-darkness. It was getting lighter outside and it would be a long day of travel. Better get underway, he resolved.

The short-cut from Rexburg on a south-easterly route took them through miles and miles of farm land along and across the Snake River to Idaho 26, and up along the Swan Valley to the huge Palisades Reservoir. Feeling that there was really nothing better to do, Naomi drove east toward Wyoming along the edge of the reservoir until they realized that going farther was pointless. She turned the truck around and retraced their travel for some distance until they came back to the tiny town of Irwin, which boasted a single combination service station and diner.

Aaron scanned the parking lot, hoping to see something of interest. A Bonneville County sheriff's car caught his attention. "Maybe we ought to take a break and talk to the deputy for a few minutes," he said. "What do you think?"

"Okay, sure, why not?" Naomi pulled off the highway into the parking lot. A tow-truck was parked near the sheriff's car with a white sedan in tow. They both looked at the car for any damage.

"*Hey!*" she exclaimed. "*That's it! That's their Mercury! Look at it!*" Aaron sat up straight and stared at the sedan, which had several streaks of ice running vertically from under the doors.

"Is that it? Are you sure?"

"C'mon, let's go in and talk to the deputy. Look! The plates are gone... it's gotta be the one!" They walked around and inspected the car for a few minutes before the cold breeze drove them inside.

Introductions and friendly greetings were exchanged with the deputy and the tow-truck operator who were seated at a table near the front windows. Some ice fishermen had reported seeing the tire tracks leading down the gravelly "beach" to what had obviously been the sinking of a car. Fresh, new ice with a light layer of new snow on it had covered the hole before the morning of the day before. It had taken most of the day to find a pair of divers willing to go down in the 45 feet of freezing water, wearing insulated wet-suits, to attach a cable to the bumper. A very large tow-truck had been needed to drag the car through the ice to the gently sloping rocky shore.

Naomi repeated for the deputy, who seemed to be getting more excited as she spoke, the long story involving the car and John and Cora Moranski. "Well, I'm sure that's the right car," she said. "They would have had to get another one first, though. We've figured they would have most likely bought one from a private owner, probably not very far from here."

"We've been checking the want-ads in the papers," Aaron added, who was, once again, excited and encouraged about making some progress. "We figured on checking the Idaho Falls papers before we have to go back home tonight."

"At least we know they came this way," Naomi added. "I'm sure the feds will be interested in that."

"It sure appears that way," said the Idaho deputy. "But we'd maybe better run the VIN number, just to make sure it's the one you're looking for."

"Yeah, you're right," Aaron said. "But I noticed the number from the dash is gone."

"Uh, huh, we'll take it into the shop and see if we can find another one under the hood. Why don't you guys give me a call in a couple of hours at the SO? We should know one way or another by then. And then, I'll get in touch with the FBI and Jackson PD."

"Sounds good!" Aaron answered. "In the meantime, we'll head into Idaho Falls and see if we can find any recent private sales of late-model cars."

"I'll bet they would've picked some kind of bland-looking sedan

like this one," said Naomi, "one that wouldn't stand out, you know...
like maybe a *lime-green Blazer!*" She and Aaron laughed at her
"suggestion" about the Blazer.

"... private joke," Aaron said with a grin. "It's a long story. They'd
probably look for some white four-door... one that would just blend
right in with the other traffic."

"That's a real good idea," the deputy replied. "I doubt I would
have thought to do that. Dang! That really makes a lot of sense." He
turned to the tow-truck operator. "Don't you think so, Duane?"

"Oh, yeah, it does," the truck driver replied, grinning, as though he
was surprised and pleased to be included in the conversation. "I'd say
that's real good thinking!"

Back in the truck, Aaron headed quickly for Idaho Falls. Before
many miles had passed, Naomi asked him, "Wasn't it kind of dumb to
run their car out onto the ice, that way?"

"Yeah, I was just thinking the same thing. What if the ice hadn't
broke?"

"But, even as it was, a big hole in the ice would be sure to grab
people's attention... and the tire tracks. It must have been just on a
sudden impulse... something they hadn't really thought through.
Moranski can obviously be very clever but sometimes he seems to go
with his first dumb idea... like putting brown hair in the wig he wore
and leaving it where investigators could find it... then not even
thinking about any blond hair that could be left in his trousers."

After another mile or so in silence, Naomi spoke again. "But
maybe like the brown hair in the wig... Maybe by putting the car in
'drive' and running it out onto the ice, he intended to send the message
that they were heading west when they really weren't. Maybe they've
doubled back on us! Maybe they got another car and they're really on
their way to Denver. They could even be there now... or anywhere!"

* * *

Not long after two in the afternoon, Aaron and Naomi were
running out of possibilities. They had checked out six recent private
car sales in the Idaho Falls area and were losing hope. The last two
they planned to follow up on would put them on the west side of the

city and into the farm land, in an area referred to in one of the ads as "New Sweden."

An elderly farmer, a Mr. Jenson, was expecting them. The man was quite conversational and related how "Mama" had recently and quite suddenly died of pneumonia. "So there wasn't any reason to keep the Chevy." He paused to wipe this eyes and blow his nose with a red handkerchief while they patiently waited. He didn't seem to quite understand why they would have come to inquire about a car that had already been sold.

"We're actually trying to find the man who bought the car from you," Naomi explained, patiently. She drew the grainy photograph from her purse and showed to the man. He excused himself and quickly left them to look for his glasses. He was gone for a few minutes.

"He surely is a trusting soul. Doesn't seem to see very well," Aaron remarked. "I'll bet she did most of the driving."

"You're probably right," Naomi replied. The man returned and looked at the photograph.

"Well, you know, that could be the man, all right. But my grandson was here. He could do a better job of recognizing the man. It was close to being dark when they came, you know... couple of days ago."

"Was there a woman with him?" Naomi asked.

"Ya, somebody was in that white car with him, I remember that. Didn't even get out of the car, that I recollect. He didn't even bother to drive the Chevrolet... just started the engine and listened to it. I don't think it had more'n eight thousand miles on it. Well, maybe a few more. But he seemed glad to have it, all right."

This greatly bolstered their hopes. "Where can we find your grandson, Brother Jenson?" Aaron asked, with confidence rising. "Does he live here with you?"

"Oh, he don't live here. Should be coming along pretty soon, though, and the granddaughter, too. They help me with the chores, you know. They'll be a comin' on the bus, right away."

"If you don't mind," Naomi said, "we'd like to stay a while and talk to them. Can you tell us any more about the car that you just sold?"

"Well, sure," the man replied. "I should even have a picture of it somewhere. We bought it just about four years ago, didn't drive it much, you know. Mostly to church and to town and back. Maybe I can find them fancy brochures the dealer gave us. It was a light color... tan, maybe, I guess you'd call it."

"Do you remember the plate number?" Aaron asked.

"Ya, I think I've got it somewhere here in the kitchen drawer, where we keep all the junk that collects over the years." Brother Jenson retrieved a large manila envelope from the drawer and proceeded to lay its contents on the kitchen table for them. From the original 1970 brochures there was a good likeness of the car. The Idaho license number appeared on several gas receipts.

"Here comes the boy, now," said the old man. "I'll get him in here to talk to you." A boy of maybe eleven or twelve years of age and a girl a little younger--both of them the picture of fair, youthful Scandinavia--burst through the front door, eager to see who was visiting their grandfather in the truck with Utah plates. They both agreed that the picture strongly resembled the man who had bought the Chevrolet.

"The only problem," said the boy, "is that this guy had dark hair. It was shorter. And he had this funny accent. Not like he came from another country or anything. But it sounded kind of different."

"Yeah, it was real different," echoed the girl. "Like he didn't know how to talk real good." The visitors smiled at each other.

"What about the white car they came in?" Naomi asked, still smiling at what the girl had said. "What make of car was it."

"It was a Mercury!" the boy exclaimed. "And the woman in it had kinda yellowish hair."

"Yeah, she had honey-blonde hair!" the girl said.

Aaron smiled, remembering when he, as a boy, knew all the car makes and models. "Sounds like they just switched hair colors. Did I mention they were clever people," he said to Naomi.

"Was there anything unusual about your car, the tan Chevrolet?" Naomi asked. "Any dents or maybe primer spots or any broken windows?"

"Oh, ya," the boy said. "The windshield had a little crack in the corner, on the right side, right in the bottom corner. It always bugged me when I was riding there in the front seat."

The little girl added, "And the back bumper has a dent in it. Grandma let my brother back it out of the driveway one day and he backed right into a post!"

"Well," the boy retorted. "It's just a little dent!"

"My gosh, Brother Jenson," Naomi said. "You've been so much help for us. Would it be okay if we kept the brochures of the car and this service receipt with the plate number on it?"

"Can't see any reason why I would need to keep 'em," he replied. "Now that Mama's gone... " His voice choked to a soft whisper and he couldn't complete the sentence. Naomi put her arm around his thin shoulders and drew him close to her for a moment in silence.

"Thanks a lot," she said, quietly. "You've been *so* helpful. Thank you, so much!"

"And you, too," said Aaron to the boy and the girl. "We really appreciate it."

From the farm, Aaron drove directly to the sheriff's office in Idaho Falls. They shared what they had learned with the deputy they'd met earlier, along with a detective. "Let me see if an FBI agent is available, right now," the deputy said. "They'll need to know right away about the Moranskis switching cars!"

"My guess is..." said Naomi, "they'll likely keep on going west to the coast of Oregon. Course they could be anywhere, even on their way to Utah... or they could even be there already." She glanced at Aaron. "But I don't think so. Do you, Aaron?"

"I really doubt it."

* * *

Naomi took over driving south in the late afternoon on Friday. Her first impulse was to stop at the first public phone and place a call to Jon Gates, the special agent for the FBI whose territory was the southern half of Utah. She felt eager to get the word out as soon as possible on the probable route of the Moranskis and a description of the car, that they would be driving, including the Idaho license plates. But she suddenly remembered Shane's patient admonitions and decided she should call him instead.

It was time to stop for gas again. So while Aaron filled the truck's gas tank, she placed a collect call to the sheriff's office. Shane was not in the office, so she spoke to Ian Cooper.

"Hey, Sheriff!" she began, suddenly wondering what he might think of her and Aaron making the trip to Idaho without saying anything to anyone there. "This is Naomi."

"Oh, yes, Naomi, what can I do for you?"

"Aaron and I are in Idaho Falls. We came up here in hopes of finding out which way the Moranskis went from Jackson." She paused, expecting either a compliment or remonstrance from Ian. But he was silent. "Well, guess what? We're pretty sure we did!"

"*You did!?*" Ian exclaimed. "On your days off? Well, so what did you find out?" Naomi related all the details of the Moranskis' escape into Idaho, the ditching of the Mercury, the car they had bought just outside Idaho Falls, and where she and Aaron figured they'd likely be going.

"You're not making this up!?" Ian exclaimed. "You're not joking? Are you?"

"No, no! I'm not, really!" she insisted, while laughing. "We're on our way back, now. I was about to call Jon Gates in Provo, but I figured I'd ought to talk to you or Shane first. The FBI up here knows all the details, already. We talked to them. Of course, they said they were working on the same theory and probably would have got the same information if they hadn't been so busy!" She and Ian had a little laugh about that.

"Don't tell anybody I said this," Ian told her, "but the FBI can be a real nuisance, sometimes. Maybe a 'necessary evil'."

"Okay!" Naomi answered, laughing. "Anyway, the Moranskis'll likely be wanting a big change of scenery, you know. Probably the west coast, wouldn't you think?"

"Well, yes, very possibly. Especially after Jackson Hole. I'll talk to Shane and decide on our next move. We'll make sure this info goes out all through the western states. But then these people are pretty slick, you know, they might even find a way to get into Canada. You just never know."

"Looks like Aaron's got the gas tank filled. I'd better get going. See you tomorrow, I guess."

"Okay. Hey, Naomi. Good job! I'll see that the county pays for your gas... and the motel, too. And I'll see that you get some comp time for it."

"Oh, well, thanks a lot, Sheriff. Bye."

* * *

Aaron was able to doze a little along the way and felt somewhat refreshed and awake by the time they got to Provo, where the gas tank needed to be replenished. He drove on through the night all the way to Cedar City where Naomi decided to wake up for the remainder of the trip to Toquerville. On their arrival, Nero, having been confined to the barn with adequate food and water, recognized the sound of the truck and began to raise a royal ruckus and wouldn't stop until they rescued him. He literally jumped into their arms, one after the other, as though he hadn't seen them for months.

* * *

They awoke not long after eight o'clock, Saturday morning to a loudly ringing telephone. "That'll be my mother," Naomi yawned and remarked as the phone continued to ring. "I'd better get it. She's probably been trying to get us for the last two days."

She was right. Becky had been letting the phone ring a long time, Thursday and Friday, thinking they might be outside looking after the animals or working on remodeling the barn.

"Hello," Naomi answered, still feeling tired and somewhat grungy from having simply collapsed into the bed after a long day and a good share of the night.

"It's your Mom! Where have you people been? I've been trying to call you for two days. Have you been up to Parowan? I was beginning to think you were... well, never mind that. Where have you been, anyway?"

"We, well, we took a quick trip to Idaho. Just got back really late, well, early this morning. I guess the sheriff didn't mention it to you. I called him yesterday before we left to come back home. We found out which way the Moranskis lit out, and the car they're driving now.

Let me tell you all about it later. Maybe I'll drop by this afternoon. Anyway, we'll both be there for dinner tomorrow."

"Well, okay," Becky said in resignation. "But I have a bit of news, too. Guess what? Preston has... " She paused for several seconds.

Naomi grinned in anticipation. "Well? Preston has... what?" she asked. "Has... what, Mom?"

"Preston has decided... he wants to be baptized. Right away. And he's been trying to persuade me to do it, too. And he hasn't even heard all the lessons yet."

"Hey, that's great, Mom!" Naomi replied. "That would be wonderful. I can't wait to tell Aaron. When will that be happening?"

"Probably quite soon, I guess. There's some paperwork to be taken care of, and all that."

"That will be so wonderful. But I thought you were going to tell me something else. Are you sure there isn't *something more* you have to tell us?"

"Oh, well... gee. What on earth would that be?"

"You know very well what I'm talking about. What about the marriage thing? You know, you and Preston? How about it?"

"Oh, that." Becky answered, feigning indifference. "Well, we might get around to that, too. He wouldn't want me to go into a lot of detail before we get it all figured out, though."

"Well, sure. I understand," Naomi responded, still smiling. "That will be so nice. I know it's been a lonely time for you."

* * *

"Washington, this is Two-eighty-nine," Aaron spoke into the microphone as he left home. "I'll be ten-eight, at Toquerville. Any contact with One-six-two?"

"He's working in the canyon today. Let me see... One-six-two, ten-twenty?"

"One-six-two, I'm at Anderson Junction, north-bound. I'm off in about an hour."

"Washington, ten-four," Aaron answered. "I'll meet him in about three minutes." Dan and Aaron switched channels.

"Hey, Dan, let's stop in at Bud's for a few minutes. I've got some news for you. Have you seen Johnny around today?" Before Dan answered, a third voice joined in.

"I'm in Cedar City," Johnny Lee broke in. "Mind if I join y'all? I'm on a contact right now. Give me fifteen minutes."

"Hey, come on down, Johnny," said Aaron. "I need to tell you guys all about my weekend!"

CHAPTER TWENTY-THREE

Around four o'clock, Ian Cooper and Shane Lowry made a special Saturday visit to the sheriff's office to meet with Aaron and Naomi. Sgt. Walden stopped by for the conference, also. It was brief, but Aaron and Naomi related all of the details they could remember. The others marveled at what the husband and wife team had learned in Idaho and repeatedly congratulated them.

"Just one thing," Ian repeated, "I know you're both young and eager and all that... and, of course, I can understand there's some personal motivation here, and that's partly why I'm telling you this. But before you go off on any more trips to find these people, please coordinate with Sgt. Lowry and me, *FIRST!*"

Aaron leaned back in his swivel chair with a halfway sheepish grin on his face and said apologetically, "Well, okay, I, and probably Naomi, too... We're definitely ticked off at these people! *Like, royally!*" Aaron stopped grinning and leaned forward. His voice choked slightly. "He tried to kill her, you know! And she had him! Right there in Jackson! He'd be locked up right now, somewhere, if the FBI hadn't tried to keep their stupid information quiet... just so they could get the credit! For cryin' out loud!"

"You're right, you're right," Walden remarked after a few seconds. "We're only asking you to coordinate... coordinate with the rest of us! Nobody's saying you two didn't do a fine job. Hey, if you hadn't gone up there and found out what car they're probably driving now and a personal description, changing hair colors and all that! Without that, nobody'd have a clue!"

"It was a fine piece of detective work," Shane added. "But we all need to operate as a team! That's all we're saying, Aaron. But... it's like you said before... where did they go from there? ... after they got the car from that farmer?"

Naomi quietly and calmly absorbed what the others were saying. She realized that most of their remarks were directed at Aaron--as though it had all been his doing. They seldom even looked in her direction. Were the men maybe dismissing her, in their sub-conscious minds anyway? Some of the blame for the Moranskis' escape was rightly hers. Several "if-onlys" ran through her mind, again. If only she'd maintained a tighter grip on his wrist and used her feet to propel them both to the surface of the pool where she could breath. If only she'd been able to rip the breathing apparatus from his mouth, it would have forced him to come up for air, too. If only she'd gotten out of the pool immediately after he broke free, she would have been able to run after him, at least keeping him in view before he disappeared into his apartment. If only she hadn't made the premature arrest, they could have watched him around the clock all night and then the FBI agents would have been able to arrest them both.

Her mind began to wander even further from the situation at hand. Lately, she reflected, thoughts of small children, maybe three or four years of age, maybe a blond boy and a girl with brown hair had quietly stolen into her mind. The little ones looked up at her with wide smiles. They were such attractive children and they were very smart and well behaved at church and loved their father and mother so much. And she and Aaron loved them. Maybe she'd just stumbled into this "man's world" by mistake and now... was it soon time to get out?

"Anyway," Ian remarked with some finality, looking around at the others. "At this point it doesn't appear that there's anything any of *us* can do. Your assumption is likely correct, they would probably have continued on west into Oregon and maybe down the coast to where the climate's warmer."

"I think you're right, Sheriff," Shane said. "After spending winters in Jackson, for... I wouldn't know how many years, they'd probably want to find someplace warmer." He paused briefly before going on. "Still the man seems to me to be the type who wouldn't just walk away and forget things. I'm betting he just might be obsessive enough... and crazy enough to come down here."

"What do you mean?" Walden asked. "Why would he do that? He'd have to be crazy! We have his picture! And a description of their car! He'd have to be crazy to do that."

"Yes, he would," Shane answered. "But he tried to kill Naomi and failed. The man is a professional killer, after all. And his wife could be, too. There's no telling what they might decide to do. And, besides that, they don't know that anybody has a good description of the car they're driving, now. I'm just saying we'd all better keep a sharp eye out for the Moranskis for a while."

* * *

The meeting broke up and everyone went their separate ways. Aaron and Naomi agreed to meet later at their favorite place for a sandwich. In a reflective mood, Naomi drove west from St. George to patrol the western reaches of the county. It would be good to make contact with Whitney Greyhorse and just maybe forget about the Moranskis for while. He would ask her about them, of course.

She stopped at the small grocery store on the reservation. The woman taking care of the store was unable to contact Whitney on the radio and invited Naomi to use the telephone to call his house. He answered, saying that he had been busy with some boy scouts on a Saturday's merit badge project but agreed to meet her there at the store.

For a few minutes they discussed what had been happening in his jurisdiction. Just routine problems. Nothing he hadn't been able to handle as the only police officer on the sparsely-populated reservation. Eventually they got around to talking about what she'd been involved in.

"So, as of now," Naomi told him, "it appears the Moranskis have maybe vanished for good, unless some police officer, somewhere, stumbles onto them. Given their history, it shouldn't take them long to have new names and a new life."

"I wonder what my grandfather would have to say about that," said Whitney.

"Your grandfather?" Naomi asked with growing interest. "What kind of insights would he have?"

"Well, maybe not especially pertaining to the Moranskis. But a lot of times he'll come out with some really interesting advice or wisdom that can shed some light on problems that I've had. What do you think? Want to pay him a visit?"

"Well... okay. We've got nothing to lose. Let's talk to him."

The shadows were long in the St. George Basin, as they departed the store and drove in two vehicles toward the grandfather's house. The winter sun was dipping behind the Beaver Dam Mountains. The dim lamp light seemed to strain to get out from old man's small, smudged windows.

After she was introduced to Nathaniel Greyhorse, Whitney conversed with the man in their native language. They paused now and then and laughed, which baffled Naomi. With some apparent finality, and with animated gestures and facial expressions, the grandfather launched into a long and somber discourse to Whitney, only occasionally glancing at Naomi. It's happening again, she said to herself.

After a few minutes, the dialogue between the men subsided and Nathaniel became more quiet and smiling.

"Well, okay," Naomi asked as they sat in her car. "So what did he have to say?"

"At first he thought it was a funny story," Whitney said. "I'm not sure why. Maybe it was the part about finding hair in the guy's pants. And your friend, Preston, Ol' 007... what he did. But then I told him the man tried to drown you, and he got pretty serious after that part of the story."

"So what words of wisdom did he offer as to where to go from here? That's what I'm interested in, right now."

"Well, he gave me this big, long spiel about some animals, I guess. I'm not real sure what he was getting at."

"But what did he say, Whitney? Come on, tell me."

"Well, to sum it all up, he just said that the badger can never become friendly; the snake can shed his skin, but he's still a snake; but then, he said, 'If you walk through a spider's web and break it up, she'll always go and build another one, almost the same as the first one'."

Naomi smiled in uneasy amusement. "So what do we know that we didn't know before?"

"Maybe it's like we learned way back in the police academy, you know. They said criminals get into habits... 'M-O'... 'method of operation'... *'modus operandi'*... they called it. He's liable to just go on doing what he's been doing."

"So," Naomi responded, "the Moranskis are most likely going to end up doing the same sort of thing, like managing a hotel or something, like they did in Jackson?"

"Yeah, that, and probably hiring out on hit jobs like they did at the jail."

"That makes sense. That would be a good angle to pursue. I'll talk with Shane about it."

Suddenly a voice on the radio broke into their conversation. "Seven-ten, this is St. George. Seven-ten, can you head up to Pine Valley? We have a report of a missing hiker. See if you can meet a party at the trail-head, up from the campground area."

"Seven-ten copied," Naomi replied. "I'm at Shivwits, now. Would you tell Two-eighty-nine to cancel our appointment?"

"Ten-four. He's here in the office right now."

* * *

By early Saturday evening Chuck and Cora Moranski had driven to Medford, Oregon, on Interstate-5. They had enjoyed the beauty of the Crater Lake area, but the cold temperatures and the presence of snow on nearby Mt. Scott reminded them too much of Jackson. The cold, clear air was a great incentive to seek a lower altitude and a warmer climate. It helped them decide to head south from Medford, at least as far as Crescent City, California. At Medford they strolled a few blocks to a nearby bar where they could relax over a few drinks. Along the way, a police car passed on the main street, and they stopped walking and turned toward a large department store window, watching the officer drive by in the reflection.

Cora picked up a local newspaper from the bar and brought it to their motel room. She spread the paper on the small desk and looked for obituaries. "I think we should be looking for some new names and get the car re-registered. This little vacation is awfully nice, but I'm getting nervous, driving around with that farmer's plates on the car."

"Yeah," Chuck replied. He'd begun watching a movie on the television. "We should get it done here in Oregon and then move on down the coast... maybe way down even past San Francisco. They say it's nice and warm down there."

"Here's a woman about my age. Died just three days ago over in Applegate."

"Are all the details there? Birth date? Parent's names? All that stuff?"

"Yeah, it's all right here. The name's Mona Rae Wallace Sherman. She was married to a Norval Sherman, who, it says here 'preceded her in death.' Whoa, talk about a slow pitch!"

"Hey! You ain't gonna call me Norval. 'Chuck' is just fine! Was she born in Oregon?"

"Yeah, right there in Applegate. Let's take this up to Salem on Monday and get it done. I'm starting to get really nervous!"

"Okay, we'll get it done. And the sooner, the better."

He said nothing about it, knowing how Cora would react, but he thought almost constantly of that woman cop from southern Utah. The one who knew his face so well, who had been watching him for several days, who had been watching and waiting--but for what? Surely she wouldn't have been there by herself! And if they'd had any evidence, why didn't they arrest me right away? Several "if-onlys" crossed his mind--again and again. If only he had taken an arm-lock on her neck in the pool instead of merely pulling her down by her bathing suit. If only he'd taken her out by some other method. Maybe he should have simply left Jackson and not tried to kill her. But then, drowning would leave no evidence! That's for sure! It made him angry. Still, he said nothing to Cora about it. She'd just nag him to "get over it." He'd take care of it later. After all, he knew exactly where to find her. And then there was that crazy old Aussie. What if he wasn't a genuine Australian, from...? What did he say? Sydney? Brisbane? He had a convincing act, all right! But why? What about him? Who was he anyway? Her father? An uncle? Maybe he would have to be dealt with in some way, too. He would give it all a lot of thought.

A Sunday visit to the Applegate cemetery yielded Norval Sherman's birth and death dates. From these they were able to find his obituary in the newspaper archives on Monday.

* * *

Sunday evening found Preston and Becky, attending a "singles fireside" at the Stake Center in Bloomington. The speaker gave a fascinating summary of the westward trek, the home life, and the spiritual atmosphere of the family of Lucy Mack and Joseph Smith, Sr. and of the religious re-awakening that had taken place in the vicinity of western New York in the early 1800s. Becky was a little surprised at how many of the attendees she knew as they mingled afterward for the traditional refreshments. She thought she detected some amount of envy among her female acquaintances as she introduced Preston. His proper British accent and impeccable graciousness seemed to have them thoroughly charmed.

Back at her split-level home they settled on the couch. Wasting no time on small talk, Preston turned to her. "Becky, I've decided to thoroughly commit... both to you and to being baptized."

His sudden directness startled her and she kept silent while clutching his hands. "I'm quite prepared to establish a baptismal date with the mission'ries, now. And I would be simply enthralled to confirm a date for you and me, too. I want to marry you, Becky," he said softly. "I love you!"

"Oh, Preston. I just wasn't expecting this, so soon. I hadn't really thought about... about a particular date." She raised her face up to his and they exchanged a kiss. "Let me think about a date. Do you think I should wear your ring now?"

"I'd be greatly honored if you would wear it," he replied, and kissed her again, somewhat longer this time.

"Last week I had a long talk with the bishop in this ward. I told him all about you and everything. He was quite encouraging, but he said I should 'study it out in my mind' and then pray for guidance. If it wasn't right, the feeling would go away and I would begin to have strong doubts."

"Has it happened to you? Did you do that?"

"Yes, I did, and my love for you has only increased, if anything."

"Good. I'm ready when you are!"

"Okay, Preston. Let's look at a calendar."

CHAPTER TWENTY-FOUR

Just before noon on Monday, Shane Lowry put in a call to the crime laboratory at Weber State College. The phone was answered by the criminalistics laboratory supervisor, Dr. Ernest Hunter, whom Shane had never actually met. After introductions were made, Shane broached the subject of the double murder inside the jail in Washington County, nearly eighteen months before, and briefly summarized the events of the past several weeks. This led to the question he wanted to ask of Dr. Hunter.

"One of your assistants, Margaret Radowicz, mentioned that you had told her about a journal article on the study of DNA, as a possible method of making a positive identification of individuals, possibly applying it to crime scene investigations."

"So you're thinking," said the supervisor, "that a DNA comparison of hair root cells from this guy's trousers, or maybe his comb, with those he left in the dumpster would positively pin it on him?"

"Exactly! That's the idea! Well, I guess you could say it would be great circumstantial evidence, anyway."

"Well, in theory, it would apparently be feasible, all right. But I don't know how fast the technology is coming along. In the journal article I was reading, it was just a short reference in one paragraph. It mentioned some place in England. Some researcher by the name of Jeffries, I think, was mentioned."

Shane's pulse quickened at the thought. "This is some coincidence, but I happen to have a friend, who lives right here in the county, with some great connections in England! If he's going to be making a trip over... "

"Whoa! Whoa! No kidding! That could work out... it all depends. Let me make some phone calls and see what I can find out. If he goes over there, maybe he could follow through on it. No doubt the article I saw has stirred a lot of interest all around the world. They'll be getting lots of inquiries, that's for sure."

"Yeah, I see what you mean," Shane replied, settling back in his chair. "Let me know as soon as you find out anything, okay?"

"I'll do that, Shane. And I'll try to see if there's any DNA research going on in the U.S., in the meantime."

* * *

Shortly after two o'clock, Shane was still involved in his reports on other cases. Naomi Gentry walked into the detectives' office and approached. He looked up and greeted her with a smile.

"How's it going?" Naomi said. "Anything new?"

"Oh, well maybe. I called the lab up in Ogden, a while ago. The director... Ernest Hunter's his name... he was there and he was telling me some more about the DNA stuff. He said he'd read about some research going on in England. He thought it sounded like they could be on the verge of a breakthrough for using it a lot in criminalistics."

"Did you say England? Are you thinking what I'm thinking?"

"Well, my first thought, when he mentioned England, was about our man, Preston. He's seems willing to do anything we might ask... and maybe a whole lot more!"

"Well, guess what. I think he and our Becky are about to get hitched. She told me he wanted to take her over there this spring, after it warms up a little."

"No kidding. Well, the sly old fox! Good for him! Good for them! She has seemed really happy today. Like she had some kind of secret. I didn't notice her hands, though. What? Has she got a ring and all that?"

"Oh, yes! And they're probably going to be baptized pretty soon, too. Preston's really gung-ho about it. And Mom is, um, going along with it. I'm sure she'll do fine, if she ever gets over the old grudges. I think she just needs a push from the right person."

"Preston's certainly the right person. I really like him. Simply an absolutely splendid, individual, I'd say." They both laughed at that.

"On another subject... I went with Whitney Greyhorse to see his grandfather, Nathaniel, out on the reservation. He's such a character. Whitney told him the story about what happened in Jackson, about Preston and me and Aaron. Well, 'grandfather' just laughed until it came to the part where ol' Chuck tried to drown me. Then he was all serious about it."

"So what was the old man's sage advice?" Shane asked, smiling.

"Well, he said something like, 'the badger can never be friendly and a snake can shed his skin, but he'll still be a snake.' Then he said, something about the spider... Oh... yeah. If you tear down a spider's web, she'll put up another one just like it."

"That all makes sense. Sounds like he's trying to tell us that the Moranskis will most likely be looking for the same kind of set-up, like the deal they had going in Jackson. Hey, maybe we should hire the old man, what do you think?"

"That's what I've been thinking. He could just hang out here and give out strange advice. But we'd have to get Whitney to interpret for us. So possibly... these Moranskis will be getting new names, and so on, just like they did before. And they'll be looking for jobs managing a hotel or something close to that. And taking on hit jobs on the side."

"Maybe I'll call Jon Gates, and suggest the FBI might pursue that theory. I'll bet anything, they're going to wind up in southern California."

"Good idea. Of course, he'll just say they were thinking the same thing, if not already pursuing it. I doubt *they'd* share anything *they've* come up with."

"Yeah, I'm sure. But as far as hit jobs go, the Moranskis could very well be out of business if the crime bosses ever find out we've pretty much identified him as our suspect-in-chief."

"I'll bet there's some way the FBI could use their informants to spread the word about our man, 'Chucky.' That would put them out of business, for sure."

"Oh, yeah. Hey, I knew right away you had good instincts for investigation. But I still say you'd better keep a sharp eye for a while. There's no telling how bad or how long ol' Chuck might hold on to a fixation about you. Just going on some of the things we've learned about him, that guy makes me think... he's maybe one bulb short of a chandelier, you know? I just have this feeling that won't go away, that he might try to come around and... Well, you just be extra cautious, for a while. Okay?"

"Okay, I will, Shane. I really appreciate your concern, but I'm sure I'll be fine."

* * *

Bureaucracies are often characterized as being slow and clumsy. One 'hand' is often said to be unaware of what the other 'hand' may be doing. Before the death certificate for Mona Rae Wallace Sherman of Applegate, Oregon, had been sent and recorded with the authorities in Salem, a replacement birth certificate had been issued. And with the new birth certificate in her possession, Cora Moranski--now Mona Rae Wallace Sherman--was able to obtain a duplicate driver's license, bearing her new name, after certifying that the original was lost. After several days in the Salem and Portland areas, they returned to the Bureau of Vital Statistics and driver licensing authority and worked a similar scheme in order to provide a 'legitimate' identity for Chuck in the name of Norval Sherman.

At Coos Bay, again using cash, they traded the tan Chevrolet for a newer Buick. Since the car they were trading in was from another state, the sales manager mentioned that he had to summon a police officer in order to verify the "VIN number" and Idaho registration. "Norval 'Chuck' Sherman" froze inwardly at the thought and he impulsively turned and stood up as if preparing to flee. "Mona Rae" impulsively moved beside him and took his hand just as the officer's car arrived.

She exhibited a calm demeanor as the young officer performed the routine task. But then the officer decided to try a phone call to the previous owners. "Just to be on the safe side," he said. Using the dealer's phone he obtained the number from the Idaho information operator and proceeded to dial the Idaho Falls number. It was all so routine, yet the newly reincarnated Norval Sherman was sweating the proverbial bullets. With palms cold and clammy and innards cramping, he fought the urge to saunter outside and disappear, while Mona Rae was sitting passively with one leg crossed over the other and swinging it slightly.

"Looks like everything is in order," the officer announced to the sales manager after speaking to the Idaho farmer's daughter. "She couldn't remember the name of the party they sold the car to. She figured it was just some guy and his wife who, she seemed to recall, were visiting from another state. Must have been Oregon, I guess. According to the daughter. Said it was just a cash deal. That's all she knew."

"Hey, thanks, officer," the manager answered. The buyers breathed easier--for a few seconds. The sales manager turned to them as the officer departed. "And where should we request to have your new license plates sent?" Chuck and Mona Rae looked blankly at each other. "Is there an address or post office box in Applegate?"

"We, uh," Mona Rae began, while forcing a smile. "We're... You might say we're in transition, we're actually leaving Applegate pretty soon, probably for California. We're not sure where we'll get to." Chuck gave her a look of concern, obviously annoyed that she had given away too much information, yet he could think of nothing to offer, himself.

The friendly sales manager gave them a way out. "Tell you what we can do then, folks. I'll give you a twenty-day temporary Oregon registration and when you get to where you're going you can re-do the registration there." The Sherman's breathed easier again. "Sure," the manager continued. "That'll work just fine, no matter where you go."

"That sounds good to us," Chuck said, trying not to sound overly eager to get away.

"You didn't have the Chevy very long," the manager mused. "I guess it didn't fit your needs, huh?"

"Oh, we liked it, okay," said Mona Rae. "We just decided we wanted something newer. We sold our other car last week and just decided we need a change of scene. Applegate is so small, you know. We just decided we want to see more of the world."

The manager nodded. "Oh, yes. I guess it is at that. Actually... I've never heard of it before!" He paused, grinned, and gave them both a questioning look, but said nothing and went back to completing the paperwork.

Twenty minutes later, the Shermans drove away in the almost-new, cream-colored, four-door Buick. A very odd situation, the sales manager thought to himself. Why would a couple from "Podunk," Oregon, buy a used car from a farmer in Idaho Falls and then return to Oregon and almost immediately trade it in for another? ... and pay cash? They must have suddenly inherited some money. Or maybe they had just sold their house in Applegate. Besides that, he wondered, they both seemed to have vocal accents and inflections that he vaguely recalled hearing during his two years as a draftee in the U.S. Army. Had these people really been raised in 'small town' Oregon?

The deal had a very peculiar feel to it. A couple of strange ones-- Norval and Mona Rae Sherman. If the police officer hadn't seemed so young and naive, maybe he would have picked up on the obvious incongruities. Oh well, he thought, we made some pretty good money on the deal.

* * *

On a Saturday afternoon in March, both Preston and Becky were baptized in a "splendid" service, as Preston called it. Naomi and Aaron had both been able to trade their Thursday shifts for Saturday off. Preston was as calm, assured, and serene as Becky was nervous and flushed as they sat, dressed in white, on the front row of the chapel with family. Paul Blackstone had come from Utah State University at Logan with a male friend and two young women. Ben and Natty Randolph were there along with many of Becky's friends. Ian Cooper and Shane Lowry and their wives were present, along with several other county employees. Three children were also being baptized whose families and friends nearly filled the chapel.

Everyone present seemed to thoroughly enjoy the service and congratulated them. It was a happy occasion, even for Becky. The missionary discussions had erased all remaining reservations that she had carried with her for so many years.

Becky's family retreated to her house for a fine meal that Natty and Naomi had prepared. After dinner a more "formal" announcement was made as to the date that Becky and Preston had chosen for a wedding--a mere month in the future.

* * *

It was mid-April before Shane Lowry heard anything back from Dr. Ernest Hunter at the criminalistics laboratory. From all he'd been able to find out, it would most likely be years before the science of DNA would be reliable enough to depend on for criminal convictions. Shane, Sheriff Cooper, and just about everyone else, still believing that John "Chuck" Moranski was responsible for the murders in their jail, were frustrated to no small degree. The FBI had made no progress in finding the Moranskis, at least, none that even their friend, Special Agent Jon Gates, was willing to share.

Naomi Gentry had experienced a renewal of interest and soon immersed herself more fully in the excitement of her new career. Still, in the back of her mind she was envious of Natty whose pregnancy was progressing on schedule. In the rapidly maturing spring, Naomi and Natty rode their horses in the green and blooming hills and mountains whenever an occasion gave them time, realizing that the time would soon come when other duties would curtail such recreation. Aaron and Ben went with them when they could. She and Natty still enjoyed a special sisterly bond that their marriages could not replace.

Then, too, there was a constant nagging thought that the Moranski business was not over and done with. Naomi and Shane still talked about it. Occasionally, what seemed to her a sixth sense told her that she should be ever vigilant. At times, even at their home in Toquerville, while outside taking care of the animals or just walking through the pasture to see the miracle of nature's re-awakening, she felt exposed and would pause to scan the far hillside, half-expecting to catch a glimpse of someone watching her from across the creek or to see the reflection of sunlight on a rifle barrel--like in a classic western movie. She even considered, at times, wearing her Kevlar vest whenever she was outside the house. There were dirt roads on the far side of the creek, and she knew that a man could hide over there in the brush early in the morning or late in the evening and easily learn her routine using field glasses. Or maybe even while holding a sniper rifle equipped with a good scope, fire off a couple of rounds before she could find cover. She said nothing of her concerns to Aaron--or anyone else.

The tradition of the Sunday dinner continued after Preston and Becky's marriage in April. She insisted that they sell her split-level house with the now-unused pasture and move across the valley to a home with a smaller yard on the bench above Santa Clara. For her, there were too many memories in her home that she'd shared with Andrew Scott, but she never mentioned that. Preston was a bit relieved to be moving with her into a different home, also. The pickup he'd been driving was traded-in for the purchase of a small sedan.

One Sunday morning, before church, she and Preston called his daughters in England and talked at length to Polly and Alicia and their little sons. At the dinner table that evening, Becky laughed again, relating to the family what one of the little boys had asked her. "The child said, 'Ah you going to be ouah new grawnd mothuh'?" she said, laughing again. "He was so cute!" The others laughed heartily.

Preston was smiling too. "They're both such splendid children. And extremely intelligent!"

"We've decided to make the trip to England in May," Becky announced at the dinner table. The others voiced their approval.

"That's good," said Naomi. "But Sgt. Lowry and the sheriff will want to talk to Preston before you go." The others looked at her. "They want you to find out as much as you can about the DNA studies that are going on in England."

"Ah, of course," Preston answered. "That would be my great pleasure. I've discussed that ever so briefly with your sheriff on a prior occasion. I'll be certain to contact him again. I attempted to discover more about it. I even went to the local college library and their biology department. Couldn't learn a single thing about it, at least as it might relate to the investigation of crimes."

From there the conversation turned toward Natty's delicate condition. "Whether it's a boy or a girl we'll just love it, anyway," she said, smiling. "We're just hoping that the baby will be healthy... and perfect in every way."

Naomi, aware that the others might be thinking of her with some degree of sympathy, said, "We couldn't be happier for you both. And we'll all love your baby, too! Have you told your mother about it?"

"Oh, yes," Natty replied, with a glance at Becky. "In fact she was able to get away and we met for lunch one day last month while our father was in some big conference up north. We've done that a few times, you know."

"Oh, that's wonderful," Becky remarked. "You be sure to keep her up to date on everything."

"I'll do that, for sure," Natty said. "It's so great to have two moms."

* * *

Naomi, as spring melted into summer, was gradually becoming even more watchful. While on patrol, she acquired the habit of checking her rear-view mirror and scrutinizing the traffic behind her far more often than before. During the three weeks that Becky and Preston were gone, she felt even more vulnerable. Many times she had the feeling that someone might be secretly watching her. On several occasions recurring dreams of drowning or being stalked bothered her. There had been no news of the Moranskis, one way or another. Still, she said nothing to Aaron about the dreams or of her apprehensions.

On a Friday morning in May, Aaron had to leave early for a quarterly meeting in Cedar City at the district highway patrol office. Naomi kissed him goodbye after a quick breakfast and began the morning chores. An uneasy feeling crept over her and she became especially watchful. The cool morning shadows from Smith Mesa were rapidly retreating when she again paused to scan the western hills while currying the horses as they ate at the manger. She thought she saw a flash, a reflection of something in the bright morning sun, from the far side of Ash Creek.

She stood, keeping Mancha between her and the hills across the creek, and intensely studied the distant brushy hillsides. Still concerned, she walked around the house to the front which faced east, went inside and got the keys to the Jeep. She paused at the door then returned to the bedroom closet and retrieved her gun belt and fastened it around her waist. Nero looked at her questioningly and she said to him, "C'mon Nero, let's go." He eagerly accompanied her to the Jeep and jumped inside.

She drove south a couple of miles to a bridge that spanned the surging Ash Creek. From there, she negotiated a dirt road that skirted patches of pasture and wound northward through scattered cedar trees to a point across the creek from their home. Nero's ears and eyes were focused forward at the sight of two men walking through the sagebrush maybe a hundred and fifty feet apart. Both men carried rifles but made no attempt to conceal themselves. Naomi stopped the Jeep and studied them as they walked slowly through the brush. Rabbit hunters, she decided.

She waved to them and they both returned the gesture. One of them looked slightly familiar. Maybe one of the young men in her ward, she thought. She continued north as far as the road would take her before it doubled back to the south. Watchfully, she returned home and continued with her routine.

CHAPTER TWENTY-FIVE

Norval "Chuck" Sherman studied his well-worn road atlas again. He'd looked at it so many times the corners of the pages were frayed and twisted. Frequently, in the night and almost all the time in the day, he feared being caught and taken away. Supposing what prison life would be like, he often imagined himself locked away, like Clint Eastwood in the movie "Escape From Alcatraz." He agonized through dreams of being locked for the rest of his life in a cramped, dark concrete cell with walls that were surrounded and kept frigid by unrelenting contact with cold, damp soil. Mona Rae often complained that he would wake her up in the night with groans and stifled screams.

From the moment Mona Rae had mentioned to the car dealer in Coos Bay, Oregon, that they would likely end up in southern California, Chuck began to question again why he had to put up with her. Her slip of the tongue had given away one of their most critical secrets. His increasingly ranting lectures to her had definitely put a cankerous and deepening freeze on their relationship. In his imagination, the law was one step behind them, and in that off-hand remark she had left a broad clue. A clue that could very well be their downfall! They had been so guarded to go to the trouble of getting another car using completely different names found in an old cemetery in that tiny, obscure town in Oregon. But after they had been so careful and planned so meticulously, she had nearly blown the whole thing with one casual statement to the used car dealer!

Yeah, the young, clue-less cop that had checked the VIN number hadn't suspected a thing. But what if the sales manager was a good friend of the chief or a good detective and they had got to talking over coffee? Just in the course of casual conversation, the dealer could mention the strange story of the couple who had brought an easily identified Chevrolet from Idaho, using the former owner's plates and traded it for another one in about a week. What if the feds had somehow connected the Moranskis to the Idaho car and came snooping around? Chuck was sure it wouldn't take long for a smart cop to connect the dots and the FBI would then be looking for them with their new names and their nice, almost new Buick, in California.

He hoped that ducking into Nevada would have shaken the authorities off their tracks. The small town of Ely, where they had settled in, made him feel a bit more secure even though he didn't care for the place that much.

At first, Chuck and Mona Rae were a bit puzzled at the way the local people pronounced "Nevada"--but quickly learned to say it with a "vadda" sound rather than the "vawda" sound that they had learned in school back in New Jersey.

Within days of getting a position as assistant manager at a small motel, Chuck, concealing several small tools in his clothing, made a clandestine visit to an automobile salvage business and obtained Nevada plates for the Buick. That, along with driving carefully--so as to avoid contact with the local police--would get them by. He was not about to call the Oregon car dealer to have the new plates sent to their Nevada address!

"Mona Rae." What a stupid name, he reflected! She just didn't get it. She hadn't seemed so dense before. Together, they had eliminated--what? How many men? And been paid well for doing so. They could, even now, be on the FBI's "most wanted" list? Yet she just didn't get it! Telling that car dealer where they planned to go! A stupid, careless remark! She was so naive. And yet, she nagged him about wanting to stop running--stop moving. The day they parted company had to come--and maybe soon.

His lengthy and demeaning lecture to her on the proverbial "loose lips" had finally gotten through, he thought, and had convinced her that they should leave Oregon in another direction. Their vision of a leisurely new life on the sunny shores of southern California was suddenly blown away by her simple, stupid, witless remark, he told himself--*and her*!

He looked over at Mona Rae, sleeping so peacefully as she always did. His anger stirred again. She had argued with him at every turn after leaving Coos Bay, never quite seeing the danger that they were in. Still, none of this would have happened--they'd still be enjoying the prosperous life in Jackson--if it hadn't been for that woman cop from southern Utah. He had re-lived that moment in the heated pool behind the lodge hundreds of times. He'd get back to her someday. He didn't know how, but he would. And when the time was right, he'd have the element of surprise on his side. He'd find a place not that far from her and carefully plan it. After all, that was what he did, and did it very well, he reassured himself.

In tormented memory, he returned to their overnight stay in a motel in Winnemucca. The dawn, that sleepless morning, had come slowly. As the gathering light had begun to illuminate the blinds covering the east-facing windows, Chuck had even considered leaving her there--just leaving her sleeping in the motel room--packing his things, putting them in the car and going. He'd leave her some money and maybe a note, and she could maybe get a ride on a Greyhound bus and go on back to her family in the east. He'd never have to convince her of anything, anymore. He'd never have to argue with her. She'd never find him. Where would she begin to look? She'd never go to the police. He would be rid of her and her constant nagging.

But then, if the feds ever caught up with her, they could pressure her and promise immunity and she could squeal on him and they would come after him with her as a witness. She would, no doubt, tell them about every hit job they'd ever done. She would be a liability--a loose end that could leave him vulnerable. No, he couldn't afford to just leave. Not with her still alive. He'd have to give it some more thought.

* * *

But he hadn't done it. Now, having been in Ely for several months, he seemed to feel somewhat more relaxed and they had settled into somewhat of a routine with his new job as night manager of the Mother Lode Motel. For some reason, they seemed to become more compatible. The small motel would have to be their home for a while.

Mona Rae had found employment with a petroleum distributing firm. She had come close to applying for a job in a small casino, working as a bookkeeper at a very lucrative salary, until being told that the state gaming laws required a thorough background investigation. She was glad that Chuck seemed to be settling down a bit after being in Ely for a few weeks.

Between them, they quickly discerned that Nevada seemed to be a world apart from surrounding states. There was a distinct feeling of a vastly more relaxed culture, due mainly to the open gambling that everyone simply took for granted, with each person much more free to "do his own thing" in virtual anonymity. They liked that. Not that having community mores were a bad thing, it was just that Nevada more closely fit well with their lifestyle. They talked about it and wondered why they hadn't chosen to settle in Las Vegas, long before. The major drawback to living in Ely was that they would have to drive or take a small plane--thus risking losing their anonymity--to a major airport in Reno, Las Vegas, or Salt Lake City, should a new assignment come along.

In recent days, feeling more settled and relaxed, Chuck had rented a private mail box in nearby McGill and made several calls from a public telephone to Rube in the Chicago area and his eastern connections, just to let them know where to contact him. But in doing so, he began to form the impression that they were being somehow vague with him. In spite of his desires to the contrary, it seemed as though he was getting something of a brush-off or a run-around. Did they know the cops suspected him in the Utah jailhouse murders? How would they have found out? It only made him hate that woman deputy sheriff all the more. He would do it. And the sooner the better.

Chuck was beginning to hate Ely, too. Having been raised in the vast urban sprawl on the west side of the Hudson River, the narrow little town between surrounding high mountains quickly spawned a constant feeling of oppression. At times, it felt as though he was being slowly squeezed between the crushing jaws of a gigantic vise. The "Shermans" soon began to realize they had very little in common with Ely's townspeople, consisting mainly of miners, cowboys, and BLM personnel, whose leisure lives seemed to be centered on the local bars and high school sports. Yet, a surprising number of small churches lined the main street.

Living in one of the motel rooms, he found new ways every day to despise the small town. Furthermore, Mona Rae was beginning to get on his nerves again.

"It looks to me like you've about wore out that map book," she observed late one evening. "What's on your mind, Chuck? What have you come up with?"

"Yeah," he replied, thinking ahead of her response. What would she find to object to now? "I've been thinking we should go on down to Las Vegas. This place is getting to me. I can't stand it here anymore! I've got to get out of here! Why don't we go to Vegas? We can get some better jobs and we can... "

"Las Vegas is mighty close to that job we did in that Utah jail... isn't it? I don't think that's such a good idea! You can't still be thinking about that woman cop! That woman you couldn't handle?" She stared at him for a moment and then rolled her eyes in disgust. *"Get over it, Chuck!"* she screamed at him. *"She can't do nothin' to us anymore! It's over! She's history!"*

Chuck leaned back in his chair and rubbed his forehead nervously. "Keep your voice down. You want to tell the whole world about it?" His first impulse was to grab her by the throat and choke off her outbursts. He'd thought of it many times and saw himself attacking her in a rage or even as she slept at night--pinning her arms with his knees and grabbing her by the throat and ending it. But what would he do with the body? He would have to give that some more thought. And if anyone asked, he would simply say that she had decided to get on a Greyhound bus and return to the East, to her family back there. Yeah, that would take care of it, he reasoned. Or, why not just pack up their stuff and head out for Vegas and dispose of the body somehow, someway?

With his pulse racing, he struggled to get control of his emotions while gripping the road atlas. He silently stood up and walked stiffly out of the motel room, slamming the door behind him, and onto the sidewalk, which was dimly illuminated by the motel's flickering overhead neon sign.

It was nearly midnight when he stumbled out of the bar and across the narrow street from the motel. The sound of screeching tires barely got his attention. Some kids in a passing car yelled obscenities at him for not getting off the highway fast enough. But he paid them no mind, found his way to the room, and collapsed on the couch, where he remained for the night.

For nearly a week neither of them spoke to the other. Slowly, a plan was forming in his mind. He would do it--and soon, he resolved to himself. And if Mona Rae wouldn't go along with it, maybe he'd just rid himself of her, too.

"I'm going take her out," he said suddenly one morning, which took Mona Rae by surprise. He went on as if there had been no argument about it. "We're going to handle it like it was just another hit job. We can drive down there and do it."

"*But Chuck!*" Mona gasped. "*She's a cop!*" Her response, this time, was more of a plea than a protest--a desperate appeal to his intelligence. He detected that and it made him feel all the more resolved. She was weakening. "*We can't do it!* All the jobs we've done before have been on bad guys! One mobster out to get another! You know that! What's the matter with your brain anyway? You kill a cop, a *woman cop*! You'll have every other cop in the country after us. We'd be hunted down to the ends of the earth. *And you'd better believe they'd know who done it!* I say let's let her be and go back east or something, maybe Florida." Her pleading tone only served to strengthen his resolve. "Come on, Chuck! We've always talked about Mexico... or Canada. Come on, please! Let's not do this!"

"We can do it and be in Mexico before anybody knows anything." Chuck responded so calmly that it surprised even him. "I've made up my mind. We can do it just like that job in Austin last spring. This dump should have maybe fifteen grand in the safe by the weekend. We can clean it out and be gone, like that!" he said, with a snap of his fingers. "We'll make it look like we was robbed! Are you with me... or what?"

"Dang it! Chuck, I'll have to think about it! Let's think about it! Okay?"

* * *

Teletype machines in surrounding states clacked out the terse announcement of the motel robbery and kidnapping--and possibly a double murder in tiny Ely, Nevada. It occurred sometime during the first week of June. Television news anchors in Reno and Las Vegas and in all the surrounding states featured the lead story on nearly every newscast for more than a week.

The manager of an Ely motel and his wife, as yet, unnamed, had apparently been abducted and robbed by unknown persons believed to be heading west from Ely. The victims' Buick had been found with blood smears inside it, abandoned among some trees along a dirt road leading into a dry canyon away from Highway 6, some forty miles west of the town. Nearly eighteen thousand dollars had been taken from the motel safe. Officers in White Pine County along with dozens of volunteers were still searching for the abductees, or their bodies, in the vicinity of their abandoned automobile and beyond.

Range cattle in the area had obliterated any footprints or tire tracks that might have shed some light on the events surrounding the car, its passengers and their abductors.

* * *

Becky and Preston thoroughly enjoyed their three weeks in England and nearby small countries. Becky marveled over and over concerning the life she was now leading, contrasting it with the lifestyle of Hildale. Now she was married to a very cosmopolitan British gentleman. She imagined, in time, taking tours of the continent of Europe and maybe other far-off places like Norway, or Hawaii, or Alaska.

Preston had arranged for the marketing of his townhouse in Blackpool. His daughters promised to see to its maintenance until the sale was consummated.

Upon returning to their home in the St. George Basin, they were both disappointed to learn that the Moranskis still had not been arrested. Becky was especially fearful for Naomi's life. And though Preston tried to reassure her, he was worried as well. Special Agent Jon Gates, when pressed for information, had revealed to Shane and

Naomi that the FBI and U.S. Marshals had learned that the Chevrolet purchased in Idaho had been traded to a used car dealer in Coos Bay, Oregon, for a nearly new Buick. The same Buick, in fact, that had been owned by a couple--Norval and Mona Rae Sherman, apparent victims of a motel robbery--in Ely Nevada. Agents sent to Ely had pretty well concluded that the Shermans were, in fact, John and Cora Moranski. Some latent fingerprints were taken and were sent to the laboratory in Washington, D.C., with their positive identification pending. But what had the robbers done with the victim's bodies?

It was no small shock for Naomi, Aaron and others, close to her, when they learned that the Moranskis had not settled somewhere along the southern Pacific coast, but were, or had been, close to southern Utah. Based on the strong possibility that the robbery and murder had been staged, all sheriffs in the surrounding area of Utah and Nevada along with highway patrol personnel were supplied with pictures of the Moranskis, a brief summary of their history and possible intentions. Their vehicle was not known. Sheriff Cooper made sure all motels, service stations, and eating establishments in Washington, Iron, and Beaver counties were supplied with the same information.

Whenever they could, Naomi and Aaron retreated to Brian Head, still their favorite place to get away. Nearly all of the snow had melted away and the winter crowds of skiers had gone back to their summer concerns. The dance floor at the main lodge still provided an enticing respite from their official duties.

At the first Sunday gathering, upon returning home, Preston announced that he was now eager to see more of the country. A day in Zion National Park, with its numerous short hikes, was his immediate choice and the following Saturday morning, when the family could all get together, was chosen.

CHAPTER TWENTY-SIX

After brooding over her crisis for many weeks, Mona Rae Sherman had eventually resigned herself to going along with Chuck's plan. Seeking help from the authorities or having her husband securely "committed" on the basis of his obvious insanity was not really an option. It began to seem plausible to her that they could carry out the murder and then go east or, possibly, even into Mexico. Still, she clung to the idea that maybe he would fail. Maybe she could find a way to make him *believe* he had succeeded. Or perhaps she could secretly do something to thwart his efforts or, at least, *warn* the woman he was seeking to kill.

As they had done near Idaho Falls several months before, Chuck and Mona Rae had purchased a second car in a private sale. About a week before the staged motel robbery and abduction, Chuck had insisted that they take the trouble to drive the 300-mile round trip from Ely to Delta, Utah, to purchase another car. They were able to obtain a late-model Ford--still bearing Utah plates.

In Delta, they had walked separately into a food market. While pretending to shop for groceries, Mona Rae followed a woman shopper who was careless enough to leave her open purse sitting in her shopping cart. While the woman studied the merchandise on grocery shelves, Mona Rae, seeing that no one was looking, walked by and slipped the wallet from the purse. She then casually made a few purchases with cash and left the store. The stolen wallet contained the woman's driver's license, several credit cards and a small amount of cash which she concealed in the trunk of the Buick and then discarded the wallet in a nearby trash receptacle. Chuck casually watched her smooth actions on the far side of the parking lot from the windows of the store and returned to the Ford when she was sitting in the Buick.

They then reversed direction and, driving both cars, nervously traveled west through fields of alfalfa and knee-high corn to the small town of Hinckley. Here, they pulled into a service station to fill up for the long trip back to Ely. The middle-aged cashier stepped out and walked around the Ford.

"Well that car looks familiar," he remarked, at last.

Mona Rae and Chuck were both seized with apprehension at his words. "Oh, how's that?" Chuck asked, trying hard to conceal his nervousness as he filled the gas tank.

"Well, my uncle over in Delta has one just like it," he said. "Did you just buy it from an older guy by the name of Peterson? On the east side of town? I heard he it for sale."

Chuck breathed easier. "Yeah, yeah, we did. 'Peterson.' That was the guy's name."

"I'd say you got a real good car there. Oh, yeah. Old Uncle Fred... They took real good care of it."

Gasoline was still running into the Ford's tank when Chuck looked through the front windows and saw the attendant back inside using the telephone. He must be just checking to make sure the car was sold and not stolen, Chuck figured.

They went inside together to purchase snacks and pay for the gas. Chuck spotted the small camera on the wall behind the counter right away, turned his face away and whispered a warning to his wife. Mona Rae quickly pivoted and walked back to the Buick. Grabbing her purse, she reached inside, closed her hand around the stock of her .25 Beretta, and, glancing back at Chuck, waited. The attendant noticed their apprehension and looked up quickly from the cash drawer.

"Oh, the camera's just a little precaution," he remarked to Chuck. "We been robbed a couple of times. Hasn't happened since we put up the camera. I read about it in a magazine once. Seemed like a good idea. The tapes run about a day and get re-cycled after a month or so."

"Hey, that's a good idea," Chuck remarked. "I guess a man can't be too careful these days, you know."

"Yeah, that's for sure," the attendant said. "You have a nice trip. It's a long ways to the next fillin' station over at the state line."

* * *

Shane Lowry couldn't wait to share his ideas and suspicions with Naomi. He felt that one of two likely possibilities would eventually prove true. It seemed feasible that the Moranskis could had been abducted and killed by robbers perhaps passing through Ely. But then, why would their alleged killers bother to remove and conceal the bodies? There were some blood smears in the Buick that were still in the process of being analyzed. Based on the idea that the victims may have been taken from the car and executed, Nevada officers were searching for their dead bodies near the location of the Buick. But they decided it was more likely, upon confirming who the supposed victims were, the Moranskis had staged the robbery themselves and by some means were "on the move" once again.

* * *

Having arranged the motel "robbery" in Ely and leaving the Buick, with a little rabbit blood smeared inside, some forty miles west of town, Chuck and Mona Rae felt relieved to be leaving. Chuck threw the road-killed rabbit into the brush, knowing large birds and other carnivores would scavenge it. After carefully staging a "crime scene" with the Buick, Chuck drove the Ford east through Ely nearly eighteen thousand dollars richer and on to the Baker turn-off on Highway 487 and from there into Utah.

Mona Rae decided to make one last appeal to Chuck to forget the woman cop and just go on to Florida. Her pleas fell on deaf ears. Chuck drove on in silence in a southward direction through Utah's west desert. The scattered ranch houses of tiny Garrison swept past on Highway 21. It was nearly midnight when they found a motel room in Milford.

By ten o'clock the next day, Chuck drove the Ford into Cedar City searching for a pawnshop. After having located the Iron County Jail, he reasoned, a pawnshop should be close by. The purchase of a hunting rifle and hollow-point ammunition took longer than they planned. While doing so, they were startled to see a police officer walk in and speak briefly to the shop owner. Feeling virtually paralyzed, out of the corners of their eyes they watched the officer visually sweep the interior of the shop, hesitate, then leave. They breathed easier.

Using the driver's license she had stolen in the Delta market, Mona Rae filled out the requisite forms and signed a certificate to the effect that she was who she said she was and a resident of Delta, Utah. They purchased the rifle and ammunition with cash.

From there, Chuck drove to the west, searching the desert and hillsides for a place to check the sight alignment of the rifle. In a large abandoned gravel pit, Chuck fired three rounds with the Remington .243 at about 150 yards and discovered that no adjustments were needed. At Enterprise, a motel room was obtained using the woman's ID that Mona Rae had stolen.

* * *

Naomi and Becky stood at the door to the small detectives' office and exchanged friendly banter with Sgt. Lowry for a few minutes. Marti Gibson approached them from the dispatch office.

"Naomi, there's call for you on line four, some woman." she said, with a smile, and turned to go back.

"Hello, this is Deputy Gentry," Naomi said, after picking up the phone in the patrol office.

"*I can't stop hi...!*" It was just a whisper. Naomi could visualize the woman's impassioned message being cut off, perhaps by a blow to her face. She heard no further intelligible words. There were muffled sounds of a man's and a woman's voices--angry, arguing voices--for a few seconds. She could hear a woman sobbing and screaming--some distance from the phone. Naomi, straining to hear, thought it sounded like a struggle was taking place.

"Hello! Hello!" Naomi yelled into the mouthpiece. There was no reply. A few moments of silence passed and then the line went dead.

Puzzled, she quickly strode back to Marti and asked, "Did you get that woman's name, or number? Or anything?"

"No, she just said she needed to talk to you... about something. She mentioned something on the west side of the county, maybe last week. I didn't ask her name. I'm sorry."

"So what was that about," Shane inquired, as he walked toward her in the hall, preparing to leave the building.

"I don't know. Marti said it was some woman that wanted to talk to me. But when I answered, she just said a couple of words then it sounded like there was somebody arguing--or maybe fighting--with her. Then she hung up. Or maybe the phone equipment cut us off. I hope she can call back. It could've been that couple that we had to break up last week... out in Bloomington. Whoa! They were nothin' but mean and vicious."

"Probably was. Or maybe it could've been a phone problem that cut her off."

"I think I'll drive out past their house and maybe just see what's going on... if anything."

But Shane was thinking that it could even have been someone trying to verify her whereabouts at the moment, or even someone trying to warn her. The Thompson woman? But then, why would a contract killer try to warn the intended victim? He considered telling Naomi of his concerns but decided against it. "Well," he said, attempting to be humorous by mocking the television cop shows. "Y'all be careful out there!"

"Roger that!" she replied, with a smile. "And you, too!"

* * *

Naomi preferred to be in her pickup to go to the western part of the county, but it was in need of repairs. After a half-hour or more had passed, Naomi left the office in a patrol car that was given temporarily for her use. Marti took another call, apparently from the same woman who'd called before. "I'm sorry," the woman said. "I think my phone is out of order. I'm calling from another phone. Could I speak to Ms. Gentry, uh... Deputy Gentry... I should say?" To Marti, the caller's voice sounded nervous and agitated.

"I'm afraid she's gone out of the office," Marti said. "She's patrolling the west side of the county this afternoon."

"Oh, that's good. I met her one day when she was out here on another problem we had. My name is Joan Gardell. I'm calling from, uh, Veyo. And I'm afraid we have another problem. Our son and some of his friends went out hunting rabbits early this morning and it's way past time for them to return. I'm afraid something's happened to them. You know, with boys and guns! Mothers worry! I was just wondering if maybe she could... maybe drive out this way, just in case there's a problem."

"Okay, Ma'am, I'll ask her to stop by and see you," Marti said. "But I'm sure everything will be just fine."

"Okay. I sure appreciate that," the woman said. "Tell her to go west from Veyo where the road goes down into the Moody Wash. We'll meet her at the bridge."

"Sure," Marti answered. "Let me just put you on 'hold' for a second and I'll see where she is." Marti wondered for a moment at the woman's words. She didn't remember sending Naomi into the western part of the county in the previous week. Furthermore, she had answered the phones long enough to know that the people of Veyo and the surrounding area would just say "Moody Wash" rather than "the Moody Wash" when referring to the nearby canyon that included Magotsu Creek. And the caller spoke with a slightly odd accent. But her concerns faded quickly and she conveyed the message to Naomi.

* * *

Mona Rae hung up the pay phone at Veyo and turned to Chuck who had been listening over her shoulder. Except for her reddened and swollen cheekbone, her face was drained and pale. "She's on the way," she said softly, in resignation, trying to control her emotions. "Chuck, please! For the last time, please don't do this! She's just an innocent young woman! She has a job to do! They've just got married! They could even be expecting a baby! She's not an evil person like all those others! Chuck, don't do it! Please!"

Chuck was way beyond anger. He struck her again with the back of his hand across her cheek that was already crimson and swollen from previous blows. She stumbled, sobbing, to the car and got in, feeling despair and defeat. They both eyed the loaded rifle lying on the back seat, mostly covered by a jacket. Neither one made a move to pick it up.

Mona Rae was still crying and desperately trying to concoct a plan of her own, as Chuck drove toward Moody Wash. On the way, the road made a switchback from south to north on the steep hillside. At the sharp turn there was a wide and unpaved observation point. Chuck stopped and got out of the car to have a look at the magnificent terrain. From the road just out of Veyo, prior to the abrupt switchback to the north, the bridge over Moody Wash was plainly visible from above. Traveling the road, the distance to the bridge was nearly a half-mile. But from the view area, directly above, it was easily within range of the Remington.

* * *

Naomi stopped to see if a family of rock hunters needed help to change a flat tire near the Arizona border on Highway 91. When Marti had called her on the radio, the name, Joan Gardell, was not familiar to her. She mentally reviewed her patrol activities of the past week on the west side. She also reviewed recent entries in her notebook and came up with nothing. She felt a twinge of concern for a few seconds, but then thought that she'd probably just forgot to make a note of any contact she might have had with the Gardell woman. While crossing the Shivwits Reservation, Marti asked her to contact another citizen in Ivins, which would require her to depart from her intended route. Whitney Greyhorse was parked at the small store and she stopped to talk. The conversation led to an invitation for him to accompany her. He left his car parked and, using Naomi's radio, notified Marti and the woman at the store that he would be riding with Naomi.

Naomi sensed that the trip to Veyo might be good for public relations at best. It hadn't taken her long to learn that overdue hunters, hikers, and a variety of other "lost" travelers seemed to materialize not long after the sometimes frantic call to the sheriff's office. Still, Ian Cooper had made it plain to all that it was a good thing for citizens of the county, especially the voting citizens, to feel assured that their sheriff's personnel were interested in their welfare and willing to help with nearly any type of "emergency."

Along the forty-five minute trip to Veyo, she and Whitney exchanged humorous stories about distressed citizens. But both seriously acknowledged that the "humor" in a given situation often depended on which side of the badge one was on.

"Have you talked to your grandfather lately?" Naomi asked.

"Oh, yeah," Whitney replied. "I almost forgot about that. I was telling him all the latest about that guy in Jackson, how the FBI had tracked him into Oregon and down into Nevada."

"So what did he have to say about that?" Naomi asked, glancing over at Whitney. "You knew they'd disappeared from Ely? The Moranskis staged a robbery and abduction up there. And now they've headed for who knows where."

"Well, Ely's not that far from here, either." There was a period of silence between them as they continued north.

"Okay, what did your grandfather have to say about all this?" Whitney's words were beginning to get to her. What was Moranski thinking? Had she simply been denying the terrible possibility? She thought, again, of the time he had nearly drowned her. Were the Moranskis on their way to find her? Could they be here now? Watching her? Stalking her? Right now? Suddenly she thought of Aaron and wanted to be in his arms to enjoy his strength and protection. "C'mon Whitney, what did he say about spiders and snakes this time?" She asked, trying to make it sound like she was joking.

"Well, he just said something like, 'the spider often bites several times, one after another' before she's finished."

"Well that's a comforting thought!" Naomi turned west at Veyo and drove slowly through the town. On the overlook above the big wash, they spotted a dark blue Ford with a middle-aged couple in it. At a glance, as had become her habit, she took note of the blonde woman beside the dark-haired man. The couple seemed not to notice the sheriff's car. These details were noted but not fully processed in her brain.

The Gardell woman had said she would be waiting further down near the bridge. It appeared obvious that the couple in the Ford had nothing to do with the rabbit-hunting situation. Still, it did seem odd that the couple in the car was only sitting there rather than standing outside the car to look at and photograph the magnificent geologic wonders. On an impulse, Whitney took out his notebook and jotted down the license number as they passed. The blonde woman, the passenger, turned to look--after the officers had nearly passed by.

Naomi drove on down and stopped in a small clearing just prior to crossing the bridge. She turned off the ignition and they sat for a time scanning the brushy hillsides ahead of them on the far side of the meager flow of Magotsu Creek that emptied into Moody Wash about a mile north of the crossing.

Suddenly, she spotted a woman in the rear-view mirror, sprinting in a zigzag pattern, out of the tall sagebrush toward them and shouting something. Naomi quickly opened the door and turned toward the woman who, she now realized, was shouting some kind of warning to her and waving her arms. Whitney was likewise out of the car. The woman fell toward them, screaming in agony, almost before they heard the crack of the rifle from above and behind her.

Naomi stood nearly paralyzed for a couple of seconds, while pulling her revolver and trying to locate the shooter. Whitney was scrambling to take cover behind the open door on the passenger side.

"Get down!" he yelled at her. As she turned, feeling as if it was all in "slow-motion," she felt a sharp tug on the back of her Kevlar vest and a horrible shock to the triceps of her right arm. Her revolver flew from her hand into the maturing June grass. Her entire right arm was now numbed and useless. Tears from the pain stung her eyes as she crouched into the driver's seat, which faced away from the shooter's apparent location. Two more shots exploded in showers of glass particles through the rear window.

"My rifle's in the trunk!" she screamed at Whitney who was still crouching behind the passenger door and bobbing his head up to try to see the shooter.

"I can't get to it! I can't see the guy! He's gotta be up on the hill, probably in that blue car we saw!" Naomi grabbed for the microphone to call the sheriff's dispatcher.

Repeated calls brought no response. Apparently deep inside

Moody Wash was not a place for easy radio communication. There were no more shots fired at them. Whitney, crouching low, ran around the front of the car, crouched behind the driver's door and scanned the upper hillside again. Seeing no shooter, he ducked around the door and pushed into the driver's seat. Naomi moved over, still clutching her bleeding upper arm.

"I'm okay. What about that woman? You better check on her!" Whitney started the car and drove it forward to where Naomi's pistol lay in the grass. He bent over to scoop it up and drove in a half-circle through the brush to position the car between the woman on the ground and the direction the shots had come from. He pulled Naomi down on the front seat to be shielded by the door. The woman on the ground was still facedown and coughing blood between sobs and groans. A small but widening spot of blood was evident below her right shoulder. Glancing warily up the slope again, Whitney slid out of the car and examined the blonde woman's wound.

"Get the first-aid kit in the trunk!" Naomi exclaimed, rocking in pain. "Take care of her first. I've only got a flesh wound. What's she got?"

"It's pretty bad! He shot her in the back, up by the shoulder." He ripped the ignition key from the switch and sprinted for the trunk. There were no more shots fired while he was in plain sight of the shooter's position. From that moment on, they both felt assured that the shooter had gone. Using bandages from her first-aid kit, bleeding was slowed or stopped for both injured women. The woman on the ground said nothing to them as they put her into the back seat and tried to make her as comfortable as possible.

Whitney took over driving. The blue Ford was gone. Once they were back up on the highway, Whitney sped south. Over the wail of the siren and the sound of the rushing air, Marti finally heard Naomi's voice.

"Washington! This is Seven-ten! Nine-fifty-three is driving! I've been wounded in the arm! It's not real serious! But we have a critically wounded woman with us! Can you send an ambulance to meet us?"

"Naomi!" Marti screamed into the microphone. A few moments of silence followed. Naomi could imagine Marti trying to get her emotions under control. "We'll get an ambulance!" The voice was a little more calm and rational. "What's your twenty?" The dispatcher's microphone stayed keyed for a few seconds and excited voices were heard in the background.

When the microphone finally closed, Naomi continued. "We're on Highway 18, almost to Snow Canyon." Whitney took the notebook from his shirt pocket and gave it to her.

"Ten-four, Seven-ten. Your ambulance is on the way now." Naomi shuffled the pages with one hand and found the tag number for the blue Ford.

"We were at Moody Wash Bridge to meet the woman. Somebody shot at us from up on the side-hill! We think it was a dark-haired man in a blue late-model Ford sedan." She paused to read off the license number. "The Ford may have gone north or south... we don't know. There was a woman in the car with him; she could be the same woman that was wounded. She's really critical. Might not make it. She was trying to warn us!"

"Ten-four, we got that." It was Ian Cooper's more calm voice. "This is most likely Moranski. We're checking out the tags now. We'll get the word out."

"That's what I'm thinking, Sheriff. Is Two-eighty-nine around the office... anywhere?"

"Yes, he's here in the office right now. He'll take Becky and meet you at the hospital. Six-seventy and I will be there to talk to you, also."

"Oh, thank you, thank you. Tell 'em I'm just wounded in the arm. I'll be fine."

A short time later Marti was more calmly broadcasting an "all points bulletin" on the blue Ford and its driver as "armed and dangerous." In keeping with former events and situations, the registered owner of the Ford was not Moranski. But the name, Fred Peterson of Delta, Utah, was not broadcast. Law enforcement officers in the Escalante Valley and the St. George Basin were alerted immediately and set up a perimeter watch on major roads leading from Veyo and beyond. A positive response was asked for and received from each of those on duty. Numerous others, off duty, were notified and responded at once by scrambling for their cars and getting out on the highways. In mere minutes, word of the shooting and a description of the car and driver were broadcast to officers in all of the surrounding states.

CHAPTER TWENTY-SEVEN

The blue Ford, registered to Frederick Peterson of Delta, went unseen for several days. From the descriptions given by the Ford's former owner, of the buyers and of their Buick, it was clear to everyone that the injured blonde woman and the man who shot her were, in fact, Cora and John Moranski--still using the Sherman's identification documents.

The abandoned Ford was discovered and reported by some campers far up a heavily rutted, dirt road at Big Pine Spring, surrounded by dense scrub oak, within about four miles of Signal Peak, which was due north of St. George. Shane's theory, which he shared with the others, was that tourists had probably unknowingly given John Moranski a ride into St. George. The question plaguing officers was, of course, where had he gone? Had he bought a bus ticket and fled the area or was he nearby and planning another attack?

It was the prognosis of attending physicians that the severely injured Cora Moranski would take some time to heal. Though fully conscious most of the time, she had not verbally responded to questions by anyone--not the hospital personnel or sheriff's officers. But from the sadness on her face and her frequent crying spells they concluded that her thoughts were in deep turmoil. She had no identification papers or photographs in her possession. The hospital personnel agreed among themselves and let Sgt. Lowry know that on closer examination the woman's hair was not blonde, but was in fact, a medium brown with an ample amount of gray in it. Shane and the others had pretty well concluded that she was, in fact, Cora Moranski and that she had tried to protect Naomi from being killed by slipping away from her husband and dashing down the hill in the tall sage brush to warn her. And it was generally agreed that her actions had been enough of a distraction for the shooter to interfere with his aim, sparing Naomi's life. Given the assumption that she had been a witness to an attempted murder by her own husband--that she had tried to prevent--it stood to reason that her life could be in great danger, as well. Deputies were assigned to watch over her, twenty-four-seven.

Meanwhile, Naomi's arm was not severely injured and within a day or two she was able to function quite well, mostly in a left-handed fashion. She was given the job of relief dispatcher on the assumption that her arm would need several weeks to heal. Upon being relieved of her new assignment by a shift-change, she walked down the hall to talk to Shane. He was about to leave for the hospital to try again to get some answers from Cora Moranski. She decided to go with him.

* * *

"I owe you a lot," she said to the woman, who stared at her blankly, after Shane introduced her. "You saved my life. And I'm really grateful for that." The two women studied one another's faces for a moment. The woman in the hospital bed looked away for a moment. "You're Cora Moranski, aren't you." Naomi said. It was not a question. The woman turned back toward her.

"Yes, I am," she said, softly. "John... Chuck... he still goes by Chuck, tried to kill me... and you, too. The man is going insane. I know if I hadn't cooperated he'd have killed me first." She paused to catch her breath then continued in a nearly imperceptible whisper. "I had a part in setting you up for it. I only wanted to be there to warn you. I'm so sorry. I just thought maybe I could keep you from getting hurt. He was just going crazy... so obsessed about it. I was thinking maybe somehow, or maybe someway, I might be able to warn you in time. He was completely obsessed with killing you, ever since he failed... up in Jackson. He's completely crazy about it and he definitely *will* try it again. I just know it. And... ," Her voice failed in a gasping, choking sob. She paused to regain her diction and continued in a whisper. "He'll kill me, too... if he gets the chance."

"Not if we can help it," said Shane. "We're keeping watch outside the room. Mrs. Moranski... what do you think your husband will try to do? Where do you think he is now? We've located the blue Ford. He drove it up into the mountains and left it. We'd appreciate any help you could give us."

"Well, he's got quite a lot of money with him. He could rent a car or even fly out of here and come back after us later. But my guess is he's right close by, just waiting for the chance. He's most likely kept the rifle. You'd best keep Naomi, here, out of sight until he's caught... if he ever is. He's just gone crazy! But he can be real clever, too, you know."

"Yes, we know he can," said Naomi. "And I really appreciate your concern for me. You really took a big gamble. You really didn't have to do that, you know."

"I'm glad you've decided to talk to us," said Shane. "You'll have more visitors tomorrow. Our county prosecutor will want to talk to you and the FBI agent will be back... now that you're talking to us."

"I'll talk to anyone who wants me to. I'm just tired of it all. I'm tired of the killing and running and hiding. I want him caught, too." She coughed very softly and the pain in her shoulder made her grimace and groan. She tried to take a deep breath, but the pain was too much. More tears flowed from her eyes. Naomi handed her a glass of water with a sipping straw, which helped with the cough.

"We'll be going now," Shane said. "You need to get some rest now. I'll be back tomorrow afternoon. I'll ask the nurse to get you something for the pain."

* * *

Aaron, Naomi, Becky and Preston all agreed that the best place for Naomi, for the time being, was at Preston and Becky's new home in Santa Clara. According to their plan, prior to Naomi leaving for the office, Preston would carefully reconnoiter the several surrounding blocks and drive ahead of her on the way to work. A Saturday's excursion to Zion National Park was eagerly anticipated. John

Moranski had either remained in hiding nearby or had left the country completely. Prosecutors, U.S. Marshals, and FBI agents were interviewing Cora Moranski at the hospital for a couple of hours each day for several days. The details of several of her husband's contract murders were discovered and documented. Everyone was beginning to breathe a bit easier.

* * *

Saturday morning seemed to hold the promise of a relatively mild mid-June day in the St. George Basin. A low pressure "cold front," holding a possibility of showers at the higher elevations, had moved across southern California's Death Valley in a north-easterly direction over Clark County, Nevada and the southwest corner of Utah. Aaron, eager for an outing with the family, arrived early at the Blackstone residence in Santa Clara.

"Come in, come in, Aaron," Preston said. "We were just thinking of preparing some sort of breakfast dish."

"Hey, great! I'm hungry, too. Are the women up yet?"

"They certainly are. They're now in the process of changing the bandage on Naomi's arm. Maybe you should have a look at it yourself."

"I'll do that." He walked into the bathroom and surprised them with a kiss for Naomi.

"Her arm looks really good," said Becky. "The doctor thought she might need some kind of a soft cast, but they've really stitched it up just fine. I think it'll heal up quite nicely... if she doesn't stress it too much."

Aaron took a closer look. "Yeah, I agree. She's tough, all right. I think she'll make it. We're really lucky! That's for sure." But what he said hardly expressed his true emotions. In his heart he wanted nothing more than to get his hands on the man who shot her--trying to kill her a second time.

Naomi smiled at him. "We have Cora Moranski to thank for that!" she said. "Of course, I did that a couple of days ago, after she started talking."

"I just hope nobody's told the reporters she's talking," Aaron said.

"If word gets out about that, he'd be walking into the hospital with a machine gun. He'd try to get her again, for sure."

"Anyway, I'll be glad to be able to get back home again," Naomi said.

"Well, let's get eating," Becky said, "and get on our way. Natty said they would meet us at the west gate around nine."

"Preston's got breakfast going," Aaron exclaimed. "I can smell the sausages."

* * *

The sun was well above the towering pink and white sandstone cliffs of Zion National Park when they finally approached the west entrance. Ben and Natty were waiting in the parking lot. Preston had kept an eye on the rear-view mirror and Aaron glanced back at times. No cars seemed to be following them. At least, not close enough to be obvious. Being Saturday, the park was somewhat more crowded compared to weekdays.

As they stopped at the Zion Park Headquarters, and got out of their cars to go inside, Naomi could not help having a twinge of envy, noting Natty's growing waistline.

"Every time I see you," she whispered, "you're looking a little bit larger. I'm so jealous, you know," She said it with a smile, but they both knew Naomi meant every word. With a slight gasp of emotion, Natty put an arm around her sister's waist and pulled her close. "I really am happy for you," Naomi said.

"Yes, I know," Natty responded, with love thickening her voice. "But you have my admiration. Everyone at the warehouse wants to know how you're doing."

"Tell them I'll be fine. I guess you'll be quitting soon."

"Yes, I'm planning to. I'd like to stay home with our little one... and maybe another."

"Now I really am jealous," Naomi said, sadly. "I've wondered a lot, even before the shooting, if this deputy thing is all worth it. Aaron and I have talked about it many times. He'd love to have children, too."

They realized they were dragging behind the others and holding them up. Preston was especially anxious to absorb all the geologic history he could and strolled about, gathering free Park Service brochures and buying several books from the gift shop. Though it had been some years, all of the others had been there many times.

But the views were, nevertheless, magnificent and the gradual rotation of the earth presented ever-changing angles for the sunlight on the multi-colored cliffs high above, slowly changing the colors and shadows. Every new stop along the way, as they drove beside the Virgin River inside the park, was a delight, even with the throngs of tourists along the roads and trails. Bees, yellow jackets, butterflies, and other insects and the darting chipmunks and squirrels caught their attention along the paths lined with fresh green oak and maple leaves that filtered the sunlight. Animal tracks--left by bobcats, coyotes, deer, and a variety of small reptiles in the pink sand as they had roamed and hunted in the nighttime silence--were a curiosity. They were a little surprised by the number of tourists speaking an assortment of foreign languages.

At lunch, the others remarked about it to Preston. "Oh, yes. I've heard all their languages. The Dutch, the Scandinavians, the Polish, Italians, and the French, of course. I would have difficulty conversing with them. The sounds are all very familiar, yet distinctive in their own way. But I'm afraid the Asians all sound and look very much alike to me."

"I'll bet many of them speak some English," Naomi said.

"Oh, I'm certain they do," Preston replied.

"Have any of you noticed that, uh, older gentleman?" asked Aaron. "He's been keeping right with us for several stops. Looks like he's having a sandwich over there under that tree right now."

"I've seen him, too," Naomi answered. "For an old man with a cane, he seems to get around pretty well. He's been with us for every stop we've made, I think."

Becky glanced over at the man. "You mean that guy in the light blue jump suit, with white hair and mustache?"

"Yeah, with the wide straw hat, Aaron observed. "It just seems a little, you know, like he's pretty much all alone."

"I know," Becky exclaimed. "I'll bet he's here remembering his honeymoon trip with his new bride... maybe... what, sixty years ago?

Maybe even more than that."

"That's got to be it," said Natty.

Ben nodded, too. "Yeah, he's gotta be one rugged old man, fer sure." It was about as much as any of the others expected him to contribute to the conversation, but he surprised them. "I wonder if he's really as old as he looks." The others turned to stare at Ben. His deeply tanned face flushed a bit as though he was embarrassed by their sudden attention. "I noticed he gets around pretty good for an old codger with a cane." His comments and his tone seemed to slightly suggest caution or suspicion. It was the merest hint of a warning, perhaps--as though Ben Randolph might be suspecting something sinister about the man. But he said nothing more. It left the others thinking about it, but no one pressed him further. Aaron began wondering if he should have brought Naomi's Kevlar vest. He began to study the old man and other tourists more closely.

Ben's poignant observations were something of a punctuation mark that more or less prompted them to end their conversation, and move on.

"Is anyone game for the trail to Angels' Landing?" asked Aaron. "There's still time for me, I'm on the 'six-to-two' shift tonight."

"I'm game," said Naomi.

"I think maybe... " Natty started to say.

Becky cut her off. "You'd better not go up there, honey!" she warned. "I'm afraid it would be too much of a strain."

"Okay," Natty said. "I know. I was just thinking I'd stay down here. We can do it later... and take our little Benjamin Randolph, Jr. in a backpack with us. I know Ben's hiked it three or four times. We'll probably drive on up to the end of the road and play in the water for a while. Then we can just go on home from there. We'll be seeing you all for dinner tomorrow."

Ben moved close to Aaron and said quietly, "I'd keep an eye on the old man if I was you." Aaron turned quickly to him and nodded while contemplating any remote possibilities.

"You'd better be there!" said Becky. The others bid them goodbye, as well, and they departed. In the parking lot, Aaron removed his field glasses from the car and Preston grabbed his camera. All four of them put on hats and departed up the trail.

Very few tourists were hiking the steep and winding trail. Most of them were young people. Several small groups walked around them at a faster pace. Many were in shorts, rugged hiking boots, and sleeveless tops. One man, wearing standard hiking gear: leather boots, khaki shorts that ended at mid-thigh, a loose, airy khaki shirt, and an Australian bush hat, seemed to be hiking alone but was in no apparent hurry--stopping frequently to take in the surroundings. Under the bush hat, he appeared to have a shaved head. His mustache was rather dark and he wore a pair of large dark glasses. Naomi looked closely at the man and wondered if and where she may have seen him before. But the magnificent landscape soon took their minds off nearly everything except where to place their feet on the steep and winding trail.

Not long after launching on the trail, Aaron looked back and was surprised to see the old man they had observed earlier also starting. He won't even begin to make it to the top, Aaron thought. But like they were saying before, the old man was undoubtedly reliving a much earlier time, perhaps when he had hiked that same trail with his new bride. He remembered Ben's observations. Maybe he wasn't really as infirm as they had supposed.

Preston and Becky began to lag behind almost as soon as they started. "Let's slow down a little," said Naomi. "There's plenty of time and we should stay with Mom and Preston."

"Yeah, you're right," Aaron replied, with a wide grin. "Do you think we could maybe talk them onto jogging with us? Maybe get 'em in better shape?" They paused to allow others to pass them. The man in the bush hat nodded without smiling as he passed them. A group of Asian tourists carrying what appeared to be some very expensive cameras passed them while conversing among themselves. Each of them smiled and nodded. Somewhat strangely, the old man with a cane was not too far behind, either. Aaron and Naomi made several stops along the way to wait for the others and to catch their breath.

About two-thirds of the way to the top, where the dull red cliffs dropped away on both east and west sides, less than twenty feet apart, they found a bench. All four of them sat down to rest a few minutes and to view the magnificent canyon and read from a large pictorial chart that depicted and named a variety of points in the deep gorge below and on the horizon. The sounds of traffic at the canyon bottom could not reach them. All was quiet and serene, but for the sighing of the breeze through the cedars, pinion and mahogany.

"I'm afraid I'm getting pooped out," Becky said, finally able to speak after puffing hard. "And I don't like the looks of the trail from here on up to the top." The others looked up the trail. Other hikers nearing the top seemed to be the size of mere insects. "My gosh, it looks like we'd be practically walking on a knife edge, up there. I don't like the look of it!"

Preston sensed her apprehensions. "It looks that way to me, too. I'm afraid I'm getting a bit queasy, myself. Perhaps you young folks should simply continue from here. We can go back down and rendezvous at the parking lot in... perhaps about an hour?"

"Sure," said Aaron and Naomi nodded. "We can do that." They all sat quietly for another few minutes.

"Did any of you notice any peculiarities concerning the man in khaki shorts and the bush hat?" Preston wanted to know. The others quickly glanced up the trail, but the man had disappeared. They turned back to Preston.

"What on earth are you talking about?" Becky asked.

"Oh, perhaps it's nothing, really."

"What was it?" Naomi wanted to know. She was becoming somewhat more than curious. Actually, each of the four of them had been thinking at times, to themselves, about John Moranski and being somewhat watchful and wary of any out-of-the-ordinary attributes of their fellow tourists. Ben Randolph's observations of the old man-- and now Preston's question--focused their minds again. The old man with the cane surprised them again as he struggled up the trail toward them, from about twenty yards away, his bent frame seeming nearly exhausted by the strain.

"The man in khaki briefs... shorts, as you call them... " Preston began, pausing to take another breath. "His face and arms appeared to be deeply weathered and tanned, but did you notice his legs?" Becky turned to him, open-mouthed. But he continued. "Now, it would appear that the bush attire was what he habitually wore. And, consequently, one would expect his legs to be likewise tanned. Well... at least, somewhat. Furthermore, if he had any hair on his legs, at all, it was virtually invisible. Yet, his mustache is very dark. I find that to be somewhat strange."

It was as though each of the foursome had supposed that only he or she was thinking of Moranski--still on the loose--and that he could be stalking Naomi at that very moment. Is that what Preston was implying? Would the man in the bush hat be hiding ahead of them--lying in wait for her? None of them wanted to say it for fear of spoiling the day in the magnificent park.

"Maybe we should all go back to the parking lot," said Becky. "The rest of you could maybe go all the way some other time. Being up this high is starting to get to me, I'm afraid."

"Want to do that?" Aaron said quietly to Naomi. "I think your mom is getting a little worried for you."

"Sure," she answered, quietly. "We can always come up here on our own sometime later. I think we really should go back with them. But how would Moranski know we were going to be here... today? How is that possible? I really don't think that it's him. It just can't be!"

"I don't think it is him, either," Aaron whispered in reply. "But your mom is really, really worried. It's not worth it. We can do this some other time."

"Yeah... I suppose you're right."

"Why don't you two get started, going down," Aaron suggested, "and we'll catch up in a minute or so. We can make it up to the top another time." He turned to Naomi and said quietly. "I think we should wait in the parking lot for that guy to come down. I'd like to get a better look at him."

"Oh, I would, too. Both Preston and I saw Moranski up close in Jackson. I wasn't even thinking... " They remained sitting together on the wayside bench for some time. Preston and Becky had disappeared down the trail, passing the old man who stood catching his wind while gazing over the edge of the cliff. Several small groups of younger hikers passed them coming and going. Finally, Aaron and Naomi stood to begin the descent to the parking lot. Just ten feet or so took them to a point that was without a retainer fence and they stopped in great apprehension about four feet from the edge to take one last look from that dizzying height. From that viewpoint, gazing eastward, a drop of nearly twelve hundred feet would put an object almost to the river's edge.

They were surprised to see the old man move upward once more. Now he would pass behind them, take a seat on the bench that they had just abandoned, and probably sit there remembering a much earlier time. The three of them were now alone together.

Aaron and Naomi stood looking at distant surroundings--still in awe of the magnificent canyon. The east fork of the Virgin River-- still high from melting snows on the peaks to the north and east-- rushed by in silence in the gaping gorge below them. The occasional whisper of a breeze passing through the ancient gnarled cedars was the only detectable sound.

As complete strangers, on a chance meeting in the wilderness often do, Naomi turned, smiling, toward the old man to greet him and to perhaps engage him in a short, friendly conversation. She felt that profound congratulations were in order--that he was able to make the effort to hike up the trail at his obviously advanced age. Would he tell them about the time he first visited the canyon?

The old man was just five or six feet behind them as she turned. His wide eyes betrayed an almost demented rage. His stance that had looked bent and fragile was now virile and crouched. Naomi stood open-mouthed and transfixed for an instant. The man seized his cane with both hands and, holding it horizontally, rushed at them as they stood close together. It was an obvious strategy--to simply bulldoze them both over the edge as they stood together, admiring the magnificent surroundings.

John Moranski hadn't counted on having Naomi turn toward him, but realizing that he was now committed, he lunged at them.

"*Aaron!*" she screamed, as she spun around and positioned her feet solidly on the bare rock beneath her. She grabbed onto the cane as best she could with her left hand and tried to push back. John Moranski was able to shove them closer to the edge of the cliff before Aaron, much larger and stronger than Moranski, could get turned and brace himself within a foot of toppling over the edge. Moranski exploded in curses directly into their faces and redoubled his efforts. Finally able to stop the man's forward momentum and move him backward with much greater force, Aaron savagely punched Moranski in the face several times before he gave up and bolted down the trail--leaving them holding his cane. His wide-brimmed straw hat tumbled to the rocky precipice beneath their feet. Aaron ran after him at once, followed by Naomi.

"He might have a gun!" Naomi yelled. Moranski was obviously not hiding behind rocks or among trees or bushes. They could see the back of his white toupee bobbing and dodging along the winding trail. Aaron ripped his own revolver from his fanny-pack, spilling his water bottle and its other contents, as he raced after the man.

"Preston!" he yelled as he ran. "Preston!"

CHAPTER TWENTY-EIGHT

Preston and Becky heard the distant shouts behind them and stopped to look back and listen. "Preston!" Aaron shouted again. "Stop him! Stop him!"

The "old man" could now be seen bounding toward them with something in his hand that Preston assumed to be some sort of firearm. He quietly motioned Becky back off the trail into the thick oak brush and partially concealed himself as well. Moranski was within two steps of his position when Preston stuck out his foot and tripped him. Moranski reeled forward and tumbled head first into a sizeable thorny bush, which concealed a large rock. His headlong plunge into the bush brought his forehead into contact with the rock and he fell limply on his left side, moaning in pain. His face, arms, and hands were scratched and bleeding. His Beretta .25 caliber, semi-automatic, had fallen free of his hand and lay under the bush. Preston quickly twisted Moranski's wrist behind his back, placed a foot on his other hand, and waited for Aaron.

Well, Aaron," Preston began, while sitting on the man and holding an arm behind him. "It seems our Benjamin Randolph had the right idea after all! A right proper disguise, I must admit!"

"That's for sure!" Aaron said. He took hold of Moranski's other hand and put it behind his back, also. Naomi arrived carrying the cane and the field glasses.

"Oh, honey!" exclaimed Becky, "Your arm is bleeding!" Blood was seeping through the bandage covering Naomi's upper arm.

"It'll stop," Naomi assured her. "It'll be okay, Mom."

Aaron turned to Becky, "Could you remove this man's shoe laces?" She looked at him quizzically. "We can use them to tie his hands."

After that had been accomplished, they all breathed easier. Preston retrieved the little automatic from under the bush and, making sure it was not cocked and ready to fire, put it in his pocket. Curses exploded from Moranski's mouth as his head seemed to be clearing. A large knot was growing on his forehead and blood dribbled down into one eye. Multiple deep scratches covered his face, neck, hands and arms. The skin of his throat had been punctured by a small twig that had snapped off as the bush had collapsed. His nose and left cheek were beginning to show some redness and swelling. Naomi took out a white tissue from her fanny-pack and started to wipe the blood away. Moranski jerked his head away and cursed at her again.

"It seems as though this man could use a muffler on that mouth of his," Preston said, calmly removing a large handkerchief from his pocket. He then took Naomi's smaller one, stuffed it into Moranski's mouth and tied it in place with his own.

"Just in case you haven't figured it out," Aaron said to the man he held down on the ground, "you're under arrest for attempted murder. You darn near got us, Moranski. Nobody would have been the wiser. This makes the third time you've tried to kill my wife. And that means I really don't like you, at all! Give me an excuse and I'll drop you over the edge, myself!" Moranski tried to wriggle free and continued a string of muffled expletives.

Naomi removed the man's wallet and began a brief inventory of its contents. There were several identification documents bearing an assortment of names and addresses. No ID for John Moranski was among them. There appeared to be perhaps $300 or more in cash. Naomi stuffed the wallet into her fanny-pack.

Without laces in his shoes and hands bound behind his back, Moranski was brought to a standing position. His straw hat was replaced on his head and the party began to descend the trail once more. Naomi, in the rear, still carried his cane. Moranski in his "old man's" attire--the light blue, short sleeved, now somewhat torn and bloody jump suit--was, indeed, a spectacle. The gag in his mouth and his hands bound behind him drew stares from tourists who stood aside with gaping mouths as the five of them passed by.

Preston and Becky reached the parking lot at the Angel's Landing trail-head before the others. They had moved the car to a shady spot and had the air conditioner going. Becky sat in the car to enjoy the cool air. Preston dug into Moranski's front pockets and found his car keys.

"It seems, from the looks of the keys," Preston remarked, "he was driving a GM car... a rental, most likely. It shouldn't be that difficult to find."

"I think he was in the gray compact, over there," said Aaron, pointing. "I noticed him driving it... back when he was an old man."

"Yeah, me, too," said Naomi. "I'll check and... "

They were startled to see the man in the bush hat and khakis approaching them from the trail's opening among the trees at the edge of the parking lot. He appeared to be ready to break into a wider smile.

"Well," he said, getting nearer to them. "It looks like you folks have just about done my job for me." Preston, Aaron, and Naomi silently glanced at each other. Moranski eyed the newcomer warily. "Name's R. J. Blevins," he said with a smile and put out his hand to greet each of them. He kept the dark glasses on. Blevins pulled a small folding wallet from his shirt pocket and displayed the credentials of a U.S. Marshal. Aaron and Naomi both examined it closely. The photograph didn't seem quite right. "Okay, the photo is little out of date," he said. He removed the dark glasses for a few seconds to afford them a better look. "But thanks for catching this man for me. I wasn't really sure it was Moranski."

From behind the man, Preston was shaking his head ever so slightly. Naomi noticed his skeptical look. Blevins removed a set of handcuffs from his back pocket and held them in readiness. "We've been one or two steps behind him ever since he took off from Jackson. We were all surprised when we found out they'd been holed-up out in Ely, Nevada. They probably could have stayed there for a long time. I'll be glad to take him off your hands, right now." He was beginning to sense their skepticism. "I can show you the federal warrant right now if you like. Got it in my car over there."

Preston was shaking his head from side to side even less subtly.

Moranski also began shaking his head even more vigorously and trying to yell out--as if to protest being turned over to a U.S. Marshal. "We've been noticing you for quite a while," Naomi said, trying to sound friendly. "If you were after this man, why were you getting so far ahead of us, up there on the trail?"

"Actually, ma'am," was the reply. "Moranski, here, dang near had me fooled, too. I noticed him, alright, but the man is clever. A very good disguise, wouldn't you agree?"

"Then you must have... Did you have your eye on someone else?" Aaron asked. "We didn't notice anyone remotely suspicious besides you, yourself. Your disguise is, um, pretty clever, too, you know. And where's your partner? I thought U.S. Marshals always worked in pairs."

"Thank you very much," Blevins said. "Actually, if you must know, it was you people that I've been watching... for several days now. And we've been watching the hospital, too. My partner's still down there. We figured Moranski'd show up sooner or later. Unfinished business, you know. He just couldn't let it go." He began to make anxious motions with the handcuffs. "Now, if you don't mind, folks, I can take this man off your hands and be on my way with him." Over Blevins' shoulder, Preston was silently shaking his head with even more emphasis. Becky stood beside him with her mouth open in silence.

"Well, maybe we'll take him in ourselves," Aaron replied. It made him quite uneasy to say it. A look of hardness came over Blevins' face. For an instant, Aaron considered a course of action to take if the confrontation became more serious. Was Blevins carrying a gun? Was this really turning into a serious problem? Furthermore, was the man really a U.S. Marshal, or was it all a clever ruse? For what purpose? Could he be one of Moranski's confederates? Or maybe just one more "hit man," commissioned to do away with one more of the expendables? "I think we'll lock him up, ourselves, for now. This makes three times he's tried to kill my wife, a police officer."

"When the local courts down here are through with him," Naomi asserted, "and the county attorney agrees, you feds can work it all out with him yourselves." Blevins' expression changed from somber hardness to a friendlier mien. Moranski, himself, seemed to relax a bit and breathed noticeably easier, as if he actually feared being taken away from Aaron and Naomi.

"Very well," the man said, forcing a smile and pushing back his hat, revealing a sweating forehead. "We'll see you in court, then." They watched him walk to his car. As he turned toward them again at his open car door to wave goodbye, Preston raised his camera and snapped a quick photograph.

CHAPTER TWENTY-NINE

For Naomi and her family it seemed as if a heavy weight had been lifted off their shoulders. Sunday dinner was something of a celebration. The Moranski threat on Naomi's life was, at last, over and done with.

* * *

John Moranski's initial appearance in court, the following Wednesday, was brief. While standing before the judge in an orange jump suit, he was apprised of the three counts of attempted murder-- specifically, a deputy sheriff of Washington County, a state police officer, and his own wife, Cora Moranski. The District judge was deeply concerned about the dark bruises and the deep scratches on Moranski's face, throat and hands until they were explained to him. Having no legal counsel as yet, Moranski was handed a list of local attorneys that the judge had on hand. The defendant was advised that he could select his own lawyer from the list, if he wished. John Moranski gave no response to the judge's words.

Cora Moranski was able to leave the hospital after several weeks and was held in jail as an accomplice and as a material witness. A doctor checked on her at least once each day. She rested a lot, of course, with little else to do, and still required pain medications. The U.S. Attorney from Salt Lake City and the Washington County attorney were discussing offering Cora Moranski probationary status, with subsequent induction into the witness protection program in exchange for her full cooperation. She would not, of course, be allowed to actually testify in court against her husband. Federal Marshals, having the duty to locate, arrest, transport and guard federal fugitives, patiently watched the court proceedings and waited for further developments. Many more charges against the Moranskis were pending.

Throughout the initial court process, attended by Aaron, Naomi, and Preston Blackstone, there was no sign of the man who had claimed to be the U.S. Marshal, "R.J. Blevins." None of the FBI agents nor any of the federal officers in attendance had ever heard of him. The photograph that Preston had taken, as Blevins turned to speak to them before getting into his car, presented a fair likeness of his face. A second photograph of the car showed the license plate of a rental unit. The FBI agents seemed glad to get copies of the pictures.

Throughout all interrogations with federal and local officers, in his rational moments, Moranski insisted that he would answer no questions until they agreed to a deal. He boasted that he could give them all kinds of leads--names, addresses, and an assortment of other connections--to mobsters throughout the United States.

Often late at night in the small cell-block he would shout-- apparently supposing that he had the attention of investigators--the names he claimed he could provide and the crime syndicates he could help take down. Occasionally, he was heard to be cursing at Cora. Still, at other times they could hear him actually crying while cringing in something of a fetal position on his bunk. Other prisoners were quickly becoming extremely irritated at him and complaining to the jailers on duty. Some loudly vocalized threats of extreme bodily harm even though he was in a separate cell. But he paid them no mind. Moranski kept up his nightly diatribes--often aimed mainly at other prisoners.

The details of Moranski's strange behaviors were relayed to Ian Cooper who, in turn consulted with the county attorney. It was decided that a local doctor, having some experience with mentally ill patients, should be called in to examine John Moranski. After two sessions with the doctor, during which the inmate actually said very little, the doctor allowed that he might be slipping into--or, possibly cycling through varying stages of--paranoid schizophrenia.

* * *

The preliminary hearing for John Moranski was scheduled for two weeks in the future. Early the following Wednesday morning, a tall man in a dark suit, wearing heavy-rimmed glasses, and an obvious dark toupee approached the front desk of the sheriff's office. His papers indicated that he'd come up from Las Vegas. His appearance and manner immediately stirred strong suspicions--conjuring recollections of one "John L. Croft, Jr." they'd had experience with. The man's Nevada Bar Association credentials, carefully scrutinized by both Shane Lowry and Ian Cooper, seemed to be in order. He told them he had been hired to represent John and Cora Moranski. Shane even took the trouble to check out the license plate on his car and called the phone number on his business card.

On being escorted from his cell, Moranski's ankles were shackled with a short chain. His facial hair had grown out and was approaching maybe a quarter of an inch. He wore a set of handcuffs on his wrists attached to a belt around his waist while shuffling to the interrogation room where he was to meet the lawyer. He cautiously peered around the door and refused to have any contact with the man. He quickly shuffled back to his cell and refused to come out. The lawyer then asked Shane to escort him back to where Moranski was, in order to make another attempt to talk to him. John sat back under the top bunk of the two-man cell in somewhat of a cowering manner, and almost totally avoided eye contact with the man. Shane Lowry's description, later, of what was happening, was the source of abundant humor among the sheriff's personnel.

Moranski's actions surprised most everyone, but it was later to be understood. After two days, given the lawyer's persistence, Moranski relented and decided to speak with the man, provided that a deputy was to be present. He refused to explain his reason for the conditional interview. After his initial and extreme anxiety seemed to subside, the deputy, who had been casually observing from the doorway of the interrogation room, was called away for several minutes. Under the table, as he faced the lawyer, Moranski's leg began to jiggle nervously as they quietly talked.

* * *

Late in the night Moranski began to feel a crawling sensation in the hair on the back of his head. While trying to sleep, he kept brushing and scratching at his hair, but the sensation persisted. Guttural sounds from deep in his throat came out at times often punctuated by bizarre shrieks. As happened before, the jail staff patiently tolerated the noise but made no response. The other inmates' reactions swung between severe annoyance and extreme amusement. It was several days before Moranski's dermal irritation ceased and he said no more about it.

The lawyer visited both John and Cora Moranski several times. A few days before the date and time for his preliminary hearing, Moranski began to feel sick. Chills and fever prompted the sheriff's head jailer to have his cellmate removed as a precaution. A colorful rash quickly covered his body with red welts. In three more days, while raging pleas and accusations spewed from his mouth in alternating screams and moans, he was experiencing severe cramps in the legs and joints. After being removed to the hospital, a sample of his blood evidenced a strain of rickettsia. His death was slow and painful.

* * *

A hearing was held in District Court concerning his death. The autopsy revealed that he died from the dreaded rickettsia, commonly called the Rocky Mountain spotted fever. The blood-engorged wood tick that had infected him was later discovered dead under the bunk in the cell he had occupied. As Cora Moranski, accompanied by Naomi Gentry, sadly watched, and began to silently cry, his body was placed unceremoniously in the ground in a wooden box by several county employees. It was in a small cemetery that for un-recalled decades had been used for the burial of an assortment of unclaimed incorrigibles.

An alert was broadcast on television news programs to campers and tourists to be careful in the southern Utah wilderness and in Zion National Park where, it was speculated, he likely had made contact with the tiny arachnid. No other cases of the fever were found to have originated in southern Utah.

The Washington County Attorney relinquished custody of Cora Moranski to the federal authorities and, gaunt and gray, almost beyond recognition, she was quickly escorted away by a pair of female U.S. Marshals. It was later learned that she spent over five years in federal prisons before being given probation and witness protection.

* * *

Later in the week, six officers held an unplanned, unofficial, and informal gathering after closing time at Bud Tulley's cafe. The mood was somewhat somber, at first. Bud locked the front door after the last customer left and declared that all beverages were "on the house." He then sat down to join in with the semi-celebratory crowd.

There were some somber moments as Naomi re-lived the terror, while telling of the attempts on her life. But hilarity erupted as Aaron recounted Preston Blackstone's private detective work in Jackson.

"Absolutely a most outstanding bit of sleuthery, I must admit!" Aaron exclaimed. The others laughed. "Is there such a word?" he asked, turning to Naomi.

"I think maybe that would be 'sleuthing,'" Dan offered.

"Well, anyway... he was, indeed, a bloody competent sleuth, I'd have to admit," Shane added.

"Y'all think maybe he learned all that from one o' them James Bond movies?" Johnny Lee asked.

"Come on, now, all of 'you all' please stop mocking my new step-father!" Naomi exclaimed, trying to sound angry. Then she added, "He's a wonderful man with a big heart!"

"Yeah, you're right," Aaron admitted. "Sorry. He's a good man, all right. But... maybe the British constables tend to be, um, just a tad more, um, creative."

"Hey, I'll tell you what," Shane said. "I've thought a lot about this. I expect, from time to time we might just stand to benefit from his advice. He's had a lot of experience." The others looked at him and finally nodded in agreement. "But we still can't say for absolutely certain that Moranski killed Barker and Conway," Shane remarked, in more serious tone. "But if it wasn't him, who else could have done it? We just might never absolutely know for sure."

"Well," Naomi began, "the hair that was found in his clothing certainly shouts that it was him. And if it wasn't him, why did he try to get rid of me in the first place?"

The others looked at her in silence. Shane spoke up. "Maybe someday, when this DNA research has advanced far enough... we'll be able to remove any possible doubt... from my mind, anyway. I know Preston is counting on it." The others looked at him questioningly. "I guess you didn't know. Preston promised the sheriff he'd pay for our trip to Jackson if our jailhouse killer was not Moranski."

After a moment of silence, Dan ventured, "That's a pretty safe bet, I'd say." The others nodded in agreement.

Nearing eleven-thirty, Barney Jeppson looked at his watch for the third time in several minutes. "Well, I'd best be movin' on," he said at last. The others looked around and acknowledged the lateness of the hour, as well.

"Hate to leave you to do the dishes all by yourself, Bud," said Dan. "But you know how it is."

"Yeah! Right!" Bud said, as he unlocked the door and let them file out. "Be seein' you around, guys!"

EPILOGUE

After much discussion, prayer, and meditation, Naomi and Aaron decided to begin a family. In time, it became necessary for her to work in the office for a while. Sheriff Ian Cooper was greatly disappointed to lose her as a patrol officer, but agreed that it was the best choice for them. He offered her an "indefinite leave" arrangement, promising she'd be welcomed back whenever she chose, provided that a position was open. Their twin boys were born late the next spring.

* * *

It would be several years before the hair samples, taken from the comb that John Moranski had left in the pocket of his wine-stained trousers in the casino in Jackson, Wyoming, would be more closely compared to hair found in the clothing he'd left in the refuse container at the Hurricane K-Mart restroom. The DNA from the roots of the hair, and from the saliva stains taken from the soda can he had used at the jail, left no doubt as to who had murdered Floyd Barker and Brody Conway inside the Washington County jail. Thus, Preston Blackstone, happily for all, was permanently "off the hook" as far as having to keep his promise of funding Naomi and Shane's trip to Jackson.

It was discussed by Sergeant Lowry and Sheriff Cooper and others that it was possible but not likely that John Moranski might have, in his turn, been murdered by the Las Vegas lawyer. The dead wood tick, found in his cell, was "autopsied" as well, and retained in evidence. Its body slowly dehydrated until it become a brittle hollow shell. Shane made a couple of trips to Las Vegas. Quiet inquiries, conferring with Clark County officers assured him that--as far as they knew--the lawyer in question was, indeed, who he said he was, a member of an apparently reputable law firm and a regular "pillar of the community."